JEANETTE'S GIFT

SHENANDOAH BRIDES ~ BOOK 5

BLOSSOM TURNER

WILD HEART
BOOKS

Copyright © 2022 Blossom Turner

All rights reserved. No portion of this book may be reproduced or transmitted in any form or by any means - photocopied, shared electronically, scanned, stored in a retrieval system, or other - without the express permission of the publisher. Exceptions will be made for brief quotations used in critical reviews or articles promoting this work.

The characters and events in this fictional work are the product of the author's imagination. Any resemblance to actual people, living or dead, is coincidental.

Unless otherwise indicated, all Scripture quotations are taken from the Holy Bible, Kings James Version.

Scripture quotations marked (NKJV) are taken from the New King James Version®. Copyright © 1982 by Thomas Nelson. Used by permission. All rights reserved.

ISBN-13: 978-1-942265-61-0

To all fellow dreamers who dare to step out of the fray...the fear...the frantic and follow your heart's desire. May your God-given talent take flight and soar on the wings of His power.

I will praise You, for I am fearfully and wonderfully made; Marvelous are Your works.

Psalm 139:14 (NKJV)

CHAPTER 1

∼

SPRING 1881
SHENANDOAH VALLEY

Jeanette Williams's body wilted and sagged, pulling her thin shoulders forward. Twenty-nine felt like ninety-nine. Until this birthday, Jeanette had held a smidgeon of optimism that she would someday marry and have a family of her own. All hope was gone. God had somehow forgotten her. The cheery frosted cake that sat on the table seemed to mock her dreary existence.

"Auntie Jeanette?" Her four-year-old niece, Geena, pulled on her hand. "Can I help you blow out the candles?"

The child could extinguish them all for all Jeanette cared. At her nod, Geena jumped up and down and smiled, the mirror image of her raven-haired, blue-eyed mama, Katherine. Seemed everyone from the youngest to the oldest was attractive—except Jeanette.

"Not until it's time, Geena," Colby said. "So quit bothering your auntie."

Jeanette glanced at the child's father before she lifted Geena into her arms. "You're not a bother, are you pumpkin?"

Geena wrapped her chubby arms around Jeanette's neck and pressed in a hug. An ache rose within. Oh, how she wanted one of these little ones of her own.

She gazed around Katherine's parlour at those trying their best to give her a birthday celebration and forced a smile. Tears bit behind her lids, and she pushed her glasses higher on her nose glad she could hide behind Geena to conceal the watery flow. Present were Pa, Katherine and Colby and their brood of kids, Lucinda and Joseph with their family, and Gracie and Matthew visiting from Richmond with their four-month-old baby. Despite being surrounded by those she loved most, Jeanette's throat constricted to an impossible ache, and acute loneliness crushed in. She stooped down to let the squirming Geena go and stood with her shoulders squared. She best get used to spinsterhood. She had a lot of living yet to do. Didn't she?

Gracie moved beside Jeanette and gave her arm a quick squeeze as if she were reading her mind. The giant knot in Jeanette's throat tightened.

"How are the students this time of year?" Gracie asked. Her knowing eyes held compassion. "I bet with the warmer spring weather, they're not too focused."

"So true." Jeanette gathered her emotions and tucked them deep. "This next stretch until the end of May is the hardest to keep them learning. We lose a lot of the older boys to necessary farm work this time of year."

"But I heard enrollment has never been higher," Katherine said. "Crazy how Agnus keeps sending disparaging remarks about your teaching style to the county superintendent. Little does she know that Colby is good friends with him, and we can counter the untruths."

Jeanette batted her hand in the air. "Agnus has wanted my

job ever since I was picked over her. She's been beating the 'it's not fair a married woman can't still teach' drum ever since she got married. And I don't disagree with her, I just don't like the way she's trying to push me out. She thinks if I weren't teaching, then the school board would be forced to hire her."

Lucinda's brows arched. "Well, you're more charitable than I would be. Besides, Lacey Spring couldn't find a more admired teacher than you. Those children love you."

"Yes, you have a gift with little ones," Pa added.

"Teaching is the consolation prize when one can't find a husband and have a family of her own." The words slipped off her tongue with a bitter tone. She had not meant to be that transparent.

The room fell silent.

Jeanette bit her lower lip and turned to her niece. "Geena, I'm ready for my birthday cake. Are you going to help me?"

Geena squealed in delight, diverting the attention from Jeanette's foolish words. If only they weren't true.

~

In the cool morning air, Jeanette lifted her head—and her spirits—determined to fight off the depressing effects of yesterday's celebration. God's mercies were new every morning, and it was up to her to find the truth in that passage. The mile-long walk to the nearby school gave her time to ruminate about the lessons and pray over the day. If nothing else, she was dutiful in her faith.

The fragrance of lilacs filled the air. She paused at the array of blooms hanging heavy over Helen Donovan's white picket fence and fingered a panicle. Dipping her head, she breathed in deeply. Ahh, now this was the closest thing to heaven she would get all day.

"Do you want a few for a bouquet, dearie? It will brighten up that schoolroom."

Jeanette looked up to see Helen rocking on her veranda sporting a welcoming smile. Despite it being first thing in the morning, her thick wavy silver hair was perfectly coiffured. "Goodness, you're up early."

"Don't know how many more beautiful spring mornings I'll have. Seemed a waste to spend it in bed." She beckoned with a wave of her hand. "Come, I'll get you some scissors. I know how much you love those lilacs."

Jeanette strolled up the cobblestone pathway toward the small but cozy home.

Helen tried three times to pull herself from the rocking chair to no avail. "Either this chair is getting smaller, or my behind is getting wider." She chuckled as her plump bottom flopped back down.

"Sit, sit. I know where they are. I'll help myself." Jeanette pulled the screen door open and walked into the familiar kitchen. Funny how at twenty-nine, an eighty-year-old woman was her best friend.

Helen had picked up the pieces of Jeanette's broken heart when she'd lost her ma, and from that time forward, Jeanette popped in regularly to visit her. She loved the older woman's company because she understood loneliness having lost her husband years before. Helen had a way of caring deeply, especially for the misfits like Jeanette. She pulled the scissors from the drawer and hurried outside. She must not dawdle. She wanted to have plenty of time to organize her day down to the last jot and tittle. She snipped at a few clusters and returned the scissors to the rightful drawer.

Back on the porch, she smiled down at Helen. "Thank you. I'll stop by again soon."

"You're such a dear." Helen lifted her spotted hand to

squeeze Jeanette's arm. "How is it that some fine man hasn't snatched you up already?"

How indeed? No man was looking for a homely woman snuggled up next to him in bed. Jeanette dropped a kiss on Helen's papery cheek and set off.

She refused to think any more about men or the lack thereof in her life. Teaching was her reprieve from the monotony, the schoolhouse the only place where she contributed to the world and had purpose. She found joy in doing it well.

She reached the one-room log schoolhouse. The door squeaked as it swung open. She would have to get Pa to oil that for her soon. She hung her cloak on the first hook in a row that lined one wall and placed her lunch pail on the bench directly below. No need to start the pot-bellied stove in the far corner on such a warm spring morning. One less thing to do. She straightened the few rows of benches facing the front.

Now, where was that mason jar? It would be perfect for the lilacs. Ah, there it was tucked on the nearby shelf. She moved across the room to the washstand and dipped water from the drinking bucket to fill the jar. She plopped her lilacs inside and took a moment to arrange them before setting the jar on her small desk. The school board could afford only a table, but thanks to Katherine and Colby's generosity, she had both a desk and a bureau to store the children's records.

She best review her preparations for the day's lessons. With grades from one to eight and ages from five to eighteen, there were a lot of wheels turning. She pulled her outline from the small carpet bag she toted to and from the school and sank onto the hard wooden chair.

As she settled in, the door creaked open, and eight-year-old Laura Wallace poked her head in.

"I know I'm early, but the others aren't coming today." She smiled. "May I help with something?"

Jeanette waved her in. "Your older brothers aren't coming again?"

"Papa says he needs the boys around the farm this time of year."

"Even Benjamin? He's only seven."

"Papa says it's time he learns how to feed the chickens and muck out the stalls."

"And the other girls?"

"Little Tessie is not feeling well today, so Sarah had to stay home to look after her."

Jeanette sighed. She couldn't blame the father. With six children to care for and having lost his wife, he must be overwhelmed. News was buzzing around town about the handsome widower and his big family who'd recently moved into the area. They had bought the old run-down Reiner place. All the attractive women, whom Jeanette couldn't hold a candle to, were a-twitter. She ought to go introduce herself. She made a practice of visiting every parent, but her stomach had twisted into an ugly knot every time she'd tried. Single men, especially a handsome man, made her tongue-tied and awkward. How would she find the strength to do it?

"Could you clean off the blackboard?" She handed the cloth to the blonde curly-haired child with cherub cheeks. "I'll do the top and you do the bottom."

Laura's smile split wide.

Jeanette had heard Mr. Wallace was a city boy with hopes of giving his family the farm life. Pa'd mentioned how the soil was fertile and, with a few bumper crops, he would be on his way. She prayed for the sake of his little ones that it would be so.

"How about I walk you home today? It's time I make my acquaintance with your pa." She forced the words out of her mouth. She had to get this done. Those kids were missing too much school. Most times a visit encouraged better attendance. Plus, it was Friday, and she would not be missed at home. Pa went over to Katherine's for the evening meal. It was Jeanette's one night off a week from cooking for him.

Laura stopped swiping at the chalkboard. "I...uh...don't think Papa would like that."

Jeanette sat in her nearby chair so as not to tower over the child. "Why ever would you think that?"

"He's not much for talking to strangers, and he tells us to stay clear of the town folk."

Now that was odd. He brought the children to church. But come to think of it, he never interacted with people. The most anyone could get from him was a lift of his hat. Of course, the women loved the mystery.

Not so with, Jeanette. She was his children's teacher and should have no qualms about visiting. She only wished her head would tell her stomach, which gurgled and complained at the thought of confronting this handsome widower.

Jeanette stood and resumed cleaning the board. "Well, I'm not a stranger or one of the town folks." She cleared her throat against the knot of tension settled there. "I'm your teacher, and I make a point of meeting all the parents. So, we'll walk together, and I'll have the delightful pleasure of getting to know you better. How does that sound?"

Laura smiled and flung herself at Jeanette. Her slender arms wrapped tightly around her waist. Startled at the reaction Jeanette bent to give the child a proper hug.

Laura melted into her arms and wouldn't let go. Soft sobs broke out until the girl hiccupped.

"What is it, dear child?"

Laura muffled into her shoulder. "I miss my grammie so much."

The feel of the child's arms around her neck broke Jeanette's heart. She knew what it was like to lose a mother as an adult. How much worse would it be for a child? She would help out in any way she could, but first she needed to see what was going on at the Wallace home. That gave her a boost of courage. She could do this. She had to do this for the children.

"Sweetie, you go ahead and cry. Missing those we love when we move away is normal." Jeanette held her until the sobs subsided. Funny that it was not her mother she said she missed. Just how long had Mr. Wallace been a widower? And why would he choose to drag the children away from the only mother figure they had?

CHAPTER 2

A soft afternoon breeze teased a few strands of Jeanette's hair free from her careful bun. She curled them around her ear. She had made a point of finishing the school day at two on the dot, which would leave plenty of time to walk to the Wallaces', have a short meeting, walk home and enjoy a quiet evening with no cooking necessary. Who was she kidding? Katherine thought she was doing Jeanette a favor when she invited Pa to supper, but in reality, it emphasized her acute loneliness.

Knots crowded the space between her shoulder blades. Was she doing the right thing arriving at the Wallace farm unannounced? From the time she had told Laura she was coming for a visit, the typically bubbly child had been quiet. What was she troubled about? With Jeanette's shy personality, she found these home visitations difficult enough without confronting hostility.

Jeanette didn't correct Laura as she kicked pebbles, scuffing up her shoes, while they walked toward the child's home. She was clearly bothered. What could Jeanette say to keep the conversation flowing? "So does your grammie live back in the city?"

"Grammie is dead, just like Mama." Laura looked at the ground and kicked another rock.

Jeanette's hand pressed against her mouth to still the gasp. So much loss for one so young. Had the two deaths happened close together? She dared not ask. She reached for Laura's hand and pulled the child to a stop. "I'm so sorry." Crouching down to eye level, she held open her arms. "Can I give you another hug?"

Laura collapsed against her, and the tears started afresh.

Jeanette smoothed her hand up and down the child's back.

Laura pulled away. "I'm not supposed to be a crybaby." She sniffed and rubbed her hand across her nose.

Jeanette pulled out her handkerchief and wiped at the trail of moisture. "It's not being a crybaby when we weep for those we love and miss. You should've seen me when my mama died just over a year ago, and I'm an adult."

"You cried?" Laura's blue eyes widened.

"I surely did."

"Then my brothers would for sure call you a crybaby."

Jeanette breathed a sigh of relief. At least it wasn't her father calling her that. "Brothers can act tough sometimes. It's their way of holding back their own tears."

"It is?"

"It sure is. Now come. I want to meet your papa." Jeanette held out her hand, and Laura's small fingers interlocked with hers. She swung her arm, causing Laura's arm to swing too. Laura grinned up at her.

"There you go, sweetie. That's just the smile I was looking for."

They reached a long winding driveway with ruts and grass growing down the center and turned up the lane. With Laura's hand still tucked into hers, Jeanette took in the dilapidated condition of the Wallace farm. The old fence showed signs of being newly repaired. A skinny donkey chomped on the grass. The roof of the barn sagged, in desperate need of attention. The structure did not look safe to enter. The small farmhouse was no more than a run-down shack. A few planks covered the broken glass in the lone window. The porch had boards missing—an accident waiting to happen. And the fields that should've been planted by now had weeds knee high, all but for a small, cleared section they'd obviously been working on. Why would anyone with six children to care for buy a place that needed so much work?

She and Laura climbed the rickety stairs to the porch, and Laura jumped over a missing plank as if it were no big deal. She swung open the door and called out. "Sarah, Teacher Williams is here."

Ten-year-old Sarah climbed down the ladder from the loft, which was open to the room below. At least the ladder looked new and the railing above secure. A wall with unpainted wood that looked considerably fresher ran down the center of the loft. Both sides could access the ladder in the middle.

"Teacher Williams, what are you doing here?" Sarah moved toward her, biting down on the nail of her baby finger.

"I'm just going to visit with your pa like I do with all the parents." Jeanette's gaze traveled quickly around the main room, taking in a large table in one corner filled with dirty dishes below the remaining cracked windowpane. Aside from the wash basin on the kitchen counter, it was covered from one end to the other with dirty pots and pans, tools, and what looked like soiled clothing. The floorboards were so filthy that Jeanette couldn't tell where one plank ended and another began. The half-boarded window choked most of the light from the room. The place could not look more depressing.

She put a hand to her mouth to cover her horror.

"How is your sister?" Jeanette hoped her shock was not obvious. She should stay and help this family, but the last impression she wanted to give was that of an old maid trying to snare a husband.

"She's...she's sleeping."

"Do you mind if I take a quick peek?" Jeanette asked.

Sarah's dark brown eyes flitted to the door. "I...I'm not sure and Papa is not here to ask. He's out in the field."

Of course, he would be out in the field. She had not thought of that. And he certainly would not appreciate a total stranger meddling in his life. Her stomach felt as twisted as a wash rag, but she couldn't leave them in this state.

"Why don't you let me ensure Tessie is fine, and then the three of us can work together on cleaning up and surprising your father with a hot meal when he and the boys come in."

Sarah's dark eyes brightened. "You'd help us?"

"Indeed, we all need a helping hand now and again, don't we?" The niggling doubt of what she was suggesting turned into a full scratch.

Sarah's gaze flicked away as if she could see through the walls to the fields beyond. "But Papa says—"

"Come on. It'll be a wonderful surprise for your papa. He's been working hard in the field all day, and you've had to care for your sister." Jeanette gave her most winsome smile, the one she reserved only for children.

"I guess that would be all right."

"Of course, it's all right." Jeanette put a bounce of confidence she did not feel into her words. She climbed the steps to the loft and turned toward what was obviously the girl's side. It held a semblance of order, whereas one peek to the boy's side, with clothing strewn atop the three straw-filled mattresses and all over the floor, told a different story.

Five-year-old Tessie lay sleeping on her mattress. Jeanette bent low to touch her hand to Tessie's brow. It was warm but not overly hot. The little child turned her head into Jeanette's hand, and she stroked the side of her face and whispered some loving words, things she thought Tessie would've heard her mama speak.

Tessie's small, skinny hand latched onto Jeanette's, and she smiled in her sleep.

Jeanette could barely find the strength to break free. A sting prickled behind her eyes, but she stuffed the ache down. There was work to do.

She climbed back down the ladder. "Your sister is fine. She probably just picked up the cold that's been going around. Sleep is the best thing for her. You did a good job looking after her today."

Sarah's head came up. A wide grin replaced her worry.

Jeanette surveyed the room. "All right, this is going to be fun. What time does your papa get in from the fields?"

"Not until near dark. He says they have to use every bit of daylight they can to get the field planted."

"Perfect." Jeanette clapped her hands. "That will make the surprise all the more dramatic. We have time. First things first. Open that door and let the afternoon sunlight pour in and give us some much-needed fresh air."

Jeanette pulled at the chain she had around her neck and opened her oval watch. It was two-thirty. By her calculation, they had four hours to work a miracle. A lot could be done.

"We begin with fresh water. Where's the pump?" Jeanette followed the girls out to the pump, each of them carrying a tin bucket.

After hours of work, Jeanette's fingers were red and raw. Her insides were jumping at the thought of Mr. Wallace walking through the door. With every passing moment, that reality became more frightening. Had she stepped too deep into Mr. Wallace's business? The troubled waters in her mind rippled with concern.

She stood back and surveyed the finished product. Every dish was clean. The tools were placed in one corner. The table was set for supper. The floorboards sparkled, and a load of laundry was hanging on the line in the cool evening breeze.

Jeanette's famous biscuits were baking in the oven, along with an egg creation seasoned with cured ham and cheese. Fried potatoes crackled in a pan on the wood stove. Jeanette was ready. If nothing else, she was resourceful.

But had she overstepped the boundaries?

Since when was helping a neighbour not the right thing to do? She prayed Mr. Wallace would not think she had designs on him. Oh gosh, she should have thought this through better. She had merely seen a need and jumped in.

Rather than stay, she could leave and the girls could explain. Yes, that was what she'd do.

No. She couldn't do that. She had to be there to take the food out of the oven in case the others didn't arrive in time. She'd gotten herself into this uncomfortable pickle, and she would have to see it through.

"Girls." She bent down and beckoned them closer. "You have been an enormous help. You should be very pleased of the work you did. Your papa is going to be so proud of you."

The two older girls beamed up at her. Blond, blue-eyed, and fair-skinned, Laura was the complete opposite to her sister Sarah, who had brown eyes, almost black hair, and darker complexion. Jeanette glanced at Tessie, who'd come downstairs and rocked in the chair by the fire, sucking on the corner of her blanket. Freckles dotted her ivory skin. The coppery tones of her curly mop glowed in the light of the fire. The children could not look more different. One would never think them sisters, but then again, no one guessed she was a sister to the four beauties in her family.

Everything within Jeanette wanted to sink into that chair and lift Tessie onto her lap to snuggle her close. She longed to soothe the angst that compelled the child to chew on her blanket. But Mr. Wallace and the boys were due back anytime, and holding the child would be far too familiar.

The door burst open, and Mr. Wallace came barrelling in

with Ben, Charlie, and Jacob close behind. "Sarah, I've told you never to start a fire—" He stopped short at the sight of Jeanette and took one glance around the room. "Who are you, and what the blazes is going on in here?"

Sarah jumped.

Laura's eyes filled with tears.

And Tessie popped her thumb in her mouth and began rocking the chair furiously.

Jeanette squared her shoulders. Her hands fisted. She would back away from most any confrontation, with one exception.

How dare he frighten the children?

CHAPTER 3

"Well, good evening to you too, Mr. Wallace." Jeanette straightened to her full height and stepped forward. The man still towered over her. That was indeed a novelty, considering she was as tall as or taller than most men she met. "I'm Miss Williams, your children's teacher." She held out her hand, doing everything within her power to still the tremble.

He reluctantly gave a short but firm shake.

Dang those glasses of hers. They were sliding down her nose. She pushed them into place without shifting her gaze. She would not cower.

Unusual light brown eyes framed by dark brows and thick lashes glared down at her. She was close enough to notice tiny hazel flecks swimming in the depth of his stare. How could his dark brown, closely cropped hair look so perfect after a day in the fields? She took in his strong features, wide forehead, full but neatly trimmed beard. And then her brain reminded her not to ogle. When she opened her mouth to speak, the words stuck in her throat. "I'm... I mean... Oh goodness, the biscuits." She raced for the oven, grabbed a towel to protect her hand and swung the door open. With a flick of her wrist, a pan of golden perfection landed on the breadboard. She could talk now that she wasn't staring at that flawlessly created man.

"I came this afternoon to meet you, as I do with all my parents, and found the girls in a moment of need."

"My girls are none of your business."

"But of course they are. I'm their teacher, and I'm heavily invested in all my students." She busied herself lifting the biscuits from the pan into a basket. "Besides, any good Christian would be propelled to take action in the circumstances."

"My circumstances are none of your concern."

She ignored him altogether and pulled the saucepan with her egg creation from the oven. Glancing over at the girls, she smiled. "Your daughters are amazing. All they needed was a little direction. What hard workers they are." When it came to being an advocate for the children, this man could not intimidate her. The look on those girls' faces was all that mattered. She flipped the potatoes in the pan.

She chanced a peek at Mr. Wallace. He gave her a steely-eyed scowl, which only made her want to laugh.

She held out the basket of biscuits. "Sarah, dear, come put these on the table. And Laura, grab the butter, will you?" She lifted the hot saucepan and breadboard and carried them to the table centering them for easy access.

"Boys, go wash up," she said. "Supper is served."

"Sure smells good, Teacher Williams," Charlie said as he headed to do her bidding.

"That's because it is. This is one of my pa's favorites." She spooned the fried potatoes into a bowl. "Tessie dear, do you feel like eating?"

Tessie was still rocking in the chair. She nodded her head.

Mr. Williams followed the boys out to the pump. When he returned, he took off his hat and placed it on the hook by the door. He did not say a word as his family bustled around him. Jeanette held back a smile.

"Gather around." Jeanette waved them over with a spoon.

The children scrambled into their seats.

Mr. Wallace followed.

When they were all seated, Jeanette glanced outside. There would be barely enough time for her to make it home before it was pitch black.

"I'll leave you now, as I must get home before dark. However, Mr. Wallace, we still need to chat about the children in the near future. But for today, take a look around and be proud of your girls. And don't forget to thank them." She grabbed her cloak and slipped out.

The minute the door closed behind her, she let out a big breath. Her body relaxed. She could finally breathe. She smiled into the dimming light. "Thank you, Lord, for gumption I know I would not have had without you."

～

*W*hat just happened?

Theo Wallace looked at the closed door and around the table. His children were digging into the food with smiles on their faces, all except Sarah, who glared at him. He glanced around the clean room. Not a dirty sock or dish in sight. The floorboards gleamed. A fire danced in the hearth. The scrumptious smell from the saucepan filled his nostrils, and his stomach growled. For the first time the place looked and felt like a home, not a pigsty, and he had been nothing short of rude.

"Papa, are you going to let Miss Williams leave without a thank you?" Sarah's tone sounded like his mother's used to when he needed a good tongue lashing.

"I am grateful. But…but…" How could he explain? The memory of his in-laws spreading gossip around the city to protect their so-called good name still burned hot. They hadn't cared how it would impact their own grandchildren, a fact that still burned his blood. He and his children were better off not allowing others to poke into their business.

Sarah's lip dropped. "We worked so hard to give you this surprise. Miss Williams thought you'd be happy."

Out of the mouths of babes. He ran a hand through his hair and blew out a heavy sigh. Sarah was right. This teacher lady did not deserve his wrath. "Jacob and Sarah, you clean up after supper and get the others to bed. I have an apology to make. I'll be back for some of that grub. Make sure you save me some." He stood and walked around to kiss Sarah and Laura on the top of their heads. "Thank you for all your hard work. Papa is very proud of you."

"Hey, we worked hard, too," eleven-year-old Charlie said around a mouthful of food.

"You want a kiss?" Jacob teased.

Charlie gave a good punch to Jacob's arm, and Jacob cuffed him on the back of the head.

Theo chuckled. "Enough boys, and thanks for all your help too." He snatched two biscuits and headed out the door. In the fresh air, he snagged a bite of one. It melted in his mouth, and he groaned. There were indeed some things about a woman he missed.

And what a woman. She hadn't taken a stick of the credit for what must have been hours of grueling work. Instead, she'd given all the praise to his girls. And not too many people stood up to him. Apparently, people found his size intimidating, but she hadn't cowered. Regal and proud, she'd stared him down, then reduced him to ashes with her matter-of-fact, no-nonsense logic.

Why had he not just said thank-you? What a dolt.

He threw a bridle and saddle on his magnificent stallion, the only luxury he owned, and cantered out of the barn. "Come on, boy." He patted Dante's mane. "We have a lady to take home." The stallion picked up speed.

Wow, that woman could walk fast. Where was she?

"Mr. Wallace?" He heard his name behind him and whirled the horse around. She came out from behind some trees.

"What are you doing over there?" His voice sounded harsher than he'd meant it to.

"I'm no fool. It's almost dark, and when I heard a rider coming, I thought it best to hide. When you passed, I saw it was you."

"You're not just a pretty face. You're smart too."

"I don't find that amusing."

"What?"

"I'd appreciate it if you wouldn't patronize me." She started down the lane, her long legs making quick time.

He rode beside her, not knowing what to say. How had he patronized her? By the way she marched alongside, clearly ignoring him, he had offended her. Again, he figured, after his rudeness at the house.

But what had he said? He wasn't all that comfortable making idle conversation anymore. His late wife, Louisa, had seen to that. Her constant prattle and self-centered conversations had left little room for comment.

But he better think of something to say, fast.

"May we start over?" he asked. "I came to say thank-you."

"Not necessary. Your girls—"

"Could never have done that on their own. We've been limping along since my mother died." He would not mention Louisa. She was not worth his breath.

"Sorry if I overstepped. I meant only to take a little of the load off."

"I should be the one saying I'm sorry. I've forgotten my social graces, and I'm not much of a conversationalist."

"That makes two of us." She gave him a wave of her hand.

"You did not offend. Now get back to your family, Mr. Wallace, they need you."

"I...I don't have the wagon. There wasn't time to hitch it up, but I'll give you a ride home." He reigned the horse in and held out his hand.

The teacher stopped and looked up at him for the first time. "Good heavens, no."

"Why not? He's a big stallion, quite capable of handling both of us."

"I don't do horses."

"You mean you don't ride?"

"That's precisely what I mean, Mr. Wallace. Now, if you'll excuse me, I need to get home before it's too dark to see where I'm going."

He was not going to let her walk home in the near dark after all the work she'd done. With a quick swing of his leg, he jumped down landing a few feet in front of her. "Come on. You must be exhausted after teaching all day and then cleaning that mess back there." He pointed toward his house in the distance. "I'll help you up." He spoke one word to Dante, and the horse stilled. "Step into the stirrup and swing your leg over—"

"I know how to mount a horse, Mr. Wallace. I merely prefer not to. Besides, I'm not wearing suitable attire."

"Don't over think it. Be spontaneous." The words were out of his mouth before he could filter what he was suggesting.

"I've had enough spontaneity for one day. I just cleaned a stranger's house, including washing his dirty underwear."

He laughed out loud. Had she just said that?

Even in the gathering dusk, he could see her cheeks bloom red. "Well then, after that horror, riding on a perfectly safe horse with that said stranger should not be a stretch." It surprised him to be bantering with her so naturally. But then again, she wasn't batting her eyelashes or looking at him as if he were a stallion that needed to be broken.

She hesitated, looked up at Dante, and then surprised him when her boot went into the stirrup. She was up and holding the horn of the saddle like a pro.

He caught a glimpse of her shapely legs peeking from beneath the slightly hiked-up skirt and the lacy stockings above her sensible boots. He looked away. Hmm, this woman was more interesting than he'd have thought at first glance.

He swung up behind her. Their bodies sank together into the curve of the stallion's back. He reached his arms around her to manage the reins. With a click of his tongue and a slight nudge of his knee, they were off.

She was trying so hard to keep distance between their bodies, her back ramrod straight.

"Relax," he said into her ear. "I promise. You're perfectly safe." He could feel her body slowly ease into the curve of his. A faint smell of wild roses wafted from her skin, the softness of her body against him...

No. He would not allow his mind to go there. He had six good reasons at home to care for, and farmland he needed to plant. There was no time for distractions. Nor would he ever be taken in so blindly again by a woman, any woman.

She pointed out directions, but otherwise they rode in silence. He couldn't help but like her. The fact that she didn't bombard him with constant chatter calmed him and reminded him of the reason he had ran after her. "I'm sorry I burst into the house like that. When I saw the smoke from the chimney, I thought Sarah had started a fire by herself, and I was scared for the children's safety. There's not enough of me to go around."

She nodded. "That must be difficult."

"And once you left, Sarah gave me a tongue lashing for not thanking you."

"Well now, Mr. Wallace, you deserved that."

"Call me Theo." The words surprised even him. He genuinely wanted to know this woman's name, and sharing his own seemed a good start. And it seemed silly after all she had done, and being his children's teacher, not to have some familiarity.

She paused. "I think it best we keep this professional, Mr. Wallace. Especially with me being the children's teacher."

"All right then, Miss Williams, but may I know your first name, now that you know mine?"

"No."

He chuckled. He did find it fun teasing this starchy, proper woman. What a refreshing change from the women in Richmond. He had the urge to break into a full gallop and not stop until she told him her first name. Instead, he tightened his arms around her, pretending a need to adjust the reins. Dante's head bobbed up and down at the intrusion.

Miss Wallace gasped.

He smiled. He should not enjoy this so much. But he did.

CHAPTER 4

Was Jeanette crazy? What had possessed her to agree to such an unladylike mode of transportation? She knew what—she felt dog-tired. Cleaning that house, and then the stress of Mr. Wallace's response after a day of teaching, had taken its toll. The temptation of getting off her feet with dusk approaching faster than she'd anticipated added to the appeal. Now, here she was up on top a very large horse—with a man.

If Agnus caught wind she was riding double with a man in the near dark—and a very handsome widower at that—well, she could kiss her job goodbye. They couldn't get through town fast enough for her liking. Not to mention, if anyone saw them, she would be mortified. Good thing it was almost pitch-black outside, and they were nearing the ranch. She would certainly walk up the drive. There was no way she wanted anyone to see such a display of familiarity.

Oh, but she couldn't lie to herself. Mr. Wallace's invitation to be spontaneous had made her want to do what he suggested. Why was that? And more honestly, she wanted to feel…something. She never took on her fears. She shied away from not only horses but all male contact. Yet here she was with a handsome man's arms wrapped around her, just inches from a heart that felt like it might beat out of her chest. Why shouldn't she enjoy a few moments of feeling alive? And oh, how alive she felt. Her hands tingled. Her arms felt on fire as he brushed up against them. And the back of her neck had goosebumps at the exhale of his every breath.

Had he heard the sharp intake of her gasp when he'd adjusted the reins?

So, this was what it felt like to be held close. There were no words to describe it. All fear of riding disappeared with his arms around her. She relaxed into the curve of his strong body. She would enjoy this moment and keep it stored for the times she allowed herself to dream.

"We're almost there." She tried to keep the disappointment from her voice.

"You live on the Richardson spread?"

"Katherine is my sister. Josiah Richardson is her late husband. She's remarried now and runs the ranch with her husband, Colby Braddock. But they've kept the name the same in honor of Josiah's memory."

"You live with your sister?"

"No. Our family has a farmhouse on the property, but there's only Pa and I left. Ma passed a while back, and all my sisters are married." She was glad she faced away from him. Heat blasted her cheeks. Nothing like pointing out her spinsterhood. "Guess I should've been a boy. Then, Pa would have someone to work the land when he's gone. He manages the farming end of the business. He's showing his age, but he's one of those men who will never stop until the day the good Lord takes him home. The way it stands, the farm will be absorbed into the Richardson spread when the time comes." Her sentences sounded breathy, and her words spilled out fast.

"Your pa is a farmer?"

"One of the best in the valley."

"Hmm."

"What does 'hmm' mean?"

Silence.

Should she ask again? No, she hated when people pushed her for information she wasn't ready to tell.

He turned the horse between the gates.

"I'll walk from here."

"Why?"

"It's best no one sees us. Don't want to start any rumors."

"I understand." He reined in his horse.

For one last second, she closed her eyes and soaked in the feel of his arms around her. He did not move or immediately dismount.

"Thank you for seeing me safely home." Her voice wavered. Could he tell she was affected by his nearness?

"Thank you for everything you did. For the first time, that house felt like a home."

His breath whispered in her ear, and she longed to turn her head toward the touch of the whiskers tickling her skin. Then he dismounted, and she sat up straight.

He held out his arms. "I'm a fast learner. I dare not tell you how to dismount, but I will catch you." His voice held a teasing tone.

She slid from the horse into his very capable arms.

He held on no longer than necessary to steady her. She received the same reaction she received from all men—disinterest.

"I best be getting back," he said. "I sure hope those boys saved me some of that great smelling food you made." He mounted his horse with one easy swing and tipped his hat. The dust kicked up around her, and then he was gone. The evening's first pale stars twinkled in the heavens as his silhouette disappeared into the thickening darkness.

If only she were beautiful—and not twenty-nine. If only she were practiced in the skill of conversation and flirtatious mannerisms instead of sitting like a statue in silence most of the way home. She shook the stars out of her eyes and turned up the drive. She had given up on *if only's,* years before. What was it about Theo Wallace that made her want to crack open the door of painful possibilities?

~

"It was so nice to have someone to help and teach me how to do things." Sarah Wallace stood beside Jeanette's desk, longing in her eyes. "It's only been a week since you came, and the house looks so messy again."

"You should be out playing with the other girls on your lunch, not fretting about the house."

"I hate the mess." Her chin jutted out, and her dark brown eyes pierced into Jeanette's soul.

"I see how meticulous you are, Sarah. You're like me, I think. You hate chaos."

"I used to help…" Her eyes filled with tears and she bit down on her lip. "I should've paid better attention."

"You had no idea your mama—"

"I don't mean my mama. I mean Grammie." She twisted one of her pigtails around her finger. "I don't remember my mama much."

Just how long had Theo been a widower? That was one piece of information the rumor mill had not provided. "Maybe your pa will meet a nice lady someday, and you'll have a new mama."

"Papa doesn't like socializing much. He says that women are more trouble than they're worth."

What a thing to say to his daughter. "That is certainly not true of all women," Jeanette said with more force than she intended. A surge of anger rode her spine at such an unfair generalization. What happened to make Theo feel that way? And why was she referring to him as *Theo* in her mind? She lifted her hand to still Sarah tugging at her braid and gave a squeeze. "You're going to be a fine woman someday soon, and that will not be true of you."

"But how will I know how to be a woman without anyone to teach me?"

The truth of that question pulled at Jeanette's heart strings, and she found herself speaking without forethought. "Tomorrow is Saturday and I have nothing planned. I'll come over bright and early to help you girls get organized. We'll make it our Saturday thing."

Sarah's eyes brightened. "You would do that?"

"Yes." Jeanette stood. "Yes, I will. Now off you go." She waved her hand. "Have some fun before lunch hour is over, and don't you worry about the house." Should she have made such a promise without discussing it with Mr. Wallace first? Oh well, she needed to have that conversation with him about the children's schooling anyway. She'd work her arrival so she came after the boys were in the field, and then he could not decline her help.

Sarah's smile split wide. Her head tilted. "Should I ask Papa?"

"Leave your pa to me. You need help, and you shall receive it. Now run along and play."

Sarah skipped out of the schoolhouse door, and Jeanette's smile crumbled. Too much weight was put on that ten-year-old, and she was going to ease it whether her papa approved or not.

~

Pa entered the kitchen, and Jeanette's head snapped up from her bowl of oatmeal. Oh bother. She had hoped to be on her way before he started asking questions.

"What'cha doing up so early on a Saturday?" Pa scratched his head and yawned.

"Can't a grown woman have any privacy?"

Pa's brows rose. "Now ya got me real interested." He shuffled over to the wood stove and poured some hot brew into a tin cup. "A girl who protects her only morning to sleep in with as much vigor as you have over the years sure does pique some interest when she's changing things up." He curled his aging hands around the coffee mug and lifted it to his lips.

"Help yourself to oatmeal." Jeanette pointed to the pot warming on the edge of the wood stove. "That's all I'm making this morning. I'm reserving my energy to help others."

Pa chuckled. "If it was Helen you were helping, you'd just say so. Come on, spill the beans."

There was no way she would get out of the house without telling him what she was up to, but could she do so nonchalantly? She was already a bundle of nerves at the thought of coming up against Mr. Wallace. He may not take kindly to her gift of charity, being the private person he was. The last thing he would want was the community knowing the dire straits of his predicament.

"Promise to keep this between the two of us?"

He chuckled. "Because I have so many people to talk to out there in the dirt between them there rows."

"If you must know, I'm headed to the Wallace residence. And I shall be gone all day." Jeanette tried to speak normally, but her voice sounded strained. Heat flooded her face.

"Wallace? Is that the family that moved into the old Reiner place?"

"Yes."

Pa whistled through his teeth. "That place needs a mighty lot of work. Old man Reiner is not known for his work ethic or his scruples. I couldn't believe what I heard in town, him bragging about what he got for that place, and how sure he is Mr. Wallace won't make a go of it."

"How would that be to his benefit?"

"He'd get his place back with whatever improvements were done. And keep the down payment and all the monthly payments. If those rumors are true, Mr. Wallace must be on the desperate side."

"Oh my." Jeanette's hand flew to her mouth. "From what I've witnessed…" She nodded.

"I've seen him at church," Pa said. "But every time I go to make his acquaintance, he's bustling his family out."

"I've only met him once before, but this much I picked up on—Mr. Wallace is a private man."

"So, why are you going?"

"If you saw that place, Pa, you wouldn't ask. Six children with no mama. There's cooking, cleaning, spring planting, so much work any man would be overwhelmed. And the barn and house look like a good wind could take them down. Quite frankly, take your pick of reasons. I've never witnessed so much need under one roof."

"Then I'll come, too. And we could—"

"No. I think he's going to have a fit when I tell him I intend to help each Saturday. Let me ease him into this."

Pa lifted his bushy brows. He had a teasing sparkle in his dark eyes.

"Don't look at me that way. You should see those little girls. The oldest one, Sarah, is only ten, and she's trying to take on the load of a mama. It's heart-wrenching."

Pa filled his bowl with oatmeal and set it on the table. He lifted his work-worn hand and grazed it down Jeanette's cheek. "Ahh, you've always been a softie, more concerned for others than for yourself. Just let me know if there's any way I can help." He kissed the top of her head before slipping into his seat. "Your secret is safe with me. But I suggest you cut across the back field and follow the path through the woods. You'll come out on the country lane that goes right by that place. Bypass town and keep the tongues from wagging."

Jeanette smiled up at him. "My thoughts exactly."

CHAPTER 5

"Sarah told me you'd be coming. Thanks, but no thanks." Theo shut the door firmly in her face. He hated to be rude, but that woman had been in his head all week. He had no intention of encouraging another such week of wondering what it would be like to have a fine hard-working woman like her at his side. Or having him questioning himself about whether he could trust his decision-making abilities regarding women.

She didn't knock again.

Good, she was not persisting.

He peeked out the half-boarded kitchen window and watched her step down off the porch. Apparently, she was leaving. That was easier than he'd anticipated. But his gut felt like a good-sized rock had dropped in. Sarah's eyes had lit up when she talked about Miss Williams and all she would learn from the teacher.

"All right boys, out to the field we go."

Jacob and Charlie groaned.

"If you want to eat all winter, then we need to get that crop planted. We're already behind all the farmers in the area." It didn't help that he had wasted time that morning waiting to deal with the Miss Williams problem.

"Does Ben have to come?" Jacob asked. "He just gets in the way."

"He can pick rocks. Besides, Sarah has enough to watch with the other two." He looked over and caught his oldest girl's eye. She was blinking back tears. Doggone it, he had no idea how to deal with girls. They cried at the drop of a hat.

He walked over and crouched in front of her, but she turned away. "Come on, Sarah, don't be mad at Papa."

"Miss Williams was going to teach me how—"

"Miss Williams had no right to promise anything without talking to me first." He stood and ran a hand through his hair.

"Why can't we accept help? We surely need it."

"Yeah," Charlie whined. "Why didn't you let Miss Williams come in? I'm tired of smoked ham and beans."

"Got to say, my mouth was watering at the thought of that meal she made last week," Jacob added.

Laura added, "And Miss Williams said—"

"Enough. All of you."

Laura jumped at the sound of his raised voice and started to cry.

Now he had two of them in tears. "Come on, girls." He bent down and held out his arms. They walked in, and he hugged them tight. "You have to trust my decision. We can't ask Miss Williams, who has worked hard all week teaching you children, to come here on her day off and do our work. That's not fair to her."

"But, Papa, she wants to help," Sarah said.

As much as he knew he was disappointing the girls, it was best they didn't get too attached to a temporary fix. Women were complicated, and except his mama, he'd not met a one who didn't have an ulterior motive.

33

No, he had no need of a woman around the house. Now, some good farming advice, that he would take.

"Come on. Times awastin'." He stepped out, and the door slammed behind him. He would hook up the mule to the plow, and hopefully, by the time the day was done, they'd have enough furrowed soil to plant.

Movement in the corner of his eyes caught his attention. He looked back over his shoulder, and there she was with a shovel, digging up the garden patch he had still not gotten around to planting. For crying out loud. Did that woman not take no for an answer? He marched over with a decided frown on his face, intending to look and sound the part. "What are you doing?"

"What does it look like I'm doing? Every family must have a vegetable garden, and you have far too much on your plate to do everything."

"No, I mean why are you still here?"

"Because God told me to stay."

"God told you?"

"Yes."

"So, you're telling me God speaks from heaven now?"

She stopped her digging and planted the spade in the earth. "Not an audible voice. He speaks into my spirit. Had I left, I would be disobeying His will."

Theo could not make sense of what she was saying. He believed in a God up there somewhere, but God had certainly never spoken to him.

"Trust me, Mr. Wallace, I'm no more excited about this than you are. Especially when I have someone as obstinate and ungrateful as you are to deal with." The frown on her face draped her words in determination.

"Let me get this straight—I asked you to leave, but you have no intention of going."

"I fear God more than man."

He shook his head. He did not get all this God stuff, and he had hours of work ahead in the blazing sun. Every moment he argued with this stubborn woman was one less in the field.

She planted her hands on her hips. "Let me put it to you this way, Mr. Wallace. I brought some seeds and intend to have this garden planted by noon. Then I will tackle the inside and the laundry this afternoon. By the time you come in at dusk, I will have supper made and be on my way."

"I don't need charity."

"Yes, Mr. Wallace, you do. We all do at times, and there's no shame in that. But you can count on me not to whisper a word of this because I respect privacy as much as you do. The only one who knows where I am is my pa, and he's a farmer like you without a penchant for gossip."

Theo didn't have a clue how to fight such logic. The need for help was obvious. When would he find time to wash the clothes and clean the house? And they did need vegetables.

"Run and tell the girls to join me." Miss Williams spoke the words like a command. "Laura was most excited to learn how to plant seeds, and I brought all the ingredients for a chocolate cake, which Sarah is going to learn how to make this afternoon." She pushed her glasses up on her nose, picked up the shovel, and began digging.

He turned to go.

"Oh, and I didn't see a hoe in your barn where I found this shovel. Do you have one?"

He turned back toward her, trying to fight back his smile. He should be annoyed and frustrated, but he couldn't seem to summon either response. The woman wanted a hoe. Not his attention or attendance for tea. Not a ride in the park or to the shops, but a hoe. She was so incredibly different from any of the women he had known in the city. Her no-nonsense approach and intelligence drew him.

Dangerous water to dive into.

"A hoe, Mr. Wallace?"

Like an idiot, he had stood there staring at her. "I'll get Jacob to bring it to you."

~

Jeanette loosened the earth with each thrust of the spade. How had she had the strength to defy Theo? God did indeed give power when He wanted something. As clear as that cerulean sky above her, she'd heard God speak into her spirit, encouraging her to follow through on everything she had so carefully planned for the day. She was quite familiar with living in the shadows, but somehow in this circumstance, the wellbeing of those children pulled at her heartstrings. Was it just the children? If so, why did her pulse quicken at the sight of their father? Like right now, as he strode so quickly with Tessie riding on his broad shoulders, the other two girls and Ben running to keep up.

Laura burst ahead and barreled into Jeanette at full speed. "You stayed." Her arms hung on tight.

Jeanette leaned down and hugged back. "I did, and you can thank your papa. Once I explained what important work we had today and how much help I was going to get from you girls, he realized what a wonderful day we're all going to have."

He mouthed thank-you to her and lifted Tessie from his shoulders, swinging her in a circle and making her giggle before he put her down. "Go ahead, Ben, ask her." Theo nudged his seven-year old son with his large hand. "But remember, no is no."

"May I stay and help with the garden? I could learn how to water the rows."

"Why, that's an excellent idea, Ben."

"But you said the garden would be my 'sponsibility," Laura said, pulling at her dress.

JEANETTE'S GIFT

"Only with your papa's permission, and the word is *responsibility*. Can you say that correctly?"

"Responsibility." The word struggled off Laura's tongue.

"How about we put the two of you in charge of the garden, a team effort?" Mr. Wallace said. "There'll be more than enough responsibility to share. Isn't that right, Miss Williams?"

"It is." Jeanette agreed.

"But Ben thinks that, because he's a boy, he can boss me around even though I'm older than him." Laura rolled her bright blue eyes and placed her hands on her hips.

"Do not. You're the bossy one."

"Do so." Laura stomped her foot, and the dust billowed.

"I guess if the two of you can't get along, Miss Williams will head home. And, Ben, you'll come out in the field and pick rocks." Theo's voice rang with authority.

He smiled at Jeanette, and she nodded, trying to stay focused. Oh goodness, that smile really was something. Her gaze snapped back toward the children. "Your decision, Ben and Laura. Either you decide to work together, or you heard your papa, I'll have to go home. And that would ruin it for Sarah, who plans to make you a yummy chocolate cake for dessert this evening."

The children looked at each other and nodded.

"All right then. Let's plant a garden. Sarah, you wash the dishes from breakfast and get the kitchen ready for our baking session. Ben, since you already know how to pick rocks, any that come up as I dig, you will remove to the edge of the garden, then rake smooth any lumps you see. And, Laura, the seeds are in that bag over there. Carefully pull out the jars and set them at the end of each row. See where I have sticks in the ground?"

She nodded.

"What about me?" Five-year-old Tessie asked. "Don't I get to be a helper?"

"But of course. You have a very important job. You will get

us a cup of water when we need one. Sarah will help you fill the cup, and I could use a drink right now."

Tessie's green eyes rounded, and her skinny legs took off running toward the house.

"I'll eat my shirt if you have that garden in by lunch," Theo said. "But then again, if this is how the good Lord told you to spend your Saturday, who am I to argue?" Theo hit her with a ready smile that made her stomach lurch.

"Hope you like the taste of linen," she called after him as he walked away.

His laughter filled the yard, and she smiled. Where was the shy Jeanette? And who was this woman with the snappy comeback?

She smiled at Ben and Laura. "All right, we're ready to build our first mound for the squash." She gathered the rich soil into a hill with her shovel. "The seeds." She pointed to the jar a few feet away. Laura ran to get it. "So, this is what we're going to do for each mound. Are you watching carefully?"

Both children nodded, their eyes big and attentive.

She pulled four seeds from the jar. "Now, as my Papa taught me, we plant one seed for the blackbird, one for the crow, one for the cutworm, and one to grow." She poked a seed into the ground as she spouted off each line of the rhyme.

The children giggled.

"Do you think you can remember that?"

"One for the blackbird," Laura said.

"One for the crow." Ben beat her to the next line, and she scowled at him.

"One for the…" Laura paused.

Jeanette kept from laughing at the child's furrowed brow.

"One for the wormy," Ben yelled.

"No, it's one for the cutter thingy," Laura shouted.

"You're both half-right," Jeanette corrected. "One for the cutworm."

JEANETTE'S GIFT

"And one to grow," the children said in unison.

"Very good."

Ben bobbed up and down, strutting about like an ornery rooster.

Laura rolled her eyes at him.

Jeanette laughed. It reminded her of days gone by when one moment she was fighting with her sisters and the next, laughing. Her life with Pa was but a shadow of the yesteryears.

"Now you try." She handed the hoe to Ben and the shovel to Laura. "Keep the mounds in a row because we're going to water them in the trench below."

~

"Well, I'll be darned." Theo stepped inside that evening, the sound of wonder on his lips. "Laura and Ben just showed me the garden, and this house looks and smells amazing."

Jeanette ignored him. She could go about serving up the meal without a tremble in her hands if she kept her eyes on the task and off of him.

"I will not underestimate Miss Williams again."

Jeanette didn't turn from the wood stove and the large pot of stew she was stirring. "Not just me, it was a team effort. Wasn't it, children?"

She smiled as they each told him a piece of the day's story. The saving grace had been that the three younger ones were exhausted after the gardening, making it easy to get the cake in the oven, supper on, and housework done. All those trips back and forth to the house for cups of water had paid off, and Tessie'd taken a long afternoon nap. God had indeed blessed their day.

"Hmm, that smells delicious." Theo's voice came from right behind her, and Jeanette flinched. He bent over her shoulder and inhaled. "Haven't had anything that smelled that good in a long time."

She stepped to the sideboard, out of his space, and moved the hot biscuits from the pan into a basket. Her hands quivered. She prayed he didn't notice. "Biscuits again. But I promise next week, I'll make fresh bread."

He was beside her again. Close. Too close. "Next week?" he whispered.

"Yes, next week." Now it was not only her hands but her voice that trembled as well.

"Hmm. We'll talk later when I take you home."

"Take me home?" She spun toward him. Then tried to back up, bumping her backside into the counter.

"I'm not going to let you leave again without us both enjoying your hot meal." His warm breath fanned her cheeks as he reached for a hot biscuit.

She caught herself just short of smacking his hand away and was so thankful. That would have been far too familiar. "I…I have to get home before dark."

"Even if you left now, it would be dark before you got halfway, and I'm not about to let you go alone." He popped a piece of the biscuit into his mouth. "So good."

"But not a good example for the children who I made wait until it was time to eat," she whispered.

He chuckled. "I suppose I have left all culture behind, but back to the subject at hand. What's the difference when I take you home? Now, or after we eat? Personally, I'd prefer to enjoy a hot meal first."

The thought of sharing a ride on his horse yet again made her cheeks flush with heat. "I don't much like your horse."

"Hmm."

That could mean a thousand things. Did he realize the truth, that the problem wasn't the horse but the close proximity to him?

"We'll give our mule, Blossom, a rest after her day in the field while we eat. Then, if it makes you more comfortable, I'll hitch her up to the wagon."

"Here." She shoved the basket of biscuits into his chest. "Can you put those on the table?"

"I'll take that as a yes." He smiled, obviously quite pleased with himself, and moved toward the table.

"Oh, and I'll need your shirt."

"What?"

"You said you'd eat your shirt if we had the garden in by noon." She looked past him at the kids. "And we did, didn't we children?"

Their heads bobbed up and down. There was something about their smiling faces that gave her courage.

"Oh, so that's why you brought us lunch out to the field…so I couldn't verify for myself?" Theo's voice held a teasing tone.

"No, I was saving you time. But we worked on telling time this morning while we planted the garden. With all these witnesses to corroborate, the story, I don't see how you can get out of it. We're going to quite enjoy seeing you eat your shirt."

Jacob and Charlie snorted in laughter.

Ben hooted. "Yeah. Yeah."

She held out her hand. "Shall I serve it with a side of stew?"

Laura giggled.

Sarah's dark eyes danced with delight.

Tessie jumped up and down. "Eat it, Papa. Eat it."

"I have to get out of this dirty thing before supper anyway." He held her gaze with a challenge. A network of laugh lines etched the curves of his eyes as he started to unbutton his shirt. When he slid it off his broad shoulders, she caught a glimpse of his corded muscles and sinewy strength. She turned away.

His chuckle followed him into his bedroom off the main room. Drat. That man knew exactly how to shut her up. She would not tease him about his shirt again. But goodness be, it was hot in the room, and it had nothing to do with the wood stove.

She filled each bowl with a generous portion of hearty stew, glad there would be plenty for the next day.

Theo returned and pulled out his chair at the head of the table.

Jeanette surveyed the seating arrangements, wondering where to squeeze in. Sarah patted the bench beside her. "Sit beside me." Jeanette slid onto the bench. Tessie immediately popped up from her chair and snuggled in on the other side. They all shuffled down to make room. Jeanette put her arm around Tessie, and the child melted into her side.

Theo's brows rose, but Jeanette didn't care. For the first time in her life, she experienced what it would feel like to have a family of her own.

"Mind if I say grace?"

Theo and the boys had already been shoveling the food in. They lowered their spoons slowly. "Sure. Seems we've gotten out of the habit since Ma's been gone." A red tinge filled Theo's cheeks.

Jeanette could barely get the words past the knot lodged in her throat. Right here in this room was everything she had ever dreamed of. She finished a quick prayer and then pushed the stew around in the tin bowl unable to eat. Her stomach clenched at the thought of Theo reading her mind.

"How can you not be starving after all the work you've done today?" Theo asked. He popped half a gravy-smothered biscuit into his mouth and closed his eyes, seeming to savor it.

She didn't want to stare at him, but somehow that small relaxation took ten years off his face.

His eyes opened. "Your cookin' is next thing to heaven."

"Thank you." The word croaked out like it'd come from a frog with laryngitis.

"It sure is," Jacob said. "Can I have more?"

"I made plenty, enough for seconds tonight and extra for tomorrow. You'll have to let me know what you would like next Saturday so I can plan ahead." Her words were met with smiles all around the table—except for Theo, whose face went sober. He looked down at his plate.

"Since you're not eating anyways, we best get you home."

The stew on his plate wasn't even finished, but he rose abruptly. "I'll hitch up the mule." He grabbed his coat from the hook and slammed his hat on his head. The door closed a little too loudly behind him.

She'd upset him. Too bad, because she was coming back next Saturday, and that was that.

CHAPTER 6

*T*heo could not contain his annoyance. Miss Williams hadn't been seated on the wagon buckboard for more than a second before he spoke. "Why did you mention next Saturday? I told you I needed to discuss it with you." He slapped the reins, and Blossom started moving.

"What's to discuss? You need the help, and the good Lord has sent me."

His hands tightened on the reins. The woman was infuriating with all her God talk. "And what's the good Lord going to do when my kids get attached to you and you decide it's time to find the next charity project? Did you see how Tessie snuggled up to you at the meal?"

"I did."

He waited for her to elaborate but she said nothing. "Well?"

"Hmm."

Oh, he knew what she was doing, using his word. The one he used when he didn't want to answer a question.

"Please… don't come." He tried to keep the catch out of his throat but could not. His kids had been through enough heartbreak after losing their grandmother, being abandoned by their mother, and all the gossip her folks had stirred up. Good thing the younger ones had no memory of that time.

"Why?" She twisted her body toward him. "What's wrong with showing a little kindness?"

"And where will that kindness be when some man snatches you up and your Saturdays are full?"

She turned forward again, but he didn't miss the hurt in her eyes nor the tightness in her lips. "That's not even remotely likely."

"Of course it's likely. Just a matter of time, I'd say."

"Have you somehow missed the obvious, or do I have to spell it out?"

"The obvious?" He didn't have a clue what she was talking about. Why were women so complicated?

"This." She pointed to her face.

He looked at it, trying to figure out what she was talking about it. There was nothing wrong. No scars. No blemishes. And he had already seen beyond those glasses, if that is what she was referring to. She had dark brown intelligent eyes. Kind and mysterious. But the glasses...that had to be it.

"So what? You wear glasses."

"Don't pretend."

She was getting harder to understand by the minute, and they were getting so off track. "There's nothing wrong with the way you look. Can we stay on topic? My children..." He had to make her understand. His kids could not weather more loss. "They've had enough loss to last a lifetime. First their mother, and then their grandmother. If they get attached to you and suddenly you're gone..."

"I assure you, I have nowhere to go."

"So that's it. You'll defy my wishes regarding *my* children?"

She placed her hand on his arm, and a shot of awareness pulsed through. "Please. Let me shine in the only way I know how. Children are all I have, and I've helped many. From extra hours in their learning process to—"

"But this is not tutoring on how to read or write."

She yanked her hand back, and he missed the contact. "No, it's teaching life skills a girl will need as she grows into a woman. Quite different from what you'll teach your sons." Words flowed out, and as much as he wanted to put a halt to her argument, he held his tongue to let her finish. "I promise, I'll never abandon your children. They'll always be in my life, no matter what the future holds, until you marry again, and I'm no longer need—"

"My children are my only concern. Marriage is not." Was this her angle, and that God stuff a ruse?

She batted her hand into the air. "Of course, you'll remarry. You're a handsome man who has stirred up a fair amount of interest with your weekly church attendance."

The fact that she thought him handsome made his heart pick up speed. He scowled at his own stupid reaction. "I don't care what kind of interest I stir up. And I only attend church because of a promise I made to my dying mother." He gritted his teeth and slapped the reins. Blossom picked up her pace. He was not afraid of the women at church. He was afraid of this woman in particular.

"I'm sorry about your ma. I lost my ma too." She patted his arm as if he were a child. A strange urge to put his arm around her and show her he was every inch a man came over him. He gripped the reins tighter.

They rode in silence. At least she didn't feel it necessary to fill every moment with chatter. He maneuvered the wagon between the gates of the Richardson ranch. "It's later and darker than last week. I would prefer to see you safely to your door."

She nodded. "A wagon is a little more respectable, should we be seen."

"And a lot less fun." He chuckled, glancing her way. Even in the moonlight, he could see the color pouring into her cheeks. She was fun to tease, and it took the attention off him. She had a way of pulling things out of him he did not want to reveal.

He drew to a stop in front of the idyllic farmhouse. If only his home looked like this. It would take some good fortune and years of hard work to obtain this level of hominess. But he was up for the challenge. His kids deserved this new start, where gossiping tongues could not rip apart their world, where crisp fresh air replaced the stench of the city streets in the only area he could afford to live.

"In light of your aversion to marriage," Miss Williams said, "I think it is all the more prudent that I come next Saturday, for the sake of the girls. There are things they need to learn that only a woman can teach them." She pushed her glasses up on her nose and gave him a no-nonsense look.

Drat, her common sense was infuriating. How could he refute that?

The screen door slammed, and a thin wiry man hopped down the porch steps with the agility of a man half his age.

"I'm glad you brought my girl home. She's twenty-nine, and still I worry."

"Pa, I'm quite able to take care of myself."

He had wondered how old she was. Twenty-nine? She looked years younger. And still not married. Why?

She jumped down from her side of the wagon before his brain kicked into motion. He should've helped her down, and he should introduce himself. He reached down and held out his hand. "Theo Wallace, sir. Thanks for sharing your daughter for the day."

"Jeb Williams." He pumped Theo's hand with a firm grip. "I don't have much say in what my girl does, but this I know—you'll never find a kinder soul on God's green earth. Even though she's as stubborn as a badger when she gets an idea in her head."

"Pa. I'm standing right here."

Theo glanced her way but kept his focus on her father. "Don't I know it."

She jutted out her chin. "It's been a long and productive day. I shall retire." She allowed a tiny smile to curl the edges of her generous mouth. "See you next Saturday, Mr. Wallace." He watched her turn and head up the stairs into the house without a backward glance. Stubborn as a badger and as magnificent as they come. He was no match for the likes of Miss Williams.

He still didn't know her first name.

"Seems I have no choice but to be her charity case," he mumbled.

"Say what, son? My hearing ain't so good."

"I was wondering what your daughter's first name is. The kids and I have been calling her Miss Williams. That seems a tad too formal when she insists on helping each Saturday."

"It's Jeanette, after my mother."

Jeanette seemed too formal for one so down to earth. Nope, he didn't think the name suited her. It didn't roll off his tongue. She was more of a Jeanie. The kind that came in a bottle and granted wishes. "Thank you." Theo tipped his hat. "I best be getting back to the children."

"Mr. Wallace?"

Theo's hands stilled on the reins.

"If'in you need any farming advice or help, I've been around for a summer or two, and I'd be happy to give you a little of my time."

"That is very kind of you, Mr. Williams. I see where Jeanette gets her generous heart from."

"If you knew my story, young man, you'd know that I've been in need a time or two. I'd consider it an honor to pass the kindness that was given to me on to another."

"Seems you taught your daughter well. She obviously witnessed that kindness over the years."

"If'in we learn to help each other, the generosity keeps going around. Hoping I'm not overstepping my boundaries, but I noticed you were behind on your planting, and your barn roof needs a little love. How about I rustle up a few hands and come by next week with my daughter?"

Was his need that obvious? He'd guess anyone walking by the place could see it would take him a month of Sundays and all the time in between just to get the field planted. Not to mention all the other tasks that needed doing. They were too numerous to mention. It was not the time for pride or suspicion. His family needed this. "I'd be much obliged, sir."

"See you next Saturday."

Theo tipped his hat and snapped the reins. Blossom plodded ahead.

Mr. Williams had said the same parting words as Jeanette before she'd disappeared into the house. How had he gone from asking her not to come at all to agreeing to not only her help, but her father's help too?

CHAPTER 7

"I felt such conviction rise up within me." Jeanette sipped her hot tea gingerly and looked around Helen Donovan's parlor, avoiding her friend's questioning eyes. Saturday was only two days away and she was worried her pa had overstepped the boundaries of a *little* help.

"The Lord works in mysterious ways." Helen dipped a sugar cookie into her tea.

"Apparently, Mr. Wallace agreed to Pa's offer to organize some helpers for this coming Saturday. I don't think he has any idea how big a group is coming. Colby even donated his ranch hands for the day. They're going to work on the barn."

Helen placed her teacup on the side table and knotted her hands together, tenting them over her generous girth. "I haven't seen you this excited in a long time. Maybe never."

"I'm happy for the family. The need is so great. If they can get enough help to get on their feet, how wonderful will that be?"

"Could it be more than just the children?" Helen's eyes twinkled. "Perhaps a certain young farmer has caught your eye?"

Jeanette swallowed hard. Helen had a way of looking into

her soul. It was unnerving. Best to laugh it off. "A girl would have to be blind not to notice Theo...I mean Mr. Wallace. I may be a spinster, but I'm not dead." She had better curb using his first name in her mind. It was beginning to slip out.

Helen chuckled.

"But I'm not silly enough to lose my head over him. He is far too handsome for the likes of me."

"Why do you do that?"

"Do what?"

"You're a smart girl. Don't play dumb with me."

"Hmm." She loved the word she'd picked up from Mr. Wallace. It covered everything but said nothing.

"Don't you be hmm-ing me, either." Helen pointed her finger. "We've shared a lot since your mama died. And if there's one thing I know, it's when you need some plain talk. You run yourself down all the time, and yet you're the most gifted woman I know. You sing like a meadowlark, you play the piano to perfection, you can decorate any room, fix any meal, sew any piece of clothing, not to mention teach a roomful of students, and yet you do not see the beautiful creation God has made in you."

"If I'm so beautiful, why then do men look past me as if I don't exist? Life is a cruel teacher, Helen, but I've learned well. Besides, I've come to peace with my reality, and I certainly don't plan on opening my world back up to fanciful dreams." If only Helen knew how much those dreams had cost her in the past.

"Do you believe in the sovereignty of God?" Helen's graying blue eyes pierced her soul. Where was she going with this kind of questioning?

"Of course, I do."

"Then I challenge your thinking. If God has the right to do whatever He wants, when He wants, and how He wants, which is what His sovereignty means, then why have you never accepted how you look? Why do you compare yourself to your sisters constantly and always decide you come up short?"

Jeanette put down her teacup a tad too forcefully and stood. She crossed the room to the window and stared out. She could not meet Helen's intense gaze.

"Or is God not allowed to be sovereign in His creation of people?"

"That's fine for all the beautiful ones to say. They've never been tested." Jeanette whirled from the window. "Look at you, Helen. You're eighty, and you're still very attractive. Something this will never be." She pointed at her face.

"We are only as attractive as we believe we are."

"That's a pile of poppycock." Jeanette threw up her hands.

"Is it? Have you ever gone through a day, any day, believing you were beautiful?"

"I live in reality."

"Do you now? I rather doubt it. If you could see yourself the way I see you, you would believe that God made you very beautiful."

Goodness, Helen was infuriating today. Jeanette wrung her hands and paced. How could she make her dear friend understand?

"Stop pacing that floor and sit—"

"I don't care to sit."

"Then at least agree to a favor this Saturday?" Helen said.

"What?"

"Who is the most beautiful woman you know?"

"Katherine, with my other sisters not far behind."

"And what makes them beautiful?"

"Why, how they look of course." Jeanette rolled her eyes.

"Stop rolling those beautiful brown eyes at me and listen." Helen patted the seat beside her, but Jeanette ignored the invitation.

"Let's take Katherine for instance. She's beautiful not just because of what the outward shell looks like, but because she's giving and sacrificial on the inside. Wouldn't you agree?"

"Yes, but—"

"No buts. You believe too many negative things about yourself, and that has got to change. On Saturday, I want you to walk with your head held high, your shoulders back, no looking down. Imagine every eye is upon you because you're the most beautiful woman in the world. And how about you wear your hair differently and add a splash of color to your clothing. Then we'll chat next week."

"Why would I do that?" Jeanette patted her familiar bun. A chill of concern spread through her body at the thought of changing anything that might draw attention. "I cannot."

"It will be a good exercise in believing in yourself, in what God gave you both on the outside and the inside."

No, she could not agree to this. She was comfortable hiding in the shadows. Just the thought wreaked havoc on her breathing. She took in a couple deep breaths to still the light-headedness she was feeling. "There's no need—"

"There's every need, and no harm in trying. Accent the positive on the outside, but even more importantly concentrate on your thinking on the inside."

"What do you mean?"

"Think upon all the things you're good at, the gifts that God has given you. And no negative thoughts allowed into that head of yours. You hear?"

"I'm not sure it's possible. I have to admit that I have a lot of negativity inside this head of mine."

"I know you do, dear. Humor me. Grant an old lady a silly wish."

The way Helen was looking at her with that pleading in her eyes, how could Jeanette say no? "Fine. But it won't change a thing."

The crinkles around her lovely eyes twinkled with merriment. "That's my girl. Now come back and finish your tea. I've raised your dander all I'm going to for one day."

~

Jeanette flopped over in her warm bed. One cognitive thought of the day, and she was up. Sleeping in on Saturday no longer held any appeal. Excitement surged through her body. She prayed Theo would graciously accept the help offered. Being the private type, he may feel overwhelmed, and Pa had gone overboard in seeking help. Half the church men were coming, and some of the ladies had already sent notes with their children to school to say they would be bringing food for the workers.

Jeanette pulled her sensible dress on and had begun wrapping her hair tightly in a knot at the base of her neck when she remembered her promise to Helen. Practicality dictated her hair be tied back, but a promise was a promise.

She swivelled in front of the mirror. The sensible dress had to stay. She would be working. However, she could do something different with her hair. The bun could be softened with a couple wavy strands down the sides. No, those strands would drive her crazy, and she was going to work. She braided her thick hair and pulled it to one side so it hung down her torso. This was how Gracie always wore hers. That small change softened her face. She gazed into the mirror and smiled—a full smile with nothing held back. The transformation was undeniable. Could Helen be right? Was Jeanette her own worst enemy? She wasn't convinced, but she would keep her word.

Jeanette tiptoed down the steps and into the kitchen. She needed coffee, at least until Pa and the sun decided to get up. With care, she lit the wood stove and readied the beans.

"Good morning."

Jeanette jumped back from the stove with a huff. "Really, Pa? Need you sneak up on me like that?"

"I was not sneaking, my girl. I must tend to the animals and do a host of other things before heading off to the Wallace place. The early bird hatches the egg."

Jeanette laughed. "You mean the early bird catches the worm."

"Whatever the case may be. I want to dedicate this day to the Wallace farm, but I have some things that must be done."

Jeanette poured coffee for herself and Pa and set a pot of water on the stove to boil. "Breakfast won't be long." She cut two thick slices of bread and slid them onto a plate, smothering them with honey, just the way Pa liked. "Boiled eggs or oatmeal?" She carried the coffee and bread to the table.

"I'll have oat..." His mouth dropped open. "Well, if that don't beat all."

"What?" Jeanette's face flushed with heat. Pa was staring at her as if she had two heads.

"Nothing." He looked away and picked up the bread.

"Out with it, Pa."

It was a moment before he said, "You look nice. Your hair and all." He waved his free hand without looking at her and took another big bite of honeyed bread.

Jeanette couldn't believe one small change in her hair could render Pa speechless. That was a first. Was it too drastic?

She couldn't do this.

Helen would have to understand. She was Plain Jane Jeanette, and anything outside the obvious was trying too hard. Everybody would know the ugly duckling was trying to look like a swan.

Oops, there she went. Negative thoughts flowed so naturally.

She made the oatmeal, served it up, and headed out of the kitchen. "Call me when you're ready, Pa."

"Aren't you going to join me?"

"No. I already ate." She hoped God would forgive her white lie, but she couldn't sit across from Pa's stare one more minute.

There was still time to right this wrong. If Pa thought it a drastic change, then others would see her efforts as the poor spinster Jeanette trying hard to get the available Mr. Wallace's attention. The thought made her shudder from tip to toe. How humiliating that would be.

Before the mirror in the bedroom, she unplaited the braid and shook her long thick hair free. With a familiar twist of her wrist, she scooped the strands that softened her face into the bun and pulled the hair good and tight. Enough of this nonsense.

Put the braid back in.

What was that urging, that tugging, that feeling she had to obey? That if she did not listen, God would be disappointed?

Today is not about your comfort, daughter, it is about truth.

No. She couldn't change her appearance, but she could work on her thought processes. Yes. That was what she'd do. She'd work on believing she was fearfully and wonderfully made, as God's word said she was.

And that braid needs to go back in.

She had been a Christian for a long time. She knew when the Spirit of God was speaking. But was she brave enough? The thought of others judging her... But she didn't want to disobey the Spirit's lead. Oh, what a conundrum. She raised her hands to the pins in her bun.

Her stomach clenched and unclenched. Her hands fell to her side.

I will give you courage. Just ask Me.

"Lord, help me. There'll be so many people there. and I don't want them to think—"

You are doing this for Me.

Jeanette pulled the pins free, and her hair cascaded down her back. Her fingers trembled as she braided it. Feelings tumbled one over another…pain, panic, pleasure.

Hair ready, she went to her armoire and opened the door. Hmm? Her dress with the yellow daises could be just as practical as her humdrum gray one. If she was going to do this, she might as well go all the way.

CHAPTER 8

Theo stood at the edge of his field and lifted his head and stared. Wagon after wagon lined the rutted driveway. People swarmed and buzzed about as if this were a beehive, not a farm. They were everywhere—in his fields, replacing the roof on the barn, on his porch securing the railings and replacing the boards. One was even on the house rooftop, patching the weathered hand-split wooden shingles.

There was a woman he had never met weeding his garden, and he dared not darken the door of the farmhouse, where Jeanette and another bunch of ladies were preparing the lunch meal.

How had one yes to Jeanette turned into this? Not that he didn't need the help, but he would now be indebted to strangers, people whose names he didn't know. How would he ever repay such kindness?

"Ain't it great?"

Theo turned to where Jacob leaned on his shovel. When had his oldest shot up in height and turned into such a young man? His startling violet eyes pierced right through, fringed with thick dark lashes. He looked like his mother, from the blond curly hair to that one slightly crooked front tooth. No wonder Theo had not second-guessed—

"Pa. Aren't you happy?"

"Yeah, son, it's great. Just hate owing all these people something I can never repay."

"I like it here far better than the city, but I was worried…"

His thirteen-year-old son had been anxious. Now, that was a hard one to swallow. "I know. Turns out your pa bit off more than he could chew." Little did his son know how aggressive the in-laws had been in trying to take the kids from him after Louisa's death. They didn't understand that, when Theo's ma died, he could no longer leave the children to work on the railroad, that farming far away from his former in-laws' clutches was the only opportunity left to provide for and keep his family together.

Jacob's eyes brightened. "But now with all this help, we'll have this field planted by the end of the day, and the house and barn repaired. It feels like we'll have a fighting chance."

Theo didn't want to come across as ungrateful, but to a man who was used to going it alone, all this help was humbling and overwhelming. He turned back toward the house, unable to meet his son's stare.

A group of women stepped onto the front porch, Jeanette among them. Taller and more regal than the rest, his eyes gravitated to her. Was she wearing her hair differently? He had been out in the fields before she arrived. Where was that tight bun? He had wondered a few times what it would be like to set that knot of loveliness free, then quickly corrected his wayward thinking. He would not let his thoughts wander today or any day. He did not trust his decision making when it came to women. Louisa had done a good job of kicking that confidence right out of him.

The sound of a cow bell rang out as Jeanette lifted her hand to shake and called out in her sing-song voice for all to come in for the meal.

Jacob threw down his shovel and bolted toward the house.

Theo didn't move, though. Instead, he watched as Jeanette turned to one side, giving him a glimpse of a long thick braid hanging over her shoulder nearly to her waist. His hands turned instantly sweaty, and his pulse skipped and tripped. He didn't like the reactions she caused. What was it about that woman? Under his skin, consuming his thoughts, even in the dead of night, entering his dreams and causing loneliness to rise up.

Theo picked up the shovel Jacob had discarded and stuck it into the freshly tilled soil so they would know where they left off on the planting of seed. With a heavy sigh, he made his way toward the group congregating on his newly boarded front porch. He'd never felt comfortable in crowds, but he was grateful for the help. Maybe he could stay on the fringes, and the need for conversation would be minimal.

The closer he got to the group, the more startling the transformation in Jeanette. She not only wore her hair becomingly, but she had on a dress with some color rather than the drab gray she typically wore. The yellow daises made her dark eyes shine.

He gave his head a shake and looked away.

Jeanette clapped her hands to get everyone's attention. "The way we'll do this…"

His eyes were drawn back to her. He was used to this take-charge woman with his children, but seeing her standing tall and confident in front of the crowd… now, that was different. At church she kept in the background, with her head down. Today was the opposite. With a stunning smile, she waited for the crowd to quiet.

"First," she said when she had their attention, "Pa will say the blessing, then you may file through the kitchen and fill your plate from all the wonderful goodies on the table. Find a spot to sit, wherever, inside or out. Some of you may have to use your wagons for a seat. Children, we ask that you give the chairs to the adults and sit on the floor." She looked at her pa and nodded.

Her face turned a delightful shade of red. Theo figured it was not easy for her to speak in front of that crowd, but she didn't look down or try to make herself appear shorter as he had so often noticed she did. He was so proud of her, and that thought scared him more than anything. Was he getting emotionally involved?

Above the crowd, she met his gaze before she closed her eyes to pray.

He kept his open. His resolve to stay clear of her was weakened by the fact that he enjoyed staring at her without her knowledge. When her pa was done praying, Jeanette's gaze landed on him again.

He didn't know what possessed him, but he smiled at her, holding nothing back.

She blushed and rushed inside.

A jolt of heat shot up his spine. He was attracted to her, and this was a complication he did not need. He headed to the pump and splashed water over his face. Something had to cool him down. He used the towel they kept handy to dry.

"Mr. Wallace." The sound of a genteel woman's voice broke through his musing. He lowered the towel.

"My name is Victoria Stanfield. I'm your neighbour."

She looked just like Louisa, his first wife. Blond coiffured curls, startling blue eyes. Petite and curvy.

"Our properties are kissing cousins to the north." She daintily waved her handkerchief in the general direction and fluttered her eyelashes at him.

He would put a stop to this one. "And Mr. Stanfield? I would like to make his acquaintance."

She looked down and placed the handkerchief to her cheek as if to catch a tear. "Mr. Stanfield passed away last spring."

He cleared his throat. "I'm sorry to hear that."

"Seems we share the same sadness. I heard your wife—"

"Hmm." He was not going to have this conversation with anyone. "Nice to meet you Mrs. Stanfield. Please, excuse me, but I must eat and get back to the field."

"But of course."

He turned and hurried across the yard toward the house. This was precisely why he avoided getting too friendly. That short conversation with widow Stanfield batting her eyes at him was all he needed to be reminded exactly why he had no intention of being sucked in again.

He entered the kitchen and surveyed the room. Jeanette stood against the far wall, seemingly in no hurry to eat. Before he could rationalize his thinking, he joined her as he might an old friend.

"You should get in line," she said. "We're encouraging the men to help themselves first so they can get back out there."

"I'm fine." He was anything but fine. A couple of summers helping his uncle obviously did not a farmer make. His stomach had been churning all morning at the thought of what a failure he must look like.

Her brows furrowed. "Are you all right? I mean with all these people?" Her soulful brown eyes bore into his. She was too perceptive, too comfortable, too deep in her understanding of him, especially for the short time they had known each other. In all the years he'd been married, Louisa had never picked up on how he was feeling. Or was it that she had never cared?

"Anything less than thank-you would sound ungrateful. But I have to tell you, people helping me without strings attached? It's not something I'm used to."

"That's how we do it here. We help each other. And it doesn't hurt that Pa has a lot of influence in the community."

"That's for sure. I thought he meant to bring a couple people, not a village."

She laughed. "He does have a way of getting over-exuberant at times. I hope you can handle the crowd for one day."

"Considering how much help I'm getting, I'm more than grateful."

She touched his arm. The yearning that one small kindness evoked complicated the road of friendship he wanted to go down with her.

"Go quick and get in the food line," she said. "Agnus, the town snoop, is heading this way. Trust me, you do not want an inquisition from her."

"Thanks for the heads up."

"It's the only good thing about being taller than most."

"I like your height." He gave her a smile. "I don't have to stoop to talk to you."

Her shoulders went back, and she stretched to full height as if to test his sincerity. "I like my height too. And if you believe that, I have a bridge in the Sahara Desert to sell you." She laughed, but the smile did not reach her eyes.

He walked to the table and picked up a plate. Her glib effort to poke fun at herself bothered him, but why should it? He dared not add concern for this woman, who was winding her way into his soul, on top all of his other worries. Maybe his head should tell his heart. The last time he went soft on a woman...

He pressed the knot in his throat down, desperate to dispel the memory. Had not Louisa cured him for good?

"Are you gonna stand there looking, or are you gonna partake?" Jeanette's Pa, Jeb, stood beside him.

Theo looked over the feast. Everything from fried chicken to beef pot pies, not to mention desserts aplenty, crowded the large table. How to choose enough to not look rude. His stomach was still complaining and would be until everyone left.

He glanced back Jeanette's way through a split in the crowd. She was tying Tessie's shoelaces. Tessie gave her a big hug and Jeanette smiled, a real smile that lit up her whole face.

His chest involuntarily squeezed tight. He had never witnessed anything more beautiful.

Theo looked back at the table, but Jeb's eyes had followed his.

"She was born to be a mother," Jeb said, the words so low he wasn't even sure he'd heard them.

Theo ignored him and filled his plate. Odd thing for Jeb to say to him. Was there a message behind that remark? No. He was only being friendly, and Theo was far too suspicious.

~

*J*eanette had given the previous day her best effort, but negative thoughts had still crept in. The critical remark to Theo about her height had spilled out without thinking. She climbed the steps of the church and walked inside. Helen was sure to beckon her over and demand a full report.

There she was with her eagle eyes, waiting. She lifted her wrinkled hand and waved to Jeanette.

Might as well get it over with. Jeanette slid into the pew beside her.

"Well?" Helen's brows lifted.

"I tried."

"And?"

"I wore my hair like Gracie always does, in a braid, and people stared at me," Jeanette whispered.

"They were noticing your poise and confidence for the first time. Of course, they would look twice."

"Ha, poise and confidence. Not likely."

"Ah, ah, ah." Helen shook her head, stopping her short.

"All right. I get it. And I will admit, holding my head high and not slouching felt really good."

"There you go." Helen patted her knee. "After years of thinking of yourself one way, it'll take some time to see yourself in the light of truth."

"Not sure I'd call it—"

"Yes, truth. You're a desirable young woman. But if you go around stooping, not looking people in the eyes or smiling, you never get to see their reaction, or their invitation."

"Oh, I've seen their reactions. Trust me." Jeanette bent toward Helen's ear. "The snickers. The nicknames growing up. The lack of anyone wanting to court me. That spoke volumes."

"Or it spoke of God's sovereignty. He was saving you for such a time as this." Helen nodded at Theo's family as they filed in.

Jeanette turned to see Tessie, Laura, and Sarah beeline her way. Theo nodded at her and slid into his regular pew near the back of the church with the boys.

"Miss Williams, Miss Williams," Laura said.

The girls crowded in, Sarah on one side and Laura on the other. Tessie climbed onto Jeanette's lap.

"Hello children," Helen smiled her welcome.

"Hello Mrs. Donavan," the girls answered in unison.

"Papa said we could sit with you, if that's all right?" Laura asked, looking up at Jeanette. She snuggled close, and Jeanette's arm instinctively went around her.

"And Papa wants to invite you and your pa for lunch. We have so many yummy leftovers from yesterday." Sarah looked up at her with hopeful eyes. "You will come, won't you?"

Helen clucked her tongue and smiled at Jeanette. "Of course she'll come."

The music started, and they stood to sing. Jeanette's spirits soared. She was invited. Her presence was desired, and it had nothing to do with work. Her voice lifted in song. After the hymn, she took a quick peek back at Theo before she sat.

Widow Victoria had somehow lodged herself right beside him. She would've had to climb over the boys to do so. And with that extravagant dress and bustle, it would have been quite the feat.

Theo caught Jeanette's gaze. She gave a faint smile and turned toward the front. Victoria was much more in Theo's league. In fact, Jeanette should be happy for him and encourage a relationship. The children would have a mother, and Theo would gain a much-needed wife and a spread with a sizable piece of land right next to his. How much more perfect could it get?

Jeanette would enjoy the children sitting at her side and on her knee, and for a moment she'd dream.

And then she would decline the lunch invitation. There was no point in encouraging any more than the necessary. Her heart could not take another fall.

CHAPTER 9

Jeanette clapped her hands above her head. "Quiet children. Quiet." She pointed to the benches in the small schoolhouse. "Take your seats. As you know, today is the last day of school before the summer break."

The boys let out a loud whoop, and the girls squealed in delight.

"Children, settle down. I know you're excited, but we have some wonderful awards to give out before you're dismissed."

A hand shot up.

"Yes, Alice."

"Are we going to have the cake you promised?" The pudgy girl eyed the large chocolate cake sitting in a pan at the edge of Jeanette's desk. She licked her lips.

"We sure are. But first things first. Sarah and Joe, could you please come to the front and wipe off the board nice and clean for the last time this school year. Peter, you and Robbie go outside to the pump and fill the water bucket please. We'll want a drink of water with our cake. And the rest of you gather around my desk here. Let the little ones come to the front and you bigger ones behind them. We're going to have some fun as we cut the cake and you receive your rewards."

The children scurried in place.

"All right now that Peter and Robbie are back, we are ready. You're each going to represent a piece of this cake."

"Don't you mean *get* a piece of the cake?" Lizzie asked.

Jeanette smiled. "Not so fast. Put on your thinking caps. We're going to pretend this cake is the student body." The children groaned, realizing they were going to have one more lesson.

"We have one big piece of cake. Would it be fair if I just handed the whole pan to"—she looked around the group —"Tessie?" She lifted the cake pan and pretended to give it to Tessie, who was so little that her head barely made it over the table. Her little arms reached out, and her eyes popped wide.

"No, that wouldn't be fair." Jeanette lifted the cake and placed it back on the desk. "But we could give Tessie a ribbon for being the youngest student this year." She held out a pink hair ribbon and handed it to Tessie.

"For me?" She smiled wide, revealing her missing front tooth.

"For you." Jeanette's heart swelled. Such a simple gift brought joy. "Now Tessie, come over to this side of the desk and stand right here." Jeanette pointed to her side.

"Back to the cake. What if I cut it in half?" She took her knife and cut the cake down the middle. I now have two pieces to give away. What if I gave one piece to Tessie and the other to George, the oldest student?"

"Not fair," Robbie shouted.

"You're right, Robbie. We want to be fair, don't we?"

George let out a loud whoop. She handed the teen a pencil. "This is for your hard work and dedication to your studies despite all your farm duties. Use that pencil to mark your building project or draw your plans for the tree house you've been talking about."

A wide grin split free.

"Come join Tessie."

He did, and Jeanette continued. "So, we have the cake in two pieces, or in half. How many pieces would there be if I cut it in quarters?"

Hands shot up all over the room.

"Joy?"

Joy smiled proudly. "That would be four pieces, Miss Williams."

"Right you are." She cut the cake in the opposite direction into four pieces. "So, let's see…would it be fair if I gave these four pieces to only Tessie, George and…" By this time the children, had clued in if their name was called, they were going to get a gift. All eyes were fixed on her. Jeanette loved the happiness she saw in every face. She had saved to buy these gifts for the children, and it would be worth every penny. "Ben and Lizzy."

She handed Ben a pencil for his helpfulness, and Lizzy a blue ribbon for the best in spelling. "Come on over." She waved them to her side of the desk.

"I'm now going to cut the cake into double the number of pieces already here. How many pieces would that make? How many more students can I add to Tessie, George, Ben, and Lizzy?

By the time she cut the cake into enough pieces for every child, each one had a gift for their effort, attendance, excelling in spelling, mathematical skills, reading, or being helpful and kind. Every child was honored for shining in some way, and every child got a piece of chocolate cake.

As the children sat around eating and talking, she wondered how she would fill her days over the summer? The house was so quiet now with just her and Pa. Theo and his six children came to mind. She could go there more often, but would he want her? Would that be too much of an intrusion of his privacy? Or worse yet, what if she offered her help and ended up falling more in love with the family than she already had? She could no longer deny how deep her feelings ran for each of the children. And what about their kind father? Someone who looked like her had no business fancying the possibility of more, but she did enjoy his friendship. Could her heart take the pleasure of being in his presence more often without falling for him?

And what of widow Victoria? Every Sunday, she wiggled her way onto the same pew as Theo. Could she be more obvious? Were the boys warming up to her? Thankfully the girls chose to sit with her. Was Theo interested in Victoria? So far, the town rumor mill had not linked the two of them together, despite their close proximity at church every weekend. Jeanette rarely paid attention to the gossip, but in this case her ears were tuned in. Seemed her name more often accompanied his. But she was no fool. Up against the wealthy and beautiful Victoria, there would be no contest.

It was her growing friendship with Theo and her love for the children that sealed her decision. The girls especially needed a woman's guidance, and she had nothing but time.

∽

Jeanette headed off to Theo's farm like she did every Saturday morning. Warm, lemony sunlight angled through the stand of maples and tulip poplars as she made her way through the forested section. A soft breeze pulled at her hair, which she'd twisted into a more comfortable bun. Birds twittered and swooped from branch to branch. Tendrils of Virginia creeper encircled the trunks of different trees, stretching skyward. Last fall's leaves cushioned the pathway. She inhaled deeply. The fragrance of new growth and rain-softened earth filled her senses. Oh, how she loved that fresh smell. Trilliums and violets, wild geraniums and jacks-in-the-pulpit opened their buds to the warmth of the sun. No wonder May was her favorite month. Everywhere she looked, spring, with its endless cycle of rebirth, brought the stirring of life and filled her with hope.

Would she be brave and offer to help the Wallace family more often? The path opened to the road adjacent to Theo's farm, and she turned up the lane toward his house.

As if he had been waiting for her, he came out of the barn and down the driveway as soon as she stepped into sight of the property. She pulled at the strands of hair that were blowing across her face. That was what she got for not pulling it tight.

"Good morning, Miss Williams."

The rich timber of his voice caused a warm knot to settle in her stomach. "Good morning, Theo…Mr. Wallace." Her face flushed with heat. Why had she allowed herself to think of him as Theo? Now she'd spoken it aloud.

"Let's stick with Theo. I like that a whole lot better." He joined her, and they continued the walk toward the house.

"Then you must call me Jeanette."

"No."

She stopped. "Why?"

He turned to face her. "You look more like a Jeanie to me."

Just the way the name Jeanie rolled off his tongue felt like a gentle caress. No one had ever shortened her name or given her an affectionate nickname. Jeanie…sounded endearing and special.

"You'll be Miss Williams in public, of course, but when it's just the two of us…? If it's all right with you, I think Jeanie suits you better." Tiny hazel flecks of mischief sparkled in his handsome brown eyes.

Was he teasing her? "Ahh, I guess that would be all right."

"Then I have a favor to ask, Jeanie, my friend."

His tone was jovial and light. But the way he was looking at her made her hands tingle and her heart flutter like a trapped bird. She couldn't hold his intense gaze. "Yes." She looked beyond him to the house.

"I think by now, I can consider you my friend, right? Being that I don't let just anyone launder my unmentionables."

Her eyes flashed to his face, and she giggled. Who was this happy-go-lucky man? He was standing so close that she could see the varied colors in his closely cropped beard.

He lifted his hand and smoothed a wayward strand of hair from her cheek.

She couldn't breathe.

"All kidding aside, I do consider you my friend. The way you and your pa have helped my family is truly above and beyond. My faith in Christianity is being restored." He stepped back and swiped a hand through his thick hair.

"What favor is it, mister...I mean, Theo? If I can help, you know I will." What was he trying to spit out?

"We'll talk about it when I take you home." He headed back into the barn.

She continued toward the house. What was that all about? Drat. Now she had to wait all day to find out.

The same weekly chaos met her as she knocked and pushed open the farmhouse door. Dirty dishes lined the counter. The floors needed a good scrubbing. At least the laundry was heaped in a pile instead of all over. That was progress. She entered with a sense of purpose.

Tessie squealed and raced down the ladder from the loft so quickly that Jeanette held her breath. The little girl ran across the room and flung herself into open arms.

Jeanette swung her up. "How's my girl?"

Tessie laid her head on Jeanette's shoulder and whispered, "I wish I was your girl, and you were my mama. Then I'd get to see you every day."

Jeanette swallowed hard against the knot in her throat. If the truth be told, there was nothing she would love more than to be a mama to these six rambunctious children and a wife to the man who'd just called her Jeanie. But that could never be.

"Sweet pea." She took a moment to sink into the rocking chair with Tessie. Rocking, she smoothed her hand down the child's back. Tessie was so affectionate and only five. She needed a mama.

"Do we have to get up now?" Sarah called down from the loft.

Laura let out a groan.

She was not an early bird. "Take your time. There's no rush."

"Can we take our time too?" Jacob asked.

"Yeah," Charlie said. "If the girls don't have to get up and work, can we sleep in too?"

Jeanette was not going to fall for that one. "What did your pa say before he headed out?" Silence filled the room. "Boys?"

"He said that Jacob and Charlie had to hurry up and get out there," Ben volunteered. "Ouch. Stop hitting me, Charlie."

"Then don't be such a tattle tale," Charlie said.

"Yeah," Jacob added. "Mind your own corner, Ben the hen. Bwak, bwak…all you do is squawk—"

"Boys, leave your brother alone and do as your pa requested."

Jacob climbed down the ladder and stomped across the kitchen floor. "It's not fair. All we ever do is work around here." From the pot on the wood stove, he slapped some pasty oatmeal into a bowl and plunked down in a chair. His elbow hit the table, and he leaned his head into his hand.

Jeanette got up from the rocker and put Tessie down. She took the girl's small hand in hers. "How about we make your brother some bacon. That always cheers him up."

Tessie nodded.

The oatmeal could go to the pigs. "How about I whip up some flapjacks and bacon. I'm sure your Pa won't mind. And if he comes looking for you, the smell of maple syrup will win him over. Deal?"

Jacob smiled. "Deal."

"Now you're talkin'!" Charlie jumped the last few rungs of the ladder. "And the sleepy-head girls don't get any. Nor the tattle tale up there." He glared up at Ben, who was looking down over the rail.

"Hmm, Charlie. Looks like crabby boys are going to be added to that list of have-nots. Or shall we do away with your not-so-charitable idea?"

He grunted. "Fine then."

"Ha ha." Ben stuck his tongue out.

Charlie raced for the ladder, but Jeanette was faster. She grabbed him as he flailed wildly. He fought back the tears filling his eyes. "Let me at him."

"Violence is not the way to solve this. You're older and more mature. I'll make sure your pa knows what happened here and how well you handled Ben's teasing."

"It's not teasing. He's a brat who needs a thrashing." Charlie yanked hard to pull free, but Jeanette held tight.

"Yeah," Jacob said. "Pa babies him, and he gets away with this kind of thing all the time."

The door opened. "What's going on in here?" Theo's voice thundered across the room.

Tessie went flying across the room to her pa. Tears streamed down her pudgy cheeks. "Charlie's hitting my Miss Williams, and I want him to stop."

Charlie jumped back from Jeanette. "I was not hitting her. I was…"

Theo's face turned red. "Charlie, Jacob, out to the barn immediately."

Jacob stood from the table. "What did I do? It's Ben—"

"You two blame Ben for everything. Out." He pointed his finger, and both boys scurried to do his bidding.

"Are you all right?" Theo moved toward Jeanette.

She bent down and hugged Tessie. "I'm just fine. Charlie didn't hurt me." She stood. "Can we talk out on the porch?" Jeanette did not wait for a reply but headed out the door.

Theo followed.

After the door closed behind him, she spoke. "I hope I'm not over-stepping, but I think your children need a day off, and you need to join them. Do something fun."

He moved closer. "They're scrapping like a pack of hyenas, and you think they need to be rewarded?"

"What I think is that they're exhausted and…"

A scowl furrowed his brow. "So now I'm a terrible father making them work every day?"

This was not going well. She hadn't meant to offend. *God, please give me the words.* "Everyone needs a rest once in a while."

"I take them to church on Sunday morning. They don't have to do anything until the afternoon."

"But when was the last time you did something fun together, as a family?"

"There's no time for fun. I'm barely surviving here with all the work."

"Theo, look around. The fields are planted, the fences mended, the barn roof new and fresh. I even see the crops sprouting in your fields. You can let up for a day."

She touched his arm, but he snatched it free and paced away.

"I'm sorry, Theo. Obviously, I'm meddling where I shouldn't. But something I can do over the summer while school is out is give practical help. It'll give me time to teach the girls all the things my mama taught me, like how to cook, sew, can the fruit, garden. I could even take them back to my place and give them piano lessons."

He stopped in front of her. "You would do that for them…for me?"

"It would help fill my days. I don't have much in my life to…"

He pulled her into a tight hug, silencing her words and filling her mind with thoughts that ought not to be there. Her breath cut off, but her skin tingled and warmed.

"Thank you," he whispered into her hair.

They stood like that for a moment. Jeanette melted into his strength, the intoxicated scent of chopped wood and manly essence filling her senses. The feel of his warmth soaked into her, making it impossible to move.

Then, as if Theo realized what he was doing, he abruptly pulled away and steadied her with a firm grasp. He gave a final pat, took a step back, and gazed over the fields. "I suppose a change of scenery wouldn't be such a bad idea. But I don't think I know how to have fun anymore. Any suggestions?"

Her throat was tight and parched. Could she even speak? "How…how about a picnic down by the creek? On our ranch, there's this lovely spot with a deep watering hole for swimming. It may get warm enough—"

"You know how to swim?"

"Yes. You don't?"

"Grew up in the city. Never had the opportunity to learn."

"How about over the summer we do a trade?"

His brows lifted.

"I'll teach you and the kids to swim, and you teach me how to ride?"

He laughed, a genuine laugh that crinkled the lines around his eyes and made them sparkle. "You mean on a real horse, not the kind that rocks?"

"Yes, a real horse. I want to face my fears." She did want to get confident enough to ride alone, but if she were honest, the thought of him cozying up behind her certainly sweetened that pot.

"A deal." He held out his hand.

She placed her hand in his and shook firmly. A tingle skittered all the way up her arm.

CHAPTER 10

Theo relaxed back on the blanket. When was the last time he'd sat under a tree and watched his kids have fun? Finding a farm he could afford with the small inheritance he'd received at his mother's death had been a challenge. And getting out of Richmond before the Calberts had caught wind that his ma had passed away had been crucial. There was no way he was going to risk having their power and influence come up against him once his ma was no longer in the picture to help. But even before that, working long hours on the railroad to provide for his ma and family had given no time at all. What a shock it had been to go from the comfort of the Calbert money and the cushy overpaid bookkeeping job to the grueling work on the railroad. But at least he had not sacrificed his kids for an easy life. Had they stayed with the Calberts, his children would've turned out as selfish as Louisa had been. He would do everything in his power to make sure that never happened. He shook the tough memories clear and focused on the good all around him.

Tessie was digging in the sand with a stick. Sarah was instructing Laura on how to combine the correct amount of water to the sand to create the perfect mud pie. The boys had their knickers rolled up above their knees and were in the water each with a fishing pole in hand. When they'd stopped by Jeanette's house, Jeb had helped the boys fasten some line and a hook to a sturdy stick. They were getting bored with not catching anything and were rough housing. It would only be a matter of time before one of them went in. Most likely, it would be Ben. But after hearing what had happened earlier from Jeanette, a good soaking would be fair payback.

He glanced over at her sitting beside him on the blanket, and his pulse skipped a beat. He wanted to pull her hair free of that no-nonsense bun and run his hands through. Then take off those glasses and kiss the lips she was currently chewing.

He snapped his head back to the children and pushed that thought away. Was he so lonely that he would jeopardize the best friendship he had experienced in years? The minute a person began kissing, trouble started. That much he knew from Louisa. No. He needed a friend, and his children needed a good woman's influence in their life. Jeanie was all of those things. She was without question the most giving, loving human being he had ever met.

"The water's a little cold for swimming lessons, but how about we put our feet in?" She smiled invitingly at him.

His throat knotted. "That sounds great." He was way too hot for comfort, and it had little to do with the sun beating down.

She pulled her shoes from her feet and removed a pair of lace trimmed stockings—pink and feminine. Not the sensible type that would have gone with her outfit. Then she stood and lifted her skirt, revealing her bare feet and slender ankles.

He tried not to stare.

She looked back. "Ready?"

He had not moved, too busy watching her. "Go ahead. I'll be right there." He turned with a swiftness to hide his embarrassment and kicked off his boots and pulled his stockings free.

She was down at the water's edge with Tessie in her arms. Wading into the water, she dipped Tessie's feet in, not at all concerned that Tessie's splashes were getting her wet or that the bottom of her dress was soaked. She laughed with his littlest girl, lifting her in and out of the water. The sight of them together brought back Jeb's words…

She was born to be a mother.

If only Theo had chosen someone like her to begin with instead of Louisa. How different his life would be.

"Papa, come quick." Ben yelled.

His fishing stick was floating away. Theo raced in to grab it and pulled up. A trout flipped and flopped on the end.

Charlie hooted in excitement.

"I caught a fish," Ben hollered. "I caught a fish."

"You caught nothing," Charlie said. "Pa had to rescue your pole."

Theo pulled his half-wet body from the creek. "The fish are biting. Maybe if you stay focused, we'll have a feast tonight." He no sooner said the words than Jacob, a little further down the creek, yanked his pole out with another fish.

"Not fair." Charlie pouted, his lip hanging down.

"You can't catch anything if you don't have your pole in the water." Theo pointed to the stick on the ground.

"Papa, I want to try." Laura pulled at his wet shirt tail.

"Girls can fish, too," Sarah said.

"They sure can." Jeanette nodded.

Tessie jumped up and down. "Me too. Me too."

"But of course, you too." She patted Tessie's head.

Tactical error on her part, considering there were only three poles and six kids, and they all wanted in now that the fish were biting. He raised his eyebrows, and Jeanie laughed at him.

"All we need are three more sticks." She reached into the lunch basket and pulled out some line and three more hooks. "First rule with children. Always come prepared." She gave him a sassy grin as her glasses slipped down on her nose. "I knew this would happen if the fish started to bite." Delight lit her face, and her eyes rounded, looking like swirls of melted chocolate.

His soul began to thaw.

A rush of feelings crushed in, and his senses ran sharp. Did she have any idea what she was doing to him? The thought of being around her more both thrilled and terrified him. And that favor he'd considered asking that morning? Impossible. To think he had almost asked her to stage a kiss and pretend to be a couple. What a lark. There would be no pretending if he allowed himself the pleasure of that kiss. He'd be a goner. He didn't need protection from Victoria, who had recently started showing up at the farm. No indeed. The woman in front of him was far more of a threat to his peace.

"Theo." She waved her hand in front of his face. "Can you find the girls some sticks?"

"Sure." His voice cracked like a young lad's. He turned away. He dared not let her see the emotion she evoked.

∼

"What a wonderful day." Seated beside Theo in the wagon, on the way home, Jeanette peered into the darkness. "Don't you agree?"

"You were right about the kids needing some fun."

"And you. Didn't you enjoy yourself?" She knew he had, but she wanted him to acknowledge that it was not all about the children. The rest had rejuvenated him too.

"I did. Are you proud of yourself, Jeanie?" He turned her way, and a shadowy grin twitched his lips.

"I am." Her voice held the growing confidence she felt in their relationship. He teased her all the time, so surely she could return the favor.

He chuckled. "I bet you are. Truthfully, I had no idea how

much a change of pace would revive me. And the kids are too beat to even bicker with each other."

"I'll come Monday to help with the chores we never got done today."

"About that."

A tangle of nerves danced inside her. Was he going to refuse her help? "Yes?"

"I was thinking that maybe we should just—"

"Would Monday, Wednesday, Friday work for you?" She would not let him refuse her support after the wonderful day they had. No, she would not.

Silence. And then... "Hmm."

There it was again, that answer that held no answer. So be it. It was better than a no.

"And maybe with my extra assistance, you could make Saturday a fun day for the children. A reward for their hard work all week."

"Would you join us? Six kids near the water are a handful. But...but only if you wanted to. No. Scratch that, it would be asking too much."

Excitement rippled through her being. "I would love to, Theo." She glanced his way with a smile.

A grin twitched at the corners of his mouth as he looked down at her.

"Oh, and what was that favor you started to ask me about this morning? You said we'd talk about it on the way home."

Theo's head snapped forward and he slapped Blossom's reins a tad harder. The mule picked up its pace.

Somehow, she had made him uncomfortable.

"Not important."

"Sure, it is." She placed her hand briefly on his arm and felt him shift away. She dropped it into her lap. What was happening? From relaxed and charming to brisk and short in a matter of seconds.

"You know that Pa and I will help you in any way we can." Maybe if she threw Pa into the mix, he would unwind. Or had he picked up on the way her soul responded to his every nuance? Was her reaction to him obvious? Making him uneasy?

"I'll be eternally grateful to both of you. The questions I keep peppering your pa with and his patience… I would've made so many mistakes without his expertise. And you…"

She peeked sideways at him, and he swallowed hard, his neck moving forward with the motion.

"You…there are no words. My children adore you."

If only *he* adored her, too.

Stop that. They were just friends, and she knew that.

"I shouldn't have mentioned that favor. You've done too much already."

"It's not as if my life is a whirlwind of activity. I'm looking forward to…" She pursed her lips closed. How could she begin to explain that his family made her come alive? For the first time, her life felt exciting and full.

He pulled the mule to a stop just outside the ranch gate and turned to face her.

She gazed up at him. The song of cicadas, the stillness of the night, and the gathering darkness cradled them in a world of intimacy. She longed to touch his face, feel the chisel of his chin beneath his closely cropped beard, run her fingers through his thick hair. Her body tingled with awareness. This was not friendship she was feeling.

He lifted a tendril of her hair that had worked free and tenderly placed it behind her ear. The tips of his fingers slid down the side of her face, and she caught her breath. She froze, waiting for him.

He kept looking at her. Not as if he didn't see her, as most men did, but as if she were desirable. When he dipped his head toward her, she closed her eyes.

His breath fanned her cheeks.

She couldn't believe something so wonderful was finally about to happen.

Then he snapped away.

Her eyes flew open, and she watched as he sat ridged and upright, facing forward. Heat flooded her face and she looked away. What a swooning fool to have thought he was about to kiss her.

"Jeanie, you shouldn't be wasting your time on my family. You should be courting men and concentrating on your future."

His voice gravelled, ripping at her heart. "But you don't understand. I'm…I'm so awkward with men, always have been." Once again, she had misread what was happening, which was absolutely nothing.

He shifted her way. "You've never been awkward with me. If anything, you've been confident and sure of yourself."

She didn't look at him. "That's because of the children. They're the buffer and the reason I persisted. They need me."

"So, we're not friends?"

"Of course, we're friends now. But I would've never been so bold without them. I assure you. You don't need to worry about me. There will be no courting of men in my future. There never has been. In fact, my friendship with you is more than I have had with any man. I freeze up. Oh, it's all so embarrassing." She twisted her hands in her lap.

"Perhaps it would be practical to add more than riding lessons to our trade? It would make me feel better about all the help you've been giving."

Jeanette ventured a peek, expecting some humor in his expression, but he was serious. "And just what, may I ask, are you thinking?"

"I could help you learn how to be more comfortable around eligible men. We could practice conversations, and I could give you pointers about what a man—"

"Are you suggesting that you teach the teacher?"

"I am." A wide grin split free. The white of his straight teeth stood out against the ever-darkening backdrop.

"Can I start with a question?"

"Sure."

"You seem to vacillate between being relaxed in my presence to being very uncomfortable. What am I doing wrong?" She desperately wanted to know if he felt any of the stirrings she did.

"Jeanie, I'm comfortable with you. But I have complications from my past. I wish I were ready to start up a relationship, but I may never be." He touched her arm.

She pulled free of his touch.

"See, that's the kind of thing I could help you with, your instinct to pull back and the way you stand in the background at church."

"You're one to talk. You're not exactly a social butterfly."

"True, but that's because I'm not looking for a woman. You, on the other hand, are a wonderful woman with much to offer any man."

"Hmm."

He smiled at her use of his word. "It's the truth."

"Oh, I know. They're lining up." She forced out a chuckle.

His voice softened to almost a whisper. "Since you confided in me, I'll do the same with you. My first marriage was a mess. I'm not even sure I know what love between a man and woman is supposed to look like, being that my dad died when I was quite young."

It was not the moment to have something tickle her funny bone, but the thought of this man, this handsome, eligible recluse offering to teach her...

She tried to hold in her mirth, but a bubble of laughter slipped free, then a full-on melody. "I'm sorry, Theo," she said between giggles, "but it struck me funny that you're going to help me?"

His rich, baritone laughter joined hers, echoing into the black of night. He snapped the reins, and the wagon rolled between the gates and up the drive. "Don't we make a pair."

"We sure do." Jeanette knew he didn't mean that literally. She best protect her heart from here on in, but she couldn't help liking the sound of that.

He stopped the wagon in front of her home and faced forward without looking at her. "On second thought. I think we should keep your visits to once a week. Better the children—"

"Better the children what? Your vacillating decisions are confusing."

He hopped down from the wagon extending his hand to help her down. She ignored it and brushed past him. He was back up on the wagon when she turned before heading up the porch steps. "Theo, there's no danger in friendship, or in me loving on your children." She whirled back towards the house and took the steps with a determined stomp. "I'll see you on Monday." She slammed into the house, not sure he heard her words. It did not matter. She would be there Monday morning whether he liked it or not.

~

Jeanette's eyes slowly opened. The room was still dark. Faint fingers of morning light brightened the curtains. Dawn could not come fast enough. She had barely slept the past two nights. It was Monday morning and time for action.

Tossing and turning, she had woken many times thinking about the fun she'd had with Theo and his children at the swimming hole, and then about Theo's honesty about his first marriage. What had happened in his past? If he questioned what love was, he must carry a deep, abiding wound. What was clear was her need to respect his boundary of friendship. Whatever had happened in his marriage had broken down trust and being trustworthy was crucial. She could do that, but she was not going to abandon those children.

However, maybe his crazy notion of a trade was not such a bad idea. If she could learn to be less tongue-tied in the presence of a man, there may be hope. She was beginning to see herself as a very capable homemaker with a deep love for children. Perhaps she did have more to offer than she'd ever given herself credit for. In helping Theo's family, she was gaining confidence beyond the confines of the school room. Why should she live a life as an old spinster when she had so much love to give? Theo's crazy idea had merit.

God, you're still a God of miracles, aren't you? Dare she believe? Yes. She would believe. She would enlist Theo's help, and maybe, just maybe, she could get out of the rut she had been in for years.

She pulled herself from the bed with determination. Every move had purpose as she washed, dressed, and made a quick breakfast for Pa. One step out of the house and a glance upward gave pause, but she refused to be dissuaded. Swollen clouds draped low. The steely gray threatened to release weighty moisture any moment. Could she make it to Theo's farm before the sky opened? She picked up her pace and headed across the field.

Why had she been so afraid of learning to ride? If only she had pushed through, she could jump on her pick of horses at the ranch and be there in no time. Fear had kept her captive in far too many ways. It was time for change.

She laughed into the heavens as heavy raindrops began to fall. What did she care about the past? She had hope for her future. She spread out her hands and whirled in a circle before pulling up the hood on her cloak. For the first time, she intended to fight for a life that was different from what she had previously accepted. Her glasses were spotted with rain, and she took them off and slid them into her pocket. It surprised her how well she could see without them. Had she been hiding behind them as well? Or did the world and everything in it just look clearer?

Theo would most likely be in the barn feeding the animals, and the children would still be asleep. Jeanette scurried across the farmyard only too happy to put off the fireworks that were sure to happen. She took the steps with determination, knocked briefly, and let herself in.

She jumped at the sight of Theo standing at the wood stove stirring a pot of oatmeal. He whirled, the spoon in his hand dripping oatmeal on the dirty floor.

After their day off on Saturday, one sweeping glance of the place told her there was much to do. She best get started.

"What are you doing here?" Theo's voice sounded nervous. He cleared his throat.

Tessie squealed from the loft and jumped up and down near the railing. "You came. You came."

"Of course, I came."

"But Papa said you weren't coming anymore."

She arched one brow at him and slipped her cloak from her shoulders. With heat flushing into her face, she turned away from his stare and shook the droplets of water off her cloak before hanging it on the peg.

The fact that he would tell the children she wasn't coming burned a hole in her heart. She loved those kids. And what was all that about offering a trade if he didn't want her around anymore? Tessie scrambled down the ladder, and Laura who normally had to be sweet-talked out of bed, was right behind. Sarah and Ben followed. They piled into her and the group of them hugged. It was like they had all accepted she would not be around and were surprised and elated.

Jacob and Charlie looked down. "Yippee, some good food," Jacob said.

Jeanette glanced at Theo, who dug his fingers through his crop of hair.

"All right children." She clapped her hands. "We'll start with breakfast, but first I must talk to your pa."

She nodded to the porch, and he followed. The minute he shut the door behind him, he launched in.

"You need to concentrate on your own life—"

"Theo, I am concentrating on my own life. I'm bored and I've chosen to fill my summer with meaningful work. Until you find yourself a good wife, there is work aplenty right here within these walls."

"You know marriage is not—"

"I know, which makes my being here all the more important. I want to help you shape your girls into women and bless your boys with a few things they would miss not having a mama—like a good meal. Plus, what about our trade?"

"I think your laughter said all there was to say about that trade. It would be crazy for a man like me, a man who had a disastrous marriage to—"

"Actually, I've been thinking about that. I do need your help. I'm so inexperienced with men. Conversation and friendship are where it all starts, right? And I'm abysmal at both. I could use the practice—"

He looked away, shook his head. When he looked back, she saw a seriousness in his eyes that hadn't been there before. His voice lowered. "I need you to go, Jeanie. I have to figure this out on my own."

Like a stone dropping to the pit of her stomach, disappointment pressed down. What could she say to that? He had every right to decline her help.

The rain hammered on the porch overhang as he leveled a determined stare.

This family needs you. The words of the Spirit emptied into her as clear as the deluge pouring off the roof. And she had instant wisdom and strength.

"You're wrong, Theo. You don't have to figure this out on your own. I'm here. God has sent me, and I see what's right in front of me. Your family needs me." She turned so swiftly that her dress whirled around her ankles. She was not leaving. Service to this family was God's idea, not hers.

He caught her hand as she reached for the doorknob, and a jolt of life shot through her.

"But you must go," he said. "I don't know how to say this. The...the children are getting too close, and as I told you before, they can't weather another loss."

She turned toward him. "They shall not have to. In case you haven't noticed, I'm a spinster with no prospect of marriage. And even if by some miracle a man wanted to court me, that wouldn't mean I would abandon the children. It's not only they who have gotten close. I have too. I pray God will grant me the opportunity to be a part of their lives right into adulthood and beyond, as long as they need me." She turned before he could see the moisture welling in her eyes and swallowed past the lump in her throat. "And if I want to spend my time where I feel God deems it best spent, then take that up with Him. Not me."

She pulled her hand free, opened the door, and walked inside. A whisper flowed from her lips. "Thank you, Jesus, for your clarity and strength." She could feel a smile lift the corners of her mouth as she cleaned a portion of the counter to work upon. Breakfast was the first task of the day, and it would be a good one. No lumpy porridge for this crew. Eggs, bacon, fried potatoes, and fresh biscuits smothered with the jar of blueberry jam she had stuffed in her cloak pocket.

This family needed her. Truth be told, she needed them more.

CHAPTER 11

*A*fter a long day, Theo sat in his rocking chair on the porch. The cool evening air was refreshing, and the downpour earlier had been just what the fields needed.

The children were all sleeping, the house was clean, the laundry done, and they'd enjoyed a scrumptious supper, thanks to one very persistent woman. How could he argue that he needed Jeanette's help? He certainly had no funds to pay her. They barely made the monthly payment to Mr. Reiner and struggled to buy the essentials as it was.

She had remained quiet on the ride home today. He'd never been with any woman who could handle silence so comfortably. Louisa had talked incessantly, never tired of her favorite subject—herself. She was the reason that what he most enjoyed about his life now were the moments not crammed with words.

But Jeanie was different. She had that perfect balance between conversation and quiet. He could have her around all the time, and it would never be too much. Truth be told, dropping her off at the end of the day brought a deep sense of loneliness.

Part of him wanted to draw her into his arms and never let

go, but the rest of him wanted to run. He had so naively fallen under Louisa's spell and look where that had led. The sting of being duped still pricked blood. He knew he was jaded and doubted if he could ever fully trust again. But was it women in general he didn't trust, or his own decision making?

If he were to ever venture into marriage again, it would be with a woman like Jeanie Williams. A woman with natural beauty on the inside and out, who didn't feel the need for constant attention. One who had no idea how attractive she was, with her thick hair begging to be freed of that bun. The day she had worn her hair in a braid down her torso… thankfully, she'd never repeated that. He had not been able to stop looking at her, which was unsettling to say the least. And the way those chocolate brown eyes melted with love when she held Tessie or taught Sarah how to cook. How many times had he found himself staring? Everything about Jeanie was refreshing after Louisa and the Richmond belles he had left behind. Jeanie was too good to be true. Why had no man snatched her up? What was he missing? Did she have a secret past that marred her reputation? If so, he was well acquainted with that kind of woman and never wanted a repeat.

His hands tightened on the arms of the wooden chair. Memories he fought hard to keep in the shadows burst into life.

"Why did you marry me, Louisa?"

He looked around their ornate bedroom with heavy velvet drapes and gilded molding. That sense of not belonging washed over him again. Even after eight years together there was no sense of security, or love, for that matter.

"Women do desperate things in desperate situations." She pulled one fancy stocking high and swivelled her leg in front of the mirror. "Six children, and they still look mighty fine."

Why was she changing her stockings at that hour? "I regret not taking more time to get to know you," he whispered, not wanting anyone outside their bedroom door to hear. The help, his nosy mother-in-law, or his controlling father-in-law. All had the propensity to eavesdrop.

A mirthless smile crawled across her lips as she turned from the mirror. "You still don't get it, do you?"

"Get what?"

Her laughter held a raucous tone. "I might as well tell you, since you're too dense to figure it out yourself. Why do you think I insisted upon such hasty nuptials? Marrying you was a coverup for what another man left behind."

He drew in a sharp breath. Jacob was not his son? "What?" His hand slammed down hard on top of the bureau. He no longer cared to keep things quiet. Yet, he loved that boy fiercely —a son in every way. He crossed the room in one swift movement and pulled Louisa up from the bed. "You've made a mockery—"

"Tsk, tsk, Theo." She pulled her arm free.

He let her go. He had to or he'd not be able to control the rage mushrooming inside his head. Her betrayal—and the way she'd so callously announced it—made his hands tremble. He clenched them tight rather than put them through the wall like he felt like doing.

With one eyebrow arched, she sat back down on the bed. "You've never been given to violence. You don't want to start now." She pulled the other stocking on. "In fact, I thought you'd be a lot more fun than you are. A good fight now and again would've spiced up the tedious boredom of living with you and all those kids." She waved her hand to the baby crying in the nursery next door. "Listen to that horrific sound. Where is that nanny to shut it up?"

"It? That is our daughter. Not an it!"

Just the way she smirked at him sent a shaft of fury scuttling up his spine. "What? Are some of the others not mine as well?"

She ignored him, rearranging her low-cut dress to show as much of her bosom as possible.

"Answer me." He had to know. Not because he didn't love each of those children with all he had within him, but because he needed to know if their whole marriage had been a sham.

She turned from the mirror. "Do you really want to know?"

"Yes."

"Honestly"—she turned from side to side in front of the mirror, clearly adoring her reflection—"your guess is as good as mine."

His jaw clenched tight as he bit back what he wanted to call her. There was little intimacy between them, though he had tried. But what a fool he had been to trust that she would be as faithful as he had been. And the way she had warmed up now and again, got all cozy after months of frigidity from her side of the bed... Now it all made sense.

"Did you ever love me, or was I just easy prey?"

"You were awfully naïve, and daddy liked you enough to take you in and give you that ridiculously paying bookkeeping job. That kept me in his good books and living the lifestyle I'm accustomed to." She placed her hat on her head and slipped in the necessary pins. "As for love...I tried. You're a handsome man, Theo, and I liked that other women envied me, but we're just too different."

With a final approving look into the mirror, she picked up her carpet bag.

"And where do you think you are going?"

She glided across the room as if she were the queen of England and stopped in front of him. "I know you'll make a far better father than I'll ever make a mother." Her dainty hand reached toward his face.

He recoiled from her touch. "What exactly do you mean by that?"

"I'm leaving you, Theo. I found myself the type of man I've always desired. Exciting. Rich. And tad bit dangerous. I'll finally be free and no longer under your thumb—or daddy's."

"What about your children?"

"Like I said. You'll make a far better father than I'll ever make as a mother. Goodbye, Theo."

His hands hurt from clasping the hard wood on the arms of the rocking chair. He stood swiftly and paced across the porch. No. Jeanie was nothing like his first wife. Louisa hadn't spent an hour helping another person, let alone day after day. Jeanie had to be different if he was going to trust her with his children.

She *was* different.

But it was frustrating how she'd told him to take things up with God. God wasn't listening. God had never heard Theo's prayers. And really, it wasn't as if a mere mortal had the right to question God and expect an answer. If he could, he would tell God what he really thought of His so-called care.

I'm here. I'll never leave or forsake you.

And there it was, one of the many verses he remembered his mother repeating, time after time. Though he'd never cared to listen, those verses poked up uninvited like weeds in his fields. Like Jeanie, Ma had believed all that rhetoric, and he had almost started to buy into it. And then, God took her when the kids—and he—had needed her the most.

How did Jeanie know God was telling her to help his family? And the way she prayed at the dinner table so matter-of-factly, as if God were sitting right beside her, waiting to answer her prayers. That kind of faith, he didn't understand.

"God," he whispered into the star-studded sky. "if you're up there, what do I do?"

He listened.

Nothing.

He'd have to make this decision about what to do with his growing attraction for Jeanie, and his obvious need for her help, like he made all others. Alone.

How could he fight Jeanie's goodness and insist she not come to help when one look around his house proved he was failing his children horribly? If he wasn't going to remarry, his children needed a feminine role model. Who better than the local teacher, whom the community trusted with their children?

He sank back into the rocker and let out a breath. His large frame caused the chair to protest with a loud creak as he relaxed. Every day Jeanie gave them was better than a day she didn't. That was decision enough.

The fact that he enjoyed everything about her, even her bullish ways, might've helped that decision. When she was right, she was right. His family needed her.

~

"You're making that up." Jeanette could feel heat pour into her cheeks.

"I am not. I sit at the back of the church, and I see everything." Theo's smile lit up his face as he rocked on his porch in the waning evening light. "And you have to try."

No, she couldn't. That new cowboy, Solomon, surely had not been staring at her or she would've noticed. And she certainly couldn't go up to him and strike up a conversation.

"Well, I sit at the front, and when I'm playing the piano, I see things too. Like widow Victoria squeezing into your row all cozy like."

He scowled at her.

She laughed. "Don't get all ornery with me. You know it's true."

"You're deflecting from the subject. We're talking about you. I have no interest in starting up a relationship, so never mind her. You, on the other hand, have a live one on the end of your hook, and you don't even see it."

"Not possible." Or was it that she kept her eyes pinned on Theo and his family whenever she could discreetly look?

"It's possible, so let's practice." Theo stood and walked over to the railing. "A deal is a deal. Pretend, I'm the cowboy. Wait." He raced into the house and back out again. He slapped a cowboy hat on and leaned against the porch post, crossing his feet in a relaxed pose. "All right, Jeanie. Give me your best smile, pretend I'm Solomon, and come and introduce yourself."

Jeanette gaped, sure that her mouth was hanging open. He looked so handsome, teasing her, standing in that relaxed stance. That cowboy hat looked mighty fine—or was it the man in it? Her hands tingled, and shivers skimmed up her arms.

"I'm…I'm to pretend you're Solomon?"

"Come on, Jeanie girl. You can do it."

She stood and rubbed her clammy hands on her dress. Her heart kicked up speed and slammed against the walls of her chest. Solomon was the last thing on her mind. The only way she could possibly do this was to joke her way through. She sauntered up to Theo with a decided sway to her hips, much like she had witnessed Victoria do. "Hello, Cowboy." She batted her lashes. "My name is Jeanette Williams. My friends call me Jeanie." She looked down demurely like she had watched other women do.

He waved his hand in front of her face. "That's not you. Be yourself, not a copy of something you've seen others do. Besides, *I* call you Jeanie. That's for me and me alone."

When she looked at him, his face held annoyance, and the giggles got the best of her. She covered her mouth to stifle the laugh. "You don't want anyone else calling me Jeanie?"

"This is not going to be of any value if you don't take it seriously."

"All right. All right." She held out her hand. "I am pleased to make your acquaintance, Solomon." She tried to imagine the cowboy at church, but the very handsome Theo was all she could see.

He caught her fingers and covered them with his. Warmth

oozed up her arm. Slowly, he bent forward and raised her hand to his lips, kissing the back softly.

A quickening tripped her heart in erratic beats. She gasped and tried to pull away.

"No. Don't yank away or you'll give the wrong message." He removed his hand slowly, and even still, she missed his warmth when he was gone.

"Now, where would you take the conversation from here?"

This practicing thing was not going well. Her insides flipped. Her body tingled from tip to toe, and her mind was not on Solomon.

"I was just thinking how handsome you look in that cowboy hat." The words came out honest and sincere. There was no coquettish lilt to her voice or tease in her eyes. She meant every word. Theo was dangerously handsome, and she was more than a little affected by his nearness.

Suddenly, he tugged her close. He didn't speak but held her against his chest. Their eyes locked, and he looked at her as if she were the most beautiful woman in the world. Never had she felt anything so enchanting in her life. His gaze dropped to her lips, and she could barely breathe. She had to pull a long breath in to combat the light headedness. The last thing she wanted to do was faint in his arms. "What…what are you doing?"

"I'm doing what you're inviting. If you play those kinds of games, you'll get yourself into trouble. You should never be that forward in a first introduction…voicing how handsome a man is." He let her go abruptly and stepped away. "I think that's enough for tonight." He hopped down the front porch steps and mumbled as he walked away. "Gotta get you home."

She wrapped her arms around her body. She hadn't been thinking of Solomon. The loss of Theo's embrace felt like a cold blast of winter had blown in. She shivered in the warmth of a lovely June evening. Truth be told, she desired the kind of trouble he was talking about if it was him in her arms.

CHAPTER 12

It was Jeanette's Sunday to play the piano at church. She had done that for years, but today was different. Reverend William had been asking her for a long time to sing a solo, but fear had always held her captive. The background had been her safety net, but as of late, refusing to sing felt disobedient.

Against every nerve that flowed, frayed, and fought within her, today she was going to do the unthinkable, play and sing a solo. Only the Reverend knew. She'd told him that she would nod if she had the courage. If not, she would begin playing the introduction, and the reverend would invite the congregation to sing along. No one but the reverend and the good Lord would be any the wiser if she chickened out.

But she wouldn't. Not today.

Her hands trembled as she sat at the piano and began to play low while the congregation filtered in, each family finding their favorite spot. She hit a few wrong notes thinking about what was to come but nothing she couldn't redeem with a little spontaneity. She smiled at Theo's family as they filed into their pew at the back of the church. The girls waved, and she nodded to acknowledge them.

Her nerves settled when it came time for the congregation to join in the opening song. But as it got closer to her allotted time, her heart hammered against the walls of her chest. Why in heaven's name did she feel she had to do this? Wasn't it good enough that she served the Lord in playing the piano and leading the children's choir? A solo. Was she crazy? Why put herself through this torture?

Reverend William went through a few announcements and then looked her way. Her head nodded, almost against her will.

"I will be speaking today on the loving grace of God. However, before we begin Jeanette is going to bring this message to you in song." He smiled at her and then stepped away to sit.

She sat up straighter and keyed the intro. She played it again. Everything within her was screaming no, no, no.

Sing to Me, the Spirit whispered.

She opened her mouth. All fear vanished as she focused on what the words were saying and who she was singing to.

"'Amazing grace, how sweet the sound…'"

Her courage strengthened as she sang. She hit the notes with clarity and ease. By the last verse, when she asked the congregation to stand and join her, fear was but a distant emotion. Never had she felt the Lord's presence more powerfully. She had a strong sense that He was pleased with her.

The hymn finished, and an ethereal silence settled over the crowd.

Reverend William stepped up to the podium and held the silence. The congregation would normally slip to their seats, but no one moved.

Reverend William lifted his face heavenward. "Well, if that wasn't the presence of the Holy Spirit brought to us through the voice of an angel, I don't know what was. Let's worship the

Lord, giving Him a round of hearty praise." The usually somber, quiet man lifted his hands clapping, into the heavens. Shouts of joy and boisterous applause echoed through the rafters as others joined in.

Jeanette slipped into her seat beside Helen and Pa. They each gave her a warm hug.

"You did the Lord proud," Pa whispered.

"That was so beautiful." Helen's arms squeezed tight.

She glanced back at Theo and his family. The children beamed, Tessie waved wildly, and Theo hit her with a striking smile that made her heart lurch.

Widow Victoria caught the exchange and glared.

Jeanette allowed a full smile to blossom before she slowly turned toward the front. She spent the rest of the service thanking God for the courage He had given her to sing only to Him. After the service, she was overwhelmed by the people who gathered around to compliment her voice and tell her how profoundly they had felt the move of the Spirit. Uncomfortable with the attention, she edged her way to the door.

Reverend William was shaking hands as people left and pumped hers vigorously. "You, my dear girl, have been hiding your gift under a bushel. The Lord is very pleased that today, you let your light shine."

As heat crawled up her neck, Jeanette practically skipped down the steps. She hurried across the church yard to where Pa and the Wallace family stood.

"And you didn't tell me you were going to do this, why?" Pa's voice held a stern note, but laughter danced in his eyes.

"I wasn't sure I could."

She glanced up at Theo, whose gaze held only admiration. "You're capable of so much more than you give yourself credit for."

"You sounded like an angel," Sarah said.

"Best part of the service," Jacob added.

Tessie pulled on her hand, trying to get her attention. "Can you teach me to sing like that?"

Theo stepped forward, picking up Tessie. "That, my dear child, is a special gift. No one can teach that."

Jeanette could not hold back her smile. She had never been happier. Obeying the Lord with the scary stuff was not turning out so badly at all. She was going to have to pay better attention to His leading.

"Miss Williams?"

She turned to see the young cowboy Solomon behind her. His tall, lean frame edged closer. Solid muscles filled his sleeve as he removed his cowboy hat. "I-I was wondering if I could make your acquaintance." His eyes darted up and then down to the ground. He fiddled with the rim of his hat.

Jeanette could recognize shyness when she saw it. It had to have taken a lot of nerve to walk up to their group.

"Certainly." Jeanette stepped away from her family and Theo's, and he fell in beside her, slipping his hat back on. They came to a stop under the branches of a large oak tree, and he turned toward her.

"Solomon Maynard's the name." He tipped his cowboy hat. "I'm new to the area and not typically this forward, but your song…it got me here." He lifted a hand to his chest.

Jeanette had no idea what to make of all the fuss. "I was so scared, but somehow God gave me the strength."

"It was amazing. Truly."

"Thank you."

"I work with Colby and was sitting with his family when I asked Katherine who the songbird was, she told me you were her sister. She was going to introduce us, but you skedaddled out of there quick. Glad I caught you outside. Hope I'm not being too forward in asking to have the privilege of escorting you home?"

"You…you want to escort me home?" Was she hearing right?

"A nice day for a leisurely ride, wouldn't you say?" He spread his hand up toward the blue sky. "Your sister said you live right next door, and I'd be honored if you'd let me accompany you." He removed his hat, splaying a hand through his thick, sandy blond hair.

This had to be a first. Plain Jeanette was getting an invite about fifteen years too late. But it was a day of firsts. Before she could talk herself out of it, she heard herself agree. "A ride in the sunshine would be lovely."

His wide smile revealed a row of straight white teeth. "I was going to hop on my horse this morning, but something told me to take the buggy. Now I know why."

Her face heated as he held out his arm.

"Just one moment. I should let Pa know."

She swung around and hurried back to the group. "I'm going to catch a ride with my new friend. I'll see you at home."

Pa gave a Cheshire grin. Tessie asked if she could come along, to which Theo immediately said, "No." He gave her a nod, but he did not smile.

She hurried back and placed her hand in the crook of the cowboy's arm, and they walked to his small buggy. He helped her up, and they set out on the road back to the ranch.

"So, what brings you to the valley?" she asked.

"Work."

"Just work?"

"Yup."

Oh goodness, this was going to be a long ride home if he only gave one-word answers and did not put a bit more giddy-up into his horse's gait.

"And you do what at the ranch?" Jeanette asked.

"I'm a hand."

Silence. She was not used to spending time with men, much less having to pull out conversation. How awkward. Why had she agreed to this?

First Pa's wagon and then Theo's with the kids rolled on by, and she wished she could yell out for them to stop so she could escape this silence. Instead, she smiled and waved. Theo gave a quick wave and then looked forward.

They plodded on in silence until Solomon pulled the reins tight and turned toward her. "Sorry. I'm not usually this tongue-tied around women. But sitting in church listening to you sing, I was moved like I've never been before. Then to find out you weren't married or even engaged… Well, it seems too good to be true. Now I feel as awkward as a teen on his first day of courting."

Jeanette felt her eyebrows shoot up. She worked hard to relax them. Was he thinking this simple ride home was courtship?

"I've said too much. What an idiot. I'm rambling on like—"

"Solomon, I'm flattered. But it was only a song."

"No. That's just it. It wasn't only a song. I've been waiting for God to reveal…" His lips pressed shut, and he looked down at the reins in his hands.

"To reveal what?" What was he saying?

His blue eyes lifted to hers and softened. "I'm bumbling. Forget I said anything. Let's get to know each other and see where God takes this." He slapped the reins, and his horse picked up their pace.

Was this man seriously interested in her?

"You'll see in time that I'm not as crazy as I sound right now." He laughed at himself.

"How old are you, Solomon?" Jeanette was sure she was older, and her age would quickly put things into perspective, ending this awkward situation.

"I'm twenty-five. I was married for about a year. Lost my wife and the baby during childbirth."

Jeanette touched his arm. "I'm sorry. That must have been tough."

"It was over six years ago, and I still miss her." He kept his eyes pinned on the road.

"That's honest."

He nodded. "That's what I'm told. I'm too honest."

"No such thing. I love that quality in a person."

"But life goes on, and I feel like God is telling me it's time to live again." He swung his hand out over the rolling hills. "It's so beautiful here, and there's so much to be thankful for."

Jeanette could not help but like the young man. He wasn't lost in self-pity like she had been for far too many years.

"And I love the work. I'm good with horses. It's my gift. Colby recruited me at a horse sale in West Virginia, asked me to come work with his thoroughbreds. I'm looking forward to a bright future."

She peeked up at him. "So, you're not just one of the many ranch hands that come and go?"

"No. It took a lot for me to leave my folks and the rest of my family. But everything about this offer felt right." He turned his head and gave her a winsome smile.

She needed to tell him the truth. "I need to be honest, I'm twenty-nine." Her words came out fast and jilted.

"And?"

"Too old for you, but I know a couple nice ladies at church I could intro—"

"I have to tell you something, Jeanette. I haven't courted a single woman or offered to escort anyone home since my Christina died. Haven't felt the slightest urge until...today." He smiled at her. "Well, to be honest, you did catch my eye a few weeks ago."

Jeanette looked across the fields to the mountains in the distance, but all she saw in her mind's eye was Theo. What would he think? Would he ever be healed enough to want another relationship? Maybe this was God's gentle way of keeping her eyes in the direction they were meant to go. But somehow Theo felt...comfortable. Like home.

Gosh, she had better nip that one and fast. Theo had made it only too clear friendship was all he wanted.

"I can see my honesty has made you uncomfortable," Solomon said. "Will you tell me about yourself? At twenty-nine and unmarried, I'm sure you have a story too."

That remark cut deep. She shivered against the chill rejection always fostered.

"Are you cold?" Solomon slowed the horse and twisted toward the back of the wagon. He hauled a blanket to the front and placed it over her lap. "There you go. Better?"

She thanked him. She had no intention of telling him her shiver had nothing to do with the weather. Even with the extra time to think, she had no story. Had she done what Katherine accused her of doing years before, allowed her standoffish ways to shut herself off from people? When Solomon had asked to escort her home, her first thought had been shock, and for good reason. She would tell him the truth. "There is no story. No one has ever wanted me. That's my story."

He placed the reins in one hand and gave her shoulders a quick squeeze with his other arm and then respectfully removed it. "I can't believe that, but I won't belittle your feelings. I can see your hurt runs deep."

Jeanette shut her eyes to hold back the tears that pressed against her eyelids.

The wagon bumped and jostled over a rutted patch. He held the silence for a few moments before touching her arm. "Would you do me a favor, Jeanette, and sing that beautiful song you sang at church?"

She took a moment to collect herself and find her voice. As the words flowed from her lips, her troubled mind disappeared.

He joined in the song. His rich baritone naturally carried the melody, and she found the harmony. They sang the song twice, their voices blending effortlessly together, bringing them to where the bend up to her house split off the main drive.

"Thank you. I'll make my way from here." She didn't want Pa scrutinizing their goodbye.

He pulled the horse to a stop. "I hope you've enjoyed our time half as much as I have."

"I have." She was surprised at how she could answer that truthfully. "And thanks for reminding me of what is truly important by singing with me. You have a wonderful voice."

"We make beautiful music together. I knew we would." The light in his blue eyes twinkled.

"Are you flirting with me, Solomon Maynard?" She swatted his arm with her gloved hand.

"I am, Jeanette. Sorry, I don't know your full name."

She laughed. "Jeanette Rose Williams."

He jumped from the wagon and came around to help her down. When she was on the ground, he lifted her hand like a perfect gentleman and kissed the back.

She didn't pull away. Thanks to Theo's tutelage, she allowed her hand to gracefully return to her side after he released it.

"I am flirting with you, Jeanette Rose Williams. You can count on that." His dimples danced. He jumped back into his wagon and tipped his hat. "Until next time." The wagon lurched forward up the drive to her sister's. She watched as he whistled his way out of sight before she took the bend to her house.

CHAPTER 13

"So. How did it go?" Theo asked the question as he drove Jeanette home that following Saturday, but he was not sure he wanted to know the answer.

All week long he had resisted the urge to prod, but ever since last Sunday, a thread of loneliness had stitched its way into his soul. He could not pull it free. Something about seeing Jeanette sitting beside Solomon on that wagon made him feel the pang of loss. He had refused to ask her all week and she had said nothing. But after spending his whole day with her and the kids at the swimming hole, in a much more relaxed state than usual, the words just tumbled out.

"How did what go?" She picked a piece of lint off her dress and folded her hands in her lap. The buggy rattled over a rut, and she grabbed the buckboard to steady herself.

"Sorry about that. I wasn't watching where I was going." He'd been staring at her to see if he could pick up any information from her expression. "I meant with Solomon, last week."

"Oh that." She waved her hand into the cool evening air. "It was…nice."

"Nice?"

"Started out a little rocky—he hardly said two words—but then he told his story, and I told mine." She laughed. "Mine was short. Unlike his, losing a wife and baby. He's been through a lot for someone so young."

"How old is he?"

"Only twenty-five. I'm much too old for him."

Theo liked the sound of that.

"He doesn't seem to think so, though. Even came by the house one evening and asked me if he could take me into town today for a tea and a piece of apple pie at the Old Angler's Inn. Apparently, Molly Angler has opened up her restaurant to the public as well as her patrons."

Theo's gut twisted. Solomon had asked her out? "Then why were you at the swimming hole with us all day?"

She slapped at his arm. "Come on, Theo. I'm not going to let the kids down. They work so hard all week helping on the farm, and this is our fun day. I told Solomon I'm unavailable, Monday, Wednesday, Friday, and Saturday. But you would've been proud of me. He kissed my hand, and I didn't flinch or pull away."

"Good girl." His words sounded flat even to him. What she was telling him made him feel as out of sorts as having his skin turned inside out. "So, like I said, he's interested." He pulled the reins too tight, and Blossom's head bobbed. Theo had better calm down and fast.

"It would seem so," she said. "Now I just have to somehow unwind enough to give it a chance."

"You're relaxed with me. You can do it."

"As I told you, having the children around was a great distraction. It eased us into our friendship."

"Or was it my welcoming charm?"

"Ha, welcoming charm. Prickly pear is more like it."

Ouch, that hurt. Along comes gentle Solomon up against prickly pear. What could he say to that? She was right. He had been obtuse. If only he could go back and make a better first impression. But how was he to know she would turn out to be such a beautiful friend? And then again, why did this matter so much to him? She deserved happiness, and he was not the person to give her that.

They rode in silence to the gate of the Richardson Estate.

"Stop, please."

He pulled on the reins.

She laid a hand on Theo's arm, and awareness flooded in. "Did I offend you with my teasing? You went quiet all of a sudden."

"No. Of course not." He could not tell her. "I guess I'm just sorry we started out so—"

"Oh, don't worry. All that is water under the bridge. Trust me. You're a great friend, and I'm going to need you to help me with this whole Solomon thing."

She smiled at him in a way that made his heart buck. There in the twilight, with the first star glinting in the dimming light, the word *friend* did not seem like enough. He turned forward abruptly and slapped the reins. Blossom lurched forward.

~

The month of June was heating up. A warm breeze whipped at Jeanette's clothing as she beelined her way through the orchard to the big house. She tightened the ribbon on her sun bonnet and pressed back her excitement. Katherine had found a new pattern for swimming gowns made especially for females in *The World of Fashion* magazine. They were going to spend the day sewing. It was time the Wallace family learned to swim, especially if they were going to continue to visit the swimming hole every Saturday.

Jeanette's life was full, and she was at peace. Theo's children needed her, and she had never felt more alive in service to the Lord. The added bonus of Theo becoming such a dear friend and the growing attention of Solomon didn't hurt either. She was beginning to feel more positive about herself. She was happy, truly happy for the first time in many years.

She skipped up to the imposing portico and knocked on the ornate door. Tulips and vines were intricately carved into the solid wood. Her eye for detail never tired of the grandeur of patterned brick, carved stone, decorative gables, and generous windows. But nothing inside her needed the life her sister enjoyed. All she longed for was purpose. And God had miraculously provided the Wallace family. She needed them as much as they needed her. Theo's friendship and the love of those children filled a lonely ache that had resided within her for far too long.

The door swung wide. "Goodness, Jeanette. You don't have to stand on ceremony waiting to be let in. You've got to learn how to barge in like Pa does." Katherine's voice tinkled with laughter.

Jeanette glided through the door and followed her sister down the hall into a nearby room she had rarely been in. Floor to ceiling windows allowed the sunlight to flood in and would be perfect for their endeavor. Scissors, thread, different prints of flannel and wool, lace and trim, all graced a large table.

"I have everything ready." Katherine squeezed Jeanette's arm. "We rarely get a good sister visit these days."

"I know." Jeanette moved further into the room. "This will be fun."

"It will, and I don't want any argument. My donation will be the material and my seamstress to help get these suits done for next Saturday. I'll call her after we have a chance to catch up."

"But that's too mu—"

"You did say you go to the swimming hole on Saturdays?"

"Yes."

"Look at this." Katherine waved her over to a magazine, completely ignoring her protest. Her beautiful blue eyes danced with excitement. "The world is finally getting wise to the needs of women."

Jeanette looked at the images and gasped. "Short sleeves and trousers that only cover to the knees? Why, that is—"

"Smart," Katherine insisted. "A dress with trousers and long sleeves is torture to swim in. Not to mention dangerous. You and I both know that."

She was right. The swimming gown looked on the edge of scandalous, but wise. The two-piece garment had a top that fell below the hips with a high neckline and short puffy sleeves. A set of trousers that covered to the knees would be worn underneath. The gown had scalloped edges trimmed with lace around the bottom of the top and matching trousers. A belt cinched in the waist. "How utterly feminine and freeing this would be to swim in." She fingered the picture. "But I fear it's too revealing."

"Fiddlesticks." Katherine batted the air like Ma used to do. "Besides, no one else will see you. The swimming hole is on our property, and I'll make sure no one interrupts your family time."

"It's not my family," Jeanette corrected. "And I must maintain modesty in front of Theo."

"Goodness, Jeanette. The flannel material alone is going to eliminate any chance of impropriety, and what's a little arm showing and skin below the knees when women are wearing low-cut gowns that show off their bosoms for all the world to see? Safety is of utmost importance as these children learn to swim."

"You're right." She could not put into words how much courage it would take to wear a suit like that in front of Theo. Katherine was a married woman and clearly forgetting how awkward it would be.

"But of course, I'm right." Katherine gave her a cheeky smile. "I'm going to make this pattern for myself and my girls, too, so we can all be shocking together." She threw her arm around

Jeanette and gave a teasing squeeze. "Now, pick out the print you want for each child."

Jeanette fingered the soft material and chose a different color for each of Theo's daughters.

"You did bring their measurements, yes?"

"I did."

"For the boys, too?"

"Don't I always listen to my older and wiser sister?"

"As if. But flip the page, and you'll see what we're making for the boys." Jeanette looked at the one-piece wool swimsuit that covered the body from neck to knees. Her stomach flip-flopped at the memory of measuring Theo with his strong muscular arms and broad shoulders—not to mention the length of his stature. Heat flooded her cheeks as she remembered how intimate that moment had been.

"What's that cute expression, all flustered and pink?"

Jeanette turned away from Katherine's astute stare. "Nothing."

"Don't give me that *nothing* story. I've never seen you so happy."

Gosh, did her every emotion show? "I...I am happy, in service to the Lord—"

Katherine let out a snort that mushroomed into full-blown laughter. "In service to the Lord. Now, that's a new one."

Jeanette put on her most indignant expression. She looked down through her spectacles perched on the end of her nose at Katherine, who was considerably shorter. "I-I..."

Katherine's hand went to her stomach, and she bent over in gales of laughter.

"Are you quite done?" Jeanette was a tad annoyed.

Katherine righted herself, a knowing smile twitching her lips. "Are you quite done... lying to yourself?"

"I have no idea what you mean. I'm merely helping with the children."

"A big strong handsome farmer, and you're the only woman in the community who hasn't noticed. Not likely. But if it soothes your ruffled feathers to believe—"

"I didn't say I didn't notice. I merely said that my focus is on the children."

"Then it's time to refocus. Come on, Jeanette. You have two very eligible men vying for your attention. Don't let fear ruin this for you."

"Fear?"

"Yes, fear. Every time any man has looked twice at you, you've pulled your hair tighter into that frightening bun you wear, and you've slipped into the shadows. Too afraid of being hurt."

"I don't remember any man in my past looking twice at me. And there's nothing wrong with my bun."

"Men have looked at you, but you've never allowed yourself to see what others see. And there *is* something wrong with the way you wear your hair. No one needs a bun pulling the skin on their face back like they're in hurricane-force winds."

"Heavens, you embellish. My hair needs to be practical."

"Don't deny it." Katherine pulled Jeanette to the mirror. "Take a look. Now, let me rearrange." She pulled the tight knot free and ran her fingers through Jeanette's hair. Thick tendrils cascaded all the way down her back. "You have beautiful hair, but no one would ever know. With this length and volume, you could wear it like I do." She refashioned a bun higher on the head and then lightly tugged at the hair to loosen and soften the look. "There. So much better and still practical." She smirked into the reflection of the mirror, clearly happy with herself.

That small adjustment of her bun from the nape of her neck to the top of her head made a considerable difference, even more of change than the braid had made.

"I dare you to wear your hair like this."

"If I change things up, will it look like I'm…I'm—?"

"You do want to get married someday, right?"

"Of course."

"Well then, all you have to figure out is which man, Theo or Solomon?"

"As if it's that easy."

"It is. Now, be honest, which way are you leaning?"

"If I thought I had a chance? Theo and I are good friends, but he told me he doubts he will ever be ready to remarry. And Solomon... I'm just getting to know him."

"Theo's first wife is gone. Life moves on and like with me..." Katherine held a far-away look in the depth of her eyes, but she blinked it away quickly. "It may take some time, but he'll learn to love again. And when he does, you could be the one. Steady. True. Loving. Like Colby was for me after Josiah."

Katherine assumed Theo was mourning the loss of his wife, and Janette was not about to reveal Theo's private life. It was far more complicated than she could share.

"Or," Katherine rattled on, "there's Solomon. Colby raves about him. He's a stand-up guy, hardworking, and Colby says anyone who can break a horse with such patience and kindness is a special man. Either way, you just need to put yourself out there."

"I don't know..."

"What don't you know? You're one of the most beautiful women I know, both on the inside and out. Yet, you've hidden behind your works, taking care of Ma, Pa, the school children, and now Theo's family. Everyone knows what a gem you are, but somehow you don't."

"I heard unkind remarks, how the Williams girls were all beautiful except for that plain Jeanette. And how—"

"And you believed them, shrinking into the background." Katherine shook her head.

"You would've too." Jeanette could hear the defensiveness in her voice, but the memories still cut deep.

"I'm not judging you, sis. I just wish the cruelty of words didn't have such power, especially with someone as kind and beautiful as you." She stepped forward and removed Jeanette's spectacles, pulling her to the mirror. "When was the last time you looked at yourself without hiding behind these things?"

Large, dark eyes gazed back at her. They held a glimmer of something she had not seen in a long time. Hope. It was amazing how that one emotion lit up what she'd always considered non-descript.

"Now smile."

A flicker of a grin kicked up the edges of her mouth, removing the serious and dour.

"Give me a full one."

Katherine tickled her ribs, and Jeanette laughed.

"Hey, what's this?" Katherine ran her fingers down the back of Jeanette's dress. "Are you wrapping your bust line?"

Jeanette jumped back, out of her reach. "It's none of your business."

"Now we're getting to the crux of the matter. You've worked hard to hide every asset you have. Why?"

"Not always. I did try. When I went to school in Richmond, Grandmother talked me into dressing like the other ladies. You know how she is. I had a whole new wardrobe in a matter of days. Men did show interest, but not the kind I wanted." Her face flushed hot as she pointed to her bustline. "They would not look into my face but…"

"Unfortunately, there'll always be those. But what does the Spirit tell you about Theo and Solomon?"

Jeanette didn't hesitate. "Theo's a good man. And Solomon treats me with the utmost respect."

"There you go. You said that with conviction. I can vouch for Solomon, and from what Pa has told me, he really likes Theo."

"You and Pa have been discussing Theo?"

"Not only him, but you and him—together."

A ripple of delight ran through at the thought. Theo and his six beautiful children would be a slice of heaven, but she could hardly admit that to herself let alone anyone else. "Well, I never."

"We're family. It's what family does. Now go behind that screen and rid yourself of that burden. Especially with summer coming on, that must be so uncomfortable."

Jeanette did what her sister asked, though she couldn't believe she was giving in. The tight linen fell free, and she pulled up her chemise and hooked up the front of her corset. Her day dress went over her head and the material cascaded over her body. She cinched up the belt. Had fear and wrong perceptions really turned men away?

With her head held high and her shoulders back, she came from around the screen.

Katherine clapped a hand to her mouth and her eyes went wide. "Oh, my goodness." She waved Jeanette over. "You have curves."

Jeanette stood before the mirror. She couldn't deny the transformation—the hair, the eyes lit with hope, the fullness of curves. She had always thought of herself as straight up and down because she was tall and had little for hips, but now she saw curves she'd never allowed herself to notice before.

She smiled a real smile.

"Wow. Let the real Jeanette step forward. Not the fearful one."

"You're assuming I'm going to make all these changes."

"Yes, I am." Katherine pulled herself to full height. "And I'm going to hold you accountable. I'm also going to pray that God gives you courage as He did me, to be the woman He created you to be."

Jeanette laughed. "No praying allowed."

"Ha, because you're afraid of the power. And to be honest, as much as I like Solomon, I think God saved you all these years from being someone else's wife because He knew this day would come. Those children. That farmer."

Jeanette gulped back the knot that clotted her throat. Could that possibly be true when she had decided long ago that God had forgotten her dreams? Could Theo and his family really be part of her future?

Katherine clamped down on her arm. "I've got an idea. Don't change a thing, quite yet. I'm going to invite Theo and his family to dinner this Friday, along with Solomon, and maybe Winnie and Robert just to mix things up a tad. It's high time we extended some hospitality to the new ones in the community." She winked. "You and Pa will be invited too, of course. And I'm personally going to see to your attire and hair."

"Theo is a very private man."

"Then it'll be your responsibility to convince him. Tell him he can't snub your family after all you've done for him."

"I will not guilt him into coming."

"Fine then. I'll pray about that too. Just ask him tomorrow and let me know."

CHAPTER 14

Theo had agreed to attend the evening meal at the ranch only because he didn't want to insult Jeanette or her family. And the kids had begged him. He no more felt like socializing after a full week of work than he felt like doing the laundry he guiltily left for Jeanette.

He needed to clean himself up at the outside pump before heading in to change. Jeanette was training him to leave the dirt outside, not track it in. And after all the cleaning she was doing, he was trying his utmost to establish new habits for himself and the children.

"Boys, come on—we have to clean up for our outing tonight." He yelled at Jacob and Charlie, who had Ben by the feet and arms.

"We'll put Ben in the water trough here for a good cleaning." Jacob laughed as they held the wiggling and screaming kid over the horse's water. "You said the next time he forgot to water the horse—"

"Stop it." Theo said, but laughter filled his voice as he splashed water over his upper body and put his head under to give his hair a good wash.

"Pa. Pa. Save me." Ben squeaked out his plea as they lowered him down.

The older two always said he came to Ben's defense. This time, he would ignore the happening. A little water wouldn't kill Ben, and maybe then he'd remember to water the animals as told.

Ben came out of the trough spitting and gagging as he swung wildly into the air.

Theo shook his head. He'd better intervene before it escalated to more. He marched on over. "Get cleaned up, before I do the same to you boys."

Jacob and Charlie went running.

Ben was next to tears. "Why didn't you stop them?"

"You had that coming, son. You've been lax in your chores and the other boys have had to pick up your slack. A little water won't kill you."

Ben's lip almost hit the ground, and his eyes burned with anger. "That's not fair. Two against one."

"It's not fair, you leaving your work for them either. Now get on into the house and change into your Sunday clothes. We're going to Jeanette's family for a fancy meal. Remember?"

Ben's eyes lit up. There was nothing like food to distract. He gave Ben's wet head a playful rub, and the boy lit out across the yard toward the house.

"And don't go traipsing through the house with those wet clothes," he called. "Take them off on the porch."

Theo walked a little slower. Parenting six children was taking its toll. Most days he felt like a failure. Thankfully, Jeanette filled in the gaps. She had a way about her...strong but gentle. Loving but firm. What didn't he like about that woman?

He should not be thinking that way. She had Solomon knocking, a man so clearly better for her in every way. He didn't come with a ready-made family or all the damage a bad marriage had done to Theo's soul.

He opened the door to find the household in an uproar. All this could've been avoided if only he had said no to a brown-eyed girl.

Tessie's sobbing could be heard a mile away. "Sarah, why is Tessie crying? She's making no sense."

Sarah lifted both hands. "Why do you always expect me to know everything?"

Did he do that to the poor girl? Yes, he did. Guilt pressed down, weighty and wearisome.

"She can't find the pink hair ribbon Miss Williams gave her on the last day of school," Laura said. "I tried to help her, but I couldn't find it either."

Jeanette would know where it was. Of that, he was sure. He crouched down beside Tessie and held out his arms. She lunged forward, sending him backwards onto the floor. He let out a chuckle and lay flat.

Tessie relaxed against him. Her sobbing ceased as he rubbed her back like he had seen Jeanette do.

"How about I help you look for your ribbon, but if we don't find it, you'll still be my beautiful girl." She had her thumb in her mouth as he stood with her in his arms. He knew better than to say anything. Since Jeanette had come on the scene, Tessie's habit had improved. Now, she only sucked her thumb when she was extremely upset.

Hmm, where would Jeanette put a ribbon? Ah yes, she'd asked him to put up shelves above each bed, so each child could store their treasures. "Did you look on the new shelf Daddy built for you?"

Tessie's eyes popped wide, and she was wiggling to get down and was up the loft ladder faster than he liked for safety's sake.

"It's here. It's here." She held the prized ribbon tightly in her fist.

"Come. I'll tie it in your hair."

She hurried back down.

His large fingers fumbled with the ribbon, and he wished Jeanette was with them, but she had come the day before, saying that since she didn't have to cook an evening meal on Friday, she would do so on Thursday. Who was he to argue with such logic and one less meal to cook? After his third attempt, Sarah came to his aid.

"No, Papa, you do it like this."

He watched her weave the ribbon into the braid, leaving colorful pink tassels hanging down.

"Aren't you a clever young lady?"

Sarah looked so proud at the compliment. If only he could remember to give them out more often.

"Miss Williams taught me."

"That doesn't surprise me." Glancing at the clock on the mantle, he headed for his bedroom. "We have to leave in five minutes or we'll be late."

Nerves tightened his shoulder blades as he opened his armoire and pulled out the same suit he wore each Sunday. If Jeanette hadn't clued into the fact he was a pauper, she would after this evening. Most everyone would have a special suit for a grand meal at one of the most influential homes in the county. Not him.

He combed his thick hair back. It was getting a tad unruly, and he hated that, but he didn't have time to take the scissors to his head.

In minutes, he had the family loaded in the wagon, and they were off. If nothing else, he would be on time. His stomach churned at the thought of formal dining. Not because he wasn't practised in the social graces but because he had left that world behind and wanted to keep it that way. His children would be sorely lacking in etiquette, if he didn't make an effort to teach them. This was a perfect opportunity.

"Now children. Remember your pleases and thank-yous.

JEANETTE'S GIFT

And never interrupt an adult when they're speaking. Only begin to eat once the hostess, Mrs. Braddock, begins. And—"

"Yes, Papa. Miss Williams already went over everything with us." Sarah flicked her long hair behind her. "Would you like us to repeat what we learned?"

"Sure."

"Do not be seated at the table until we're invited. Do not…"

Theo's mind wandered as his daughter recited the rules. Of course, Jeanette had explained the essentials of proper etiquette. What he left to the last minute, she'd covered ahead of time. His family needed her in more ways than he could list. A burst of air pushed through his lips in a heavy sigh. He was getting way too dependent upon her. What would they do when she moved on? It was only a matter of time before Solomon snatched her away. Even though she promised to never abandon his kids, no man would want her caring for another man's household.

The two brick pillars of the Richardson spread came into view all too quickly. The children chattered incessantly. His hands felt clammy against the leather reins, and he alternately brushed them on his pants.

Instead of taking a left to Jeanette's home, they took a right and plodded up to the grand stone mansion perched on a knoll. The row of sturdy, evenly spaced maples that lined both sides of the graveled drive covered them in a canopy of shade. Canted early evening rays slivered through the weighty branches.

Theo rolled up to the white colonnaded portico in his humble wagon and pulled to a stop. Dread nipped at the back of his neck. He had grown to love Jeanette's company, but put in a room full of strangers, he'd rather not.

The children jumped down, oblivious to his angst.

An old man ambled their way, his hair stark white against the dark skin. "You must be Miss Jeanette's good friend." He waved Theo down, taking the reins. "I'll tie this here lambchop to the hitching post fer you and git one the boys to water and feed her." He rubbed Blossom's nose gently. "Now, go on yonder. They're all waitin' for you." He waved in the direction of the house.

The old man could barely walk and obviously could not see. Blossom was an ornery mule, not a lamb. Theo wanted to jump to his aid, but that would most likely offend. He shook his head at Jacob, who looked about to do the same.

The large door swung open, and Jeanette swept out onto the portico.

Theo's breath caught in his throat. A vision of loveliness stood before him. Her long hair was piled up on her head with ringlets framing her face. The look created a softness he wanted to sink into. Her spectacles were missing, revealing the beauty of her dark eyes so often hidden. Her cream-and-burgundy ensemble, trimmed in lace, was certainly not that of a teacher, or an everyday work dress. It was the first time he'd seen her in anything form-fitting, and he tried not to stare. Her long slim torso, slender waist, and generous bust line—how had he missed that?—made him turn away to catch his equilibrium.

He looked at his children, whose mouths were hanging open.

Tessie was the first to move. She bounced up the steps. "You look so pretty, Miss Williams." Her eyes were as round as saucers.

Sarah and Laura followed. Sarah reached out and touched the velvet burgundy on the gown. "It's so beautiful. You're so beautiful."

She said the very words Theo wished he could voice.

Jeanette glanced at him, and the best he could do was smile. Words still would not come.

She swished the bottom of her dress, and the girls oohed and awed.

"Turn around. Turn around," Laura begged.

She twirled in a circle as if she were dancing, the folds of the material swirling around her, revealing the fact she was all woman. Gone was the teacher, the helper, the worker-bee. A swath of thick tresses cascaded down her back. What would it feel like to run his hands through...no he could not let his imagination go there.

His pulse raced. A crazy chaotic beat thumped inside his chest.

Her laughter filled his head and his heart. She topped it off by looking squarely at him, in no hurry to look away giving time for her smile to seep into his consciousness. The upturned corners of her mouth changed from impish to inviting, as if meant only for him. Rarely had he witnessed such a smile on Jeanette's face, and never with such unabashed intent.

Was she flirting with him?

Whether she was or not, she awakened a tangle of emotions he had done his best to bury. His carefully erected wall began to crumble. He was as tongue-tied as a schoolboy.

"When's supper?" Ben asked. "And what are we having?"

Though Theo had specifically warned the children not to ask for food, he could've kissed Ben for breaking the trance that had him spellbound.

"That's rude to ask." Sarah pointed a finger into her little brother's chest. "Don't you remember anything?"

"It's all right," Jeanette said, bending down toward Ben. "We're not inside yet, and it's just me."

"Don't look like you. Where's your specs?"

"Ben." Theo hissed between his teeth, finally finding his feet to move up the steps. "You don't—"

"We're having roasted chicken, honey glazed ham, and potatoes just the way you like them. And my spectacles are right here." She pulled them out from the inside of her glove and placed them on her nose. "Better."

"Yes," Ben said.

"No, no," Sarah and Laura said at the same time.

She stood up and turned his way. "What do you think, Theo?"

Her smile widened to reach her eyes, and she took the glasses off and put them on again.

He could not speak, silenced by the close proximity to her loveliness. "I..." She was flirting with him. Two could play at that game. He leaned in, close enough to catch a scent of wild roses. "I think you look beautiful either way," he whispered in her ear. His heart hammered against the walls of his chest so loudly that he was sure she could hear it. He had not flirted with any woman for so many years, and yet somehow it felt natural with her. Maybe because the truth was not hard to express.

"What did you say, Papa?" Tessie pulled at his hand.

She blushed a perfect pink and whirled around, entering the hall. "Come along, children. Katherine's family has been waiting all day for you. Jacob, you remember Seth from school? And Laura...Jillian is your age."

"What about me?" Tessie asked.

"There's Georgia, whom you met at school, and Geena, who's only four. They can't wait to show you their dolls after we eat."

Her words were spilling out fast and breathy. Was she reacting to him as much as he was to her?

She led them into the dining room, where a long table with a centerpiece of flowers graced the middle. Tantalizing smells wafted from the kitchen. Fine china was set in each spot. He sure hoped his children would be careful and not break a dish.

He caught sight of another couple, and beside them, Solomon. Theo's stomach dropped. No wonder Jeanette had dressed to impress. It had nothing to do with him. Of course not. He had made it only too clear that he was off limits. How could she know that lately, he had been second-guessing the decision never to remarry?

Katherine made the introductions around the group, but

when it came to Theo and his family Jeanette stepped forward taking the lead. "May I introduce Theo Wallace, who most of you have met, and his lovely family? I'll go from the oldest to youngest." She said the words with adoration in her voice. "These children have stolen my heart. Jacob." She nodded to each of Theo's children in turn. "Charlie, Sarah, Laura, Ben, and Tessie." The children beamed, and everyone laughed when Tessie stepped forward and did a curtsy.

"Now where did you learn such good manners?" Katherine asked.

"You're a queen?" Tessie asked.

Katherine smiled down at Tessie. "No, I'm just Miss Williams's sister."

"But you live in a castle."

"We talked about Queen Victoria the other day and what a courtesy represented," Jeanette said. "I explained how Queen Victoria lived in grand homes and—"

"Like this one." Tessie threw her arms wide.

Theo could feel the heat climbing up his neckline, and he pulled at his cravat. "My children don't get out much." It was clear Jeanette's family was far more affluent than he'd imagined. What would she want with a poor farmer whose family would work her to death?

Jeanette glanced at Theo as if feeling his discomfort. "But she's so adorable." She bent forward to give Tessie a hug.

Could she read his mind too? She had taken the focus off him.

"Gather around," Katherine said. "We are ready to eat." She clapped to get the children's attention and told them to choose any spot they wanted at the far end of the table. They piled into place. Theo was happy to see Katherine's children were as rambunctious and rowdy as his own.

Katherine said, "Theo, would you like to sit beside Jeanette here?" She indicated a spot, then turned to Solomon. "and you can sit, right across. Colby and I will sit across from Winnie and Robert. I just have to yell at Abe and Delilah that supper is being served. They don't hear so well these days."

Solomon's instincts were fast, but Theo's were faster. He pulled the chair out for Jeanette just as Solomon's hand reached out.

Jeanette looked up at Theo with her beautiful brown eyes so full of warmth. "Why, thank you, Theo. You're a perfect gentleman."

Solomon barely hid a scowl as he made his way to the other side of the table.

Theo shouldn't have felt so good about that small win, but he did. The feeling didn't last long when he noticed the way Solomon was looking at Jeanette. What was Theo doing playing the part of a courting man as if he were in a competition? Solomon was clearly the better choice.

The old man Theo met as they pulled up toddled slowly into the room with a woman who looked about the same age, likely his wife. They held each other's hands and moved with the help of canes in their other hands. They sat side by side not far from Theo. "My name's Abe, and this here's my lovely wife, Delilah." He smiled at her as if they were young lovers.

"So, this is Jeanette's young man," Delilah said loudly, looking at Theo.

Jeanette reached over and patted her arm. "He's not my man, Delilah. He's a good friend, and his name is Theo Wallace."

"Ha, that be a good one." Delilah chuckled.

"What did she say?" Abe asked.

Delilah turned to Abe. "She says they're just friends." They both laughed.

Theo chanced a glance at Jeanette, whose cheeks were blooming red. He didn't have an objection to being called her man. He would be the blessed one if that were true. But he should set things straight. "I think the man across from me would better fit that description." Theo nodded toward Solomon.

They both turned toward him. "Ah, dat makes sense," Delilah said. "A fine woman like our Jeanette having to pick between—"

"Enough teasing," Colby smiled at Abe and Delilah. "Abe, would you please say grace?"

Colby and Katherine's relaxed behavior helped the knot between Theo's shoulder blades to ease. He took a deep breath and slowly exhaled. He could do this.

Hands were reached out, and Theo took Jeanie's. He didn't hear a word of the prayer with her palm so warm and perfect in his. Everything about her felt right. Adrenaline tore through his veins like liquid fire. He gave a light squeeze and she responded back. It had been a long time since he'd felt anything but lonely at a social gathering. But tonight, with Jeanie at his side, a sense of completeness came over him. He dared not dissect that emotion too closely.

CHAPTER 15

Jeanette stood to full height and looked out over the farm yard. She placed her hands in the small of her back and stretched. With her height, bending over the trimming and cutting of the children's hair was no easy task. "Come on, Ben. I did as you asked," Jeanette cajoled. "You're the last in the line-up."

Ben had a pout on his face. "Pa hasn't had his hair cut."

Theo laughed as he came up the porch steps. "That won't work, Ben, because I'd love a haircut. I hate it when my hair gets unruly."

"Then you go first."

"No, Ben," Theo said. "Sit down and get the job done. If Jeanette has any steam left, I'll have mine cut after we eat."

A jolt of panic raced up Jeanette's spine. There was something intimate about the thought of cutting Theo's hair.

"How about it?" Theo looked at Jeanette with hope in his eyes.

"A…a break would be good after I'm finished with Ben." She looked away and patted the chair. "Let's do this."

"Aw." Ben plunked down.

"This won't take long if you cooperate. Now, help me out by lifting your head."

Jeanette wasn't sure how she got through that haircut and the evening meal. Her mind was centered on how she could get out of cutting Theo's hair. She could tell him she was too tired. No, that wouldn't work. He'd just ask the next day now that he knew she had that skill.

"All right, children." Theo's voice rose above the chatter. "I'd like all of you to share in the meal cleanup, then ready yourselves for bed."

He smiled at Jeanette, and her hands broke out in a sweat.

"Are you up to getting rid of some of this for me?" He smoothed a hand through his thick hair.

Jeanette swallowed back the lump in her throat and nodded. Best to get it over with rather than fret. After all, she had cut her pa's hair for years.

"Children, Jeanette's going to cut my hair out on the porch. No fighting. You hear?" He carried his chair out the door.

Jeanette followed, gripping the scissors in her pocket. She could do this.

The sun hugged the western ridge, but the longer days provided canted light that spilled onto the porch. Unfortunately, there was plenty of light.

Theo sat tall in his chair. She didn't have to bend low as she did with the children. As her hands moved over the hair at the nape of his neck, they began to tremble. Good thing she was behind him so he couldn't see the effect his nearness caused.

She smoothed a hand through his hair. It felt just as she had imagined. Soft. Thick. Inviting. She shouldn't be enjoying this so much. "You have such...such thick hair. It works better if it's wet." She hated that the words stumbled out of her mouth.

"You want it wet?"

"Yes. Go soak your head under the pump."

He stood and turned toward her. "You're not just saying that so you can get a good laugh."

"Ha. That would be funny. But no."

He took the steps two at a time, stripping his shirt off as he went.

Goodness that was not a great idea. The view of his wide shoulders and rippled muscles drew her attention. The scissors in her hand clipped rapidly back and forth. She could not take her eyes from him as he bent his head and pumped the water, then stood and shook off the excess. He slipped on his shirt as he made his way back but didn't do up the buttons. Her furtive glance traveled up his wide chest to the unexpected humor in his eyes. The pulse in her throat fluttered like the wings of a butterfly.

"Is it wet enough?"

She could barely speak, and he seemed to know it. "Sit."

He plunked back down, and she moved behind him, where his all-knowing eyes could not see the tremor in her hands as she began. Each clip brought her closer, around the side of his chair, until she stood in front of him. Her reaction to his nearness was not restricted to her alone. She heard the intake of his breath as she leaned closer.

He shifted, obviously affected by her.

She touched his arm. "You must remain still unless you want…"

He looked up and met her eyes. "Unless I want what?" His gaze was focused on her mouth.

What was he inviting? He gave her a look no man had ever given her. Whatever it was between them, a play of emotion sparked and flared. "A…a mistake."

He touched her free hand. "A mistake. No, it would not be a mistake."

What did he mean by that? The way he held her gaze made her melt. She wasn't experienced enough to know how to respond, but a warm knot settled in her stomach. She moved out of his reach and set the scissors on the side table. She needed a moment and a random conversation to calm whatever was happening within her.

She glanced over at the rocking chair on the porch. "I've been meaning to ask you. That rocking chair and the table in the kitchen are beautiful pieces of furniture. Were they your mother's?"

"I made them when the kids and I were living with Ma."

"You made them?"

"Don't sound so surprised."

"But Theo, they're beautiful. People would pay good money—"

"I couldn't make them fast enough to earn a living, so I had to go work on the railroad." He stood. "Are we done?"

"No. No. Sit. I needed to stretch." She rolled her neck in a circle and stretched her head from side to side. Good. She was feeling more herself. "Now, let me check to see if I have the sides even." She moved with confidence towards him. She could do this. With both hands, she smoothed her fingers through his hair, checking the length on the sides. But that kaleidoscope of feelings rose again…tingling hands, shortened breath, racing blood.

He closed his eyes, and she relaxed. The touch became a light scalp massage.

"Hmm, that feels so good." He rolled his head from one side to the other, and her hands slid to his shoulders.

"You're so"—*beautiful. Oh my, she had better reign those thoughts in* —"tight. From all the farming, I guess. I often work Pa's knots out. He says it helps ease the pain." She was rambling, she knew.

"Feel free." He lowered the open shirt, so it fell down his back to his elbows. The corded muscles splayed beneath her fingers made her breath catch.

She kneaded the tension in his neck, able to pinpoint the knots and work them out. The drop of his shoulders melting under her touch gave her a sense of fulfillment. But what started out as practical need became anything but. The feel of his skin and his woodsy scent filled her senses. Intoxicating. He was far too handsome, and this experience was nothing akin to helping ease her pa's ailments.

He let out a deep breath. "I know you're probably exhausted, and I should take you home."

He obviously had no idea the heaven she was in. "Shh. You work hard every minute of every day. Just relax."

He sank into the chair, and it was all the encouragement she needed. Somewhere along the way, the sun slipped behind the ridge and the shadows deepened. Like the ribbons of vivid red and orange filling the distant horizon, she never felt more alive, more vibrant.

He settled a hand on one of hers and drew her around to face him, rising. "Thank you." His gaze fell gentle and made her feel every bit a desirable woman. If she were not mistaken, his look was that of a man to woman. The strength of emotion that seared through terrified her.

"I have no idea why you're not already married. You're…" His words faded, and he turned away, yanking on his shirt. "I'll get the wagon ready to take you home." His voice went from tender to gruff, and he was off across the yard before she could decipher what had happened.

They didn't speak for a number of miles and her discomfort grew. She had to get the comradery back. All that touching and feeling had heightened her awareness and the glaring fact at how awkward she was with men. She couldn't begin to understand how to read what had happened.

"Theo?"

"Hmm."

Maybe if she brought Solomon into it, he would know how

to help her. "I don't know how to read men. Take Solomon for example. He's held my hand, but nothing more. Does that mean we're only meant to be friends? Does he not find me attractive? If that's the case, then I would get that." Her words tumbled out, frayed and awkward.

He pulled Blossom's reins, bringing the wagon to a stop. His hand ran through his freshly cropped hair, and he let out a sigh. "Why do you do that all the time…put yourself down?"

"I don't—"

"You do and it makes me sad. You're an amazing woman, but you seem to be the only one who doesn't see it. I can't tell you what's happening between you and Solomon, but I assure you of this, you'd be hard pressed to find any man who I think would be good enough to deserve you."

She looked up at the canopy of twinkling stars above. All of creation seemed to know what to do—except her. Her throat thickened. "I wish I were not so… backwards with men." She turned away and swiped a tear from her eye.

"Jeanie. Look at me."

She slowly turned his way. The soft moonlight illuminated his handsome face. His eyes gentled, and he touched her face as if she were made of glass. "You're not backwards. You're easy to talk to. You're the best friend I've ever had."

"You don't think…that…that it might be because I don't know how to flirt and—"

"Shh." He placed a finger over her lips. "There's nothing wrong with your innocence. In fact, it's charming and quite refreshing. Solomon is most likely taking his time because he respects you. He's willing to get to know you first. That doesn't mean you're unattractive."

"Then why have I never been kissed?" She snapped her head in the opposite direction, unable to hold his gaze. "I'm so embarrassed. I have no idea why I told you that." She stumbled down from the wagon and started to run. She had to get away. What a fool to reveal so much.

"Jeanie, stop."

She kept running, stumbling thanks to the tears blurring her vision.

Suddenly his arms were around her, and he turned her into his chest. She pressed her tear-stained cheek against his heart. He let her cry, soothing his hand up and down her back as he would a hurting child. Except she did not feel like a child. She felt every nuance of his touch with heightened awareness.

He leaned away from her, wiping the tears from her cheeks with the pad of his thumb.

"What's wrong with me, Theo?"

He shook his head. "I would tell you if there were anything you could change, but as I said earlier, I have no idea why some man didn't snap you up long ago. If only I had chosen so well the first time."

She looked deeply into his eyes and saw nothing but sincerity there. Her gaze dropped to his lips, and she wondered what it would be like to be kissed. Really kissed. Not just a peck on the cheek.

"You said you'd help me...teach me." She looked down, unable to hold his gaze, but she needed to know. "Will you teach me how to kiss?"

His breath hitched. "I don't think that's—"

"Please Theo. I'm twenty-nine years old, and don't know the first thing about it." She lifted her head, and his lips came down on hers so fast it surprised her. Hard, yet soft. Demanding yet delicious as they moved over hers, coaxing a response. She had no idea what she was doing, but she mimicked his movements. The sensation was overwhelmingly beautiful. She never wanted it to end. Moments passed before his mouth left hers in tearing slowness. His hands cupped her face with such tenderness, his breath mingling with hers. "Oh, Jeanie, we should not have done that."

No. He was not going to apologize for the most wonderful experience of her life. Her first taste of intimacy and what a kiss it had been. Like dancing in flames, the searing response had spread through her whole body, leaving an ache for more. "Did I do it right?" She stretched her arms around his neck and did what had been haunting the portals of her mind from the moment he called her Jeanie. She pulled his head back down to hers.

He groaned and met her, kiss for hungry kiss. Her fingertips tingled as they moved over his broad shoulders and played with the curls at the nape of his neck. His hands moved like a gentle caress from cupping her face to smoothing over her hair and down her back. If she was dreaming, she never wanted to wake up. She experienced excitement, elation, ecstasy. The elixir was dangerous and intoxicating.

He ripped away from her embrace. "This lesson is over." He took her hand and practically dragged her back to the wagon.

So, it had only been a teachable moment for him? Yet for her, every fiber of her being was singing. He obviously hadn't felt what she had, or he would've never wanted that to end, and he certainly would not have called it a lesson.

What was happening to her? Was she falling in love with him?

She climbed up into the wagon, and he followed. With a slap of the reins, they were moving. He didn't say one word.

She loved his children, and they needed her help, which meant the two of them somehow needed to get beyond what just happened. Maybe it was the haircut, or the shoulder rub, or a perfect starry night, but she wasn't in the least bit sorry. She touched a hand to her swollen lips and smiled. She had been thoroughly kissed when she had expected only a quick peck. Surely, he had felt something too.

She wouldn't think about that right now. She had to make things comfortable between them again.

She waited until the wagon came to a stop in front of her house before turning to him. "You're a very good teacher, Mr. Wallace," she said with deliberate sass on her lips.

He looked down at her in surprise and burst out laughing. "And you're a quick learner, Miss Williams."

"And that will be all we shall say on the matter, agreed?" She smiled at him, extending her hand. "Shake on it."

"Agreed." He shook her hand, and the tingling started all over. She ripped her hand free, hopped down, and hurried up the porch steps without a backwards glance. Whatever had happened between them could be dissected another day. For tonight she would have sweet dreams.

CHAPTER 16

June melted into the sticky heated days of July. Another glorious Saturday with the Wallace family down at the swimming hole brought an unbridled surge of happiness. Time seemed to stand still when Jeanette was with them. A hot breath of wind blew across the creek, pulling at her bun. She had tried hard to make it less severe, but she was not as experienced at the art of hairstyling as Katherine was.

"Come on, Miss Williams," Sarah called. The three girls wore their new swimming gowns and waited at the water's edge for her.

"Give me a moment." She placed a few leftovers back into the picnic basket, pulled the checkered cloth over, and stood. Another gust of wind ripped at her hair. A braid would work better. She untwisted the bun and shook her head so that her hair fell free.

"You have beautiful hair." Theo stood close. She hadn't heard him come up behind her. He lifted a tendril and then quickly dropped it.

His kind words were like a soft whisper of a breeze,

breathing life to faint embers in her soul. Did he mean it? She began to twist the thick locks into a braid, and he stilled her hands.

"Leave it."

His touch sent shivers racing up her arms and back down her spine. Ever since their kiss, she could not be anywhere near him without a reaction. "I…it's not practical for swimming."

"Does everything in your world have to be practical?" An easy smile touched the corners of his mouth, deepening the laugh lines around his eyes.

She didn't know how to answer. Did he want her to leave her hair hanging free? She never did that.

"Papa. Mama. Come." Tessie jumped up and down.

Jeanette's head snapped toward the child. What had Tessie called her? Her eyes flashed back to Theo.

His eyebrows rose and his face blanched.

Jeanette sprang forward. "Tessie, I'm not your mama, I'm—"

"Sorry about that." Theo was right beside her.

Tessie moved forward, pulling on Jeanette's hand. Her soft green eyes pleaded. "Will you marry my papa so that you can be my mama?"

"Tessie." Theo's voice was firm. "Miss Williams is kind enough to help us, but she is not your—"

"But Sarah told me that if you and Miss Williams get married, she would be my mama." The child's eyes filled with tears. "I want Miss Williams to be my mama. Please, Papa?"

"So do I," Jacob said. "We'd have good eats every night and—"

Theo lifted his brows at Jacob giving him a look that spoke volumes.

"I agree," Charlie echoed.

Sarah and Laura's heads were nodding.

Theo's Adam's apple bobbed, and red flushed from his neck into his face. He was clearly mortified at the thought.

Ben, looking for the perfect stone to skip, was the only one oblivious to the drama.

"Children. Children." Jeanette was determined to set this straight, for Theo's expression spoke a thousand horrified words. "That's not how marriage works. It takes two people who love each other, and your father and I are only friends. I'm courting Solomon, remember."

Theo turned to her. "I'm sorry. Can I have a moment with my children?"

Jeanette quickly braided her hair and slipped into the cool water. She swam out, away from the family, giving them privacy.

She was the outsider, of course, and the way Theo had dismissed her only served to remind her of that. When he had told her he was not ready for a deeper relationship, he had meant every word. Yet that kiss had caused a shift...a longing. A desire to meld these wonderful kids and their handsome father into her future.

She liked Solomon, and their friendship was growing, but her heart did not pick up speed when she saw him, nor did her body tingle at the slightest touch. She had been about to end that relationship, in hopes...

Jeanette chanced a peek in their direction. Tessie was sobbing, and Theo was trying to console her. She was glad she couldn't hear the conversation. It would be far too painful.

~

"*D*rop me off at my house." Jeanette's voice sounded courteous but distant to Theo as she bundled up the blanket and picnic basket. "There are enough leftovers for your evening meal, and I want to go home."

Theo stepped closer and kept his voice low, hoping his children wouldn't hear. "It's not you, it's me." He wanted to somehow communicate that he was the messed-up one, not her. She would make a wonderful mama for his children. And truth be told, he wanted her for himself, but his past failure in marriage haunted him, a failure she knew nothing about. Nor should he even allow these thoughts when she had a far more suitable suitor.

"Whatever *it* is...whatever this is, me helping out with the children." She waved her hand toward the water, where the kids were still playing. "It's confusing them. And I need time to think and pray about the wisdom of continuing."

Pain clawed at his chest, but he could not think about himself. He had promised to help her in her courtship with Solomon, not have him and his family get in her way. Besides there was the problem of his finances. He could barely feed his family, let alone take on a wife, and all the things she would need.

"I'm sorry, Jeanie." He reached out to touch her arm, but she jumped back. He dropped his hand to his side.

"Don't touch me, and don't call me that."

"I'm sorry."

"And stop saying you're sorry. You have nothing to be sorry for. You made yourself clear from the beginning."

"Please—"

"I'll be waiting in the wagon." She turned and headed off.

He had overstepped the boundaries. He shouldn't have told her to wear her hair down. He shouldn't have flirted with her so shamelessly. There'd been chemistry between them ever since that kiss. Heck, it had been there a lot longer than that.

But if she were interested in him, wouldn't she have waited to see what he told the kids? The way she had been so quick to jump in and say that they were only friends answered that question. Obviously, things were going well with Solomon, and he needed to respect that.

He called the children, and they came running. They piled into the wagon, Tessie instantly crawling up on Jeanette's knee.

Jeanette gently seated Tessie's little bottom on the seat next to her. "You're dripping wet, sweet pea."

Theo knew it had nothing to do with Tessie being wet. They were all wearing wet clothing, and it was still baking hot outside. Tessie had sat on Jeanette's lap many times coming home after a swim.

She was distancing herself. And maybe that was for the best.

A lead weight settled in his gut. What if she never returned to his home? The kids would be devastated. And so would he. It wasn't just the delicious meals, the clean house, and his happy children. It was her. When Tessie'd called her mama, it had hit him hard. She was their mama and a darn good one at that. Everything she was and did drew him in. Challenged him to live. Begged him to trust again. But then Louisa's words would pour over him, and he'd remember his poor choices and the consequences that had led to where he was today. He had little to offer any woman—a brood of children who would not be hers, some not even his. A farm barely scraping by. Continual hard work.

Meanwhile, she had a handsome, uncomplicated cowboy courting her. No. He had to back off. No more flirting. No more sitting on the porch talking into the cool of the evening. And no more kissing. Never. Ever.

He took a sideways glance at her sitting next to his girls, and his thinking changed. Why not fight for her? She loved his children—that much was evident. And if their kiss was any indication...maybe she could grow to love him. For he had done things differently with Jeanie than he had with Louisa. He'd learned from his mistakes. He'd taken his time. He and Jeanie had become close friends. This attraction he felt for her was genuine and had progressed in the right order.

But had he waited too long?

He wanted to respect her wishes and take her straight home, but he needed to talk to her, to present the possibility before Solomon and she got any closer. He slapped the reins of Blossom and picked up his pace, sailing right past her driveway, as he did every Saturday.

"Theo."

He ignored her.

"Theo, drop me off, please."

"You're not coming back to the house?" Sarah's voice wavered. "You said you'd help me let down the hem on my Sunday dress for tomorrow."

Theo hid his smile. Good. She wouldn't renege on a promise she'd made. He pulled the mule to a stop, hoping she would not jump down.

Jeanette turned to the back of the wagon. "Can't it wait?"

"It's the only decent dress I have, and it's getting too short. Last week, Flora Bunsen and Ivy Turton were pointing and laughing."

Theo wasn't about to intervene, though he knew he should tell Sarah that Jeanette had done enough.

Jeanette turned her body straight ahead and nodded. "You're right, Sarah. That is important." She waved her hand forward without looking at him.

Theo forced his lungs to push out the air he'd been holding. He didn't pray much, but he was willing to try anything.

God, give me a chance to explain my feelings.

CHAPTER 17

Stupid girl. Stupid, stupid, girl. When would she learn? With every stitch of the hem on Sarah's dress, Jeanette berated herself. She loved these children, but she could not let herself fall for another man who would never be hers. Truth be told, she would do anything to be their mama, but the way Theo had set the children straight, that could never be. She must concentrate on reality and be thankful that God had placed Solomon in her life.

Theo and the boys were out feeding the animals.

Tessie was curled up on the throw rug on the floor with a thumb in her mouth. And Jeanette had sent Laura and Sarah out to the raspberry patch to pick some berries for dessert. She had a few moments to beg God for wisdom. How would she find the strength not to run out on these kids—keeping her promise—and still manage to be around Theo, yet control her run-away heart? He had been honest from the get-go. But she had allowed herself to hope, to dream that this family just might be her destiny.

She'd been so, so wrong.

A knock at the door made her jump. Who would be knocking, and how did they miss everyone outside? She wove the needle into the hem and carefully placed Sarah's dress down. The knock sounded again.

This wasn't even her home. She felt odd answering. The hinges squeaked as she pulled the door open.

The smile on widow Victoria's face vanished. "Goodness, you're here a lot." She swept in as if she owned the place and deposited a pie on the table. "Theo loves my cherry pie. Tell him I saved the last of the cherries just for him."

They were on a first name basis? Jeanette's stomach lurched and fell. Theo had said he was not ready for a relationship, but there Victoria was, this beautiful lady, bringing him pie, even knowing his favorites.

"Where is that fine man this evening?"

"I'm not sure," Jeanette said.

"Yes. Yes. I know you're merely the maid, but I thought you'd know."

"Maid?" Jeanette wanted to wipe that smug look off her face with some wise words, but she bit her tongue.

Victoria waved her white-gloved hand as if to dismiss her. "Yes. Theo told me you were working for him. I assume you're trying to make a little extra over the summer?"

"Hmm."

Why would he tell Victoria that Jeanette was working for him?

Was that what she was to him? Just the help? Not even given the title of friend. Oh, that one crushed to the point of pain. But then again, he was most likely embarrassed to admit he needed charity. She wouldn't fault him. A woman like Victoria would never understand.

"The good Lord knows he needs the help until he can find a suitable wife. Thankfully"— she put a dainty hand to her hair and primped— "I have the means to make Theo's life much easier. And the way the children are warming up to me, it won't be long until your services will no longer be needed."

Jeanette's hands fisted. She wanted to take that pie and dump it over the arrogant woman's head. Fat chance it was a cherry pie *Victoria* had made. Jeanette doubted she had baked anything in her life. The daughter of a rich land baron had married a man who made his wealth on the railway. There had never been a shortage of money, status, or ease in her life. And why did she have to be petite, blond, and beautiful, all the things Jeanette was not?

Tessie stirred and stretched at the sound of voices. She sat up and rubbed her eyes.

"Oh my. I didn't see you there." Victoria scurried over to Tessie as if she were quite comfortable in the house. "What are you doing on that dirty floor? You poor child. Come give Victoria a sweet hug." She held her arms out, and Tessie walked in.

The child hugged her, then eased her way over to stand partially behind Jeanette's skirt. Her thumb went back in her mouth. Jeanette's arm automatically circled the child's shoulders, and she gave a gentle squeeze.

Victoria shook her head. "It's going to take a lot of work and money to make fine ladies and gentlemen out of this family, but thankfully I'm up to the challenge."

As if the children weren't good enough as they were. It took everything Jeanette had not to give the woman a piece of her mind. She raised her chin and bit out her words. "I personally feel they are beautiful children, with good manners and—"

"Oh yes, from a commoner's point of view, I can see why you haven't corrected the obvious." She pointed to Tessie's thumb in her mouth. "But not to worry. There'll be plenty of time to teach them all proper etiquette."

"You're quite confident," Jeanette said with honeyed sarcasm.

"I decide what I want, and rarely does life disappoint."

If only Jeanette could say the same. All she wanted was for this woman to go. "Theo may be out in the—"

"Good heavens. Why on earth are you using his first name? Most improper for the help to do."

Jeanette gritted her teeth. She wanted to lash out, but what would be the point? Against Victoria, the likes of someone like her would never win. This day was going from bad to worse. "I best get back to my work." Jeanette turned and walked to her chair. She picked up the dress and sat. "Sarah needs her dress for tomorrow, and I need to be on my way before dark. Good day, Victoria."

Victoria was obviously not used to being dismissed. She sputtered and tsked, then turned, stepped out, and slammed the door.

Tessie shuddered.

"Come here, my dear." Jeanette put the dress aside and held out her arms. Tessie crawled up on her lap and snuggled in, and Jeanette kissed her head. How would she ever say goodbye to these sweet ones? But with Victoria in the picture, it seemed it was just a matter of time, and not much, if her guess was correct. Her heart felt as heavy as a sack of rocks.

The door swung open, and the children poured in.

"Where were you all?" Jeanette asked. "Mrs. Stanfield was just here."

"We know," Jacob said with a smirk.

"We hid." Sarah admitted.

"We don't like her much," Ben said. "But Papa says we have to be polite. So, we hide if we see her coming. That way we don't have to pretend."

"Where is your father?"

Charlie rolled his eyes. "He's out there talking to her, and she's all lovey-dovey." He batted his eyes and sashayed across the room. His lips pursed and he kissed into the air.

The girls giggled.

"How often does Mrs. Stanfield visit?" Jeanette kept her voice level, though her stomach churned and soured. So that was how things were shaping up. No wonder Theo had been so shocked that afternoon. It wasn't that he wasn't ready for a relationship. It was rather that the children had been focusing on the wrong bride.

"She usually shows up the days you're not here," Jacob said. "Brings some sort of dessert. We surely do like that." He licked his lips.

"We saw them kissing in the barn the other day," Laura said. "We didn't mean to spy, but Sarah and I happened upon them."

It took all Jeanette had to press back the ache in her throat. A sting prickled behind her eyes. Somehow, hearing it said so directly made her realize the truth, that there had been a part of her that had hoped when the day came for Theo to want a relationship, he would seek one with her.

It was probably the reason she'd remained so formal with Solomon.

"Papa's not going to make her my mama, is he?" Tears shimmered on Tessie's long lower lashes.

"We all want you instead of her," Laura said.

Heads nodded around the room.

Everything within Jeanette wanted to get up and run, but instead she did what a lifetime of practice had equipped her to do. She shoved down the bitter disappointment and thought of the children more than herself.

She put her finger under Tessie's chin and raised the child's face. "You love your papa, right?"

Tessie blinked. A tear rolled down her chubby cheek.

"And you want your papa to be happy, don't you? And that goes for the rest of you too." She looked around the room, and they nodded. "Then you have to do your best to give Mrs. Stanfield a chance, for your papa's sake. It's his choice who he marries, not yours."

The door opened, and Theo entered.

Jeanette gave Tessie a hug and set her on her feet. "I must finish Sarah's dress and be on my way before dark."

"Stay and eat with us," Theo suggested.

"No." Her answer was immediate and more snappish than she'd intended. "I will walk."

"Please stay. I'll take you home. Besides, I have something I need to discuss with you."

She jutted her chin. Was he going to tell her that her time with his family would soon be over?

"Fine." She might as well get it over with so her head and her heart could get on the same page. She went back to her stitching, but the more she thought about it, the angrier she became. She was going to give him a piece of her mind—kissing another woman and flirting with her the way he had that afternoon. He had no business telling her how to wear her hair or complimenting her as if he truly meant she was beautiful when he had the likes of gorgeous Victoria on his arm. And how dare he call her the maid? She was so much more than a maid to his children.

Her fingers stitched faster, stabbing at the fabric. She was tired of being used. But how could she blame Theo? She had allowed it. In fact, she'd insisted it was God's will that she help his family. Had she even heard from God, or was that all just another way her subconscious had tried to get what she wanted?

The needle jabbed into her finger, and she cried out. Blood oozed from the wound. She hurried to the kitchen basin to avoid getting blood drops on the floor or Sarah's dress.

"Are you all right?" Theo asked.

He was right behind her, close enough for her to smell the day's sunshine on his skin. She froze.

He reached around her to press a cloth against the droplets. The heat of his body surrounded her.

She didn't move, didn't breathe. If only she had the right to turn in his arms and kiss the cheek so close to hers. The thought brought a tremble, a longing so deep she wanted to weep. What was happening to her? It took Victoria's words, and realizing that Theo had healed enough to start up a relationship, to come to terms with the fact she would never be his choice.

She jerked her hand away and twisted free of the close proximity. "I'm fine. It'll just take a moment to clot." She reached to the shelf above the basin and pulled out a clean strip of cloth she had prepared for injury and wrapped her finger tight. Whatever Theo wanted to say, the conversation could not come soon enough. She required her personal space, and he needed to learn how to give it. He was still hovering.

"Sarah." Jeanette crossed the room, ignoring him. "You can finish that little bit of hemming left to do. I'll watch to be sure you're doing it correctly."

CHAPTER 18

Jeanette stepped out onto Theo's porch. Evening light brushed softly over the fields as she waited for him to tuck Tessie into bed. Did she want to hear what he was going to tell her on the way home? Not really, but it was necessary.

The door squeaked as it opened and shut. She kept her gaze fixed on the horizon.

"It's time I make good on my end of our bargain," Theo said.

She turned. "What bargain?"

He took the steps two at time and beckoned she follow. The dark silhouette of his broad shoulders against the waning light were indeed a distraction.

"We'll take Dante."

"No." Her answer was swift and sure. There was no way, after the day she'd had and the news she'd heard, that she was cozying up against Theo on his horse.

He spun. "But you said you wanted to learn to ride. No better way than to get comfortable on a horse, and Dante is—"

"No, thanks." She cringed at the tremble in her voice.

"A deal's a deal. We're all swimming, even Tessie is close."

"I no longer care to learn to ride. And it's been a long day. I just want to get home."

"Good then. It's much faster on the horse. And I already got Jacob to unhitch Blossom and saddle Dante up."

What was it about this insufferable man? Could he not take no for an answer? "But we have to talk."

"We can talk and ride. You didn't have any trouble last time." He disappeared into the barn and came out leading Dante by the reins. He held out his hand. "Come on, Jeanie, face your fears and ride with me."

She hated the way he used that nickname with such tenderness and longed to correct him, but she had bigger things to worry about. She was afraid all right, and it wasn't fear of the magnificent beast who pranced and sidestepped in front of her. But it had been a long hard day, and she was not going to make Theo switch up the animals. She swung up into the saddle, glad she wore her swimming trousers beneath her dress for propriety's sake. The powerful ripple of the stallion's muscles beneath her, and then Theo's strong arms encircling her, caused panic to edge up her throat. This was far more dangerous than the last time they'd ridden the stallion.

He settled the spirited horse, which was straining at the bit, and whispered in her ear. "Take the reins. I'll hold on with you."

She unglued her hand from the saddle horn. First one and then the other gripped the leather straps. His large hands covered each of hers. Like dancing flames, a searing sensation raced up her arms. Warmth curled in the pit of her stomach. She had never felt anything like this with Solomon, and why did she now, when Victoria was on the horizon?

She pulled tight on the reins, and Dante's head bobbed. The horse stepped back.

"Easy does it."

Theo's breath fanned her neck, and a shiver of delight scuttled down her spine.

"Relax."

How was she to relax when Theo, not Dante, was the source of her tension?

"I...I don't think this is a good idea."

"Give a slight squeeze of your knees into his flanks, and he'll know you're the one in charge, not me."

She nudged the horse's sides, and Dante started to move. She instantly pulled back on the reins, and the horse halted and snorted, shaking his head.

"Try that again," Theo said. "Be prepared for movement. Keep the reins loose. Pulling back tells Dante you want him to stop."

"I do know that much." Her voice sounded short.

"All right then, give it another go."

She pressed her knees, but this time Dante did not move. She tried again, afraid to do it too hard.

"Relax against me before you try again. Dante can feel your fear, and he's decided not to listen."

Theo didn't have a clue. Relaxing against him was only going to increase her angst.

"Trust me, Jeanie."

There he went, using that sweet name again in a way that melted her heart. Oh goodness, she was in a pickle. They had so many things to talk about, but instead of delving into all that had happened that day, she was learning to ride. The day could not have gone more sideways. She'd best get this ride over with and fast.

She relaxed against him. The solid strength and warmth of his chest permeated the thin calico material of her dress. His arms cradled her close. His faint woodsy scent combined with leather and horse wafted on the warm summer breeze.

"There now. That's my girl," he whispered.

If only she were his girl. Goodness, she should not be thinking that way. The thought of beautiful Victoria pressed in, and she set Dante in motion. They rode in silence. The gentle clip-clop of Dante's hoofs and the song of crickets were the only sounds between them. She was enjoying the feel of her hands enfolded in his just a little too much. He was not hers and never would be. She turned her head slightly. "May I try by myself?"

"Sure." He slowly let go of her hands and folded his arms around her. She took full control of the reins, but she'd never felt more out of control where her emotions were concerned. His hands encircled her waist, intimate and warm. She felt protected and cherished. He leaned forward, and his breath tickled the hair on the back of her neck. "I'm sorry about this afternoon."

She couldn't talk about this now. "Shh. I'm concentrating."

Dante was a dream to ride, unlike the ornery mule she had tried to learn on all those years ago. He responded to the slightest direction. Bright stars glinted in the dimming light. Darkness drew a blanket of seclusion around them. A warm breeze played with the tendrils of hair that had worked free of her braid.

Everything was perfect for a moment in time.

She could feel the pound of her heart reaching for Theo, begging him to notice she was a woman, not just his children's schoolmarm. She wanted him to choose her over Victoria.

He smoothed a tendril of hair around her ear, then gently slid his strong fingers down the curve of her cheek to her chin. "Your hair is tickling my face."

The unexpected touch made her pull too hard on Dante's reins, and the stallion stopped.

Theo's shortly cropped beard tickled her neck. Shivers danced over her skin. Her throat went parched and tight.

"You're doing so well. I'm so proud of you." His arms tightened, and he gave her a squeeze.

She nudged the stallion and continued on, glad to see the

gate posts of the ranch in view. She pulled Dante to a stop, leaned forward, and patted his neck. "You're a good boy."

"Thank you," Theo quipped.

She sat up and elbowed him. "Not you."

"Ahh, come on. I know you're upset about this afternoon, but I can explain." His voice sounded smoky and raspy and oh so masculine. "Please don't be angry with me."

She wanted to give into his pleading, but she needed answers.

"Just drop the reins," he said. "Dante has been trained to stay put when the reins are dropped." Theo's arms disappeared from around her, and the loss was palpable. He dismounted. She followed, but his hands circled her waist from behind, and he lowered her the last few feet. She turned right into his arms, but he didn't move away as expected. A look of yearning, desire even, flickered in his eyes. His stare grew hot, and he drank her in as if she were the most beautiful woman in the world.

"Jeanie—"

"Don't." She twisted away.

He grabbed her hand. "What? I want to tell you—"

"Look, I know I'm not Victoria, just the maid you so-called hired, but I deserve respect. You should not have flirted with me this afternoon, nor should you be doing…whatever you're doing now."

"So, you have deep feelings for Solomon?"

"I'm not talking about Solomon. I'm talking about Victoria."

"Victoria? What does she have to do with this?"

Dante snorted at Theo's sharp tone then dropped his head to chew on some grass.

"Oh, don't play dumb." Jeanette pulled her hand from his grip. "The children told me she's been dropping off desserts and apparently receiving kisses in return." Her tone dripped with what sounded like jealousy, but she couldn't pull them back.

Theo's jaw tightened. "I have not kissed her."

"So, the girls lied when they said you two were kissing in the barn?"

He stepped close enough for her to see the flashing hazel flecks in his eyes. "She kissed me, not the other way around. Big difference. And had the kids stuck around, they would've heard when I asked her not to do that."

"Kind of like what I did to you? And it meant nothing?"

"Your words. Not mine."

What did he mean by that? "So, you're not ready for a relationship?" She held her breath. What did she want him to say? That if he was ready, he would choose her?

He paused too long.

"I get it," she said. "You asked Victoria not to kiss you because she's desirable and beautiful, and you don't want to get carried away. You may think I'm desperate just because I'm the old spinster, but that doesn't give you the right to flirt with me and trifle with my emotions. I deserve respect."

He stepped close and placed a palm gently on the side of her face.

Tears fought to be released, but she would not cry in front of any man, ever again.

"If you believe that you're just an old spinster Jeanie it's not just me who's damaged. And if you think that I would have two women on the go, then you don't know me at all." He dropped his hand and turned toward his horse. In one swift movement he was on his steed and galloping away.

∼

Jeanette stomped up the drive but let herself quietly into the house. Tears bit behind her lashes. All she could think about was getting to her bedroom, where she could let them fall in earnest.

"Jeanette, is that you?" Pa's voice called from the parlor.

She hurried on by and started up the stairs, pretending not to hear him.

Pa followed her to the bottom of the steps before she could get out of sight. "I have something to tell you."

She stilled at the top but didn't turn around. "Can it wait until tomorrow?" Her voice cracked. "I'm exhausted."

"I suppose. But it greatly affects Theo's farm. I wanted to run this by you."

Jeanette gripped the top rail so hard that the wood bit into her hand. Could this day get any more complicated?

"I think you'll want to hear this."

Jeanette let out a sigh and retraced her steps down.

"What is it, my girl? You look like—"

"I don't wish to talk about me." Her voice wavered.

"If something happened—"

"Just tell me what you heard and let's get this over with."

"Go to bed, my dear. I can see you're exhausted. This can wait."

"A minute ago, it was of utmost importance." She walked past him into the parlor. "Obviously, you think it can't wait."

"A minute ago, I didn't know my girl was on the verge of tears, and that's way more important to me."

Jeanette couldn't hold back any longer. Every moment of sorrow she'd stuffed down for years let loose.

Pa pulled her into his arms.

Guttural sobs came in waves, pouring out of her. Now that she'd started weeping, she was not sure how she was going to stop. "I'm sorry, Pa..." she said between gulps.

"That's all right, my daughter. Let it out. Sometimes a good cry helps." His strong wiry arms held her tight.

Her sobs slowly subsided, and she pulled free. She crossed the room and sank onto the settee. "It's just been such an emotional day."

"Do you want to talk? It does the soul good to let others in. You've never been too good at that."

"One learns fairly quickly in life that letting people in results in pain."

"Or joy, and everything else in between. Talk to me, girl."

"I'm not sure I understand. It's all so confusing." She leaned forward and settled her elbows on her knees, covering her face with both hands.

Pa's body weighed down the settee next to her. His arm came around her.

"Is it Theo or Solomon? I'll take whoever it is out behind the barn and give them what for."

She looked up through a watery haze. "Not funny."

"It's Theo and the children. You love them, don't you?"

"No. Yes, I love the children but... Oh, I don't know." She clutched his arm. "Why would you ask?"

"You've invested a lot of time, and you're a fine young woman who—"

"If I'm such a fine woman, why has no man ever wanted me?"

"Sounds like you have two of them interested."

"You're wrong about Theo. Victoria will be the one he chooses."

"Now, how do you know that?"

"She's elegant, beautiful, and has the means to give that family everything they need and more. And I found out today that she's been visiting them regularly."

"Even so, I wouldn't be so sure about who he'd choose if'n I was you. I see the way Theo looks at you when you're not watching, and that goes for Solomon too. The way I figure, you're going to be the one having to choose. But if Victoria is interested in Theo, it makes what I have to tell you more complicated."

She lifted her head to face him. "Just spit it out."

"Old man Reiner is going around town bragging about how he'll have his farm back by the fall. And he's quite delighted with all the improvements that've been made."

"Why would he say such a thing?"

"Seems Theo borrowed quite heavily from him, and I happen to know Theo's tab at Alston's General Mercantile is quite substantial."

Jeanette snapped to her feet and paced. "This town is nothing but a rumor mill. But I didn't think that Winnie or Robert would be the type to tie Theo's personal money matters around everyone's nose."

"No, you have that wrong. The Alstons operate that store with utmost discretion. I thought what I could give would—"

"You've been putting money on his account?"

"Yes. But I didn't want anyone to know. Unfortunately, what I've been able to spare is not making much of a difference. Robert reluctantly told me that the balance is high, and he's not sure how much longer he can extend credit without a substantial payment."

"But if the Alstons are keeping this confidential, Mr. Reiner wouldn't know."

"He doesn't know for sure, but he's watched every visit Theo makes to town. Robert says he follows Theo into the store and lingers in the background. He would see that Theo puts everything on credit and, then he struts around with the Farmer's Almanac, delighted that it's calling for a drought. The crops are already wilting under this heat, and Theo doesn't have a system in place to water. He's relying solely on rain. As you well remember, it took us years to build all the trenches and irrigation ditches to feed the field with water from the creek."

"Oh goodness." Jeanette stood, paced to the window, and then sat back down. If only there were something she could do.

"We need rain, but short of a miracle, we're not about to get any. A failed crop would do that family in unless…"

Jeanette finished what Pa didn't want to voice "Unless he marries Victoria." A pang of loss sliced through. How would she ever let those children go? And their father?

"'Tis true, Victoria's money would solve one problem, but there's more to life than money. You need to talk to Theo."

"What would be the point? It would only embarrass him? It is what it is, and he knows his situation better than we do. We'll pray for rain. God can give a bumper crop."

"I agree, prayer is important. But I think Theo needs to know Mr. Reiner's intentions. Maybe he'll be more careful in his spending."

Jeanette shook her head. "I see the way they live. They have nothing beyond the essentials. Theo's horse Dante is about the only thing of any value."

"That's tough to hear. I was hoping there was a little wiggle room."

"Even the meals are carefully planned for the meat to stretch as far as possible. I've made sure of that. But they're growing children and good eaters."

"I'll be prayin'." Pa scratched his thinning head of hair. "But can you think of anything else practical I can do?"

"No. But there's something I can do."

"What's that?"

"Encourage Theo to love again. I could talk up Victoria and all she can give them to the children. Then, if it comes to a decision, that relationship will feel natural." The brave words flowed from her lips, but the pain was like a hot stone lodged in her chest.

"But—"

"Is this not what a good friend would do? I have the power to set the stage and then exit. Besides, I'm used to being the moral support rather than the leading lady."

"Ahh, daughter. I wish you wouldn't speak of yourself in that way."

"'Tis true. You and I both know this will be the greatest expression of love for that family I could give."

"And what about—?"

"There's nothing else to discuss." Jeanette stood, pressing her fingers to her temples. Her head pounded. "If you don't mind, Pa, I'd like to go to bed."

Where she could break down in peace.

CHAPTER 19

Jeanette lay on her bed, gazing into the dark. Shadows danced on her ceiling from the movement of the tree branches swaying in the breeze. Moonbeams drenched the room in silvered light. She had been restless for hours. What a way to be described.

Damaged.

That was what Theo had called her. Damaged.

"Oh God, I don't want to be damaged anymore. Please take this from me and heal me from the inside out." Her whispered prayer joined the breath of the wind outside her window.

My daughter, I am here.

Had she been her own worst enemy? Had she been the one sabotaging her own life, believing things about herself that were not true?

You have.

The Spirit was speaking into her soul. Loving. Guiding.

And He wasn't finished. *It's time to acknowledge truth and step into freedom.*

Her body trembled as grief crushed in. She had ruined her chances of happiness by her negative thoughts and low self-regard. Here, she had blamed God for making her plain and had not realized how destructive those thoughts were. Who knows how many opportunities had passed her by while she averted her gaze or held back in the shadows? She closed her eyes, and tears pressed free.

I am your Redeemer. I can work all things for good for those who love me and are called according to my purposes...even your mistakes.

She swiped the tears from her face. "Lord, forgive me for the past. What would you have me do going forward?"

Love yourself, as I love you.

"Please give me wisdom. Help me break these harmful patterns inside my head."

I will give you strength. You are mine and I am Yours.

Jeanette took a deep breath. She knew this would be a battle, but she was confident that God would help her have the victory. The thought brought peace.

The moonbeams on her ceiling winked, and her eyes grew drowsy. She was God's, and He was hers. For the first time in her life, it was enough. She was not asking for more.

~

"Coming for a ride, Jeanette?" Solomon's dimples creased, and his smile widened. He held out his arm as they descended the church steps. "It's a hot one, but maybe we could stop and dip our feet in the creek."

"All right. Why don't you take me home first, and I'll fix us a picnic basket and put on my swimming gown?" She had to get Theo and his children out of her head. What better way than to stay busy. Keeping her distance from Theo the past couple weeks had been no easy feat.

"You know how to swim?" Solomon's eyebrows lifted.

"Yes, but don't tell anyone. Some people think it's unladylike, but I think it's absolutely divine on a day like today."

He leaned in and whispered. "Your secret is safe with me. I enjoy a good swim myself."

"And I know just the spot. Nice and private."

She had declined attending the swim the day before with the Wallace family. Instead, she'd encouraged Theo to invite Victoria. Then, she'd been irritated all day thinking about them together.

Victoria could make a world of difference in those children's lives, especially considering there was a very real possibility that Theo could lose his farm and his home without her financial help. Though Jeanette had pleaded for rain, asking God over and over, another day of brilliant blue arched the sky.

She shook her head to dispel the troubling thoughts. She had a handsome cowboy on her arm, and she should keep her mind focused on her future, not Theo's.

Solomon helped her onto the buckboard and hopped up beside her. She smiled at him, and he leaned in close. "You keep that up, Miss Williams, and you may find I never want to take you home." His laughter, a warm rich baritone, floated across the church yard.

Theo's head snapped up from his buggy, and he looked their way. A frown bunched his brow. He gave a quick wave when he realized she was looking at him and then headed out with his family.

She shifted closer, and Solomon placed an arm around her shoulder, giving her a squeeze before snapping the reins.

The blue sky with wisps of white promised another scorcher. A perfect day for a swim. Had Theo and the kids enjoyed their day without her? Tessie could do the doggie paddle now, which made them all officially swimmers. She was so proud of them.

"You're quiet."

If only she could get the Wallaces out of her mind, but she could hardly tell Solomon that. "Just wondering how warm it's going to get. What about you? Do you have anything profound and riveting to share?" Funny how, with Theo, both silence and conversation were comfortable. She never felt this nervous energy, this pressure to fill the quiet.

"Sunny skies, a beautiful girl, and the promise of food. What more could a man want?"

"I have some leftover fried chicken from last night, and I was thinking I could wrap up some biscuits, pick some fresh peaches, and throw in the rest of a chocolate cake I made yesterday. How does that sound?"

"Mighty fine to this old cowboy." He tipped his hat.

"Well, giddy-up then. Let's get this picnic under way."

Solomon slapped the reins a bit harder, and they picked up pace. "Where is this watering hole?"

"It's not far from the farmhouse."

"Could we walk?"

"Oh, yes."

"How about I drop you off and take the wagon back to the ranch. I'll let this poor nag run free rather than be harnessed up in this heat and meet you back at the house. Give you time to rustle up the grub."

She nodded, happy to soak in the summer day in silence. She reached across the wagon and, for the first time, initiated contact by placing her hand on his arm. He looked down and his eyes brightened. He took the reins in one hand and folded his hand over hers. "Nice," he said.

Nice felt so bland. The mere memory of Theo's touch while riding Dante…a pair of hands covering hers, arms encircling, a soft *Jeanie* in her ear, seared hot in her mind. She hadn't been able to contain the tremble then, but now? *Nice* came up short and very disappointing.

Solomon pulled up to her front porch, and she slid her hand away. "I won't be long." Jeanette hopped down from the wagon and skipped up the stairs and into the house. If only she could muster up a bit more enthusiasm.

She filled the picnic basket with lunch and then headed up the stairs into her bedroom and threw on her swimming gown with a long skirt over top the shorter trousers. She untwisted her bun, braided her hair, and swung the long thick strand behind her back.

Her reflection stared back at her. Something was different, and it had little to do with her looks. The prayer she'd said after Theo called her damaged—and God's response—had resulted in a remarkable difference in her thought patterns. She had strength to accent the positive and dismiss the rest. She squared her shoulders, lifted her head, and gave her reflection a smile. God was good, and she had hope.

After hurrying back down the stairs, she added the finishing touches to the picnic basket. All she needed was that pretty checkered cloth on the top shelf. Her tippy toes and a long reach gave her just enough height. Ha, today she even liked being tall. Though the thought surfaced that she looked straight at Solomon rather than up at him, it didn't matter. Could it be she was learning to love herself for who she was? She smiled. All this progress, and it was not attributed to either Solomon or Theo. Truth was, she was not sure either of them would fit into her life. For the first time her contentment did not feel tied to a man and wow, did that feel good.

"Watcha smiling about?"

She jumped at the sound of Pa's voice behind her and whirled around. "Goodness, Pa. What are you doing sneaking up on me like that?" Her hand touched her chest.

"I'm not sneaking. Didn't you hear Solomon rapping on the screen door?"

Jeanette shook her head. "I must've been upstairs changing."

He stepped back and regarded her. "Haven't seen you smile

like that in a long time. Could it be that young man waiting out on the porch?"

"No Pa. Actually, it has to do with something deeper than a man. But I must run because a man is waiting." She gave him a sassy grin. "I made a plate for you." She pointed to the table and kissed his weathered cheek.

"Have fun," he yelled after her.

Oh, she intended to. It was a beautiful day. She stepped outside and took Solomon's arm, and they headed off.

At the secluded watering hole nestled in the center of a stand of birches, Solomon threw out his arms. "What a great spot. I know the others will—"

"No, please don't tell. It's kinda the only spot us girls have to swim in private. You men can swim anywhere without condemnation. It's different with women. Colby and Katherine keep this quiet. It's the family—"

"I understand completely. I'm just glad I'm considered family." He gave her a wink. "Let's swim before we eat." He kicked off his cowboy boots and peeled off his outer layer, leaving a pair of knee-length trousers and an undershirt, and jumped in.

Jeanette slipped off her over-skirt and dropped it to the blanket, she stepped forward to the water's edge.

Solomon's head popped up from underneath the water, and he stood. His eyes gaped wide, and a low whistle slipped from his mouth. "Wow, Jeanette."

One look at his expression, she hurried in and lowered her body under the water, swimming for the deep. She had tried to tell Katherine this swimming gown was too revealing, but Theo had never said anything. Come to think of it, she hadn't seen his expression when she'd first donned it because she had been too preoccupied with the kids. Had he thought it scandalous too?

Suddenly Solomon's arms were around her, and he pulled her close, laughing. "Stop swimming for a minute, girl."

She relaxed, and her feet settled on the ground. She was neck deep.

"I didn't mean to offend. You just look so amazing." Solomon closed the distance between them, and before she knew what was happening, he was kissing her. His lips barely touched hers before she froze. All she could think about was getting away. She twisted in his arms, separated herself from him, and swam.

What was wrong with her? That kiss felt nothing like the one Theo had given her. She hadn't wanted that one to end.

He laughed and swam up beside her. "Good thing you're a wise woman. I should not be kissing you when you look so…"

She laughed, giving herself time to think. "What? When I look like a woman ready for a swim. What did you expect? That I would swim in a full gown and drown myself? This pattern is the latest fashion, and it's high time women have something safe to swim in." She knew she was babbling.

"I agree. Truly, it's just that you're so enchanting, yet so humble. It's like you don't even know—"

"Jeanette, Jeanette."

Jeanette's head snapped to the bank, where Laura waved frantically.

Jeanette moved toward the edge of the water as Theo's kids came over the knoll one by one, screaming and laughing their way into the water.

"Papa's going to be so happy to see you," Tessie said.

"He said you wouldn't be here today." Sarah's eyebrows lifted as Solomon moved beside Jeanette.

"Where is your Pa?" Jeanette asked.

"He's trying to find a nice cool spot for Blossom," Laura piped in.

"What are you doing here?" Tessie looked at Solomon with a scowl. "This is our swimming place."

"Tessie, that is not very charitable. Solomon is a friend of mine." Jeanette turned to Solomon. "The children come swimming here most every Saturday. They're not used to seeing anyone else. Tessie doesn't mean to be rude"—she turned back to the child—"do you, sweet pea?"

Tessie shook her head, jamming her thumb in her mouth.

"No need to explain." Solomon crouched down in the shallow water to Tessie's level. "Do you mind sharing your secret swimming spot with me today. It is an awfully hot day."

She nodded. "We never got to come yesterday, so Papa promised he would bring us today."

Jeanette couldn't help but smile. Apparently, Victoria had not taken her place with Theo and the children the day before.

"Oh. Sorry. Didn't meant to interrupt." Theo's voice sounded gruff. "Come on, kids, we gotta go." He pointed his hand back toward where he must've left Blossom.

"It's all right," Jeanette waved him over, "You can all stay."

"Yay!" the children screamed. They didn't wait for more of an invitation and began splashing around.

"I checked with Colby and Katherine this morning at church," Theo said. "They didn't mention you and Solomon would be here trying to have a private moment." Theo walked down the bank, eyeing Jeanette. His voice was sharp, and his gaze held no warmth.

Her face flushed with heat, and it had nothing to do with the blazing sun.

Solomon laughed. "Trust me, company is good." He looked at Jeanette in such a way that the heat burned all the hotter.

"Don't let me disturb you." Theo passed them and dove in.

"Are you sure I'm welcome?" Solomon asked. "The kids and Theo seem right put out."

"Come on." She grabbed his hand and pulled him deeper. "There's no better way to win the heart of a child than a game. We'll teach you the rules of our water tag."

He laughed. "Ok, I'm in, but how do we make that one friendly?" He nodded at Theo who was scowling.

Why did he look so grumpy? He had encouraged her to seek out Solomon's company, and he certainly did not ask her permission to spend time with Victoria.

~

Theo walked between the rows of corn in the hot sun. Perspiration trickled down his back. The heads were wilting, the growth stunted, and the soil rock hard. If they didn't get rain and soon, he could very well lose the farm. If that happened, how would he feed his family? He could never take them back to Richmond and their cold grandparents. No. He would rather die than have them take over and raise up another Louisa. His children were too important.

Fear bristled up his spine.

Good thing he had not spoken his desires that moonlit evening not so long ago. He had almost blurted out how Jeanette had restored his trust in women. How he trusted her beyond the boundaries of friendship and believed she would be the perfect mother to his children. How he wanted to pursue a relationship with her.

Was he ever glad that his tongue had gotten caught in his throat. He had taken a breath to still the raging wildfire in his soul and the urge to kiss her senseless. He'd wanted to get his words just right, knowing he was competing with Solomon. But then she had babbled on about Victoria and her right to be respected. Jeanette clearly did not welcome his advances. Why should she when she could have a successful man with a good job, rather than one with a ready-made family and about to lose everything.

He kicked at the dust. His kids' laughing and splashing in the swimming hole the day before had been excruciating to watch. Jeanette with that man, that add on…that rival.

No, Solomon was not a rival, he was Jeanie's choice. And she had chosen well. The way Solomon had interacted with the children proved he was a natural, and the looks he bestowed on Jeanette? There was no mistaking he was taken with her.

If only Theo had not allowed that one kiss under the stars... that one impulsive craving its moment to breath. But when Jeanette looked at him with those big tear-filled brown eyes, he did what he'd desired to do for a long time. He gave in to temptation. He'd tasted. He'd enjoyed every second. She'd asked him to teach her, but he'd been far from a teacher. No, he'd been the smitten one. And all it had served to do was, give Jeanette the courage to step out of the shadows, leaving him thirsty for more.

He had waited too long to reach out for the goodness that had been right in front of him. And now, how could he begin to think he was the better choice when he was on the verge of losing his very livelihood?

He didn't know how he was going to get her out of his head, but he had to.

CHAPTER 20

The hot, sticky days of July melted into the baking heat of August. All prayers of summer rain lay dead in the scorched dust bowl of Theo's field. Along with any wishful thinking that Theo would be willing to take her on as his bride. He had more than enough mouths to feed.

Jeanette wanted to believe in miracles, but God didn't seem to be in the miracle-granting mood. It was time for action. She could help this family, and she would.

She had never been to Victoria Stanfield's home, but if the driveway winding up to her house was any indication, it would be as grand as Katherine's home, maybe even as luxurious as Jeanette's grandparents' mansion in Richmond. Good thing she was educated in the etiquette of both worlds. She could fit in as a schoolmarm, as a maid—as Victoria had dubbed her—or as a lady graced with the finer things of life. Today, she was dressed in the drabbest of gray. Her bun was back to a tight coil at the base of her neck. Her spectacles were perched on her nose, not hidden in her pocket.

She must present that of a serious teacher.

For the past month, she had wrestled with what to do, but

with each sweltering day her decision became clearer. No more fanciful thoughts of Theo, the children, and a cozy life together. That was not to be. Besides Theo had done a good job of distancing himself, so proper and formal, as if she were a guest in his home, not a friend. All was as it should be.

The stark white Victorian manor came into view. Bay windows with plantation style shutters spilled out on both sides of the bow porch. She wanted to hate the home, but everything screamed *welcome* and *charm*. From the roof cupola to the ornate balusters and the window pediments, all spoke of distinctive millwork and unlimited wealth. Flowers hung in baskets. Copious blooms in an array of colors all beautifully appointed and pleasing to the eye filled large ceramic pots. The smell of jasmine floated on the breeze. Jeanette gathered the folds of her sensible gray dress into her hands, and mounted the steps.

The Spirit within quickened. A nudge. A stirring.

No, my child.

She was overcome with the distinct feeling that what she was about to do was not what God wanted. She pushed away the thought and moved across the veranda. With a trembling hand she lifted the door knocker and let it drop. God had not made it rain, despite her many prayers. Surely a little help was not out of line. Besides, she couldn't force Theo's hand. He would have to decide. But she could add a little assistance.

The door was opened by a dark-skinned man, well-dressed in a navy suit of finely milled cloth. His waistcoat, in contrasting checkered material, exuded wealth.

He bowed slightly. "How may I be of service?" he said in impeccable English. "Do come in out of the heat." His hand swept forward as he invited her into the lavish entryway. He closed the door behind her.

A grand crystal chandelier sparkled in the sunbeams demanding immediate attention. With one sweeping glance,

Jeanette took in the rich moldings, deep baseboards, and cheery yellow wallpaper with pink roses that graced the walls above the wainscoting. Rugs that looked like they came from a faraway land felt plush beneath her sturdy shoes. The furniture, rich in history and quality, complimented the grandeur. If this is what the mere entrance boasted, what would the rest of the home look like? She had made the right decision. The children and Theo would have every opportunity money could offer.

But will they be loved?

She pushed that still small voice within, away. "Is Mrs. Stanfield in?"

"She is. May I tell her who is calling? I don't believe we received a calling card. Nor do I believe she sent out an invitation." His message was pointed, yet he flashed her a friendly smile. His handsome face revealed a perfect set of white teeth.

"I do apologize. I did not prearrange this visit. Would you be so kind as to tell her that Miss Williams, the local schoolteacher, is here?"

He bowed slightly. "Please, follow me and have a seat in the parlor while I see if she has time to see you." He led the way into a nearby room and promptly disappeared.

Jeanette twirled slowly around. The chaise lounge, settee, and chairs were all upholstered in the same rich burgundy tone. The walls were painted in sugar-cookie yellow. Perfect symmetry flowed from the candlesticks on the sideboard, the lamps on the end tables, the wall shelves with antique plates to the delightful bay window with welcoming seats. A grand fireplace with a decorative mirror hanging above finished off the room. Victoria had impeccable taste.

Jeanette's hands began to tremble. She clasped them together and slipped down to the edge of a chair. With her posture straight and her shoulders back, she was as ready as she would ever be.

Victoria swept into the room, and Jeanette rose.

"Do sit." She flapped her hand like the wing of a bird at Jeanette and took a seat directly across from her. Her fingers picked at an imaginary piece of fluff on her elaborate outfit. "To what do I owe this pleasure?" She looked up, but her eyes held no warmth.

Jeanette slipped back onto the chair. "I would like to help you."

"I was not under the impression I needed assistance."

The way she said the words made Jeanette feel small and insignificant. What was she doing, thinking that the likes of Victoria would value her expertise?

Jeanette rose. "I'm sorry, I thought maybe I could help you get to know Mr. Wallace's children, a sure way to his heart. But I don't want to waste your time. I'll see myself out."

Victoria stood. A flicker of interest lit her eyes. "Please forgive my curtness. You've come all this way. The least I can do is offer some tea and hear what you have to say." She picked up a bell on the side table and gave it a jingle. A woman entered immediately, as if she had been hovering right outside the door. "Yes, ma'am."

"See to a pot of tea, and those wonderful scones Martha baked this morning."

"Yes, ma'am." She curtsied as if Victoria were the queen and left the room.

Goodness, how would Jeanette be able to convince Victoria without offending her that she would have to learn to relax if she was going to take on a farmer with six children?

"Tell me what you're thinking." Victoria leaned forward as if every word out of Jeanette's mouth were suddenly of utmost importance. What a change in a matter of seconds.

"I know the children well. I could tell you what their likes and dislikes are. I could encourage them to see you as their future mo...ther." The word got caught in her throat. She was thankful the maid took that moment to roll in a fancy tea cart and pour them both a cup. They must've had hot water at the ready for tea to emerge that quickly.

The maid left the room, and Victoria waved her hand. "Do go on."

Jeanette took a ladylike sip, placing full attention on the tea as her grandmother had taught her. She placed the teacup in the saucer before continuing.

"From the little I know," Jeanette said, "I believe Mr. Wallace may need a little encouragement to open his life to love again."

Victoria raised her perfectly arched brows. "Just how long ago did he lose his wife?"

"I'm not sure."

"Oh, but of course not. You wouldn't be on familiar enough terms to ask such a question."

If only Victoria knew. Familiarity and friendship were what she had enjoyed with Theo until he had decided to change that.

Jeanette pushed down the memories of their previous easy comradery and continued. "I'm sure you'd understand what losing a spouse is like."

"Indeed, I do."

"Well, you'd have that in common, and I could bring it to Theo's attention how blessed he is that you've shown interest in him. And how good this would be for the future of his children."

Victoria's beautiful blue eyes narrowed. "Why would you do this for me?"

"Truthfully, I love the children. Well, I love all children." Gosh, she'd better pull herself together before she fell apart at the thought of not being in those children's lives "And they need a mother. Mr. Wallace won't be able to handle all that needs to be done when I'm back to teaching again in September."

"You are right about that. Quite frankly, I'm not sure how the rumor mill hasn't picked up the fact you're there most days. You are, after all, the community teacher, and propriety is of utmost importance."

Jeanette's shoulder blades tightened. She didn't need to lose her teaching position as well.

"Must be the fact that I've made it clear to everybody you're no more than hired help."

Jeanette bit her lip and forced out, "Thank you."

"Oh, don't mention it. You'll be returning the favor by helping me with this"—she set her teacup down and waved her hand—"little problem."

Problem? Was that how Victoria viewed the children? "You do love children, don't you?"

A flash of panic passed over Victoria's expression. She lifted her tea to take another sip. When she put it down, she was all smiles. "Of course, I do. I've always wanted a big family, but my Richard and I couldn't have children."

Jeanette let out a sigh of relief. Victoria had not been around youngsters, and Jeanette could help with that. How stiff and awkward she had been with Tessie. But that could be improved upon with a little knowledge of how children respond and what they need.

"If you're serious about wanting to be Mr. Wallace's wife…" Jeanette choked the words out through strained lips. That was hard to say. "Then come over on the days I'm there. I'll smooth the way with the children. The rest shall be easy for you, being that you possess all the womanly attributes any man would desire." Jeanette gave her best smile.

Victoria pulled her head up and nodded with an air of regal poise. "I do have a lot to offer."

Jeanette nodded. "I'm sure Mr. Wallace will be captivated." Those words tore from her mouth. If only she had the means to help Theo's family. But there was no point in *if onlys*.

"A farmer is well below my social standing, but one look at Theo, and I was interested in a man for the first time since my Richard passed. With Theo by my side, both he and his family will be elevated to a prominent place in this community.

Jeanette was bothered. Theo was not a man who needed to be elevated. He was a humble, kind man who loved his family passionately and knew how to work hard. Wasn't that enough?

"I'll let you in on a secret." Victoria leaned forward as if they were now the best of friends. Her vibrant blue eyes held a violet hue that would draw most any man. Theo was probably struggling with her charms and taking it slow to stay respectful.

"I've done some digging into Theo's past. His mother came from an influential well-to-do family in Richmond. She left it all to marry a penniless man. So, Theo comes from a good pedigree. Apparently, he had numerous women in Richmond who were more than willing to give him a pass on his father's insignificance and his mother's lack of good judgement. Must be his handsome form. He is a fine specimen, is he not?" She twittered. "Surely even someone like you couldn't help but notice."

Someone like her? What did Victoria think, that Jeanette chose a life of spinsterhood? She clenched her teeth. Did Victoria really believe she was dead to the world around her? She would not even grace that insult with an answer.

Victoria prattled on, clearly unaware of the sting of her words. "Well, I'm glad to see you haven't set your cap on him yourself. I was a tad worried about you being infatuated when Theo admitted how many times a week you were available. Monday, Wednesday, Friday, isn't it?"

So, they'd been discussing her, and Theo had felt he had to explain her presence. He'd conveniently left out their family picnic and swimming each Saturday. "Mr. Wallace needs help. Being a spinster, who would have more time in the summer than I? Not to mention the fact that I already knew the children from teaching them."

"True. But soon Theo will have all the help he requires." She spread her hand, gliding it around the room. "As you can see, we lack for nothing around here." She stood. Her petite, curvy figure was highlighted by her expensive tailored skirt and jacket.

Wealth and beauty, both things Jeanette could not give any man. Just being in Victoria's presence caused Jeanette's stomach to clench tight. Theo was a lucky man. Jeanette placed her teacup on the side table and stood.

Victoria moved toward the parlor door, signifying tea was over.

Jeanette joined her, and for the first time in weeks, her body wilted, and shoulders rounded. She felt like a giant next to the petite beauty.

"All right then, Julie, I shall meet you tomorrow at Theo's."

"My name is Jeanette." She fought the urge to drop her head and forced a smile.

"Oh, forgive me. I was trying desperately to remember, and it just wasn't coming to me. I knew it started with a *J*, but everyone refers to you as spinster Williams. Not that I wanted to do that."

"Most people do remember my name, having grown up in this community." Bitterness crept into Jeanette's tone.

Victoria patronizingly patted Jeanette's arm. "No offense my dear, it's much like I'm referred to as widow Victoria."

Once again, Jeanette had been reduced to invisible. Emotions simmered near the surface. She had to get out of there before the moisture biting behind her eyelids gave way.

She followed Victoria down the hall to the grand entrance and forced a cheerfulness into her voice. "You have a beautiful home," she said, determined not to end on a sour note.

"Thank you. I did all the decorating myself."

Of course, you did. You and your bags full of money and an army of helpers. Jeanette smiled through her jealousy.

Victoria opened the ornately carved door, and Jeanette walked through.

"Oh, and Jeanette, let's keep this our little secret."

Jeanette whirled around. "I don't think that's a good idea. If you were agreeable, my next stop was to the Wallace farm to discuss this with Mr. Wallace."

"Goodness, no. These kinds of things are best left between women. Theo would never understand why I don't intuitively know what to do with children. Men just assume all women know. But I never had siblings or the opportunity to be around the dear ones." She pulled out her handkerchief and dabbed at the corner of her eye. "Please, Jeanette." There was pleading in her voice.

Jeanette knew all about humiliation. She didn't want to inflict that on anyone. It had to have taken a lot for Victoria to admit such vulnerability. "All right."

Victoria stuffed her handkerchief back in her jacket pocket and smiled through a veil of tears. "Thank you." She reached out and squeezed Jeanette's hand. "You're a dear, but I must run. I have a tea this afternoon I must organize. The ladies expect no less than the very best."

Jeanette stepped off the portico. A dull ache pressed on each temple. She was a lady, but she'd never been invited to one of Victoria's afternoon teas. Why had the whole visit made her feel like she'd taken a few steps back? Her confidence had shrivelled in the presence of Ms. Victoria Stanfield.

CHAPTER 21

"Children." Jeanette clapped her hands over the noise at the breakfast table. The room quieted. Now that Theo had headed to the barn, she could make her plans known before the boys followed their father out. "I have a surprise for you."

Eyes brightened all around the table. "A special dessert?" Ben asked.

"A special visitor." Jeanette worked up a weary smile. The sooner she accomplished her goal and removed herself from this household, the sooner she could begin to heal from the immense loss of saying good-bye to this family. Summer was screaming along, and she only had the month of August to accomplish this goal.

"Who?" Tessie bounced up and down on her seat.

"Yeah, tell us who?" Charlie said. "I tend to agree with Pa. I don't much like unnecessary visitors."

"Victoria Stanfield is coming for the better part of today and..."

Their smiles vanished, and the boys groaned.

Charlie rolled his eyes. "Mrs. Stanfield, she ain't—"

"She isn't..." Jeanette corrected.

"Ain't. Isn't. It all amounts to the same thing. She's no special visitor. She's here all the time." Charlie's brows knit together in a formidable frown.

"And...and she doesn't like me." Tessie's green eyes filled with tears.

"She likes you, Tessie. Mrs. Stanfield has just not been around children much. She's coming to learn all about you."

"Why?" Sarah asked through narrowed eyes.

Jeanette had agonized over this question and how to present it to the children.

"Yeah, why?" Jacob looked just as suspicious as his sister.

"She's a lovely lady who..." Jeanette stalled. Words of wisdom would not come, though she had prayed for them. Why wasn't God speaking to her concerning this matter?

"Who what?" Jacob's voice rose in volume.

"Whom your father may be interested in. And you've all told me you would love to have a mama."

"We told you that thinking it would be you." Sarah crossed her arms, slamming them against her chest.

Tessie's chin trembled, and a fat tear slid down her cheek. "Don't you want to be our mama?"

Jeanette bent down and hugged Tessie, then lifted and settled her on her hip. "I'd love to be your mama, but that's not how it works. It's your pa's choice. And if Mrs. Stanfield has taken a shine to your pa, you should be thankful. She has the means to give you not only what you need, but what you want. Boys, you'd have your own horses, and the money for education to become whatever you want. And girls, there'd be toys, dolls for you, Tessie, new dresses for you, Laura and Sarah. Plus, the training needed to become ladies."

"I plan to be a farmer like Pa. Don't need more schooling." Jacob's eyes flashed with annoyance.

Jacob wasn't experienced enough to realize, there would not

be a farm if not for Victoria. The crops were wilted in the field with no rain, and old man Reiner was chomping at the bit to get his property back.

"And I have you to teach me how to be a lady," Sarah said.

"All I'm asking children is that you give her a chance, for your pa's sake. He deserves some happiness."

The children looked at each other. Sarah was the first to nod. "If this is what Pa wants, but he's been much happier since you've been here, maybe—"

"I'm temporary help, and Mrs. Stanfield could give both financial help and companionship." The words sounded like nails scraping over the chalkboard of her heart.

Jacob got up from the table and moved toward the door. "I'll agree to whatever makes Pa happy, but have you ever considered that it might be you?"

Jacob's thinking was wrong. Jeanette swallowed back the knot in her throat. If she made Theo happy, then why had he kept his distance this past month? They were growing farther apart, not closer together.

He slapped on his cap and swung open the door.

"Jacob."

He swung around, a scowl on his face.

"This goes for all of you." Jeanette flung her hand out. "Don't say a word of this to your pa. It would embarrass him. Let's just see what unfolds. Whatever is meant to be will be. The only thing I'm asking is that you give Mrs. Stanfield a chance. All right?"

Jacob nodded. "Just glad I'll be out in the field."

Charlie followed. "Me, too." He slammed the door behind him.

Tessie stuck her thumb in her mouth.

"You did what?" Helen unstitched her fingers, which were resting on her ample stomach, and sat upright in her parlor chair.

"It...it is hopeful," Jeanette admitted. "Victoria started out as starchy as they come. She didn't have a clue how to even converse with the children. But after a few days and following my suggestions, she's winning them over. The children are warming up to her."

"But why?" Helen shook her gray-crowned head.

"There's some confidential information I can't disclose, but it's imperative the children warm up to her, for Theo's sake."

"And this is something Theo has agreed to?"

Oh dear. She shouldn't have confided in the old woman. She was too sharp and too discerning. "Not exactly."

"What then?" Helen leaned forward, picked up her cup of tea, and took a sip. "Take your time. I have all day."

"Theo doesn't know I'm trying to help Victoria—"

"Ha, just as I thought." Helen set down her tea too quickly, and some splashed onto the side table. "You're trying to sabotage your chance at happiness once again. Somehow, you always have to be the sacrificial lamb."

Jeanette tended to the clean-up using her cloth napkin to swipe up the spilled liquid. "It's not as if I had a chance with Theo anyway. Besides, I have...Solomon."

Helen placed her hand over Jeanette's. "Why do you believe you have no chance with Theo? And it's odd to me that you worded it that way, unless you *want* a chance with him."

"That's not what I meant." Jeanette pulled free of her hold and sank back into her chair.

"Really? And the way you tacked on Solomon as an afterthought, like you're not at all sure about him."

Jeanette kept her eyes pinned to the floor.

"What's really going on inside that heart of yours?"

"I...I..."

"You don't even know." Helen clucked her tongue. "You're not being honest with yourself."

"Theo and I are just friends."

"Are you sure?"

"I'm sure." Jeanette answered with a sharper tone than she'd intended. Helen was irritating her, and she was having a hard time tempering her rising dander. She needed encouragement, not judgement. "If I could tell you the whole story, you'd see what I'm doing as a kindness to Theo and his family."

"I'm not so sure I see Victoria Stanfield as a kindness."

"That's harsh."

"It may sound harsh. But I'm looking at the fruit of her life, as it says in Scripture to do, and discerning if she is living her life for God. I can assure you from a lot of interaction I've had with her over the years, I'm not wrong about Victoria. She talks the talk but does not walk the walk. And I'll say no more lest I enter into gossip, other than to ask if you prayed about this before rushing in?"

Jeanette could not look the kind old soul in the eye and lie. She had skimmed over the prayer, telling God what to do. Surely Victoria was the one for Theo. She could save his family from financial ruin. Also, the plan had been confirmed by no rain and Victoria's delight at the idea. Hadn't it?

"I take it from your silence that the answer is no."

"I prayed. But I got no answer other than the circumstances, which made it clear what I needed to do."

"What you need to do is get down on your knees and pray. And you'd better talk to Theo and have him confirm that this is something he wants."

Panic bit at the back of Jeanette's mind. The thought of talking to Theo about Victoria felt daunting. How could she have that conversation without telling him she knew of his dire circumstances? How could she find the words to encourage him to turn toward Victoria when her own heart felt...what? If she were honest, she'd admit she felt at odds with the idea.

"I was merely helping Victoria—"

"You must talk to Theo. If he finds out you've involved his kids without his permission—"

"But Helen, he knows Victoria and has allowed her around the children. It's not as if I were introducing someone new."

"Doing anything behind his back will risk his trust in you. Is that what you want?" Her kind blue eyes bore into Jeanette's over the top of her glasses. "Don't ruin that wonderful *friendship* you have." Helen's mouth turned up in a knowing smile.

"But Helen, I have prayed. Maybe not in the way you suggest, but I have been praying." The smell of the mint in her tea suddenly turned her stomach sour. Theo's crops wilted more each day. "If you knew what I do, you'd understand. My plan to help Victoria makes more sense every day. If Victoria is not the one for Theo, then God knows what He needs to do."

"So now you're telling God what to do rather than trusting Him?"

"You're not helping. I'm not trying to tell God what to do."

Helen sat back in her chair, her eyes closed as if she were praying.

Jeanette waited for the wisdom that often flowed from the old woman's lips. Maybe God would give her a better plan. She was certainly open to suggestions.

Helen's eyes popped open. "Our ways are not His ways, and His ways are not ours."

That Bible verse was not what she had been hoping for. It was too abstract. Too static, when all she wanted to do was fix the situation. Her spirits nose-dived. Her good intentions were to help, but nothing felt right.

∼

Jessie had let it slip to Theo that Victoria had been visiting while he was out in the field. When he questioned the others, it came out that Jeanette had organized the whole thing. All he could get out of the kids was that it had something to do with his happiness and that they had to give Victoria a chance.

Why would Jeanie do this?

That rankled. He was in no position to pursue Jeanette, but it hurt like blazes to think she was pushing another woman on him. Whatever they had between them obviously didn't mean as much to her as it did to him. Hadn't their friendship at least warranted a conversation?

Jeanie wasn't wrong in her choice of men, but acknowledging the truth wilted his soul as surely as the crop in his field. Solomon was a successful horse trainer with a great future at the Richardson spread, whereas Theo was about to lose his farm. Solomon had no responsibility from his past. Theo had six children. And Solomon had experienced a wonderful marriage. His had been a disaster from start to finish.

Theo waited in the shadows of the barn for Jeanie. She strolled up the drive humming a tune. He was drawn to her like the birds to early morning song. His attraction had to end, but how? He had worked hard this past month to keep his distance. There'd been no more twilight conversations on the porch. He had taken over cleaning up after supper, organizing that Jacob give her a ride home before dark. He had even switched the family swim days to Tuesday or Thursday, knowing she would not be around and declined her help on Saturdays. Yet, there she was looking like sunshine, peace and happiness all wrapped together. His pulse bolted into rapid palpitations.

He had to stay on task. He aimed to find out what she was up to. Didn't she understand he had enough to worry about with the drought and the failing crops? Just as he had told her, God didn't care to answer his awkward pleas for help. And the last thing he needed were complications involving Victoria.

He stepped into the early morning light. "Jeanie." Drat. He shouldn't have used that name. It was too intimate.

She jumped at the sound of his voice and turned his way. "Goodness, Theo. I was in my own little world, and you scared the living daylights out of me." She laughed nervously.

"I need to talk to you—alone." He motioned to the barn.

She moved across the yard and followed him inside. "What is it?" They stood in a shaft of morning sunlight streaming through the open door.

"I've been told Victoria's been visiting while I'm out in the fields. The kids said something about her getting to know them better? Why would you do that without talking to me first?"

She blanched, confirming she knew this would not sit well with him.

"I-I was going to talk to you—"

"Then why didn't you?" He tried to curb the annoyance in his voice.

"Well, you haven't exactly been available and, uh... Victoria confided in me a while back that she was interested in you. And with your circumstances, I thought it would help—"

"*My circumstances?*" Did she know he was about to lose the farm? It all made sense. He couldn't blame her for not wanting any part in what was about to unfold.

"I'm sorry, Theo. I shouldn't have meddled." She turned to leave, and he reached out to grab her hand.

Somehow, he pulled her into his arms.

She gasped.

They were inches apart. Her sweet breath fanned his cheeks, beckoning him closer. Her hands warmed his chest. Could she feel the crazy beat of his heart beneath her fingertips? Solomon's face came to mind, and Theo's voice turned gruff. "You should have had a conversation with me."

"I know. But you've seemed distant, like I did something to offend."

He wasn't offended, he was afraid. She made him feel way too much.

"Well, did I?" The waver in her voice undid him.

She could never offend. She was one the kindest women he knew. He lifted her glasses from the tip of her nose and smoothed the back of his hand down the side of her face. Her skin felt delicate and silky beneath his fingertips. Her lips so... ripe for the taking.

What was he doing?

He dropped his hand and whirled away. He had to cool the hot blood racing through his veins. He had almost kissed her. His boots clicked a steady beat against the wood floor as he paced in the barn, allowing his body to calm.

"Give me back my spectacles." She held out her hand.

He still had them clutched in his fingers. "No, not until you tell me why in the blazes you're encouraging my children to get to know Victoria. Especially when I confided in you how I felt about getting into a relationship."

"How long has it been since your wife passed? Isn't it time—?"

"This is not about her passing. She walked out on us without a backward glance." The truth spilled from his lips, and hot shame covered him.

He was telling her what he swore no person would ever know.

"So she's not dead? You're married?" Jeanette's face turned ashen.

"Louisa died right after she left me for another man. They found her body in a back alley and called me. Her so-called lover had a lust for foolish women and murder. I told the children that their mother had died. I kept the fact she'd abandoned them a secret."

Jeanette moved toward him. The next thing he knew, he was in her arms. She soothed her hands along his back as if he were a child. "I'm so sorry for your loss."

Everything about this woman felt different than Louisa. She was a dangerous combination of compassion and genuineness. He could trust a woman's arms again, if hers were the arms wrapped around him for the rest of his life. Couldn't she see that she was the one he trusted? If only he had figured that out sooner. Before Solomon.

He had no right, but he wanted to fight for her.

A surge of excitement flared, only to be doused by reality. What was the point in dreaming? He had nothing to offer her. Nothing at all. Soon, he wouldn't even have a home for his family. His life felt like he was balancing on a log above a deep ravine. A spike of anger ran up his spine at this God who was supposed to care. Why could nothing turn out for him?

She pulled back. "I'm sorry for pushing Victoria on the children. Can you forgive me?"

"Why did you do that?"

"Victoria likes you. She's beautiful. And she has the means to help your circumstance."

There was that word again. It was worse than he thought. If Jeanie knew about his precarious financial situation, then the community must be gossiping.

He stepped away as a wave of embarrassment swept over him "So you know?"

She nodded.

"And you thought I'd just naturally turn to Victoria because she has money?"

"No. I thought you cared for her as much as she cares for you. I know she's not a natural with children. I was merely trying to help."

Was she really that blind? Couldn't she see what was right in front of her? The way she stirred him to the very core. The fact she was the perfect mother for his children. But he had waited too long, and she was Solomon's girl.

"That kind of help I don't need. When she came by one day with dessert, she threw out the names of boarding schools she was researching for my children."

"Boarding schools?" Jeanie's brow scrunched up adorably. "That doesn't make sense. She told me how much she loves children, how she's always wanted to have a family."

If he was going to be successful in keeping his distance, he needed to come across firm. "My children are everything to me. And if you knew me at all, you'd know I would never subject them to anyone who doesn't love them as much as I do."

"Theo, I'm sorr—"

"I don't want your apology, Jeanette." He drawled out her name so there was no mistaking his intent at formality.

Word must be circulating around town at what a failure he was. He was not about to draw her into his unlucky vortex, where even God had forsaken him. First Louisa's betrayal, then his mother's death, and now the weather and the destruction of his livelihood.

No, she deserved much better. He'd been right to steer clear of her.

He put a harshness into his voice. "I won't banish you from the children because they love you and I know you love them, but stay out of my personal affairs."

Her head dropped.

"Let me handle my own sorry life. You hear?"

She looked up and nodded. Tears pooled on her lower lids, and it took everything he had not to pull her close and renege on everything he had just said. His hands clenched until he felt the press of glass against his palm. He handed her the bent pair of spectacles and stomped away.

CHAPTER 22

Jeanette dreaded Victoria's knock at Theo's door. She'd gotten herself into this mess, and now it would be her responsibility to honor Theo's wishes and get herself out. Just the thought of all Theo had suffered and how her meddling had made things worse made her heart hammer louder than Victoria's rap against the door.

The doorknob rattled. Jeanette had purposely latched it so Victoria could not enter until Jeanette was ready. She needed time to slip out onto the porch, away from the children's ears.

"Sarah, can you watch the others for a moment?"

Sarah looked up from the picture she was drawing on the new chalk slate Victoria had given her and nodded. Jeanette took a quick glance around. Ben and Laura were playing a game of jacks, and Tessie was watching Sarah draw yet another horse, Tessie's favorite.

Jeanette unlatched the door. "I need to talk to you, outside." She had to push her way out before Victoria swept in.

Victoria huffed. "Whyever was the door locked? My time is too precious to waste."

Jeanette closed the door behind her and walked to the far

end of the porch, ignoring her tirade. "Theo pulled me aside this morning when I arrived."

"So?" Victoria's hands went to her small waist.

"He found out from the children about our little arrangement and was not at all pleased."

"What do you mean? The children love me, and soon I'll—"

"He was most upset that I would invite you over without his permission."

"Oh, that." Victoria batted her hand in the air. "Men just don't understand the—"

"I cannot permit this to continue behind his back. You'll have to discuss this with him directly."

Victoria's eyes narrowed. "So, you're no longer willing to help me?" Her voice had an edge to it.

"I'm not willing to go against Theo's wishes. If he would like me to help you, I'd be more than happy to do so." Jeanette was not about to tell her any of the personal things that Theo had shared. That was up to him to disclose.

"Do you have designs on him yourself?" Victoria cast a questioning eye her way.

The inquiry took Jeanette by surprise. "This is not about me. I'm merely passing on Theo's wishes. Besides, I'm courting Solomon."

"I have noticed how you call him Theo, and others have too. People are talking."

The thought that she was the subject of town gossip mortified her. She could feel her spirits plummet.

Dear Jesus, help me. I know that my love for these children is real even if others do not. She squared her shoulders. "The rumor mill rarely has truth to tell, and I choose not to listen to it."

"But you should." Victoria's beautiful violet eyes widened. "You don't want people to think that you're only helping out with the children in hopes of drawing Theo in. That would mar your reputation and would not sit well as the teacher of this community."

Jeanette stood tall towering over the much shorter woman rather than slouching in defeat. She was no longer going to make decisions based on what other people said. "Victoria, the Lord knows how much I love those children. I do not have to defend myself against such nonsense." Her words brought a burst of confidence. She was finally standing up for herself.

Victoria lifted her chin. "It's not me of course. You've been nothing but kind, and I've done my best to still the wagging tongues. Now, let's just forget about Theo's wishes for the time being. Eventually, he'll see that we only had his best in mind. Can we just get inside? I feel the children are warming up to me beautifully."

Courage surged through Jeanette. She was no longer willing to buckle at the first sign of conflict. "You best take this up with Theo." She let his first name slip off her lips intentionally. He was her friend, and she had every right to call him by his first name, even if he was disappointed in her at the moment.

Victoria's brows lifted. "And just what do you expect me to do until my driver returns?"

"I suggest you find Theo in the fields and have that much-needed conversation. Or you could walk home. It's a lovely day."

"Why, that is just rude."

"I'm not trying to be rude, and I do apologize for the inconvenience. I should've talked to Theo first, like I had planned. In the past, I've been too easily swayed into doing what others want, rather than what I feel I should. Now, if you would be so kind as to excuse me?" Jeanette swept by her with her head held high and starch in her spine. She let herself back into the house with all the grace and composure she could muster. When the door quietly closed behind her, she smiled from the depth of her soul.

"What are you smiling about?" Sarah asked.

Jeanette came back down to earth to find all the children staring at her. Just how long had she stood there? "I'm just happy," she said. "Jesus answered a prayer in the most unexpected way." She had not been overpowered by Victoria's persistence, nor had she worried about the gossip or let it debilitate her as it always had in the past.

Tessie pulled at her hand, wanting up. She swung the child into her arms and twirled her around. Tessie giggled.

"What prayer?" Ben asked.

"Something personal."

"Per…sunble?" Tessie mimicked.

"Personal. It means something private, something that only God and I need to know."

"I like it when God makes you smile," Laura said. "You're so beautiful."

For the first time ever, Jeanette could agree from her heart. "Thank you, Laura. That is a very kind thing to say. God does make us all uniquely beautiful in our own way, doesn't He?"

~

Theo walked the rows of corn and wheat. The sun had baked the earth to dust, and his crops were stunted and dried. It had rained a little a few days earlier, and he'd thought it would help but looking over the fields, he realized there was little hope. It was too late.

What would he do to feed his family? He owed more to Alston's General Mercantile than he could ever repay without a bumper crop, and he would have nothing to live on for the winter months. Not to mention the monthly fees to Mr. Reiner. If he missed even one payment, the contract clearly stated Mr. Reiner could take back his farm.

Theo was about to lose everything. Where would they go? How would he feed his family? A jolt of fear darted up his spine.

The thought of Victoria crowded in. Was she really his only hope for a roof over his children's heads? Could he fake loving her for the sake of his family?

No, he couldn't.

But what good would standing on principle do when he couldn't feed his children, when they didn't have a home? The thought made his stomach lurch. He groaned, covering his hands over his face. "Why, God. Why?"

"Pa, what are we going to do?"

Theo turned to see Jacob right behind him. Jacob's eyes were large and filled with worry. He'd clearly heard Theo's lament.

"I'm not sure, son. But I don't want you to trouble yourself about this. That's my job. I've always taken care of you, and I'll continue to do so." His voice sounded wooden, lifeless, even to his own ears. Jacob didn't need to know about him using the last of his money to buy the farm and planning out each month carefully so they could survive until the crop came in. Which would not happen now.

"I'm not a child, Pa. I can see what's happening. The crops are failing, and you need money."

Theo ruffled the spikey hair on top of Jacob's head. "I have a plan." May God forgive his lie.

"Is it rich Mrs. Stanfield? Because there she is." Jacob nodded to the edge of the field, where Victoria waved frantically above the stunted corn stalks.

Theo's heart plummeted into his dusty boots. He had enough to worry about without a confrontation with Victoria. Jeanette had most likely done what he'd asked, and now Victoria was offended and upset.

"Seems she's determined to talk to you. She's heading this way right through the corn."

"You go brush Dante and tell Charlie to help Ben haul water into the garden. At the very least, we'll have vegetables." With few weeds to pull due to the lack of rain, he had to find something for the boys to do. And he certainly didn't want them listening in on this conversation.

Jacob nodded and yelled over a few rows to Charlie. They headed toward the house.

Theo turned toward the woman as she struggled through the rows trampling the crop as she went. Her ridiculous dress looked fit for a ballroom, not a corn field. Jeanette would never be that insensitive, no matter how poorly the crop was doing. If Victoria was his only hope, he was in deep trouble.

"Theo. Theo. I must talk to you." She waved her handkerchief like a flag.

"I'll come your way," he hollered. "Meet me at the barn."

She turned back, her bustle twitching like the tail of an angry cat.

Two meetings in the barn in one day. And by the time he was done, he'd most likely have another woman angry with him. But if he was as honest with Victoria as he wanted to be, what would he do to provide for his family? Jeanette would soon be back to teaching. Her help on every front would be minimized. Besides, he couldn't expect her to keep on as she had been, not with Solomon in the wings. Decisions had to be made. Marriages were arranged with far less motivation. The question was, could he endure another loveless marriage for the sake of his children?

And what would he do with his feelings for Jeanette?

How had he gone from telling Jeanette this morning that he no longer wanted Victoria around to contemplating a relationship. Jacob's fear-filled eyes, and the dust bowl he was tromping through, had spoken. Another scorching day in full bloom and the God he had called out to numerous times remained silent.

He rounded the corner into the shade of the barn. "Victoria," he called. He would not go into that barn alone with her. The last thing he needed was her insinuating impropriety and trapping him into marriage. He'd fallen for that ruse once. Funny how he had not thought twice of that scenario earlier in the day with Jeanette. But then, he trusted Jeanette.

She came out of the shadows. "Do come here." She waved him inside.

"This conversation best be done in the open. I have children watching, and I want to set a good example."

"When a man and woman are courting, a little privacy is to be expected."

"Courting?"

"Surely you're not going to play blind to my obvious affection. And as you now know, I've made the effort to get to know your kids. What I don't understand is why Jeanette is saying you no longer want me to spend time with them? I thought you'd be pleasantly surprised."

He should give her some credit for caring to make the effort, but he was not going to have this conversation where Jacob could hear. He offered his arm and led her across the yard to stand under the maple tree, then stepped back so her hand fell away.

"You have nothing to say?" Both her hands were planted on her hips.

"I'm not sure what you expect."

"Am I wasting my time? Because I assure you, I have numerous other gentlemen who would be overjoyed to receive the attention I've lavished on you."

"I have to admit, your comment about placing the children in boarding schools really put me off. I love my children, and want them in my home and in my life."

"But, Theo"—she stepped close, widening her eyes in surprise—"that was only if they desired higher education. Nothing against spinster Williams, but the quality of her teaching is far inferior to what they could obtain in the larger cities." She batted her eyelashes at him. "Surely, you don't think

I was suggesting boarding school for any of them who did not desire to go?"

"I did."

She placed her dainty hand on his arm. "I'm sorry you don't know me better than that. If I was bent on shipping the children off, why would I make such an effort to get to know them?"

What she said did have merit. "I'm sorry, Victoria. With all that's going on, the responsibility of family, the farm, and this heat wreaking havoc with my crop, I just don't think it's a good time."

She placed her hand on his arm.

"I know, it's been a terrible year for growing, but you don't have to worry about any of that, I have the resources to—"

"That's just it, Victoria." He had to be honest before he gave in to the temptation of having his financial problems solved for him. "This is not how I would want to enter into a relationship. You'd be left wondering if I was only marrying you to reap the financial benefits."

"Oh, I assure you, there would be some other very delightful benefits."

Her laughter grated on his nerves. "I'm a farmer, Victoria, and I can't see our lives—"

"You haven't always been. Everyone knows you came from the city. Is it that important to you?"

"It is. I actually love working the land, seeing life burst from the soil. And my children like it here, the fresh air, the wide-open spaces—"

"Then you shall become the most successful farmer in the county. Your land butts up to mine, and there's lots of room to expand. We could amalgamate with the latest and greatest in inventions, including a water system to ensure this never happens again." She gestured to the dying fields. "Not to mention receiving all the help you need. With little old me cheering you on of course."

Her smile looked genuine. And what she was suggesting was certainly appealing.

Jacob came out of the barn leading the stallion. "Hey, Pa, do you want me to let Dante out to graze now that I'm done brushing him?"

"Sure, son. Thanks."

"Oh my, what a magnificent stallion." Victoria moved forward. "May I...?" She looked his way for approval.

He was shocked that the prissy Victoria had such an interest. "You like horses?"

"Goodness, yes." She went up to the stallion, pulled down on the halter, and gave the large animal a pet on the nose. Dante nuzzled in for more. "I'll take this fine animal to the paddock for you, Jacob. You go on in and get out of this horrid heat."

Jacob gave her a forced smile and headed off toward the house.

Theo came up beside her. "I would've never guessed."

"See, Theo? Just give us a chance and you'll find yourself more than a little pleasantly surprised. My daddy raised the finest horse flesh, and from the time I was a little girl, I have enjoyed riding."

"You have?"

"Indeed. You bring that fine horse over one day, and we shall go for a gallop. I'm not dressed for it at the moment, but I assure you, you'll have a tough time keeping up." Her eyes sparkled with laughter.

This was a side of her personality he had not expected. Maybe, just maybe he could...

But Jeanette came to mind, and the mere thought of her clogged his brain. "Regarding our relationship. Honestly, I'm not sure—"

"Just give us a fighting chance. If in the end you feel nothing for me, then at the very least you'll have made a friend." She looked up at him with pleading in her eyes. "How about we just concentrate on getting to know each other?"

He could do that. He could try, anyway.

But, truly, if he was going to spend more time with the woman of his choice, it would be the one who didn't have to work at capturing his heart or that of his children.

CHAPTER 23

Jeanette stood at Theo's counter chopping some carrots in preparation for the evening meal. Victoria had just arrived with her coachman toting a Gladstone bag in hand. With a sharp rap on the door, they both entered. Victoria nodded her way, and Jeanette gave a quick hello, then carried on with her work. According to the children Victoria's visitations had been daily. Jeanette knew her time with the family was winding up.

"Come children, gather round." Victoria waved her dainty hand as her coachman set the bag with a decided thump on the table.

"Thank you, Leonard. That shall be all until you pick me up at 4:00 sharp. And don't forget to load those other two items I instructed."

He nodded and headed out the door.

"Now, I know Jacob and Charlie are out in the fields with their father, and I have something special for them, too, but the four of you can receive your gifts now."

Tessie bounced up and down. "A gift. I love gifts."

"Oh yes, I have something picked out especially with each of you in mind. Tessie, you being the youngest and the cutest little girl ever, the first gift is for you."

She patted the child's head affectionately, and Jeanette's heart squeezed tight. She did not want to feel jealous, but a pang of something not at all pleasant stabbed through.

Victoria pulled a baby doll from her bag, and Tessie's eyes doubled in size. "For me?"

"Yes, my darling girl. All for you. But you must handle your baby with tender care, because her head is made of porcelain, and she'll break if you drop her. Do you think you can manage that?"

Tessie nodded her head, holding out her arms.

"I be careful."

Jeanette couldn't help but think how that gift would have better suited Laura, who was a few years older. The probability of Tessie not dropping that doll going up and down the ladder to the loft would be slim, and asking her not to sleep with it would be impossible.

Tessie took the baby carefully in her arms and walked over to Jeanette.

"Look at her shiny hair." Tessie smoothed a finger over her swirling porcelain curls. Jeanette had never seen a more attractive doll with it's pink bonnet and frilly matching dress.

"She is beautiful, Tessie."

Tessie moved slowly across the room and carefully slid her small bottom onto the rocker. "I rock my baby."

Victoria beamed.

A bitter taste rose in Jeanette's throat from the pit of her churning stomach.

"Now for you, dear Laura."

Laura crowded in.

"I know how much you love to help baking, so, I brought you your own supplies." From the bag, she pulled a glass bowl, with measuring cups, measuring spoons, wooden spoons and a

The Virginia Housewife cookbook. "All of this and a promise to get you whichever ingredients you may not have so you can try any recipe in the book."

Laura lifted each item as if they were the most precious things she had ever touched. She turned and threw her arms around Victoria in a burst of gratitude.

"Oh." Victoria laughed as she stumbled back a step. "Goodness, can I assume you like this?"

Laura nodded into her chest.

Victoria patted the child's back awkwardly and pulled away. "Now, who's next, Ben or Sarah?"

Jeanette pressed her lips tightly together. Her hands clenched the folds of her skirt. She wanted to be gracious, but goodness, it was hard.

"Ben can go first," Sarah offered.

"You are such a giving child." Victoria touched Sarah's cheek. "But I should not call you a child. You are a lovely young lady."

Sarah stood up taller and gave a heart-stopping smile.

Jeanette lifted her eyes into the heavens. *Please Lord, give me strength to do this. To be happy for these children, for Theo and Victoria.* She prayed, but peace did not come.

Victoria pulled out a round toy with a string and handed it to Ben. "A return wheel," he screamed. "No way. Tommy has one of these, and they're so much fun." He snatched the toy, wrapped the string around his finger, held the return wheel in the palm of his hand and flicked his wrist. The wheel left his hand, rolled to the bottom of the string, and magically returned to his hand. He repeated the motion, his face a bundle of joy.

"Say thank you," Jeanette reminded.

"Hey, thanks so much," he said between catches.

"And now for you, sweet Sarah." Victoria pulled out a bundle wrapped in brown paper and string.

Sarah took the package gingerly, as if it were a recovered

lost treasure, and set it on the table. Carefully, she undid the string and fingered the brown paper.

"Open it. Open it." The others cried.

Even Jeanette stretched to see over the bodies now in her way.

Sarah unwrapped the paper and pulled out a cream-colored dress. Layers of crinoline and satin unfolded to the beautiful pink scalloped edges. A complementary rose sash and bows on each sleeve with a matching parasol completed the ensemble, which would make any young lady swoon. Sarah held it up against her body. "Oh, it's too perfect. Wherever shall I wear such a gorgeous dress?" The way her fingers splayed gracefully over the folds of material, Jeanette could tell she was pleased.

"Why, to church of course. And I'll have you over for a nice afternoon tea at my house with some of the other young ladies in the area if you like?"

Sarah's eyes brightened.

"Why don't you go in your pa's room and try it on. We'll see if I got the size right." Victoria pointed to the bedroom, and Sarah skipped away.

One look around the room at each child, totally mesmerized by their gifts, and Jeanette turned back to the carrots chopping vigorously. Even if she wanted to, she could never afford to give the children such extravagant gifts.

She jumped at the sound of Victoria's voice.

"I do believe I'm learning what they like, don't you agree?" Victoria had a satisfied look on her face. "And I have a new fishing pole for Charlie and a toolbox for Jacob with the basic essentials. Theo told me Jacob loves to work with his hands. My coachman will bring them later."

Jeanette spoke between clenched teeth. "You did a fine job, Victoria. You are indeed learning what each child loves." Her words belied the heavy rock that had settled in the pit of her stomach.

~

*T*he long stretch of thickened air and suffocating humidity gave way to a refreshingly cool late August morning. Dried grass crackled with each step as Jeanette headed to Theo's farm. Soon, she would be traveling in the opposite direction to the schoolhouse each morning, and Victoria would have a wedding band upon her finger.

Since Theo had told her he had changed his mind and it was all right for Victoria to visit, the distance between them grew. She understood why their close relationship ebbed while Victoria's relationship with him flowed. Though everything made common sense, Jeanette's heart ached. She would miss the daily activity of the Wallace residence. For the first time in her life, she had felt what it would be like to be a mama and part of a family...all except the best part, a husband. Her cheeks burned with heat at where her mind went, and the fact that the man she considered was not Solomon.

Even the children were warming up to Victoria. Her constant gifts carefully tailored to suit their personalities seemed to outweigh the fact that she still did not have a clue how to interact with them. All was as it should be. Theo's crops had died in the field, not even fit for animal consumption. Jeanette knew what most people did not, that Victoria was Theo's only way out of the dire straits he was in.

She slowed down and enjoyed the shade of the forest before it opened to the road across from Theo's farm. A black stallion snorted in the distance. Was that Theo on the path? It was. Against her will, her heartbeat increased, clip-clopping as fast as Dante approaching her.

Theo reigned in and smiled down at her. "Good morning, Jeanie."

He had not called her that for many a day, but the way he

said her nickname with such warmth brought back instant intimacy.

"You fulfilled your promise, and all the Wallaces know how to swim, even Tessie. I, on the other hand, never got you comfortable riding a horse. How about one more lesson before..."

"Before what?"

His voice trailed, and the amusement in his expression faded. "Before I sell him. I need the money, and you know why." He dismounted in one fluid movement and landed in front of her.

She stepped out of his magnetic realm and turned away. "It's not necessary, Theo. I know how stressful this summer has been for you, and teaching me to ride is—"

"Important to me. I'm a man of my word."

His hands rested on her shoulders, and he gently turned her to face him.

She could barely breathe. The proximity was doing weird things to her insides, which were flipping and flopping.

"Please, Jeanie."

If only she were *his Jeanie*.

She had tried to focus so hard on Solomon, but not once in his presence had she felt like she did at this moment. There was no way she was getting on a horse with Theo.

She moved away and lifted a hand to Dante's head. The stallion pushed in, and she rubbed his nose.

"See, even Dante loves you." The whisper of his voice tickled her ear. He was standing way too close.

"I'm sorry you have to sell him." She kept her eyes on the horse.

"I have much bigger worries than selling Dante now that the crop is gone." His voice held defeat.

"I'm so sorry, Theo." She didn't know what else to say.

"So am I. I wanted to give the children a life away from the city, away from the gossiping tongues of Richmond society. Things were coming out about their mother, and I wanted a new life, a better life. I've failed them."

"You have not."

"I have. But I'll never regret trying, nor regret meeting the one special person I would've never met otherwise."

Tears stung her eyes. She was glad he couldn't see her face. Victoria was a lucky woman. And if he accepted what she offered, he could keep Dante and have ten other thoroughbreds if he desired.

"You've been a true friend, Jeanie."

Tiny pricks of life danced over every nerve ending. She turned, soaking in the sight of him. His strong features, his neatly trimmed beard, and his warm hazel eyes, which pulled her in. The air between them crackled with energy. The warmth of his body, so close to hers, seared through the thin material of her day dress. She was unable to bear the closeness and stepped out of his reach. "And Victoria."

He ran a hand through his windswept hair, and a lock fell across his tanned brow. He needed another haircut but just the thought of that last one sent heat rushing to her face. She ached to reach forward and smooth that wayward curl into place. She should not have these feelings when Victoria was that special woman, and Solomon...dear sweet Solomon. Goodness she was in a mess.

"With Victoria, I have to work hard at conversation and—"

"You'll have security. The children will have a wonderful home."

"Then you know I'm going to lose the farm?"

She nodded.

"And you know what I have to do?"

"Yes." The word barely slipped through her lips, choking through the pain that slammed into her soul. The weight of grief and loss pressed in. It took everything she had not to burst into tears. She was about to lose the Wallace family to Victoria.

He stepped closer and lifted a hand to the side of her face. His fingertips gently caressed a trail from her temple to her chin.

She had never felt anything so intoxicating. All she wanted to do was step into his arms and never let go.

He let his hand drop to his side. "I wish things could have been different. For the farm, for my family, for…I even prayed," he said. "But it seems God doesn't hear—"

"He hears you, Theo. The Bible says He knows the desires of your heart." In that instant she knew what the desire of her heart truly was. It wasn't Solomon, it was the man standing right in front of her. But she had sold herself short, never believing it was possible he could love her. Why now, when he was telling her that he had to marry Victoria, did she feel ready for more? She lifted her face to his daring to look deep into his eyes.

In one swift movement he pulled her into his arms and held her so tightly that she could barely breathe.

"I doubt He hears me or things would be much different now." His words were muffled into her hair.

What was he saying? That the desires of his heart were to keep the farm? Or could it possibly be that she was part of his loss? No man had ever held her with such intensity. If only she could read his mind.

"I can never thank you enough for all you've done for my family this summer," he said. "The children love you, and you're the best friend I've ever had."

Ahh, that was it. Gratitude. Friendship. He was not feeling what she was. Her disappointment felt bitter churning in her gut like a batch of sauerkraut. Why did her love for him have to become so clear at this inopportune time? She had to get away before she made a fool of herself and begged him to love her. "Theo...I must go." Her voice cracked and a tear slipped free.

"I'm making a mess of this. I've made you cry. I wanted to thank you and let you know how much I respect all you've done. I've been distant because it was my way of coping with... with the way things have turned out. But. I couldn't just walk away without thanking you and saying goodbye in person."

She could see the angst on his face. She knew what she needed to do, turn back home and quick. She reached up and kissed his cheek. "Goodbye, Theo." With only an inch separating their lips, her body froze and tingled from tip to toe.

He groaned and slid his lips over hers, crushing her body against his.

A blaze of intensity ignited, and she felt passion on the brink of no return for the first time in her life. She wanted more. She wanted all. She wanted the world and its pain to go away. She wanted to lie down in the cool grass and have Theo at her side.

Like a blossom, her heart opened in that one kiss, speaking what words could not. She loved him. She truly loved him. Not just his children, not the idea of him, but *him.* Her hands went to his chest, where she could feel the strong beat of his heart pumping beneath her fingertips, then to the thick hair at the nape of his neck.

He groaned against her lips as she opened her mouth to his and joined in a dance as old as time. His touch made her melt and soar as he cupped her face in his large hands and kissed her again and again. Never had she felt more desirable, more beautiful.

He slid his hands around her hips to her back, and she knew that, if she encouraged him in this moment, he could be hers.

But it would be all she'd ever have.

Theo had to provide for his family, and she needed to be true to her God, to her convictions, to who she was on the inside.

She had to send him away.

She ripped herself free and they both stood with ragged breaths, trying to fight their way back to earth.

"I wish things were different. I had no right to do that."

She pressed her fingertips against his lips. "I understand your circumstances better than you think. I will not return to your farm. You and the children have Victoria now. We both know what you need to do." She turned and walked away.

He let her.

CHAPTER 24

What had just happened? His body ached with a crushing loneliness as he watched Jeanette disappear. She was the woman he should be with. Everything about her brought life to his soul, to his family. What a difference between the women. Victoria talked incessantly. Jeanie seemed to know when he desired quiet. Victoria worried about a breeze messing her perfectly coiffured hair, Jeanie could swim, work, and play with the children in complete abandon without worrying over her appearance. And she didn't need to. She was so naturally beautiful.

It wasn't just her ability to bring life and order out of chaos, her joyous laughter, her intelligent conversations, her loving arms wrapped around the children...around him. It was so much more, something he could not define.

It was like Jeanie had been made for him, and he for her.

How could he possibly consider another? Jeanie filled his thoughts, his dreams. Though he had tried to distance himself from her in the past few weeks, one moment alone had snuffed out all his efforts.

He should not have kissed her. He had meant only to give

her one more horseback riding lesson and thank her and say goodbye. She deserved to hear in person how much he appreciated everything she'd done. But he had underestimated the power of being so near her, with no children or animals or crops begging his attention. It had been overwhelming.

He swung up on his saddle, fighting the urge to ride after her and beg her to marry him. But he had nothing to offer her. No income, not even a home. Besides, she had Solomon, who was so much more uncomplicated than he. Not jaded, destitute, and homeless. Yet, that kiss had proved she cared for him. What a fool to get between them, knowing he couldn't pursue her. He didn't want her to remain a spinster. She had so much love to give. Yet he didn't want Solomon to have her either. It was enough to drive him crazy.

The truth remained. He didn't know how he was going to feed his children much less take on a wife. Unless the wife had the means to provide for them all, as with Victoria.

Indeed, Victoria was beautiful on the outside, as Louise had been, but what if their relationship never deepened? Time was running out, and he was not connecting with her. He had tried to be honest with her about having no feelings, but she just kept saying that he would grow to love her. But would he? Could he find more things in common with her if he quit comparing her to Jeanie? Or was he doomed to another loveless marriage?

Fear wrapped itself around his throat, thick and rope-like, making it difficult to breathe. He dug in his heels and slapped the reins. Dante surged forward. A good gallop was what Theo needed. Hopefully, for a moment anyway, he could outrun the anguish circling in his brain and clear his thinking. There had to be a way out of this mess, but his money was gone, and Mr. Reiner would be sure to call when he missed the September payment. Even if he sold Dante and had enough for another month, there were far too many months before next year's crop, and he still had to pay his debt at Alston's General Mercantile. They had been so good to him.

He could see no way out of this mess that didn't include Victoria and her sizeable fortune.

∽

Jeanette slammed the screen door and ran up the steps to her bedroom. She flung her body across the bed and sobbed into the pillows. How would she ever say goodbye to that family? Little Tessie with her copper curls and cuddly arms. Sarah and Laura with their endless questions and eagerness to learn. Ben with his mischievous lively penchant for trouble. Charlie, a miniature Theo in both looks and temperament. Serious Jacob, so strong and willing to help in any way. Her sobs grew louder, and she buried her head in her pillow to stifle the sound.

And Theo, the first man who had taken the time to get to know her, who called her his best friend, who kissed her in broad daylight as if he never wanted to let her go. Why had he kissed her? Had he felt the same intensity of emotion she felt?

"Jeanette." A knock rapped on the door and Pa's voice filtered through. "May I come in?"

Jeanette gulped back a sob. "Not now, Pa." Her voice cracked.

The door creaked open and Pa poked his head in. "Sometimes it helps to talk."

"Pa, there's no helping this situation. It is what it is."

He ignored her, lowering his slim frame to the edge of the bed.

She swiped at her tears and pulled herself up to join him.

"Is it the Wallace family?" He handed her a handkerchief.

She nodded, blowing her nose.

"Theo's losing the farm?"

"Yes."

"Is the family moving away?"

"I think Theo's going to propose to Victoria."

"Victoria. When did that come about?" His bushy brows rose in surprise.

"She's been coming by the house. The children have gotten to know her, and it makes sense." She hiccupped between sobs. "Victoria can give them a home, a chance at a future."

Pa gave her shoulders a squeeze. "But you're crying, my girl, when this should be good news for that family. Unless it's as I thought—Solomon is not the one, and you feel more for Theo than you want to admit?"

She nodded. There was no point in denying the obvious.

"The way he looks at you, I could have sworn he felt the same about you."

"He appreciates me. Even cares for me, but it doesn't matter what he feels. He has to save his home and Victoria is the one with the money and the beauty."

"You're just as beautiful, and if you love him—"

"Pa, what I need now is honesty, not platitudes. It's not exactly like I've had suitor after suitor. I'm single for good reason."

"Because God has a plan—"

"No, because God made me *plain*. But thankfully, I can finally accept—"

"You're not plain. You have—"

"Pa, I shall never regret my time with that family." Her sobs had subsided, and she took a deep breath for strength. "I've learned so much. That experience gave me the confidence to see myself as someone with more than I ever gave myself credit for."

"'Tis true, you have much to offer."

"And the way those children fell in love with me as much as I did them? I'd make a great mama. I know that now."

"You will."

"I'll continue to love them into adulthood." A fresh sob slipped free. "Whatever that looks like now that Victoria is in the picture, but for all their sakes, I need to let them go."

Pa patted her knee.

She dabbed at her eyes with the crumpled handkerchief. "And...and having a man like Theo for a friend, well that was something I would've never done being so shy, but those kids, they brought out the fight in me. Even the courage to court Solomon..." The thought of the sweet, gentle man who'd so patiently been at her side. "Oh pa, what about Solomon?" Her head fell into her hands. "I don't want to hurt him, but I know now, I can't...I just can't."

"Solomon will be fine. He has no shortage of attention from the women. I've felt for a while now that there wasn't a spark between you two."

"Why can't I fall for him?"

Pa squeezed her arm with a strong grip. "God has a plan."

Jeanette angled away and popped up from the bed. "Stop telling me God has a plan. If He had a plan, why would He hold back the rain? Why would He cause a hard-working man like Theo to have to grovel or be forced out of his home? And why would He allow me to fall in love just in time to pass Theo off to Victoria?"

Pa held out his arms, and Jeanette collapsed against him. He held her in silence. Even he had no words of comfort to give her.

~

September should have been a month of harvest, instead Theo slammed his tools into a nearby wooden box. Old man Reiner had given him two weeks to vacate.

Two weeks.

How in the world was he to accomplish that with nowhere to go?"

"Hello."

Theo looked toward the door of the barn. "Jeb, what are you doing here?" He stood and wiped the grime off his hands with a rag. His eyes flicked to Jeb's wrapped-up foot and the cane he was leaning on. "What happened to you?"

"Went over on my ankle in the field. Hit a rut and was on my backside before I could say snapping turtles." He chuckled. "Hurts like the dandy. And getting in and out of the buggy is downright laughable."

"Sorry to hear that. You should be home resting that thing."

"Came to see if we could help each other out, seeing you're in a fix, too."

"So, you know about the farm?"

Jeb nodded. "Old man Reiner is making it quite public. Thought maybe you could use a job? Unless the rumors I hear are true and you're marrying Victoria?"

Despite how humiliating it had been, Theo had asked Victoria for financial help, hoping to have another season to turn his farm around and give their relationship time to develop one way or another.

She'd declined, insisting that immediate marriage would solve all his problems. Her intent was to pressure. To Rush. Her callous response had bothered him so much that he couldn't stomach the thought of proposing, despite his dire circumstances. On his way back from her house, he'd remembered Jeanie's words, that God cared, and had begged Him for wisdom. And he'd realized then he wanted his kids to see real love in the home, which meant he could not make the same mistake he'd made with their mother.

He did not love Victoria.

Theo's laugh sounded hollow. "Nope, that won't be happening. Decided last night I was going to head your way and ask either you or Colby for a job. Seeing as I love farming, I was going to start with you. Crazy that you beat me to it."

"Not crazy at all. God is at work, even if I'm not happy about the way He had to get my attention." Jeb laughed, lifting his foot as evidence of God's *work*. "Truth is, I desperately need help. Besides this foot here, these old bones are creakin' and snappin' in places I've never felt before. 'Bout time I start heeding the signs."

"I still haven't figured out living arrangements for me and the kids," Theo said, "but I'm hoping to find somewhere that has an old barn or shed, so I can make furniture in the winter months and hopefully feed the gang."

"Our farmhouse feels pert'nigh empty most days, and the good Lord says to take in those in need."

"No, I couldn't."

"Trust me, son, I've been there myself. I understand your predicament. And Jeanette is the most giving person I know."

Just the mention of her name brought sweat to his palms. Theo moved across the dirt floor to where Jeb stood. "She won't mind six children and their father living in her house...the cooking, the cleaning, the people continually in her space?" Jeb wasn't thinking straight. The wiry man with his thinning gray hair was showing his age.

"It would only be for a season. Give you time to get on your feet. If'in we work well together, then we'll discuss options in the spring. For now, the farmhouse is big enough. There're four bedrooms upstairs. One for Jeanette and one for me. You can take the big one and share it with the boys, and the girls can have the other one. And I have a great big barn so you can build your furniture."

"Surely you don't want that kind of chaos in your home at your age."

"Having life in my home is not chaos. Anyway, I'm giving back what someone once gave me. Our home was burnt to the ground during the war. Left me and my family homeless. A helping hand and a new opportunity were given to me. I shall never forget Josiah's kindness, nor the love of my Father God."

"You believe in God's love?" Theo hadn't seen much of that in his life, but he wouldn't argue the point. Not to a man who was offering to embrace his noisy brood.

"I do. And I feel God wants me to offer the same as I was given—a home and the means to provide for your family. If you like farming, then there's opportunity for the takin'."

"But why me? There are many more qualified than I am."

"I have no sons to take on the responsibility. You and your boys could be a great help."

"We'd be helping you?" He found that difficult to believe.

"After seeing how hard you've worked and how fast you've learned this past summer, despite the distressing circumstances, I know you're a natural farmer. And like I said, I know when God is speaking."

"To be honest, I'm feeling enormous pressure. Mr. Reiner has given me only two weeks to pack up and get out."

"Well, now the pressure's off. And I know Jeanette will understand. She loves your children and wants the best for you all."

"You mean you haven't run this by her yet?" The hope inside him plummeted. To have honest work without feeling like a kept man, and to be able to provide for his family—it was a tempting offer, but he could not accept without talking to Jeanette himself.

"She knows about my injury and was fretting last night. This will be a perfect solution for me and for you. What's the worry?"

If Jeb knew the wild attraction he had for his daughter, he would not be asking that question. Theo's gut tightened into a knot. Would he be able to keep a respectful distance? "Let me talk to Jeanette. I want to be sure this intrusion is all right with her and to let her know that she's in no way obligated to agree."

Everything within him wanted to say yes, yes, yes. To be in her presence daily. To give his children the security. To build a future so that someday he would be in a position to—no he should not entertain the impossible.

"She'll be fine."

"Let me see that for myself before you talk to her. Her reaction will speak words she may not otherwise say." How could he expect her to wait around for him to rebuild when Solomon was knocking on her door? How could he disrupt her life so selfishly?

"I know my daughter." He lifted his hat and scratched his head, studying Theo with knowing eyes. "But suit yourself. Talk to her first."

"And you'll promise not to give her advance warning?"

"I promise." Jeb held out his hand, and Theo gave a hearty shake.

"Thank you for offering, even if it doesn't work out."

"Like I said…" Jeb smiled, and the laugh lines around his eyes crinkled. "I know my daughter, and she loves you…all. She'll want to help your family."

No matter how difficult his circumstances were, Theo would not, nor could not, pressure his good friend into something she didn't want.

Ha, friend. Who was he kidding? Just the thought of Jeanie and that kiss they'd shared recently made his heart kick and the blood scream through his veins. If he had any reservations at all at taking Jeb's offer, it was the thought of being too close, too often.

CHAPTER 25

Another school year was once again underway, and autumn crisp filled the air. The children were excited and eager to learn. Seeing Theo's children was the hardest part of Jeanette's day. The thought that she would not be part of their lives other than for the few hours at school made her almost sick to her stomach. Any day now she was expecting the wedding announcement of Theo Wallace to Victoria Stanfield.

She stepped out onto the schoolhouse steps. Leaves fluttered to the ground underneath the sugar maple, dressing the landscape in gold and orange. If only she could put some of that color into her dreary life. She jangled the bell in hand, and the children came running.

When they were all in the schoolroom, Jeanette clapped her hands. "Children. Time to settle down. We'll have our story time now."

Reading a book right after lunch always seemed to calm the jitters and make the afternoon more productive. The problem was in finding a story to read that was interesting to all ages with a lesson to glean. She knew just the one. It fit the mood of her day. She went to the side bureau and pulled out Hans Christian Andersen's Fairy Tale Collection. His writing had exploded upon the American scene, and Jeanette had read everything he had to offer, including tidbits about his personal life. She shared a similar story. Unrequited love. Unpopular growing up. That of the Ugly Duckling...the perfect story for today.

Cracking open the book, she took a deep breath. The distinct smell of the sprigs of lavender she had pressed between the pages wafted up. Voices faded, and she waited until there was absolute quiet before she began.

"The Ugly Duckling, by Hans Christian Andersen. 'It was lovely summer weather in the country, and the golden corn, the green oats...'"

Jeanette finished the story, closing the book with a decided snap.

Lord help me share the true message of this story. It's been such a struggle to believe in myself, to allow that inner transformation of thinking of what is good and pure and lovely rather than being negative about myself.

"So, who can tell me the life lesson in this story?"

Lizzy held up her hand.

"Yes, Lizzy."

"The other animals should not have made fun of the poor ugly duckling just because he was different from them."

"That's right, Lizzie. In the story, the author used barnyard animals, but let's use people to better understand this concept." Jeanette's eyes circled the room and landed on Flora and Ivy, the two girls who relentlessly teased Sarah. Both the girls were from well-to-do families and were jealous of Sarah's natural beauty. "Flora, can you give me an example?"

"I, uh...don't know what you mean exactly." Flora looked at Ivy, and they both glanced at Sarah and snickered. She knew exactly what Jeanette meant.

"Hmm, maybe someone else can explain this concept to Flora so she can understand."

Laura put up her hand.

Jeanette nodded for her to answer.

"The story was teaching us how to treat others who are not the same as we are. Like when a fancy dressed guest visits our farmhouse..."

Was she thinking of Victoria?

"...that person may be of little help, but still we must be kind and patient."

That was interesting. Instead of Laura thinking that the fancy dresses were something she wanted, she saw it as an impediment to practicality and a need for kindness and patience. "Good answer, Laura...where we live, the clothing we wear, the skills we have, are all distinct and show our individuality. What are some other differences?"

Tommy lifted his hand. "I'm teased for my big nose, but Pa says all down the line of Hartfield's there ain't—"

"There isn't." Jeanette corrected.

"There isn't a Hartfield without a healthy sized nose. And it builds character." All the kids laughed as he stuck his nose in the air and joked about himself.

Jeanette smiled. If only she had embraced her uniqueness with such confidence. "You're right, Tommy. We can be teased for the way God created us, or the family we're born into. But all God sees is how beautiful each of His creations are." For the first time, she really meant what she said, teaching from the heart, not the head.

Alice's hand shot up. "The ugly duckling was really a beautiful swan and lived happily ever after when he found other swans, but life doesn't always turn out that way."

Jeanette understood exactly what the plump girl was referring to. Life was not fair. All were not created the same. "I think the point of that story was to make us realize we should not be unkind to someone who is different than us. Especially based on their looks, their clothes, all the outward things that mean so little. It's what's inside that counts." She tapped her heart. "How will we choose to treat each other? What kind words can we speak? What generous deeds can we do? How can we make a positive difference in someone else's life?"

Alice smiled, her dimples dancing. "Mama says that kindness is the best quality any girl can have."

Ivy and Flora snickered.

Jeanette sent them a pointed look.

"Your mother is very wise, Alice. So, for the rest of the week, I'm going to have a little contest. I want you to find ways to be kind, generous, and giving. And when one of your classmates shows kindness to you, I want you to share that with me. I will keep a tally until Friday at the end of the day, and we'll have a little gift for the top three students. We'll also share how that kindness made us feel."

If only her peers had been kind to her. Then maybe she wouldn't have battled the self-image problems that plagued her into adulthood. She was finally learning to see things about herself that were beautiful on the inside and the out, but she still had much to learn. One of the best things about being a teacher was the power to shape and mold the lives of children on a more positive path. She'd do her best to make sure they treated each other with respect, despite their differences.

∼

That afternoon, Jeanette pulled her cloak from the hook and slid it on. She peeked out the one window in the schoolhouse at the billowing dark clouds. She would be lucky to make it home before the clouds opened. She picked up her carpet bag and lunch pail and headed for the door. Swinging it wide, she jumped at the wall of a man directly in front of her.

"Theo, you scared me."

"Hello, Jeanie...Jeanette."

They both spoke at once.

"Truth is, I've been standing out here since I sent my kids home, not knowing how to have this conversation but knowing I must." Theo brushed a hand through his crop of hair the way he always did when he was nervous.

She'd not talked to him since that day in the forest, but it was as if not a moment had passed. Her body remembered, and shivers skimmed over her flesh. The wind whipped across the school yard, stirring up a cloud of leaves and dust. She pulled the hood of her cloak up.

"Can it wait? I have to get home before the storm." She had no desire to hear about his upcoming nuptials.

"I'll walk with you." He slid in beside her as she headed down the steps. "Your pa came to see me."

She stopped and spun his way. "He did?" She didn't think pa was getting around much these days with his twisted ankle. And whyever would he be visiting Theo? The thought that he might have said something about what they'd talked about knotted her stomach.

"You have no idea what I'm going to talk to you about?"

"Should I?"

"Good."

Now, what did he mean by that? He must've worked out whatever confusion he possessed that day he'd kissed her and popped the question to Victoria. He looked decidedly more relaxed. She could not bear gazing into his eyes one second longer and resumed walking.

He reached out and gripped her hand.

"Give me one moment."

She turned toward him. "The sky is about to open up. Make it quick."

"I don't care what the sky is about to do, but I do care about what you think."

She looked up into his soulful brown eyes. Tiny hazel flecks flickered like the lightning flashing in the clouds behind him. A slow rumble grumbled in the distance.

"Your pa offered me a job, apprenticing at your farm. And if I do well, I may have a future. It'll give me a way to provide for my family. And I'm even going to take your suggestion to heart and make some furniture over the winter to sell."

"That's wonderful news. Will that allow enough income to keep your farm?"

"No. I missed the September payment, and Mr. Reiner has given me two weeks to get out."

Her spirits sank. For a split second she'd thought he was not marrying Victoria, but the truth was he just didn't want to enter marriage empty handed. Now she'd not only have to see Theo working their fields, but he'd be married to Victoria. Why hadn't Pa discussed this with her? How cruel could life get? "So, when's your wedding?" Her words slipped out with little enthusiasm.

"Wedding?" His brows knit together.

"To Victoria."

"There's no wedding. Everything about Victoria felt like a repeat of the first time. I felt if I went ahead with that, I would not have learned a thing. If I ever do get brave enough to marry again, it will be for love. And I do not love her."

That information made her want to do a jig. It took everything she had to keep her voice calm. "You're not marrying Victoria?"

"No."

"Then what are you going to do?"

"That's what I came to speak to you about."

Fat raindrops landed on her face.

He held out his hand. "Come on, let's get back in the schoolhouse until this rain stops."

She placed her hand in his, and they ran. Nothing felt more

natural than her fingers entwined in his. She laughed as the wind whipped her cloak off her head.

He was not marrying Victoria. Oh, goodness, that made her happy.

They scampered up the steps into the schoolhouse and slammed the door.

He dropped her hand and paced at the front of the room.

"Theo. What is it?" She stepped toward him, but he held up both hands and closed his eyes.

"How do I ask this of you?"

"Ask what?"

His eyes opened, and he came close enough to place a hand on each shoulder. "Promise that you'll be honest with me? I wouldn't want anything to jeopardize the friendship we have."

He was making their friendship status clear, and her spirits sank. Still, she nodded.

His words came out in a rush. "Your pa invited us to move in with you. He said there are two empty bedrooms, one for the girls and another I can share with the boys. Just until next spring. It'll give me time to get myself on my feet. I know it's asking a lot, all of us in your home, especially when you've already done so much."

"Yes." Her answer came out so fast, it jarred even her.

"Are you sure?"

"Of course." How could she say no, knowing his plight? She had an opportunity to live out the generosity, giving, and kindness she preached to her students and help a family in need. Yet all she could think about was how wonderful Theo's lips would feel upon her mouth. Who was she trying to kid?

She'd better reign in her wayward thoughts and fast. He had called her friend, and she'd best act like one. Especially if he was going to move in. With a quick squeeze to his arm, she stepped away.

"How can I say no?" The smile on her lips felt glued in place.

"Besides, I've missed the children horribly." She could honestly make this about the children.

"And they've missed you. But I think we need to talk about what happened that day in the woods."

Jeanette could feel her face heat up.

"I've wanted to tell you I'm sorry. You have Solomon, and I have my issues. I didn't respect—"

"Let's not!" She shook her head. "Let's not talk about this. The children need a home and we're good friends. We don't need to complicate things by…by…whatever that was."

"I agree." He spoke so fast, the hope in her chest deflated. She had her answer. He regretted what had happened that day.

How would she keep their relationship in the friendship category, feeling like she did? She would have to. Anticipation bit the air, her insides jumped. She didn't have to let on how the thought of being in his presence every day both excited and terrified her. After all they had been through, Theo's family needed an oasis, a soft landing. She could not let her emotions get the best of her. She hoped she was not making a huge mistake. She should have at least asked Theo for some time to pray about it. But time was not something he had.

And Solomon. She should've told Theo the truth about her lack of feelings for Solomon, but out of respect, she could not. She needed to talk to Solomon first.

CHAPTER 26

"Pa, how could you do such a thing without talking to me first?" Jeanette sprinkled some brown sugar over her porridge and then pointed her teaspoon in his direction. "Theo put me on the spot. But now that I've had to time to think—"

"See, that's exactly why I didn't talk to you first. You do too much thinkin'. Sometimes, it's just good to do and let the chips fall where they may." He scraped at the remainder of his porridge in the bowl and shoveled in another bite.

"Let the chips fall? I'm not a woodcutter. I'm a teacher who has to watch everything I do and say in this community if I want to keep my position. What will the gossip mongers make of an unmarried man living in our house?"

"So now we're going to worry more about the rumor mill than doing what is right and good in the sight of the Lord?"

She took a spoonful of porridge in her mouth but could barely get it down.

"You know full well that Theo's options were slim." Pa slammed down his spoon onto the table.

"People may talk."

"Let them talk. I'm here, and so are six children. If that's not enough eyes to keep you two walking the straight and narrow, I don't know what is. Who in their right mind would make a thing of that?"

"I can't afford to lose my job. It's the only thing that's truly mine." Jeanette choked on a small bite and swallowed the fear clogging her throat.

"Then it's time you take a risk on something bigger than your job."

"That's not your call."

Pa's eyebrows knit together. "I didn't make this decision. Seems you did that when Theo asked."

"But I had no time to think—"

"We're going around and around the same mulberry bush. Mark my word, you'll be thanking me before this is all said and done. You don't know it yet, but the Lord has His plan." Pa stood up from the kitchen table and hobbled with his bowl to the wash basin.

Guilt pierced through. Pa needed help, and Theo desperately needed a job and a home for his family. Jeanette chewed her lower lip. "Seems more like *you* have a plan rather than the good Lord."

"Me and the Lord are like this." Pa pressed his finger and thumb together lifting them in the air. "Have a good day, darling daughter, and don't forget it's your last day of peace and quiet." He chuckled his way out of the kitchen.

Oh, how she wanted to both hug him and give him a piece of her mind. On one hand, he had orchestrated circumstances that had the potential to rip open the gaping wound of her bleeding heart and make it haemorrhage. But on the other, she had time to pursue the man she loved.

She would be around his children every day and be the mama they needed. That was a good thing. But how would she see Theo every day and not fall deeper in love? The longing was already a mountain. The desire, a river of restless current. The yearning, an ocean of endless waves. She was a mess, and they hadn't even moved in.

First things first. Talk to Solomon. Pray. Then, decide where God was leading. Theo had not chosen Victoria. He said he would only marry for love. Could they move beyond friendship? She had the memory of a kiss that held promise.

～

"Solomon, let's walk." Jeanette took him by the hand and pulled him up from the rocking chair on the porch.

"Sundays are for lazin' around."

"Come on. We won't have too many nice days like this left before old man winter blows in." She forced the cheery into her voice and took his arm.

"I like it when you boss me around." His cowboy hat slid further down his brow, and he pushed it up with one finger and gave her a heartwarming smile.

Oh dear, he hadn't a clue what was about to happen. And she didn't want to be on the porch having this difficult conversation where Pa might hear or interrupt. Theo and the kids were moving in the next day, and privacy would be at a premium.

He threw his arm around her. "Anything that makes my girl happy."

A barb of guilt pierced her soul as they headed down the steps, and across the yard towards the orchard. They walked in silence between a row of apple trees. The pungent smell of fallen apples wafted up amid the crackle of leaves beneath Jeanette's feet. Life would've been so much easier if only she had fallen for him.

He tried to move in close, but she pulled away. "Solomon. I have to be honest." She stopped and faced him.

"'Bout what?" His brows bunched.

"This relationship is just not deepening for me."

He pulled the hat from his head and drew a hand through his crop of hair. "I know. I get it." There was hurt in his voice. "I was trying to be respectful and give you time to warm up to me and all. But it seems that didn't work."

"I'm sorry."

"Makes sense now why you never let me kiss you properly. Never had to work at that when I was courting my Christina. In fact, we had to work at *not* touching each other too much, until we got married, of course." He let out a half chuckle. "Then it was sheer heaven."

Jeanette now understood what he was talking about, and it wasn't Solomon who had taught her that lesson.

"You deserve someone who loves you like Christina did," she said, "and I know there are many young ladies at church with their eyes on you."

"And I've noticed a certain farmer with his eyes on you."

Jeanette's pulse picked up speed. If Theo cared, he had a funny way of showing it. Reiterating their friendship status and speaking of major issues did not invite a girl in. "I also want you to know, before it gets around the rumor mill, that Pa has invited the Wallace family to move in with us."

"Move in?"

"You do know Theo lost his crop, and that Mr. Reiner took back the farm?"

"I heard something about that."

"Pa is going to give Theo a job, and we're going to help the family get through the winter."

That's kind of your pa, but is that all there is at work here…kindness?"

"What do you mean?"

"Come on. You know what I mean." His tone held disbelief.

"I admit, I do care about Theo and his children, but Theo and I are only friends. He has made that very clear."

"Only friends?" he said, with a smirk and a slight shake to his head.

"Yes."

"You feel nothing for him?"

Words got stuck in her throat. She was not about to admit to Solomon what she hadn't yet told Theo. But she didn't want to lie.

"Solomon. You once asked me what my story was. Well, here's a great example. It's always been this way with me. Unlucky in love. The person I fall for never falls for me. And, if you're honest with yourself, you haven't fallen for me either." The truth caused an ache to flower in her throat. She swallowed the pain.

Solomon's shoulders dropped and he kicked a rotten apple with his boot. "Funny how life goes. After all I've been through, I really wanted a mature woman, not a doe-eyed adolescent. Are you sure this couldn't evolve into more? I admire you more than—"

"You said it. You never had to work at it with your Christina."

"You and I are somehow just better at friendship than courting, aren't we?"

"Seems that's the way it is for me with men. I truly wish my heart had fallen for you."

"And mine, for you."

He held out his arms, and she walked in. He hugged her tight and lightly kissed the top of her head. "Will we still sing that duet we've talked about?"

"Absolutely." She backed out of his hug and swiped at the tears on her cheeks.

"Come on girl, don't cry. God has a plan for us both." He gave her a hug. "Hope that Theo figures out what a gem you are.

I watched you with his kids, and you're everything I want for the mother of my children."

He swung an arm around her shoulder and steered her between the rows toward the house.

"Solomon, you're a good friend."

They stopped at the edge of the trees, and he turned her in his arms. Before she could stop him, his lips came down hard and purposeful against hers. He did not rush.

Everything within her wanted to pull away, but she didn't want to offend.

Finally, he lifted his head. "Anything?"

"I wish—"

He laughed. "Me neither. But I had to be sure. It's not every day a man meets a lady as fine as you." He stepped out of her embrace and tipped his hat. "Goodbye, my Jeanette Rose."

Jeanette watched him disappear through the orchard toward the ranch. She touched her fingers to her lips. Oh, how she wished she felt something for Solomon, but there was nothing. Yet, the memory of Theo's mouth on hers brought an instant smile to her lips, and heat flooded her face. Gosh she was in a pickle. How was she going to have that man in her home, so accessible and handsome? Good thing she worked all day.

She prayed as she walked across the yard. *Please, God, help Solomon. He's had so much sorrow already. Send the perfect partner his way. And God, please guard my sorry heart from falling deeper in love with a man who may only ever want friendship. Give me wisdom. And Lord, thanks for allowing me more time with those children. I truly love them.*

∽

As Theo stepped out of Jeb's barn to get a drink at the pump, he caught sight of Jeanie and Solomon at the edge of the orchard. He moved back into the shadows. Earlier at church, Jeb had told Theo to bring over whatever he needed to store.

He'd come to start the moving process. He hadn't come prepared to have his soul ripped open.

They obviously didn't realize he had rolled his wagon into the barn.

He could no more say yes to marrying Victoria after kissing Jeanie than he could forget the power of attraction between them. Her response had burnt his self-control to ash in a matter of seconds. His desire for her had been dangerous. Had she not pulled away, he was not sure what would have happened. Louisa had never kissed him with such passion or moved his soul to the brink of no return.

Now, he spied on their private moment, unable to turn away. Their kiss burned like a live coal, searing and hot in the pit of his stomach. A bolt of pain ripped through.

Apparently, the kiss he'd shared with Jeanie, which had stunned him senseless, meant nothing to her. There she was, enjoying Solomon as if it had never happened.

Theo's arms crossed and slammed against his chest. If there was a God in heaven, this was another example that He sure didn't care about Theo. Guilt speared him through. God may be saying no to the woman he wanted, but He had just provided a job and a home for his family. He should be grateful. His arms dropped to his sides.

"Goodbye, my Jeanette Rose" Solomon's words drifted across the yard, landing hard. Theo had never thought to ask what her middle name was. Though they had spent far more time together, Solomon already knew her better than he did. The man obviously understood how to woo Jeanie in the way he did not.

"Jeanie Rose." The name slipped off his lips. How suitable that his Jeanie was named after a beautiful flower. But she was not *his* Jeanie.

A surge of raw envy coursed through his veins at her smile and the touch of her fingers to her mouth. She looked as if she had just tasted magic. It sent his mind bending in crazy circles, chaotic, confused.

His anger should be more directed at himself. He hadn't snatched her up when he'd had the chance.

He wanted her to be happy, yet he felt like he was ripping apart at the seams. Had he hoped that she'd felt that kiss between them as intensely as he had? The thought that she hadn't brought a loneliness that scorched its way straight through to the bone.

But then, what did it matter? He was in no position to court her. His finances were depleted. He had no worldly possessions. He was proud that he had said no to Victoria, even if it left him penniless. He finally felt able to trust his decisions in matters of the heart. And seeing Jeanie with Solomon was a sign. He was not the one for her.

Not to mention the giant leap between Jeanie's faith in God and his. There she was, praying her way across the yard, her eyes lifted into the heavens, her lips moving. She found God so accessible and real. He looked up toward a shaft of light dancing through a slit in the barn roof. He couldn't seem to get his prayers past those darn rafters.

CHAPTER 27

"I love it here." Laura wrapped her arms around Jeanette's waist as she washed the supper dishes. All three girls were helping her by drying.

Jeanette looked down and smiled. "And I love having you here too."

"Even with the added work?" Sarah asked with a catch to her voice.

"You're all so helpful. And yes, I wouldn't trade this time for anything." Funny how she meant those words even though the rumors had started with Agnus riding the "replace Jeanette with me" bandwagon, stirring up trouble. Even still, everything about helping this family felt right.

"Ivy said that we shouldn't be here unless you and Papa get married," Sarah said. "She says its ina...propate."

The tremble in Sarah's voice now made sense. She was worried that this good thing that had happened to her family would soon be over. "Don't you worry about the runaway tongues. There is nothing inappropriate going on here."

"What's inappropriate?" Theo walked into the kitchen.

Jeanette's throat went dry and tight at the sight of him. "It's nothing." She waved a sudsy hand at him. "Just some folks with too much time on their hands."

"Meaning?" He raised his brows.

She frowned at him above the children and shook her head.

"Hey girls, it's my turn to help dry. You go on and get ready for bed. I'll be up soon to read a story."

They didn't have to be told twice. They were off and running. The stomping of feet and the chattering of voices echoing behind brought a smile to Jeanette's lips. She felt part of something bigger.

Theo picked up the towel and wiped the dishes. Silence soaked the moment in a peaceful rhythm of wash and dry. He didn't press her to expound on the conversation that had just taken place. He waited patiently while she mulled over what to say.

"Tongues are wagging," she whispered.

"Let them."

"But I didn't realize this would touch the children's lives too."

"That day Victoria knew for sure it was over between us and that my future would never include her, she was furious. Especially when I told her I'd be working and lodging here. She made some threats." He slammed a dish down a little too hard. "I'm so thankful her true colors came out before I made another colossal mistake."

"You made that decision before you knew."

"You're right. I did. I guess I'm learning."

"You are."

Jeanette kept her head down, pretending to concentrate on the washing, though there were no more dishes to wash. Her hands moved through the sudsy water. All she could think about was the fact that he did not see Victoria in his future.

He leaned close enough for her to feel his breath on her ear. "Why are you smiling?"

She glanced up at him. "I-I… Well, you two just didn't seem a fit."

"I agree. Victoria was quite happy to have me beholden to her, but I couldn't enter into any relationship where I can't provide a home for my children and my wife."

Her breath hitched and her chest tightened. Victoria was no longer in the picture, but his problems were. It mattered not a whit to Jeanette what he owned or didn't own, but she understood the need he would feel as a man to provide for his own. If they were to ever have a chance, she needed to respect how much that meant to him and not rush anything.

A charged moment ran between them as he stared down at her. So much was left unsaid, but if she started talking, she would not be able to stop.

"Go. Read that story to your girls. I have a game of checkers I promised the boys." She flicked the cloth in his direction.

"Are you sorry you took us in?"

Lines of worry furrowed his brow. "Sorry? Not at all. Now go."

He squeezed her arm. "You're a good friend. I don't know how I'll ever repay the kindness you and your pa have extended."

He could start by seeing her as a woman, not just a friend. But how could she communicate that? She would then be like Victoria, demanding more than he was prepared to give.

She could pray for wisdom. She could pray for favor. She could pray for strength to pursue the one man she wanted more than life itself. And she could be patient. At twenty-nine she understood that word all too well.

Hmm, it felt an awful lot like God had just breathed a plan.

*J*eanette bustled into the Alston General Mercantile. Her order of school supplies should be in, and if she hurried, she could make it home in time to make Theo's favorite dessert, apple crisp with clotted cream. The crisp autumn apples and her ma's secret recipe were always a hit. They had enough brisket left over from the night before to slice onto bread for the evening meal, a lighter fare that deserved a heavier dessert for the hard-working men. Actually, she had only one man in mind.

She entered the store and glanced around. Winnie must have popped into the back because she was nowhere to be seen, but Victoria and Agnus were thick in conversation. They stood on the far side, obviously waiting for Winnie's return. Jeanette waved a hand, but they didn't see her.

"I'm waiting to hear back from the county superintendent," Agnes said. "This is an outrage. Them all living together without a wedding band on her finger." The woman's triple chin creased into folds as she scowled.

"Can you blame him? Who would want to put a wedding band on that woman's finger?" Victoria waved her fan back and forth in front of her face. "Poor Theo. Not wanting to be coined a kept man with my money, he begged me for time to earn his keep. This job was the only thing he could find. And Jeb, determined to marry off his homely daughter, concocted this scheme."

"Despicable, to be sure, and completely immoral."

"I'm sure we don't have to worry about a handsome man like Theo succumbing to impropriety," Victoria said, "but I agree that it does not look good and shouldn't be allowed."

"I will be sure and see to that."

"Not exactly anything to be tempted about there." Victoria snickered with her gloved fingers touching her mouth. "But I wouldn't put it past that spinster and her conniving pa to set up something that pressures the poor man into wedlock. That's the only way she'll get a man."

Agnus harrumphed. "Indeed."

Tears filled Jeanette's eyes, but she swept them away. This was why she took one step forward in confidence only to slide two steps back. People were so cruel.

"And I will not stand for it," Agnus shook her finger. "That woman does not deserve to be the teacher of our innocent and vulnerable children."

"I found it." Winnie slipped through the curtain that separated the front from the back and held up a package. "Oh, hello Jeanette, I'll be right with you. Just have to finish this transaction with Victoria."

Agnus and Victoria whipped their heads in Jeanette's direction.

Heat flooded to her face. But why should she feel embarrassed? She was so done with gossip and cruelty, and the only way she was going to stop it was to stick up for herself instead of turn and run.

Dear God, give me strength.

She prayed her eyes didn't glisten with unshed tears as she lifted her chin and squared her shoulders. With each step closer she gained gumption.

"Good afternoon, Victoria, Agnus. I did wave when I came in, but you were too deep in conversation to notice."

"I...well...good afternoon," Victoria answered sheepishly.

Agnus turned her head, refusing to acknowledge her at all.

"We truly did consider all aspects of propriety when Pa and I made our decision to help the Wallace family, but the Bible verse that states we give Jesus a cup of water when we help the needy became the most important factor. Would you rather those poor children not have a roof over their heads?"

"Certainly not," Winnie said. The woman had no idea what Jeanette had overheard, her expression open and honest.

Agnus kept her nose up and her head turned in the opposite direction.

Victoria fanned her perfect face a little too furiously. "Why, I do declare. Do you really think I would let my Theo and his precious children flounder about without a home?"

Jeanette hated the way she let *my Theo* roll off her tongue. He was not *her* Theo. If he were, there would be a ring on her finger.

"I offered to give him the money to keep his farm afloat over the winter until the next harvest, but being the upstanding man he is, he didn't want to accept charity. Such independence is to be honored, though it forced him into the job your Pa offered. But for Jeb to coerce him into moving in with you… Well, that is most indecorous, indeed."

Jeanette straightened to her full height and looked down on both women. "I assure you, there was no coercing necessary. If there was any pressuring going on, it was from you, Victoria. Theo told me the truth, that you demanded he marry you rather than extend a helping hand. He was indeed homeless, and not because he was too proud to ask for help but because both you and Mr. Reiner refused to show compassion or generosity.

"Meanwhile, Pa offered work and a home to a family in need with no strings attached. If the two of you have a problem with that kind of Christian example, then take it up with God."

Jeanette turned toward Winnie, whose smile was shining. "Winnie, I shall come back another day for my supplies, when the air is not quite so toxic."

She heard both women gasp as she walked out. The crisp autumn air invigorated her. Or maybe it was the fact that, for the first time in her life, she had stood up to cruel gossip rather than run. *My goodness, that felt wonderful.*

CHAPTER 28

In the evenings after the children were settled, Theo and Jeanette had gone back to their summertime routine and sat on the porch talking. He loved the still nights, with nothing but the sound of the wind rustling the leaves of the nearby trees and the company of his best friend. As long as Solomon was in the picture, and no means to provide a home, that was all there could be.

But this was the best part of his day.

A comfortable silence rested between them. He had never experienced such peace in the presence of a woman. Her companionship dispelled his acute loneliness.

"Look at that moon." She stood by the railing, gazing up.

He joined her.

A cloudless night frosted the landscape with a full moon floating on the edge of the early evening sky. A yearning to throw all caution to the wind and draw her close came over him, as it did almost every night. But he had been able to keep his hands from reaching out by reminding himself of Solomon. Tonight, however, the longing was almost unbearable.

A thick braid hung down her back. Strands broke free and

blew across his face each time the breeze kicked up. Almost from the moment he'd met her, he had yearned to run his hands through her untethered glorious head of hair. He had dreamed of her lying beside him, her hair fanned over his pillow.

He dare not go there in his imagination when she was only an arm's breadth away.

"I ran into Agnus and Victoria the other day at the store."

"Hmm." Good thing she distracted his wayward thoughts with conversation.

"They didn't see me enter and were deep into gossip about our living arrangements and my impropriety. Seems they had a lot to say on the subject."

"Nothing those two say would be worth listening to."

"Nevertheless, there may be trouble coming."

He swallowed against the tightness in his throat. "What kind of trouble?"

"Agnus has written a letter to the school superintendent. Who knows what she implied, but from what I heard, it will not be anything good."

"And how does Victoria factor into this?"

"She's spreading the lie that she offered to give you money to keep your farm, but you took the job with Pa instead because you're too honorable to take a handout."

"She said that?"

Jeanette turned toward him. "I know that's not the truth, because you told me—"

"It's not exactly a lie, but she's twisting the truth."

"Meaning?" Lines furrowed her brow.

"She did offer money, but only after I'd agreed to work for your pa and had your offer of a home for my children. When she could no longer manipulate me into an immediate marriage, then she was willing to give what I had asked for in the first place."

"Why didn't you take that option? You could've kept your farm." Her voice wavered.

"Because I would've been indebted to a woman I can't trust. I've done that once before, and like I told you, I will never do it again." He couldn't stop his fingers from lifting and brushing the wayward strands that blew across those lips he so desired to kiss.

The second his fingertips connected with her warm skin, he snatched his hand away. His fingers felt as if he'd held them over a flame. "I chose to come here and give up the dream of my own farm because I trust your Pa." He stepped closer, so close that his body almost touched hers. "And I trust you. That means more to me than any piece of land."

She turned away putting distance between them. "That's the kindest thing anyone has ever said to me." There was a catch in her throat as if she were near tears. "Trust is what one should expect between real friends."

Friends. His thoughts were not that of a mere friend. But he couldn't speak of the turmoil within. She had Solomon, and he had nothing to offer. She deserved so much more than he could ever give. This reality always brought his ardor into check. He would concentrate on being a good father and working hard to ensure he had a future in farming.

"I hope I don't lose my teaching position." Her voice wavered. "It's all I have. The way Agnus and Victoria went on about the way I look, like I'm the homeliest—"

"Don't believe that vicious gossip. You're... Well, I'm sure Solomon has made you aware of how beau—"

"Solomon and I are not... We're just friends."

"What do you mean? I thought you two were courting."

"We're not seeing each other anymore." She turned away and looked back out at the evening sky.

Was he hearing right? His heart bolted to his throat. If she wasn't seeing Solomon, could it mean...? Yet what would he do about all the issues that plagued him? Finances? Future? Family? His disappointment and anger toward the God she served?

"What happened?"

"Seems the closest I can get to any man is friendship." Her face turned a delightful shade of pink even in the waning light, but what really stirred his soul was the lone tear that trickled down her cheek.

He wanted to tell her that he was way past friendship with her, but what would that change? He instead gave her shoulder a quick squeeze and turned her toward him.

"Come on. Give me a smile." Teardrops splashed from both lashes as she half laughed and cried. He brushed away the moisture with the pad of his thumb.

"Theo, you don't have to—"

"What?"

Her skin shimmered in the slivery moonlight as if caressed by dancing moonbeams. He was losing the battle.

"Console me out of obligation because you live here now."

"I'm not... I feel no obligation." He crushed her body against his in a fierce hug. Everything within him wanted to kiss her tears away, but if he started, he would not be able to stop. He leaned away just enough to look at her. "Jeanie, I sincerely care."

She choked out the words. "Yes, you care. Solomon cares. But it's just as Victoria said, plain Jeanette. Who would ever want to marry her?"

What could he say? He was in no position to marry anyone. But couldn't she see, couldn't she *feel*, how attracted he was to her? There was nothing plain about her.

She pulled out of his arms. "I can't talk about this any longer. Good night." She turned and disappeared into the house.

He longed to stop her and tell her that it wasn't her, it was him. That, though he trusted her implicitly, though he had a confidence in her that he'd never imagined sharing with a woman, he had nothing to offer. Until...maybe next year. If he worked really hard, if he poured himself into being indispensable to Jeb, if he earned the right to keep this job and knew he could support his family, then he could let her know how deep his caring went.

Hope curled around the edges of his weary mind. Maybe a time would come to act upon the love pounding in his soul.

The realization hit him. Yes, he loved her. He laughed into the moonlight. He was in love, truly in love for the first time in his life.

He would have to be much more careful. With his growing attraction, the evening, the moonlight, and Solomon no longer in the picture, her loveliness could be far too dangerous a package.

~

Jeanette put her face into her pillow and sobbed. Why had Theo felt it necessary to console her? That hug just made her feel all the lonelier. Did he feel sorry for her? Did he feel obligated? What a fool to have shared so much. And he was too much of a gentleman to lie, to say he felt anything more than care for her...the kind of care a friend would give.

Victoria's words echoed in her brain: *"Who would want to put a wedding band on her finger? Not exactly any temptation there... Jeb wants to marry off his homely daughter."* Jeanette tried to pray those words away, to stand on the things she was learning about herself that were far more valuable than looks, but between the combination of Solomon not feeling anything, that conversation in the store, and now Theo's obvious desire to remain friends, the battle was raging. Would she ever feel good enough to fight for the man she wanted? Or better yet, feel good about herself, with or without a man?

Like the wind that had picked up and now moaned outside

her window, she let out a groan of sorrow. She had ruined everything by getting so personal. Now, once again, even their precious friendship would be strained. Tear after tear flowed as she wept out the years of pent-up pain. But somehow, all the previous shunning seemed small compared to the reality that Theo could never feel more for her than friendship.

A hand touched her arm. "Jeanie. Please don't cry."

She twisted around on her bed, startled by Theo's voice. With tears still streaming down her face, she sat up.

He eased down beside her.

"You shouldn't be in here. If Pa or the children…"

"I know. But I've been standing outside your door for fifteen minutes praying your tears would stop. I couldn't bear to leave things as they are."

"I'm sorry. I was just remembering what Victoria and Agnus had said about…about…the way I look…and…"

"Shh, my darl…Jeanie." He gathered her close and rocked her. With her ear pinned against the wall of his chest, she could hear the rapid thump of his heart. Had he been about to call her his darling?

If only she had the right to pull him down beside her and drink of his comfort, his passion, his…

"I have something to tell you that I've never said to any other woman nor felt as intensely as I do right now. But I need you to look at me." He stood and pulled her up beside him. With his fingers laced in hers he walked to the window and opened the curtains, so the full moonlight shone in. He faced her, gently lifting her chin with his finger. "You need to see that I mean this from the depth of my soul."

Her pulse fluttered, and a drop of sweat trickled down her spine. Had God given her sleep, and was she dreaming the most wonderful dream?

"Are you listening?" he whispered.

She nodded.

"You're the most beautiful woman I have ever met, both on the inside and the outside. There is nothing plain about you. You're truly extraordinary in every way." He lifted his hands to each side of her face. The tips of his finger slid across her temples. "Any man would be blessed to have you as a marriage partner. No, let me be honest. I wish the timing was right, but—"

"Theo, I shouldn't have mentioned my desire to marry." There it was again, that word *but*. She didn't want to hear his *but*. She wanted to remember the conversation as it was right here, without excuses. "I know you're just a friend. I was merely wondering if I came across as dull or plain."

His brows furrowed.

She turned out of his embrace and walked to the bedroom door. "You'd better get out of here before this little visit causes trouble. But thanks for caring, my friend." She tried to make her voice sound matter-of-fact.

He followed her across the room.

She reached up to give him a chaste kiss on his cheek, one hand on the doorknob.

But he pulled her against him. His lips moved slowly across her jaw.

She could not breathe as he enveloped her fully into his arms, then covered her mouth with his. His lips moved over hers with an intensity that spoke of need, seeking her response.

The joy of doing what she had been aching to do for weeks was intense. He was in no rush and didn't stop until she was a puddle of no resistance. Every fiber of her being craved him. She wanted him to take her to that bed and lay her down to do whatever it was that people in love did.

Suddenly, he stepped back and removed her arms, which had still been locked around his neck. "Good night, my beautiful friend." There was a grin on his face.

Friendship was the farthest thing from her mind. And based

on the look he gave her, he knew it. She could think of nothing to say.

"Best we finish this conversation in the light of day. But finish it we must. I have much more to say. Sweet dreams, my Jeanie." He slipped into the hallway. With a quiet click of the latch, he was gone.

Everything within her screamed for his return.

CHAPTER 29

*J*eanette flipped over in her bed. The faint pearl-gray light of dawn filtered through the open curtains, and the happenings of the night before crashed in.

Had Theo really snuck into her bedroom, risking so much, to console her? Had he meant what he said, that she was the most beautiful woman he knew?

A warm knot settled in her tummy, and a genuine smile split free. It didn't matter what Agnus or Victoria thought—or anyone else, for that matter. God had used Theo to reveal to her that beauty reached far deeper than the skin. Somehow, he saw her as God did, fearfully and wonderfully made.

Her cheeks burned hot at the memory of his kiss. That was no chaste peck between friends. Like the one in the forest, it was passionate, intense, and altogether the most beautiful moment of her life thus far. He had been as moved as she was, she was sure of it. But how would she face him this morning? What did it all mean?

Her breathing shallowed at the thought. Was she to encourage a deeper relationship? Should she come right out and tell him she was madly in love with him? If he thought her beautiful and could kiss her like that, she must have a chance. But what was the meaning of his *but?* The word that always ensured her dreams never came true.

Jeanette rolled over in bed. It came to her, just what she needed to do. There was no getting back to sleep. She might as well get up and prepare Saturday breakfast for the gang before heading to Helen's. She would be just the person to talk to.

Jeanette rose and readied herself for the day. She put on a cheery yellow dress to match her mood. She softened the look of her bun with a few tendrils hanging down and pinched some color into her cheeks. When she gazed into the mirror above the washstand, she tried to imagine what Theo saw. Her flattened mouth lifted, and a forced smile emerged. No. A smile should not be forced but should come from the heart. She stepped closer to the mirror and closed her eyes. With a deep breath in, she thought about what God's word said about her and how Theo had echoed the same message. The birth of a smile from deep within broke free, and she opened her eyes. They lit up with a delight that made them sparkle. A bubble of laughter slipped free. Her smile revealed a set of nice white teeth and changed her expression to that which she had to concede did look rather becoming.

She left the bedroom and practically skipped down the steps and into the kitchen. A hum slipped from her lips as she lit the wood stove and put the coffee on.

"You sound cheery this morning." Pa came from the direction of the back porch and plunked down on his chair. "Be a dear and bring me a cup of that brew, will ya?"

Jeanette poured him a coffee and brought the steaming cup his way.

"Funny thing. Theo is already out in the barn working, and he's whistling' up a storm too."

She was not about to get into her personal life with Pa. As

much as she loved him, he could not begin to understand. *She didn't understand.*

"Putting two and two together, I'd say that maybe a few happy sparks are igniting."

Jeanette felt heat pour into her cheeks. "Stop it, Pa. It's none of your business." She tried to stifle the smile kicking at the sides of her mouth, demanding freedom.

He put up his hands. "Hey, just saying, it's hard to miss the humming and whistling duo." He chuckled.

Tessie wandered into the kitchen, her hair sticking up in every direction. She was dragging her favorite blanket. "I'm hungry."

Jeanette picked her up. "Well, my sweet pea, what shall we make you for your first breakfast, which you can eat long before the others wake. How about a piece of bread and honey?"

Tessie nodded. Her smile was swallowed in her cherubim cheeks.

"My favorite too." Pa reached out his arms. "Should we have some together?"

Jeanette put Tessie down, and she ran over to him. He lifted her on his knee. They looked so perfect together. A sleepy-eyed girl with a kindhearted grandpa snuggling her in the warmth of his hug. In such a short time every one of the kids had taken to Pa. He was a natural, playing games, telling his crazy made-up stories, or just good at listening to them and asking questions.

She smoothed the fresh butter and a thick layer of honey on the bread.

"Can you make me one of those, too?"

Jeanette started at the sound of Theo's voice, so near to her. How had he entered without her hearing? Well, she was rather preoccupied. She snuck a peek. "Sure."

He leaned in whispering. "Thank you, beautiful." He moved to the stove and poured himself a cup of coffee.

She feared her burning cheeks were blooming red. With two

pieces of bread ready, she moved across to the table and set them before Pa and Tessie. "Thank you, beautiful," Pa said loudly.

"Thank you, beautiful," Tessie mimicked.

Had Pa heard Theo? Not likely with his hearing problem, but he was good at reading lips, and he had probably been all eagle-eyed. Sheer panic seared through her, but Theo chuckled. He didn't seem to mind.

Jeanette crossed to the counter and concentrated on slathering another thick piece of bread with butter and honey.

Theo leaned against the counter nearby, sipping his hot coffee. "Is that one for me?"

"Here." She handed him the plate.

"Thank you—"

One lift of her brow told him he dare not say more.

"A quick breakfast this morning, and then I'm off to visit Helen. With teaching and all the extra happenings around this place, I've sorely neglected her."

"I'm headed into town for supplies," Theo said. "Do you want a ride?"

Quite frankly, she needed some space. She needed time to digest what happened the night before, Theo's kiss and his *but*. "No, thanks. I love a brisk walk in the morning." She glanced his way to see that his smile had disappeared.

"Why don't you ride in with Theo?" Pa said. "You can walk back for your fresh air. It'll give you more time with Helen."

She wanted to throttle him. Pa knew exactly what he was doing, throwing them together at every turn.

What could she say? Pa had made it impossible to turn Theo down. "Sounds reasonable, but let me get a pot of oatmeal on and fry up some bacon for Jacob. Oh, and make some ham and eggs for Ben. They're his favorite, and he doesn't even mind them cold."

"You don't have to cater to the children," Theo said. "You're spoiling them, and what will happen when it's only me and them?"

Jeanette's head snapped up. She could not keep her upturned lips from wilting. She bit her tongue to swallow back the words she wouldn't say in front of Pa. But that was just the kind of remark that shut her down. Did Theo think she wasn't emotionally involved? She loved his children with all that was within her. And what about the way he had kissed her the night before…?

Yet he was still seeing his life alone. She was in no rush, but she had hoped it meant something.

Jeanette stared at him, and he stared back. She turned away with a jut of her chin and a flick of her head. She slammed the cast iron pot onto the stove a little too vigorously, causing some of the water to splash out. The hiss and pop of the bubbles on the heated surface matched her mood.

Pa cleared his voice. "We're having a checkers tournament this morning, girls against the boys, with me on the girls side helping Tessie here. Ain't that right?" He bounced Tessie on his knee, and she giggled.

"Isn't that right," Jeanette corrected without thinking.

Pa made his eyebrows dance. "Ain't that right, Tessie girl?"

Tessie giggled all the more.

Jeanette moved about the kitchen with precision and speed. She had to get out of there. Last night, she had not wanted to know what Theo's *but* meant, but after the way the evening ended and what had transpired this morning, she needed answers. And he had better be prepared to give them.

~

For the first time, her silence did not feel comfortable. Theo could feel the heat of her disapproval as she sat with her starched spine at the edge of the buckboard seat as far from him as she could get. But what was he to say? He wanted to court her like she deserved and then ask her to marry him, but he had nothing to give her, not even a home. She had insecurities, but so did he. His inability to provide a roof over his children's head, and his previous wife's disparaging remarks, burned deep. She had always laughed at the job her father had given him, calling it token employment despite how hard he worked.

Last night he'd forgotten himself. Jeanie's tears, her obvious pain from unkind remarks, he understood only too well. He had wanted to bring healing, but what had transpired and his desire for her had complicated the situation. How could he explain without trampling her fragile state? Enough people had already done a good job of damaging the way she felt about herself. He sure didn't want to add to the pile. Should he tell her he loved her? But then what? Ask her to wait for an undisclosed amount of time to get his life together? That seemed so selfish and self-serving. Or should he just keep a respectable distance and leave the door open for someone else to love her like she deserved?

Oh God, help me. Give me the words. Help her to understand. He had been trying to talk to God rather than rail at Him. He knew if Jeanette and he were ever to have a relationship, God would be a big part of their lives. For the first time in his life, he had seen the hands of kindness extended in the name of Jesus through Jeanette and Jeb. He wanted to believe that God cared about the details, but this was another caveat. He had a long way to go.

"Jeanie, we need to talk."

"What's the point? You obviously don't realize how invested I am in your family."

"I'll try to explain." But could he? In truth, he had said what he had to slow down the runaway train he had boarded the night before.

She shifted her body towards him, and fire blazed from her sparkling eyes. "Go ahead."

"I don't want my problems, the things I need to work through, to impact you."

"Oh, you mean the *buts*. Jeanie you're a good friend, but… Jeanie, you're beautiful, but… Jeanie, don't spoil the children because, as soon as I have money to get out of here, I'll be gone."

He pulled the reins hard and brought the wagon to a halt. He turned toward her. "That's not it at all. I've made a mess of this, and I'm sorry."

"No. Don't say you're sorry. Figure out what you want from me and let me know. But until that time, no more evenings on the porch, no more touching, or kissing, or calling me beautiful. No more." She hopped off the wagon.

"Jeanie."

"And no more Jeanie. It's Jeanette and I'll walk the rest of the way."

He sat in the wagon as she marched down the road ahead of him. Tall and magnificent. She was everything he wanted for himself and his children. But he had much to accomplish first. Last night, he'd been so bent on making her believe she was beautiful that he had forgotten the timeline, the things he needed in place to even be a good father, let alone a husband and a man worthy of her. Instead, her very essence had eclipsed all else. He would not let that happen again.

She was right. He was the problem. He didn't mean to take her kindness for granted. And of course, she would think things were moving in a certain direction after he'd kissed her like he had and then flirted this morning. It took a moment of clarity, seeing her dote on the children, to realize he could never ask a woman as grand as she was to wait in the wings for him to get his life together. He had unwisely put the horse before the cart. Best to leave her be, as she requested. What would it gain to let her know how he really felt if he could not act upon it? With them living together, that would be sheer lunacy. Distance was indeed wisdom.

He snapped the reins and plodded forward. As he passed her, a sharp pang of loneliness sliced through.

CHAPTER 30

"I'm tired, Helen." Jeanette wrung her hands as she paced the small parlor floor. "Tired of specks of happiness in a dust storm of pain. Tired of being a woman who will only ever befriend a man, never find love. Look at what happened between Solomon and me."

"We both know that the end of that courtship had everything to do with your feelings for Theo."

"No. It had to do with the fact we never got past the friendship state."

Helen sat on the settee and patted the seat beside her. "Come, my child."

"That's just it. I'm not a child. I want a woman's life. Is that too much to ask of God?"

"I love you like you're my own child. I hurt when you hurt. Come, let me pray with you." She patted the seat again.

Jeanette was too angry to pray. For a fleeting moment, she'd thought she was beautiful in the eyes of at least one man, desirable even. She'd believed Theo could learn to love her. Then, as had happened with every other dream, reality came crashing in. In kindness he had tried to console her but it seemed kissing

JEANETTE'S GIFT

meant something different to a man, or maybe just to a man who'd been previously married. At twenty-nine she should understand the ways of a man with a woman. Instead, she was no more experienced than her teenage pupils.

She plunked down on the settee next to Helen.

Helen took her hand and squeezed, bending her head and closing her eyes. "Dear Jesus, we come to you asking for wisdom. Father, you know everything, and we understand so little. And so we come."

Silence filled the room. Jeanette had no words, neither did she feel like praying out loud. She had prayed far too many prayers already, begging God for the desire of her heart—for a man who would love her, for a family, for that which she felt she was created. From looking after Theo's children and being a teacher, she knew she was gifted with children. Why was the road to marriage next thing to impossible for her?

Helen raised her head. "I sense in the Spirit that God has wonderful things ahead for you, but you must be patient. Two words stand out, *healing* and *truth*."

Jeanette puffed out an exaggerated breath. How could she tell her friend that two obscure words like *healing* and *truth* were not exactly the wisdom she was looking for? And hadn't she been patient enough?

"But Helen, Theo kissed me. Really kissed me. He told me I was beautiful, like he really meant it. Then, in the next breath, he told me not to spoil the children with their favorite foods because how would he manage when he's on his own again? What does that mean? I need God to give me wisdom regarding that."

Helen rubbed Jeanette's back and patted her knee with the other hand. "I know, dear. Life can be complicated, and nobody wants to be told to have patience."

"But I've been patient. I'm not exactly a spring chicken." Jeanette half-laughed between broken sobs. "Surely, God knows this." She wiped the tears with her handkerchief and swiped at her runny nose. "I need to know if it's safe to love those children or if they're going to be ripped from my life."

"It is always safe to love."

"Come on, Helen, you know what I mean."

"Love comes at a price, a cost. Are you willing to love regardless of the outcome, or do you want to protect your heart more?"

Jeanette buried her face in her hands. "That's just it. I do love them. I can't stop loving. And the longer they stay, the deeper it grows. It scares me how much I love them."

"That kind of love is never wrong. But you must trust God with the outcome. Trust Him enough to love, even if it hurts, even if it is not self-serving, even if it's just for a season."

A pang of sorrow sliced through at that thought. She wanted to see them grow up, attend their weddings. She longed to be their mama.

"Those children need you right now. Today. You're placed right where God wants you. It is not by happenstance. This is heavenly ordained."

"But what about me?"

"That's a question each Christian asks along the way when God asks them to do something that may or may not have their desired outcome."

Jeanette closed her eyes. She wanted to close her ears and her heart too. But no, she had done that for years, and it was a cold and lonely existence. Giving to this family brought purpose and life into her world. She would never regret that. And no matter what happened, she would always be part of their history, their story. She wanted to leave an indelible mark of love.

She opened her eyes. "You're right. I can choose to shut down, or I can choose to love, come what may."

Helen patted her knee. "That's the truth I was talking about.

Let God be God and trust Him even when you don't have all the answers. And that goes for the children's father as well. I know you love him too."

Jeanette didn't even attempt to look shocked. She nodded. "This is so much more than the infatuations I've had in the past. Being so close to him yet worlds apart is agony of the soul."

"I daresay he needs your unconditional love, just as the children do. You know, the kind that doesn't demand too much, too soon. He's a man who has lost a lot—a wife, his mother, and now his farm, the very livelihood to feed his family. That would be hard on any man."

Her conscience pricked. She had been thinking only of herself. What about what he needed? He required time to sort out his life, and she could give him that. In the end, if they found their way together, that would be wonderful, but she had to let go of all her expectations. She could, however, do one thing different, something she had never done before. She would fight for the man she loved. She would allow him all the time in the world he needed, but she would be waiting and ready when he was.

"I think I can pray now." She hugged Helen and bowed her head. "Dear Father, help me. Give me strength to put myself aside and just love as you have so freely loved me. Give me patience. Pour your unconditional love through me to share with this family. Thank you for trusting me with such fragile work. I ask for courage today, and for help to not worry about the outcome. Amen."

"Amen and amen." Helen pulled Jeanette's hands into her wrinkled weathered fingers and squeezed tight. "You are such a beautiful lady. I hope you know that."

Jeanette heard Theo's sincere words echo in her head. She thought of the love that God had given her to bestow upon Theo's children and how they lapped it up. Her giftings of teaching, decorating, playing the piano, and singing came to mind. Beauty could be found in many forms.

She smiled at Helen. "Yes. I believe I am."

~

Since that day of surrender at Helen's house over a month before, Jeanette experienced a freedom she had never felt before. October's leaves fell, and November's chill arrived. She was at peace. There was no ulterior motive for her love or acts of service, rather a knowing that she was right where she was supposed to be, doing what she was meant to do.

She hung up the dish towel after another lively evening meal and set out to make her rounds, hugging each child good-night, even the older boys, whether they liked it or not. They were sprawled all over the house. Pa was teaching Jacob and Charlie how to bank the fire for the night. Ben practiced his skills on the return wheel.

"Look at this trick I learned." He thrust out his toy with a flick of his wrist. It spun on its string from one side of his body to the other before he snapped it back into his hand.

"You're getting really good at that." She would have to get over the fact that it reminded her of Victoria. After all, she had only herself to blame for that one. She had gone ahead of God and invited Victoria into that family.

Ben beamed at her praise.

She approached Sarah, who was cozied up in a chair reading *Gulliver's Travels* and kissed her head. Sarah looked up at her and smiled.

She thought twice about interrupting Theo who was tucking the girls in upstairs but decided that if she was going to love well, she would do what came naturally.

She poked her head into the girls' bedroom. "I came to say goodnight."

JEANETTE'S GIFT

Theo was in the middle of the bed with a girl tucked into each side. How wonderful it would be to rest her head against his strong chest at the end of the day. She stilled her wayward thoughts and reminded herself of the goal. This was not about her.

"Will you say our prayers with us?" Tessie asked. "Papa's done the story, and I like it when you pray with us."

Jeanette looked at Theo, who nodded. She entered.

"Goodie." Laura added. "Move over, Papa. Make room for one more."

There was no way she was going to squish into that bed with them. "How about I sit on one side while you pray, Tessie, and then I'll move over to the other side while Laura prays? That way I'll be able to hug you both good-night."

She sat and placed her hand on Tessie's small, folded fingers. "Go ahead, Tessie. I know how good you are at this." She smiled down at the child and closed her eyes.

Theo's hand touched both of theirs with a squeeze. She almost jumped out of her skin, and his hand was gone in an instant. He hadn't touched her since she had asked him not to over a month before. One small touch, and warmth penetrated her skin like a coal burning its way into her heart.

"Dear Jesus."

Tessie's sweet voice brought her back to earth.

"'Now I lay me down to sleep, I pray the Lord, my soul to keep. And as I live for you each day, I pray thee, Lord, to guide my way.' Amen."

"Good job, sweetie." Jeanette pulled her hand free and leaned close. She kissed Tessie's forehead and gave her a hug. The feel of her tiny arms around her shoulders warmed her through to the soul. The thought that Theo was watching the whole thing brought heat to her cheeks. She rounded the bed and sat beside Laura. "Now your turn." She picked up Laura's hand, careful to keep it out of Theo's range, but Laura pulled their joined hands onto her lap and placed her Pa's hand over top them all. His thumb found the inside of Jeanette's wrist. Surely, he could feel the frantic uptick of her pulse. Shivers skittered up her arms.

"Dear Jesus. Be with Grammie in heaven, and my mama who I can't remember. Please bless my daddy and don't take him just yet, 'cause we really need him."

Oh, goodness. The child was afraid of losing her last parent. Jeanette could barely stem the tears biting behind her lids.

"Bless my new grandpa, Jeb. I really like him, and thank you for this home. Please don't make us have to move again anytime soon. Bless all my brothers and sisters. But Lord, most of all, bless the mama I pray will someday be mine. You know who I mean. Amen."

Jeanette's eyes flew open and landed on Theo. His eyes met hers, but he wore a sad look.

She hugged Laura with all her might. Laura would not let go. "You're that mama," she whispered into Jeanette's ear.

Jeanette kissed her cheek and popped to her feet. "Good night, my loves." She scurried from the room, tears streaming down her face. Down the steps she ran, grabbed her cloak at the door, and slipped out onto the porch. The cool air bit at her cheeks, and she bundled the cloak more closely around her. Those children had experienced so much loss. Was she doing right by them, filling in as a mama who may never be theirs?

God, I don't know. I don't understand. I thought You told me to love unconditionally, but in the end, will I be just another disappointment to their prayers, another loss those dear children must endure?

She moved to the banister and raised her head to the sky. A thousand twinkling stars studded the canopy of black. Wisps of clouds scuttled across the silvery moon. All looked as it should in the heavens, but what about down here on earth? Every decision she made impacted those dear sweet children. *God, am I doing the right thing?*

I love you. I love them. Trust Me.

A peace, a knowing, flooded in, and her anxious heart calmed. She dried the tears from her cheeks with her sleeve. No more crying. God loved those children even more than she did, and He loved her.

The screen door creaked open. "May I join you?" Theo's voice broke into the stillness. "I know you come out here each evening to have some alone time, but...that prayer."

She nodded but didn't look his way. Her body tingled with awareness as he joined her at the railing.

"I knew my kids were affected by all the loss, but that prayer..."

Her hands gripped the wood railing so hard that it bit into her flesh.

"How insecure they must be." His voice sounded strained.

Her throat went tight and parched. What could she say? She'd been thinking the same thing. "Kids are resilient, as long as they're loved." She ventured a peek.

"I love them all right, but I couldn't even keep a roof over their heads." His voice cracked, and she looked up. A muscle jerked in his jaw.

She no longer cared about her well-laid plan not to touch him. She needed to console her friend. She snugged into his side and her arm instinctively wound around his waist. "I'm so sorry." He turned into her hug facing her. His large frame engulfed her, and she tucked her trembling body into the warmth of his arms. One moment bled into another, but she was not inclined to move. Obviously, neither was he. Somehow, that hug said what words could not.

Finally, his arms dropped, and he leaned both hands on the banister, looking into the dark.

"I know Laura wants you to be her mama, but what have I to offer?"

Everything within her wanted to convince him they had all they needed right under this roof. Pa would be delighted to have them marry and stay forever. But the Spirit was directing her to remain quiet and not voice what she desired.

"You don't have to figure that all out now. Your children are safe. You're working hard to provide for them, and Pa and I love having you around. Just take this time to heal." Helen's two words came to mind. God had asked her to trust him, and though she had thought it was her who needed the healing, she realized in that moment it was Theo.

"You're the best friend any person could have," he said.

Somehow that declaration didn't even disappoint. Friendship was a sure foundation, and she would choose to be happy with that.

"No. Let me at least be honest." He turned toward her. "You're so much more than a friend, Jeanie girl. I don't quite know how to put into words all you mean to me. But maybe in time…" His voice rumbled with an intensity she wanted to kiss from his lips. His woodsy scent, the feel of his breath fanning her face… All beckoned, but the Spirit said *wait*.

They both stepped back at the same time. "I think a walk would be good. I've got so much to sort." He stepped forward and kissed the top of her head like he had with his girls, then turned away.

Across the porch, down the steps, she watched him go until his silhouette faded into the black. Her body ached to run after him, to hold him, but it was as if heavenly arms were holding her still. God had this.

CHAPTER 31

Jeanette stood in the kitchen immobilized. All she could think about was the letter she fingered in her pocket. She pulled it free. The paper trembled in her hands as she opened it to read once again. Was the school superintendent, Mr. Gilliam, really going to put her under the microscope at the end of the week with the likes of Agnus and Victoria present? Imagine those two busy bodies getting the superintendent all fired up. All for what? Helping a family in need?

She had not a thing to worry about. Nothing improper or immoral had gone on. She raised her hand to her lips at the thought of Theo's kiss.

If Mr. Gilliam knew, would it jeopardize her job? But no, she had every right to court whomever she pleased. It was only if she became engaged that she had to notify the school board. Plus, she and Theo were not courting. What were they? Friends certainly. But honestly, more than friends. Their situation was unique, a blending of families under one roof, and the added responsibility of maintaining propriety being the local schoolteacher. Mixed with her obvious attraction to him and his—

what? She was not sure what that declaration of *more than friends* had meant.

With so many questions in her own mind and heart about their relationship, how would she do under scrutiny? Would she blush? Would she bluster? Or would she remain calm and matter-of-fact?

A trickle of sweat inched down her spine.

She slipped the letter into her apron pocket and rubbed at her temples. Soon, the day would erupt in activity, and she needed to get breakfast on and supper organized for when she arrived home from a day of teaching.

"What is it, my girl?"

Jeanette started at the sound of Pa's gravelly voice.

"Pour me a brew?" He lifted his tin cup. "And tell me what troubles you."

"It's nothing." She filled his cup and hers.

"If you think I'm gonna believe that expression means *nothing*, then you take me for a fool."

She plopped in a chair at the table. "Fine then." She pulled the letter from her pocket and slid it across the table to him.

He unfolded it and read, his bushy brows knitting together. "Seems like the two of you will finally be forced to speak truth to one another."

"What do you mean?"

"Come now, daughter. You and Theo have been dancing around—"

"Did I hear my name?" Theo walked in and headed for the coffee pot on the wood stove.

Jeanette snatched her letter back hiding it on her lap, and shook her head at Pa. Heat rushed to her face. The last person she wanted in on this discussion was Theo. He had enough on his plate. This was her battle to fight.

"By the look on my daughter's face, I reckon you best ask her." Pa stood, lifted his coffee cup to his lips, and winked. "I'll be in the barn. Call me when breakfast is ready." The slamming of the back door left the two of them in silence.

"What was this about dancing?" Theo asked.

Jeanette stood and slid the letter back into her pocket as he looked down to fill his cup. "Katherine's Christmas ball is coming up. There will be dancing." She hated to misdirect the conversation, but it was for the best. He didn't need this added worry.

His eyes lit up in response. "So, you want to know if I can dance?"

She began making breakfast. "Well, can you?" Heat rushed to her face. She was a terrible liar. She lifted an egg from the basket and cracked it on the side of the bowl. And then another.

His hand came over hers as she reached for a third. The next thing she knew, she was being twirled around the kitchen floor to an off-tune song he was trying to sing. "I may not be able to sing, but I can dance."

He whirled her around, and she giggled.

"One does not grow up in Richmond among the who's who without a solid grasp of this art."

She stumbled in his arms, stepping on his toes, but his grip tightened, and he lifted her off the floor, making her feel as light as air. His lead was superb. Not that she had much experience at all. She could count the dances she had in her lifetime on one hand. "It seems you're a much better dancer than I." Laughter filled her voice.

"So, you'll allow me to accompany you to the dance?"

She hadn't thought that far ahead. The annual dance was always a painful outing, one she attended only to please her sister. To think she would finally be escorted, and with the man of her dreams? What was there to consider? "I'd be honored to go with you, Theo."

"That's settled. Now you can agree with your pa when he says we've been dancing." He slowed to a stop with her still in his arms. One hand brushed the side of her face, and she held her breath. Just how much had Theo heard? She would give up her job in an instant to live life with him, if only he would ask.

"Papa." Tessie stood in the doorway, holding her old rag doll by its arm. The one Victoria had bought her had crashed from the loft into a thousand pieces, just as Jeanette had feared. Tessie's morning hair was tousled and stuck in every direction. "What are you doing?"

"He's teaching me to dance," Jeanette offered.

"Teach me. Teach me."

Tessie ran in, and with one swoop she was in Theo's arms, but he never let go of Jeanette. He whirled them both around. Tessie giggled and Jeanette's heart warmed. They were so perfect together. If only dreams came true.

"What exactly are your intentions concerning this family?" Mr. Gilliam's stern, unyielding expression sent a shiver down Jeanette's spine. She looked around the small schoolhouse room and back at the county superintendent. His head, balder than a coffee bean, was accented by the lines grooved deep across his brow.

She was thankful for Colby, who sat beside her. He was on the school board, and his presence brought the moral support she needed. He and Mr. Gilliam were longtime friends.

Agnus and Victoria sat across from her, glaring. They were the ones spearheading this inquisition.

"My father and I have only one intention, to help a family who did not have a roof over their heads."

"You must admit, this arrangement is highly unusual and does not sit well with some members of the community. These two ladies"—Mr. Gilliam pointed at Agnus and Victoria—"are not the only ones concerned at the questionable respectability of this situation."

Jeanette's throat tightened to the point she could barely swallow. Who were the others? She had more to worry about than she anticipated.

"And there are allegations I must investigate." Mr. Gilliam's eyes narrowed as he pulled a pair of glasses from his pocket, slid them on the end of his pointed nose, and looked down at the paper in front of him.

"Allegations? Of what nature?" She hated that her voice wavered.

"It's not a pleasant part of my job to have to ask such personal questions." He lifted his gaze from his notes. "It says here that the children have been talking to their friends about the swimming lessons you gave them in the summer, in the company of their father. Then the family moved in with you and your pa, and it's understood that the bedrooms are all on the same level." Mr. Gilliam's eye flicked up and down on his notes. "And just recently Tessie was telling anyone who would listen that she joined you and Mr. Wallace dancing in the kitchen. Is this accurate?"

Heat burned from Jeanette's neck to her hairline. "All of that is correct. But there's nothing improper about any of those scenarios. Twirling around a kitchen giving a child a taste of happiness is hardly a need for concern. Is it?"

"You are teaching the children of this community. A higher standard is required."

"But—"

"Miss Williams, you signed a contract fully aware of the importance of your single status. If you wish to change that status, we will ask for your resignation."

"I am not engaged, nor do I have any promises to that nature."

"You understand you have stated your allegiance wholly to the responsibility of teaching the children of this community?"

"Yes."

"So, nothing has changed between you and Mr. Wallace?"

How could she answer that question? What would Mr. Gilliam think if he knew there had been more this past summer, horseback rides in the dark, shared kisses, and walks in the moonlight? But then what did all that mean? Theo had committed to no more than friendship.

Victoria jutted her chin in the air. "She may want things to be different. And her father is trying to fandangle a certain outcome, but I'm doubtful that Mr. Wallace would fall for something so obvious. However, the fact that the local schoolmarm is living under the same roof with a widower and sharing bedrooms on the same floor should be an outrage to all."

"Be honest, Victoria." Colby spoke for the first time. "The whole community knows that you've had your eye on Theo. You're just put out because he didn't choose you. Bitter does not look good on you."

Jeanette wanted to throw her arms around her brother-in-law.

Victoria's mouth opened in a perfect O. "He merely needs time to get his life turned around, to feel worthy of my attention. And that woman and her father are trying everything in their power to entrap him."

"Would it help if Katherine and I offered our home to the Wallaces?" Colby looked at Mr. Gilliam. "We would've done so immediately, but we've been in the throes of a large renovation. It will be done before the Christmas ball, and we could—"

"Wait just a moment. That does not excuse the immoral behavior that has already occurred." Agnus focused her beady eyes on Jeanette. "This woman's character is questionable. Following in the steps of her sister, she is."

Jeanette sat up straight as a pin, her head held high. "How

dare you level such accusations against me or bring my redeemed sister into this?" Her hands clenching into tight fists on her lap. "I've been an upstanding member of this community my entire life, and I have done nothing to be ashamed of. Can you say the same, with your shameless attempt to secure my job?"

"Are you telling me this little arrangement has not led to inappropriate kissing?" Agnes asked. "Or Mr. Wallace visiting your bedroom?"

Victoria's head snapped in Agnus' direction. "Of course, it hasn't. Look at the woman."

"Ladies, ladies. Stop." Mr. Wallace held up his hand.

Jeanette longed to wipe that smug look off Victoria's face with the truth, but that would jeopardize her job. She hoped her heated face didn't tell the story and that their bickering had deflected further interrogation.

"So, you and Mr. Wallace are just friends," Mr. Gilliam asked. "He hasn't made advances or kissed you?"

Jeanette's gaze dropped to her lap, and she smoothed imaginary wrinkles from her day dress. As a good Christian, how could she answer truthfully without scandal breaking out? Without losing her beloved teaching position?

"Go ahead." Colby rested a hand on her shoulder. "Tell Mr. Gilliam the truth. He's a fair man who is here to help you."

Jeanette lifted her head. She could not lie. "He kissed me, but only because I was upset, and he was trying to comfort me."

"Well, I never." Victoria flapped her handkerchief furiously in front of her face.

Mr. Gilliam nodded slowly while she held her breath. "And I'm assuming that, with your father at home, there would be no danger of Theo entering your bedroom?"

Oh gosh, this was not going well. Sometimes her Christianity and the need to tell the truth was most inconvenient. "Once, Theo did enter my bedroom."

Victoria gasped.

"I knew it," Agnus said. "She had that guilty look."

"But nothing inappropriate—"

"See, her morals are so loose that she doesn't consider a man in her bedroom inappropriate." Agnus wagged her finger.

"Agnus, Victoria, and Colby, can you please leave the room? I'd like to speak to Jeanette alone." Mr. Gilliam pointed toward the door.

They stood to take their leave. Victoria gave Jeanette a snide look, and Agnus shook her head in disgust, her double chin jiggling.

Jeanette had done it now. The truth would cost her the one thing that had given her full confidence, teaching the children of Lacey Spring.

"Miss Williams, I think you understand what I'm required to do. With deep regret, being that you have been the best teacher this county has ever had the privilege to hire, I must relieve you of your teaching duties."

Tears blurred her vision. "Just like that?"

"Based on your admission of having a man in your bedroom, you must understand, there is little I can do." His eyes beheld genuine sympathy.

"Surely you'll let me ease out of the role. Say good-bye to the children?" Her cheeks burned as embarrassment crawled up her spine.

Mr. Gilliam shook his head. "Agnus Belford has offered on numerous occasions to fill in if needed. She will take over until we find a suitable permanent replacement."

Jeanette sniffed and pulled out her handkerchief. "But...but I love those children."

"I know you do. But we must maintain utmost morality, and this situation has placed yours in question. For your sake, I would suggest that you and Mr. Wallace get married post haste. It will mitigate the rumors that are sure to fly."

He didn't understand. No one understood, not even her. How could she explain that they had never spoken of marriage?

Her beloved teaching position was gone, and so was her reputation. The sheer embarrassment of the town gossip that would indeed follow with the likes of Agnus and Victoria involved sent a shudder through her body.

"I'm sorry, Miss Williams." Mr. Gilliam stood to leave. "Can I get you a drink of water?"

"No, just give me a moment."

"I will let myself out. Colby will take you home when you're ready. Don't forget to gather your personal items."

She sat there clenching the chair with her hands so tightly that they turned chalk white. And here she had tried to help Victoria. Even pushed Theo and the children on her. How wrong she had been. Neither of those women had an ounce of kindness. The fury, the grief, the shock spiraled into a vortex of emotion. With trembling hands, she gathered her things and placed them in her bag. With one last look around the cozy schoolroom, she walked out. She would not cry. Not until she was alone.

CHAPTER 32

*H*ow would Jeanette tell Pa? His daughter would be considered desperate and immoral, and it would break his heart.

She sat in silence beside Colby as the horse plodded closer to home. The wagon bumped and jostled along the rutted roadway back to the farm. The sky was swollen with thick gray clouds as miserable as her mood. She pulled her cloak hood up to protect against the wind chill.

"I know it's not my place," Colby asked, "but do you love Theo?"

"Yes."

"Then, my recommendation is to tell him. Don't live a day apart longer than it takes to be married. Life is too short."

Fine for Colby to say. He didn't understand the complexities. "You're assuming he loves me in return." She looked out over the landscape without seeing anything.

Colby chuckled. "Pretty sure by the way he glared at Solomon at church for months on end that his heart is worn on his sleeve. Trust me, I know what it's like to have it bad."

Jeanette's pulse tripped and bubbled like a swift-running

creek. Had Theo worked through the pain of his first marriage enough to trust again?

"And don't worry about the gossip. Anyone who knows you knows you're an upright Christian woman. If you weren't, you would have lied in that meeting. Though Theo entering your bedroom for any reason was indeed unwise."

"I agree. But how am I going to tell Pa? How am I going to keep from making Theo feel pressured into marriage to save my reputation?"

Colby pulled the wagon to a stop in front of the farmhouse. "Some men need a little push to realize what they have to lose."

A push? No way. She was not going to do that. She wanted a family of her own, but not enough to take a husband who didn't want her.

Colby touched her arm. "Do you want me to come in and talk to your pa with you?"

"As much as that would be comforting, I need to handle this myself." She could not admit to Colby how embarrassing the conversation would be. The last thing she needed would be another set of ears. But she had to get it done. By tomorrow, every kid in the county would know they have a new teacher, including those in her household.

"Sometimes, the worst things have a way of bringing about the best." Colby hopped down and came around to her side of the wagon. "When I left for Richmond, not able to spend another day living around your sister without us being together, I had no idea my absence would inspire what I'd been waiting years for. She was in much the same doldrums as your Theo, looking back too much to look forward."

Colby had no idea what looking back was like for Theo, and all the damage he had endured in his marriage. Jeanette took his hand and stepped down. "Thanks for your support today."

"I'll be praying for you. And if you think it will be better for you to have the Wallace family move in with us—"

"No. Those kids have been through so much already. Another drastic change would be too hard on them. And at this point, it won't bring my job back anyway."

"I wasn't thinking about your job but your reputation."

"That's the least of my worries. I'm used to unkind remarks, and it just so happens I know the truth about myself."

"Good for you." Colby patted her on the arm.

"Please tell Katherine. I know she'll understand. And I'd appreciate your prayers."

"You can count on that." He gave her a quick hug before jumping up on his wagon.

Jeanette headed up the porch steps into the house. She had to find Pa.

The kids were sprawled all over the house in different rooms, but no Pa and no Theo. Jacob said they were out in the back field making plans for the spring planting. Of all days for the two of them to be late in coming in. A needle of concern stitched its way up her spine. How would she break the news to her pa, to Theo, to the children? A headache pressed upon her temples.

She peeled potatoes and carrots for the evening meal with shaky hands. The reality of losing her teaching position was slowly sinking in, and dread weighed heavily in the pit of her stomach. Her brave words to Colby were being tested. She could hear the tongues wagging in her mind. The desperate spinster taking advantage of the poor widower, trapping him into marriage.

She could run away to Richmond and find a teaching position there. Grandmother would take her in.

No, her reputation with the school board would follow her, and how could she leave Theo's children. But oh, the horror of this all coming out and Theo thinking he *had* to make this right.

Even when dusk fell, Pa and Theo did not come in.

Jeanette pulled the roast from the oven and sliced it into

thick generous pieces. She had a hungry bunch eyeing the food. Everything was ready for the evening meal by the time the two men sauntered inside, chattering about which seed for which field.

"It smells heavenly in here," Theo said.

"Yup, my daughter can cook up a pot roast like no other." Pa hobbled across the kitchen and plopped down in his chair. "That was a bit too long on this foot." He bent over and rubbed at his ankle. "This getting old is for the birds. Healing takes twice as long."

"Are you all right?" Jeanette moved in to take a look.

Pa waved her away. "No fussing allowed." He swung his foot under the table. "Bring on the grub, darling daughter." He grabbed his fork in one hand and the knife in the other and held them in his fists on both sides of his plate. "Hungrier than a hog in a feed of corn husks."

The children laughed as they joined him at the table. Theo sat at the other end with a smile on his face.

All that was about to change. Somehow, she had to find the strength to let them know. The children would no longer have their teacher. Pa's standing in the community would take a beating. Her good reputation was gone, and Theo would no doubt feel pressure to make everything better by marrying her. Exactly what she did not want.

∼

Theo watched Jeanette bring the food to the table. He knew her well enough to sense that something wasn't right. Her face held a strained look, and she kept biting at her lower lip. But why? Was it all getting too much for her, the cooking and cleaning up after his family, teaching full time, volunteering to help with the music at church? How could he ever repay her for taking on the role of the children's mother?

He was making her a gift at the moment, but that was small potatoes to all she had done.

There was a tremble to her hands as she set down the plate of meat. Something was very wrong.

All through the meal, while Jeb and the kids chattered, she said nothing.

Bands of tension wrapped tightly in Theo's chest almost as if he could feel her angst.

Pa turned to her. "How did that meeting go today?"

Jeanette's eyes widened. She shook her head.

"What meeting was that?" Theo asked.

"The school superintendent had a few complaints about the living arrangements," Jeb said. "Spurred on by a bunch of busybodies, if you ask me."

"Pa, I don't want to talk about this right now."

Jeb obviously didn't clue into the panic on Jeanette's face.

Theo's stomach dropped. That meeting had not gone well.

"Why?" Jeb looked at his daughter with kind eyes filled with concern. "Surely the superintendent could see through the gossip. Nothing immoral is happening under this roof."

"My services will no longer be needed at the school."

Theo watched as those sitting around the table erupted into questions, everyone speaking at the same time.

"They fired you?" Jeb's brows knit together as if he was trying to piece the puzzle together.

"What? You won't be our teacher anymore?" Sarah's eyes grew bigger than saucers.

"Don't ask me to go to school, if that's the case." Jacob added.

"Me neither." Charlie slammed down his fork.

"Yeah. No school for me." Ben chimed in.

Laura's eyes filled with tears, and Tessie burst out crying.

"Stop, children." Theo held up his hand and turned to Jeanette. "Why would they let you go?"

"It's considered improper for your family to be living here

when we're not…" She could not finish the sentence. Too much like asking for a proposal.

"They don't want us here?" Laura's voice wavered.

"It's not about you kids." She smoothed a curl from Laura's eyes. "It's about a widower and a spinster, your pa and me, not being married but sharing the same home."

Theo pressed on the knuckles of one hand, and they popped and groaned. What was he to say? Jeanette was paying the price for his problems. He should take his family and go. But where?

"Then tie the knot," Jeb said matter-of-factly. "You two seem to have everything figured out, 'cept the best part."

Jeanette's cheeks bloomed crimson. "Pa."

Laura jumped up from the bench and came around to Theo. "Ask her, Pa. Ask her to be your wife and our mama."

One by one, the children crowded around him, begging he ask her.

Theo would love to marry her, and Jeb and the kids sure didn't mind. It seemed that a gift had been dropped into his lap, a problem bigger than all his reasons not to marry her. He needed to save Jeanie's reputation. After all, it was his fault she was in this mess, not hers.

He tried to press down the excitement of no longer having to fight his love for her, but he couldn't. Blood sang through his veins at the thought. Not to mention the best part—his children would have a beloved mother. And as for providing, he could work hard and make sure Jeb was paid back for every kindness. It all made perfect sense.

He looked across the table into her beautiful brown eyes. "Marry me, Jeanette. It seems like a logical solution, does it not?" The minute the words were out of his mouth, he wanted to pull them back. What a horrible way to ask a woman for her hand in marriage.

Tears gathered in stormy eyes that scowled at him above her glasses. She said nothing but got up from the table and hurried down the hall. The slam of the front door shook the pictures on the walls.

"That's not how you do it, Pa." Sarah's hands fisted, and she stomped her foot.

"Yeah, you didn't even tell her you loved her." Laura said. "The prince always tells the princess he loves her."

"That's just dumb fairy tale stuff," Ben scoffed.

"It's not dumb—"

"Enough!" Theo's voice boomed. He stood, unsure if he should run after Jeanette first or settle his upset family.

"Go on, son." Jeb waved his hand. "Your girls are right. I'm thinkin' the delivery of that proposal was less than romantic. A woman likes to be wooed."

What an idiot he was. He had made the proposal sound so logical and unfeeling when his lungs could barely expand in her presence. There was nothing he wanted more than to make her his wife.

CHAPTER 33

Like a child, Jeanette ran to the barn to weep in private, entering her old haunt, the stall where the hay was kept. It was pitch dark, but she felt her way and plopped down on a stack of straw. Her head dropped into her hands.

Theo didn't love her. He'd marry her to save her reputation, to provide a mother for his children. But love wasn't a part of the equation.

Tears slipped down her cheeks, and she angrily swiped them away. Why had she imagined something different? The only way she'd finally received a wedding proposal was because the man felt pressured. And wait until word got around that she admitted they had been kissing and Theo had been in her bedroom. The gossip mill would surely surmise that the spinster had finally trapped a man.

"Jeanette, are you in here?" The rich timber of Theo's voice filled the barn. A spill of lamplight washed over the walls.

His large frame cast a shadow as he held the lantern above his head. There was no way she was talking to him right now. The sting of humiliation burned hot. She couldn't face him. The lantern light brightened as he came closer to the stall where she hid. A sneeze tickled her nose, and she pinched her nostrils closed, but not before a stifled sneeze escaped.

The movement of the light stopped then receded. She breathed easier as the sound of his footsteps on the wooden planks headed in the opposite direction. The hinges on the barn door squeaked closed, but the light of his lantern did not disappear. He hadn't left but merely hung the lantern on the post. His steps grew louder.

The pounding of blood thrummed in her ears.

"Jeanie, I know you're in here. Please talk to me." His large frame filled the entry of the stall where she sat curled in the hay.

"Please go."

"We need to talk."

She stood in a flash of fury, brushing sprigs of hay from her clothing. "Talk about what, Theo? The fact you feel cornered into making a marriage proposal?"

"I—"

"And for your information, even if we did marry, I would still lose my position." She smoothed her rumpled skirt. "Married women are not allowed to teach."

"So, you don't want to marry me?"

Bitterness twisted in her gut. "You've shared with me how much you hated being pressured by Victoria. How would this be different?"

He said nothing.

"See, you have no words."

His brows knitted together. "I have lots of words. But I'm not sure you're ready to hear them. If my family staying here means the loss of your job, then we must go. It matters to me that you feel happy and fulfilled, and if teaching does that, then I would never want to stand in the way."

"You don't understand. It's too late."

"Is there more?"

JEANETTE'S GIFT

"I was asked outright if we had kissed, and because we share bedrooms on the same floor, Agnus made a point of asking if you had ever been in my room. I answered honestly. Not to trap you into a marriage proposal, but because I could not have lived with myself if I'd lied."

"Then we must marry. Your reputation will be ruined, and I take responsibility for that. I was the one who went into your bedroom. I was the one who kissed you."

"We kissed each other, Theo."

"We did."

He smiled for a brief moment as if remembering the shared pleasure, but then grew serious.

"Look, I'm sorry for the way that proposal came out earlier." Theo swiped a hand through his thick hair. "I've never been good with words unless I have time to think and prepare, but I do want to marry you."

A tremor tripped up her spine but the words she most wanted to hear did not follow. She stared at him, waiting. "Why?"

"The children love you, and you're everything they need—"

"No. I will not marry you." She was not going to become his wife out of some sense of responsibility or even for the children.

"Let me finish. Your reputation—"

"No again. I get that your first thought is of your children. You're an amazing father. So, rest assured you can continue to live here, and I'll continue to be the person I have always been to them. And as for my reputation, I don't care what the community says about our living arrangements. I know I have remained moral."

"Please, Jeanie."

"There's no need for a proposal. Pa was telling me he'd like to build your family a cabin on the property come spring. He sees a real future working with you, and the children will have the stability they need. So, you don't need to feel any pressure to marry me on account of them.

With winter baring down, they've been through enough, and I won't have them uprooted again. However, I will not marry you." She lifted her chin and walked past him.

"Jeanie."

She turned back toward him. "And please, do not call me that." She kept on walking.

~

Theo stood in the cool of the barn long after Jeanette had left. He went to the back where he'd set up his woodworking and ran a hand down the smooth arm of the rocking chair he was making for her.

Why hadn't he been able to spill out what he really wanted to say—how much he loved her, how much he needed her? How much he longed to have her as his wife and had for quite some time.

Instead, his first marriage and the abysmal failure he had been had filled his mind. Louisa haunted his memories. He had never been able to make her happy, no matter how hard he tried. Would it be the same with Jeanie?

Her immediate refusal was like a battering ram to his heart. But she was nothing like Louisa.

He'd used his children as a buffer against expressing the raw emotion he felt. It was frightening to need someone as much as he needed Jeanie. Louisa had never evoked half these feelings.

God, please help me. I don't know how to do relationships and I don't know how to ensure I don't make the same mistakes.

Love in marriage takes two hearts, not just one. Louisa never gave you hers.

That reasoning thought brought a calm, a truth that could not be denied. Why had he never realized that before.

Louisa's unkind words were not truth.

There it was again, that inner assurance. Something that his mother had always talked about. God was speaking to him. But there was a wall, some unfinished business.

You have been angry at Me.

Theo didn't deny the truth pouring into his soul. He *had* been angry. Though he went to church each Sunday, fulfilling his promise to his ma, he felt no peace. Things were not right between him and God. It was the reason he had gravitated to Jeanie and her faith, and it was the reason he rubbed up against it.

He was not a good fit for her. She deserved a godly man.

Remorse filled his soul, and he dropped to his knees in the light of the low burning lantern. He had been so angry at God for what life had served up that he had failed to see the blessings right in front of him. *God, I'm so sorry. I stopped trusting You a long time ago, after Pa died. I went my own way and made some bad decisions, Louisa being the biggest. And yet You have never left me. Every time I've been at my lowest, when Louisa left me, when Mama died, when the farm was taken, You have provided the next step. Help me now. I love that woman.*

A peace he had never experienced before flooded in, around, and through him. His eyes opened to what life had given him through a different lens. Six amazing children. A home for his children, and a job he loved. A man he could look up to and learn from, a man he would feel honored to call father-in-law if only. And the perfect soul mate, a woman of integrity, strength, and so much love, his beautiful Jeanie. A prize worth fighting for.

Thank you, God, for the blessings I have turned a blind eye to. Forgive me for my sins, my unforgiveness toward Louisa, my anger at You, and my mistrusting ways. Lead me forward in wisdom. Theo raised his hands to the heavens. The weight of unforgiveness fell from his shoulders.

I am healing those broken places, those words of untruth spoken over you. Trust that I gave those six children to you, knowing they would need a father's love. Trust that Jeanette is a far different woman than Louisa, and that I have saved her for you, and you for her.

Lord, I do trust You. Now that I can see clearly all you have given me. I see a future. I have hope.

Theo jumped to his feet. He could not contain the joy. *God, did you really keep Jeanie just for me, for my children, for this moment in time?*

Yes.

His feet did a jig on the wooden planks. He had a woman to woo, and a God who would ensure he did it gallantly. He would take it slowly but steadily and shower her with so much love that she would not question his sincerity the next time he proposed.

~

Jeanette slammed the ball of dough onto the counter and punched it down hard.

Theo had been nothing but friendly and respectful the past two weeks, even whistling around the house. His peaceful demeanor served only to remind her that she was right in her decision not to marry him. If he felt anything for her, wouldn't his heart be at least half as broken as hers?

She had woken that morning frustrated, knowing she loved him but knowing, if he couldn't tell her he loved her, too, that she had to let him go.

Breadmaking was a perfect way to let off some steam. She turned the dough over and kneaded with both hands until beads of sweat trickled down her spine.

What was she going to do with her life? No more teaching to fill her days. How she missed those young faces. Was sensitive Alice doing all right? She hoped the others were not teasing her.

And was Lizzy keeping up with her reading? That Tommy, what a lark. He had made her laugh almost every day. She sure missed him.

She pushed those thoughts aside. They were too difficult. It wasn't the teaching she missed as much as the children.

Had she said yes to Theo's marriage proposal, she could be very happy filling her days caring for the children and possibly having one of their own. Her cheeks flushed hot. She dare not let her mind wander there. As it stood, she aimed to lose them all come spring, but love them she would, forever and for always.

Theo had taken her at her word and had gone on as if nothing had happened, clearly delighted he hadn't been pressured into more. Most evenings after he got the kids to bed, he disappeared to the barn, lost in his world of furniture making. She should be happy for him, since she'd encouraged him to pursue that gift. Truth was, she missed their evening conversations. But then, what had she expected? That she would be worth fighting for? That Theo would tell her he loved her and beg her to marry him? She would just have to find her happy ending in loving herself as God wanted her to and pouring her love into those children. That was her prayer, but pursuing that peace was a daily battle.

She'd been worried the children would be negatively impacted by all that had happened, but they hadn't said a word about being concerned they would have to move again. They also accepted the new teacher in town with good attitudes. Thankfully, Agnus had not been allowed to stay on, for the children had confided to them how stern and unkind she had been.

Meanwhile, the gossip spread, and some of the looks Jeanette received while walking down the street were comical on the days she could get past the hurt. Oddly, Pa seemed unfazed by the growing rumor mill and the loss of her reputation. And the strangest of all was that there'd been no inquisition from Reverend William. He'd made a point to tell her he would not entertain any disparaging remarks about her reputation.

On one hand, it was as if God was protecting her, but on the other, it felt like a stormy tempest brewed within a low-lying cloud.

She stoked the fire, ready to bake her bread, and slammed the door of the hatch harder than she'd intended. The clang reverberated throughout the kitchen. The day was starting out with her hot and bothered. Maybe she should have spent more time with God rather than rush downstairs to make bread.

"Good morning, Jeanie. Is everything all right?"

Jeanette whirled around and scowled at Theo. "I asked you not to call me that."

He moved near until he stood close enough to see the trouble in her eyes. "You will always be Jeanie to me. I only use that name in private, but if you're really uncomfortable..."

A wash of feverish heat that had little to do with the stove spread over her.

"I will respect your wishes. But I want you to know I've not given up on us. I hope in time you'll allow me to call you Jeanie again."

Not given up on us? What did he mean? She turned back toward the counter, picked up the wash rag and wiped with fervor. She was far too irritated for conversation this early in the morning.

"You seem like you need a hug." His arms slid around her waist from behind, and he pulled her slowly against him. Every brain cell objected with vigor, but her body betrayed her. She leaned back against him. Her breathing shallowed as his head lowered. She could feel the whisper of his breath on the back of her neck. They stood without speaking for a long moment.

"Thank you for all you do. It does not go unnoticed."

She turned, and he stepped back dropping his arms.

"What are you doing?"

"Just saying thank-you, something I should do more often."

That was not what she meant, and he knew it. Why had he held her so tenderly? Fragile almost, like a glass doll.

He lifted a tendril of hair that had worked free in her attack on the bread dough and curled it behind her ear. "You look so beau—you have flour smudged." His thumb tenderly wiped her cheek.

She fought the urge to lean into his hand.

What was he doing, calling her beautiful? And...was that longing in his eyes? The way he was looking at her lips sent a tremor tripping up her spine, but he did not touch her again.

There was so much she wanted to ask, but words stuck like tree sap in her throat.

"Have a good day, my beautiful Rose." He turned and walked away.

A sigh shuddered through her body. Had Pa told him her middle name? My, it sounded sweet rolling off his lips.

Theo looked over his shoulder and smiled. "Tell Jacob when he wakes up that I'll be mucking out the stalls, and he should join me as soon as he can." He headed down the hall.

There was that whistle again.

Oh, dear Lord in heaven. What just happened?

CHAPTER 34

⚜

*T*heo spread the last coat of finish on the rocking chair. The thought that maybe, just maybe, someday his Jeanie Rose would rock their baby here… It made his heart melt.

Should he sit her down and tell her in plain English his intentions were to marry her? Or should he woo her slowly and let her come to that conclusion not by words but by his actions? He had bungled so much already. Every step from here on in had to be God-breathed.

How peaceful it felt to ask God for wisdom and not fight His answer. He no longer worried about failure, just woke up each morning with a prayer on his lips and a willingness to do his best. God was speaking to him daily through the Bible and during his prayer time. This morning, he had felt the Spirit urge him to hold Jeanette for a moment with nothing more than the warmth of his arms. She hadn't sent him packing, so maybe there was hope. But wow, that had been difficult once she turned his way. She'd looked so beautiful, all disheveled and doe-eyed with flour smudged across one cheek. Everything within him had wanted to pull her close, but he obeyed and treated her with the utmost respect.

The children and Jeb had been sworn to secrecy. He'd been honest with them about his intentions after that abysmal marriage proposal. The children were most agreeable, accepting their new teacher without grumping, helping out where they could, all too eager to make sure their Pa had success the next time around.

"Looks mighty fine."

Theo whirled around at Jeb's voice.

"Yeah, it turned out even better than I envisioned. I hope she likes it."

"She'll love it."

"Seems like such a small token of thanks after all she's done. And how will I ever thank you?"

"You just love my daughter like the treasure she is, and that will be all the thanks I'll need."

"I'm working on it, starting with my relationship with..." he pointed up.

"Yup. That's the best place to start. Glad to see you've made your peace with the Almighty. It's tough when we're angry at Him."

"Was I that transparent?"

"Let's just say, these past few weeks you've looked like a weight has been lifted off your shoulders.

"It has. Now I know that God had a plan all along, bringing me to this valley, to this home, to this woman."

Jeb chuckled. "Now, all you have to do is convince my somewhat stubborn but beautiful daughter that you're not marrying her out of guilt after going into her bedroom." He laughed.

"I'm sorry, sir. But that's no laughing matter to me. You have no idea how bad I feel."

"No need to explain. But I look at it differently. As long as that girl could hide behind her teaching position, she was content to fade into the background. Can't tell you how many times she missed the fact that one man or another was interested. She had herself convinced that teaching was all she had. Could be that God had to take that from her to open her eyes to the world around her and the other things she excels at."

"I pray I can be part of that world. But I want to take it slowly and respectfully."

Jeb clapped his shoulder. "Don't be going too slow. She's twenty-nine, and I want more grandbabies." He chuckled his way out of the barn.

∽

Jeanette jotted down some more notes and surveyed her sister's ballroom one last time. She'd begin decorating as soon as all the supplies were in. She nodded at Katherine. "I think this room is going to be the best I've done yet."

"That's wonderful, but we've forgotten one last thing."

"What?" Jeanette's pencil was poised to write.

Katherine pulled a measuring tape from her pocket and moved closer. "Your measurements for the costume."

Jeanette batted her hand away. "You have my measurements, and I'm not joining in the costume party. I'll wear one of my Sunday dresses, and that's that."

"I didn't keep the measurements from last time, and you most certainly will have a new gown. The costumes are half the fun. Tessie has begged to see you dressed as a princess, and I'm here to ensure that little child's request is granted."

"What, are you the fairy-godmother?"

"Nope, just your sister who insists you stop living in the shadows. Besides, you're spearheading all the decorating for me. A costume is the least I can do as a thank-you."

"I'm hardly in the shadows with all the gossip circulating."

"All the more reason to dazzle. If they're going to talk, let's give them something different to talk about. I'm going to oversee hair, clothing, and your cosmetics."

"I don't care to dazzle."

"Ahh, but you shall." Katherine wrapped the measuring tape around her waist and jotted down the number on a piece of paper.

"Must you?"

"I must." She measured from the floor to her waist, around her bust, and across her shoulders. "That should do it. Leave the rest to me, or rather to my fairy godmother seamstress." Katherine chuckled. "You know me. I'd rather be outside riding than sewing."

Her sister was much too bossy. The last thing Jeanette wanted was to draw attention to herself. "Keep it simple, I hate—"

"I hear you have an invite to the ball," Katherine said.

"Now, how do you know that?"

"I have my sources."

"'Tis true. Theo asked me a while back, but after all that's happened—"

"Oh, there's no doubt he is escorting you. At least that's what he told Pa and Colby. Now, all you have to do is open up your heart." Katherine hugged her.

"Things are not that simple."

"I think they are. It's clear to everyone with eyes that Theo has been smitten with you from the beginning—and you him. It's why you didn't fall for Solomon."

"Hmm." If the man was so smitten, why didn't he say so?

"And don't hide behind that 'hmm' of yours. Promise me you'll dance and show those gossipers that their words have little power."

"That I will. If there's one thing I've learned this past year, it's to break free of what people think of me. And believe it or not, with or without a prince charming, I'm at peace with life just the way it is."

"I can see that. You look different. More confident and…" Katherine stood back with a finger to her lips. "Don't know how to describe it. Maybe the best word is happy."

"I am." Jeanette was surprised at how quickly she agreed and how much she meant those words. "Anyone who doesn't know me well enough to know my good character can keep their assumptions. I will no longer give their remarks power over my life."

"Still, there's no harm in showing those wagging tongues a thing or two. You shall not only be a true sensation on the inside as you have always been, but on the outside as well."

"Please, don't overdo it, you know I'm not that frilly, fancy kind of girl."

Katherine's laughter echoed through the empty ballroom. "Ha, the frilly and fancy lives within every girl. I was the biggest tomboy of them all, so I should know." She turned with a decided swirl to the bottom of her dress and sashayed to the ballroom entrance. "All you need is a little encouragement. And I'm here to ensure you have the best night of your life."

~

It was three days before Katherine and Colby's Christmas ball, and Jeanette was thick into decorating mode. Missing her students, the challenge was a wonderful distraction. The first thing on the agenda for the day was a trip to Alston's General Mercantile. That tulle she wanted to drape from corner to corner across the ballroom had better be in.

She untwisted the tight knot of her bun at the back of her head, which she had done without thinking, and loosened some strands. With care, she refastened it higher on her head, giving a much softer look. She slipped on her winter bonnet and smoothed her hands over her sensible jacket and skirt. After one last look in the mirror, she stepped out of her bedroom into the hall and almost collided with Theo.

He steadied her with his hands on her shoulders.

"Oh, sorry Theo."

"I'm not. Nice way to start the day."

She turned toward the steps, his closeness too sweet, too tempting, too everything it should not be.

He walked with her, keeping his hand on the small of her back.

"Where are you headed this morning in such haste?"

The heat of his hand created an unnerving distraction as they descended the steps. She didn't want Pa or the children to happen upon them and see such casual intimacy. "To the store in Lacey Spring to pick up some material for the party." She shrugged out of his touch at the bottom of the steps.

His hand dropped to his side. "I have to go to town. I can take you."

"Thanks, anyway. I'm riding in style today. Katherine said it looks like snow, so she's offered her driver and her covered carriage."

"Well then, it's my lucky day too. May I join you?"

The thought of being alone in the carriage with Theo brought a jolt of panic. She had worked so hard to keep a healthy distance. She finally felt at peace with life just the way it was. She didn't need anything to upset that lovely balance. But how could she refuse?

"I guess it will be fine."

He laughed. "Don't sound so excited. When are you leaving?"

"I want to get an early start, so Pa said he would make a pot of oatmeal for the children when they get up. With school out for the holidays, I expect everyone but Tessie to take advantage of the privilege of sleeping in."

"They sure can't do that in the summer months with all the work. I'm so thankful to have this stability—"

"Yes. I'm fully aware of why you're here." Her voice sounded sharp. "And of course, Pa and I are happy to help. He has a stack of books to read with Tessie when she wakes up. He loves that little girl." That sounded better. More easy-going. She opened her locket around her neck and glanced at the time. "Katherine said her driver will be here at eight. That's in five minutes. Just enough time to get my boots and cloak on." She turned swiftly and made her way down the hall. Why did he have to keep reminding her why he was there? Yes, she loved him, and always would, but it was freeing to not need to make anything happen. He need not worry.

The driver pulled up, and she led the way out the door. Even the touch of Theo's hand helping her into the carriage brought an annoying response. Her body betrayed her common sense. She trembled at the proximity when he chose to sit beside her rather than across from her.

The carriage lurched forward. The crunch of the gravel beneath the carriage wheels cushioned their silence. She kept her gaze pinned outside the window as they rolled toward town.

"Did I say something back there to offend?" Theo asked.

Oh goodness. How could she answer that? She shook her head.

"What I was trying to say earlier is how thankful I am for God's provision, for your pa's generosity." He folded his fingers over hers. "And for you."

She pulled her hand free, unable to still the quiver of response he would surely feel. She didn't need to hear another *I'm so thankful for your friendship* speech.

"It's far too early in the morning to get into deep discussion." She put starch in her spine and shifted her body toward the window. "It most certainly feels like snow, does it not?"

"It does."

She breathed a relieved sigh when he remained quiet and the town finally came into view.

"What errands do you have?" she asked, turning his way.

He had an odd look on his face. "How about I meet you back at the mercantile when I'm done? I won't be more than an hour."

"That sounds perfect." She jumped out of the carriage the minute the wheels stopped rolling.

CHAPTER 35

Jeanette entered Alston's General Mercantile, hoping that the early hour would afford her an empty store and Winnie's undivided attention. She pulled her list out of her reticule and surveyed the last-minute things she needed to complete the decorating with the tulle being top priority.

"Good morning, Jeanette," Winnie said. "You'll be pleased to know the tulle you ordered is in."

Jeanette clapped her hands. "Splendid. I was a little worried I'd have to settle on the satin, but the tulle will give more of the airy feel I was looking for."

"You're so talented. How do you come up with a different theme each year?"

"I don't know. God just gives me ideas, and I can see them in my head before the creation."

"Not me. Even arranging my showcase here is a challenge. Which reminds me. I have a beautiful hair comb that came in, and I thought of you." She opened the glass showcase, with its collection of jewelry, trinkets, and hunting knives, and pulled out a white pearlized filigree hair comb. "You've done so much for the community, teaching, playing the piano at church, and now taking in the Wallace family. Robert and I want you to have this as a thank-you."

Jeanette fingered the ornamented work that had been crafted to look like lace. "It's beautiful, Winnie, but I couldn't."

She moved from around the counter and hugged her. "I insist. After all that's happened, you need to be reminded that not everyone believes the rumors or agrees with the school's decision."

A lump rose in Jeanette's throat. "How very kind, but—"

"No buts. Just say thank-you." Winnie's youthful laugh filled the store.

"It's so lovely. Thank you. And thank Robert for me."

"I will. Now, let me run to the back and get your tulle while you gather whatever odds and sods you still need."

Good thing Katherine and Colby were paying the bill. Without her teacher's wage, she had to save her last few pennies. With a basket in hand, she moved about the store, past the men's dungarees and leather brogan shoes to the shirtwaists and corsets. She fingered a lace chemise and wondered what it would feel like to stand before a man in so little. Heat poured into her cheeks. She would never know.

"Do tell. Wherever would you have use for that?"

Jeanette turned around to see that Victoria had entered the store.

"By the color in your cheeks, I dare say your thoughts were impure."

"I will not further this conversation with a response." Jeanette walked past the woman with her head held high. The clicking of heels behind her told her that Victoria was not finished.

"Tell me, how does a woman like you do it?"

A spike of anger rode up Jeanette's spine, and she whirled around towering over the smaller woman. "A woman like me?"

"Everyone thinks you're so pure and holy, but I see the way you've entranced Theo. You must be quite the charmer in the dark. Of course, a man would need the black of night to—"

"You may believe that your money and your looks ensure entitlement, but nothing gives you the right to attack my good character. I may never marry nor have riches, but I have honesty and kindness. I know I haven't done any of the things you're insinuating. Besides, you claim to care about Theo and his children, yet your tongue-wagging has proven the opposite. I, on the other hand, have loved Theo's family like God would have me do."

"Pff." Victoria waved her hand. "It would take a lot more than loving his unruly brood to have him eating out of your hand like he is."

"Victoria, you can leave my store at once if you wish to say one more unkind word." They both turned. Winnie held a bolt of tulle under one arm. With the other, she pointed to the door.

Jeanette lifted her hand. "It's all right, Winnie. Some people don't believe that showing God's love unconditionally is the most powerful gift one can give. But I know I've done it well, and God is pleased. What people think of me is of little consequence."

Victoria huffed her way to the door, the click click click of her heels snapping across the planked floor. She turned, determined to have the last word. "You'll miss my business, Winnie. Indeed, you shall." She slammed the door so hard that the wall shook.

Winnie giggled. "Seeing as Victoria loves shopping and we're the only store for many miles, I'm not worried." She hugged Jeanette. "I didn't hear most of that exchange, but what I did hear was you handling her with class and grace. I'm so proud of you."

Jeanette's insides were still jittery, but the truth of the words God had given her resonated. She did love Theo's family well, no matter what the outcome. God was pleased with her. And she was at peace.

She offered Winnie a smile. "Now, where were we? Do you have a ball of sturdy twine? I need to drape the tulle…"

~

Jeanette held out her packages and Theo deposited them on the seat of the carriage and helped her in. Once again, he chose to sit beside her instead of across from her.

"Place your feet on the foot stove." He held out a blanket to cover their legs. "I made sure the driver had a hot drink and a chance to warm up, and that he placed warm coals in the stove for himself and for you. It's getting colder by the minute."

Against her will, her pulse quickened. "Thank you, Theo."

The carriage rattled over the hardened earth. Light snowflakes drifted to the ground. She ventured a peek his way and found he was staring at her. Their breath frosted between them.

"It's snowing." She stated the obvious, longing to ease the strain.

"Does this mean you've woken up enough for some deep discussion?"

His slow, easy smile melted the resolve guarding her heart. "You mean to pick up where we left off earlier?"

"I was prepared to wait, knowing I'd have a captive audience on our return trip. I'm interested to hear your creative excuse this time." His voice held a teasing tone.

She looked away. Best she gets this over with because he had no intention of letting it go, whatever *it* was. "I'm awake."

"I'll take that as a yes."

She turned toward him. A lock of hair fell across his brow.

She longed to run her fingers through it. His light brown eyes glowed warmly with a softness that pulled her in.

"I'm not so good with words, and I bungled that marriage proposal something fierce. Can you forgive me?"

She wanted to stay angry with him, but he'd felt pressured. "You're forgiven because I do understand." The words felt strangled from her throat.

"I don't think you do," he said. "You're the only one I've shared anything with about my first marriage, but you don't know the half of it, and you need to. Will you allow me to explain?" He waited in respectful quiet.

Did she want to know? She looked at her hands knotted together so tightly that her knuckles were turning white. "Go ahead."

He cleared his throat. "Louisa was older, more sophisticated, and stunningly beautiful. I was young and easily taken in by her charm. When she wanted an immediate marriage, I naively thought she loved me and couldn't wait. The fact that every man wanted her fueled my youthful ego. Unbeknownst to me, Louisa was already pregnant."

Jeanette did everything not to raise her brows in shock. "So Jacob—?"

"Is not my biological son, and neither are some of the others, which I didn't know until she confessed the day she left me."

Jeanette gasped. She had wondered at how they all looked so different and had such wildly different temperaments. Now it made sense.

"But they're mine, each one, and I love them more than my own life."

"They're wonderful kids, Theo. You've done a remarkable job."

"Louisa came from a wealthy family and was terribly spoiled. We had nannies and maids, and she had little inclination toward motherhood. The only thing she was good at was getting pregnant and obviously having men on the side. As I told you before, in the end, she picked the wrong one."

Jeanette kept her gaze focused on her lap for fear he would see the moisture building in her eyes. She didn't want to distract from what he needed to say. But she reached out and placed her hand over his. He covered it in the warmth of his own. Her heart ached for him.

"I promised myself I would never put my children at risk of being with someone who didn't love them. The Calberts, Louisa's parents, wanted the children, but they would've been brought up the same way as Louisa had been, spoiled rotten, selfish, and raised by a nanny. I didn't want that for them. When I wouldn't give them up, Mr. Calbert fired me, and although I was learning and doing quite well at accounting, he told everyone in the community that I had stolen from him. No one would hire me.

"I went to work on the railroad, and we managed until Ma died. Then, my world spiraled out of control. I was angry. At Louisa, at her parents, at Ma for dying, but mostly at God, thinking He had abandoned me. To get my children as far away from the Calberts' influence and the gossip surrounding their mother's death, I took my small inheritance and moved here. I had worked a couple summers with my uncle and loved working the land, but you know how that went."

Jeanette slid her hand out from his and pulled a handkerchief from her pocket. She pushed up her specs and dabbed at her eyes. There was no hiding what she felt for him and all he had suffered. "I'm so sorry."

"Don't be sorry. There was a reason I was brought to this valley, to the grace God had prepared for me. You came into my life." He pulled her hand back into the comfort of his. "My Jeanie Rose, the best friend I've ever had, an angel sent from heaven. You brought life, order, and so much love into our home. You treated my children as if they were your own, and you tirelessly continued, even when it meant losing the job you love."

Jeanette couldn't tell where this was leading. Was she a good friend, or was she more? A thrill pulsed through as dread simultaneously churned in her stomach.

"You have never once called me boring or dull like Louisa did."

"She called you that?" Jeanette understood the pain of unkind words and the power they had over a person.

"And a whole lot more," he said. "Louisa wanted someone rich and powerful. She wanted to be the life of the party. And I wanted to be at home with my wife and children. The two of us were like oil and water. Funny how, when the farm failed, her unkind words came back with a vengeance. The fact I couldn't put a roof over my children's heads haunted me. I believed that if I wasn't able to provide a home, earn a good income, and shake my past, I wasn't fit to take on a wife."

Had he wanted to take her on as his wife?

"It wasn't until I found you crying in the barn after that abysmal attempt at proposing that I realized my biggest failure was the way I'd let my past control my future. The way I hurt you dropped me to my knees. I made peace with God that very night."

"I knew something was different, all the humming and whistling. It was driving me crazy, thinking you were so happy that you hadn't been pressured into marrying me. It's nice to hear it's God not—"

"Oh, Jeanie, I'm so sorry. I should've told you. But I thought you were angry with me, and not without good reason. Plus, you'd just lost your job. I wanted to give you respect and space. I also needed some time to work through forgiving Louisa and her parents. I needed freedom from my past so that I could be the man I want to be, the father I need to be, and hopefully in the future, the husband God wants me to be."

Was he saying what she thought he was saying? Hope flooded her being as she looked into the sincerity of his eyes.

"Can we start over, Jeanie? We have a solid friendship, but will you allow me to court you, to woo you, to take this relationship far beyond the borders of friendship? Including allowing me to escort you to the ball, if you'll still have me?"

Was she dreaming? Did she need to pinch herself?

"We can take things as slowly as you like," he said. "I want to earn your trust."

She had waited a lifetime to hear someone say they wanted more than friendship with her.

"If you need time to think and pray, I understand."

She smoothed her hand over his closely cropped beard, looking deep into his questioning eyes. "Yes, we can start over. And yes, you can court me, and woo me, and escort me to the ball as long as..." She smiled.

"As long as what?"

"As long as you don't mind me stepping on your toes. I haven't had too much practice dancing."

His eyes twinkled with pleasure. "I would be honored, no matter how much toe-stepping there is." He held out his arm and invited her close, and she snuggled up against the warmth of his body. His strong arms wrapped around her. "Hmm."

There he went using that word again. "What?"

"This feels like a slice of heaven."

She looked out at the dizzying sea of snowflakes wrapping them in a cocoon of intimacy. "Hmm, I couldn't agree more."

CHAPTER 36

"Come." Theo pulled Jeanette by her hand across the yard to the barn. She so seldom went into the barn that she hadn't noticed the last two stalls had been closed off. "This is new." She entered the room, which had been transformed into a workshop, and took a deep breath. The smell of sawdust and shellac filled her senses.

"Your father graciously suggested I have a clean environment away from the straw and animals. Colby donated some of his men who do fine carpentry. I learned a lot from watching them finish this up. They added a window to let fresh air in when I'm putting on the wood finish."

Theo had his tools hung neatly on the wall above the workbench. A couple of shelves held bottles of finish, rags, and smaller items. Different types of wood were stacked neatly in piles at one end of the room. Everything was orderly and precise. "Very nice. I'm so proud of you for pursuing this."

"I'm glad you approve. You get my first piece created in this space. It's in honor of your encouragement to me and a small token of thanks for all that I can never repay." He walked over to something that was covered by a large blanket. "Now close your eyes, and no peeking."

Jeanette pressed her eyes shut. The thought that he had made something specifically for her brought a sting to her eyes. She was deeply moved.

She felt his hands guide her forward. "All right." His deep voice held a timber of excitement.

She opened her eyes to the most beautiful rocking chair she had ever seen. "For me?"

"You said you loved the one on my porch, but I added a few extras." He pointed to the hand carving on the upper back of the chair. "Roses, in honor of your name."

"Oh, my goodness, Theo, this is amazing." She ran her fingers over the deep rich wood molded and fit intricately together with dove-tailed joints. The roses brought mist to her eyes. "It's so lovely. No one has ever given me anything this beautiful."

"Beautiful, like you. So loving. Kind. And giving." He pulled her close, and she raised her face to his.

"You could make a girl fall head over heels if she weren't careful."

"Here's to hoping you're not too careful."

Their banter, the touch of his hands, and his woodsy scent sent a yearning racing through her. And the way his body brushed up against her…hmm, she was in deep water.

His stare grew hot, and his look made her feel every bit a desirable woman.

She lifted her lips to his, and he didn't disappoint. What started sweet turned urgent and needy. She could feel the pounding of her heart and the tug of it reaching for him, for all of him.

"Jeanie, my darling."

She could taste her name on his lips as he pulled away.

"If I don't stop now, I won't be able to." His voice was husky, drenched in longing. "So how about you give the chair a try."

Without his support, her shaky legs sank into the comfortable curve of the chair. She rocked slowly. With her eyes closed and to the rhythm of motion, she dreamed of holding her own baby, rocking their child to sleep in this very chair. A smile curled her lips upwards.

"Do you like it?"

"More than I can ever say." She kept on rocking.

"How about I move it into the house? You can tell me where you want it."

"Give me just a moment to soak this up in the silence, in the place your hands created such a beautiful gift for me." She kept her eyes closed. So, this is where he had been each evening. Working on something for her.

"Take all the time you like." He laid a gentle kiss on the top of her head.

She heard his steps recede and the door to the workshop close behind him. Her heart lifted, as light and airy as a feather dancing in the wind. That exchange had been a whole lot more than friendship.

~

Theo's pace picked up at the thought of seeing Jeanette. He hurried down the path that cut through the orchard on route to Katherine and Colby's. He was missing her presence at the house something fierce, being that she was so busy with the decorating for the ball. Oh, did he have it bad. Never had he felt anything so all-consuming for any woman. Nor could he believe the depth of his happiness and peace. For the first time in his life, he understood what it meant to leave his future in God's hands. Yes, he would work hard and do everything he could to provide, but it was no longer something he felt he had to accomplish on his own strength. Now, he trusted in a God who cared.

The thump of the door knocker was a tad more exuberant than needed, but that was what happy people did.

Katherine opened the door. "Theo, come in."

"I'm here to help."

Her laughter echoed down the hall. "Oh, that's a good excuse to see my sister."

"Am I that obvious?"

"Absolutely. But I understand. This decorating has monopolized her time. She's in there slaving away." Katherine pointed to the ballroom. "It's never looked so good. Tomorrow should be perfect." She winked and turned in the opposite direction. "I'll leave you two alone."

He took a deep breath in. He had a few moments alone with her—no kids, no distractions, nothing but his girl.

His eyes moved around the room taking in the magical transformation. A beautifully decorated Christmas tree graced the center of a raised platform. The scarlet bows and dazzling glass-blown baubles drew immediate attention, but he only had eyes for her. There she was, on top of a ladder, fussing with the tulle she had purchased in town a few days before. A surge of awe washed through. How did she create such loveliness everywhere she went? He watched her for a moment, and his pulse thumped in crazy rhythm. Everything she did—from the smallest of kisses on Tessie's cheek, to a pat on Jacob's back, to standing precariously on the top of a ladder messing with netted material—was beautiful. She was beautiful. Her flushed cheeks, her hair busting free of that bun she insisted on wearing, the spectacles teetering on the tip of her nose.

He moved across the ballroom to the base of the ladder. "Need some help?"

Her head jerked his way, and her spectacles went flying. "Goodness, Theo, you scared me." She lurched forward and stumbled down a few rungs before her dress caught. The next moment, she was right where he wanted her, in his arms.

Her startled expression made him laugh out loud. "I got you."

"Put me down this instant. What if someone were to—?"

He lowered his head, briefly touching her luscious lips, and slowly slipped her feet to the floor. He definitely had her attention. Her arms circled his neck, and her fingers played in the hair at his collar. He lifted his head. "We'll tell them we're practicing our dancing for tomorrow evening." With a gust of energy, he whirled her around the floor. "Sing to me, Jeanie. Give us some music."

She slapped his chest, but she was laughing. "Stop that."

"Isn't this what a man does when he's trying to woo his girl?"

"No, he helps her finish her decorating."

"Ahh, so I can be of service?"

"If you're not scaring me off ladders and whisking me around floors."

He laughed and slowed until they were barely moving, his arms still wrapped firmly around her slim waist. A surge of adrenaline coursed through his bloodstream at the way she was looking at him.

"You love me, Jeanie girl, don't you?"

"Oh, you want me to admit that before—"

"Before what? I tell you how much I love you?"

"You do love me, don't you?" Her voice held a sassy tone.

"I do, with all my heart." He cupped the sides of her face with his hands and gazed into her eyes. There was no mistaking the love he could feel pouring from that deepest part of her. His lips met hers with an intensity he could barely control. With aching slowness, the long and lingering kiss ended.

"It would be wise to stop now." His words came out strained. Every nerve ending ached with a need for more.

"I know exactly what you mean." She moved out of his arms.

"Now, bring your height and your brawn over here and help me get the star on top of the tree."

~

"Children, gather around." Theo waved his hand. "Jeanette's gone to her sister's to get ready for the ball, and Grandpa Jeb will bring you at the appropriate time. A bath is a must—"

"Do we have to? I hate baths." Ben's lip stuck out.

"Absolutely, and they'll be no putting up a stink. You hear?"

"Yes, sir." Ben saluted him like a soldier, and everyone laughed.

"You're a scamp."

"If it was me, I'd call him a brat," Charlie said with a smile on his face.

Ben's hands clenched, and his face reddened. He lifted his fist.

Charlie grabbed his small arm and laughed. "You never learn, do ya? I was only teasing."

"Don't start, boys, this is a special day, and we won't have any of that."

They nodded and even looked contrite. Theo's heart swelled. This was going to be a fantastic day.

"I'll be leaving earlier than you to help Jeanette with last minute details. Be sure and wear you Sunday best." Theo turned to Jacob. "I expect you to assist Ben if he needs help with his bow tie, and Sarah, can you help with your sister's hair, ribbons, and such?"

"Of course, Pa, you don't even have to ask."

"If you have trouble, do not fret. Katherine said she'll have someone available to help with last-minute details." He patted her head. "You're such a dear. Thank you."

"Are you nervous?" Laura asked.

"The old ticker is pounding for sure." He hit his chest, and they all laughed. "Sure hope she'll have me."

"She's going to look like a princess, Papa." Tessie's copper curls bounced as she jumped up and down, tugging at his hand. "I can't wait to see her dress."

"Nor can I." He swept Tessie into his arms. "We shall dance around the ballroom floor like this." He whirled her around the parlor with her giggling all the way. The other children laughed.

"And then I shall… Whoops can't say, it's a surprise."

"Ahhh," Laura cried.

"Come on, Pa, tell us, tell us," Sarah pleaded.

"He's gonna kiss her." Ben puckered his lips and smooched into the air.

Theo slid Tessie to the floor and ruffled Ben's unruly mop. "You'll all just have to wait and see. But do you remember what we practiced?"

Heads nodded.

"Good, then all that's left is for everyone to be on their best behavior, and for me to redeem the mess I've previously made."

CHAPTER 37

The effort Katherine had made washing Jeanette's hair in rose water, slathering special creams on her skin, even insisting on new underclothing, all feminine and lacey, was truly too much. But Jeanette had found herself enjoying every moment. Other than a peek at the dress as Katherine and her maid helped her into it, she hadn't been permitted to see it, but it was way too elegant and extravagant to be considered a costume, that much she could surmise.

"Keep your eyes closed until I tell you." Katherine led Jeanette across the room and then stopped, turning Jeanette just so. "You may look now."

Jeanette slowly opened her eyes to the full-length mirror. She gasped. Then blinked them shut and opened again. Was that really her?

She touched the endless folds of flowing material to make sure she was not in a dream. Ruffle upon ruffle swagged and tucked in layers of stunning creamy white satin. The sleeves were short and puffy, fringed in tassels that swung elegantly as she moved. The high neckline was adorned with a beautiful cameo on a band of solid material from which sheer silk gathered elegantly down to the scooped neckline of the gown. Her cleavage was faintly visible for the first time in her life, but only to one who looked closely. A blush rose to her cheeks. "But it's too—"

"Too what? Beautiful?" Katherine slid her arm around Jeanette's waist and gave a squeeze. "Not for my sister. You're going to be the belle of the ball tonight."

Jeanette couldn't pull her eyes from the mirror. Was that really her in a tight-fitting bodice that accented a slim waist and voluptuous figure? She turned her back toward the mirror and saw a row of tiny pearl buttons that ran from the v-shaped back to a soft sloping bustle with a long, sumptuous train. "Why would you spend so much money on this gown? It's a costume party."

"Every costume party needs a princess. Your only job tonight will be to find your handsome prince. I'm betting that a certain fine-looking farmer who is already captivated by your kindness is going to be swept away by your beauty. Now, come sit." She pointed to a chair beside the dressing table. "All that's left to do is your hair, and I'm going to call Mariam to do that job while Rose helps me get dressed and fixes my hair."

"What about the filigreed hair comb that Winnie and Robert gave me?" Jeanette asked.

"I have it right here." Katherine tapped the jewelry sitting on the dressing table. "Amazingly, it's a perfect complement to your ensemble." She winked. "What a coincidence." That smile told Jeanette her sister was holding back information. But before she could press for answers, Katherine disappeared out the door and Mariam stepped in.

"Are you ready for the finishing touch? I see your gown is absolutely stunning." She touched the tassels, which delicately swayed with every movement.

"Yes, please."

How effortlessly Mariam pinned her hair into a fashionable

coiffeur on top of her head. She twisted an elegant braid, which crowned the knot, allowing a glorious riot of long ringlets to cascade down. The creation was stunning.

Katherine returned wearing a striking aqua green velvet dress from medieval times. Her black hair flowed free in a hundred ringlets with a small crown of jewels on her head. The laced-up bodice, square neckline, and elegant gold trimmed sleeves that draped down from her forearm to the bottom of the dress wrapped her in aura of mystery. A cream-colored netting graced her shoulders.

She twirled in a circle. "Do you like it?"

Jeanette relaxed. Katherine had always been the one everyone couldn't wait to see. Her natural beauty and flair for picking the perfect gown was the talk of the town. Tonight would be no different. Thankfully, with Katherine dressed like that, people would barely notice Jeanette. "You look lovely, as always."

Katherine moved across the room and gently touched Jeanette's head. "Your hair looks fantastic. Mariam is a true artist, and you have such beautiful hair to work with."

"I feel a tad overdone. Are you sure I'm not overdressed?"

"There's no need to fret. I think you're ready to stop being the wallflower, don't you?"

Jeanette touched the ringlets softly cascading down to the magnificent gown. How could a dress and hair style make such a difference? Or was it more than just accenting the outer shell? Could it be that God had not made a mistake in His creation of her?

Katherine set her hands on her hips. "Well?"

"I'm ready."

"Good to hear." Katherine lifted a pair of elegant white gloves from the bureau. "And last but not least." She flipped the elbow length gloves to the inside and showed Jeanette the small lace pocket. "For your specs, so you have them if you need them."

"You've thought of absolutely everything. From the tip of my evening slippers to the top of my head, you've transformed plain Jeanette into what I truly feel, beautiful."

"You are, and always have been beautiful." Katherine squeezed her arm. "Believing in yourself was the missing link."

~

Theo stood close to the door. He could barely take in the crowd and the stunning ballroom. All he longed to see was his girl. He brushed a trickle of sweat from his brow. The music had started, and there was still no sign of Jeanette or Katherine. His insides jumped. What he was about to do was way outside his comfort level, but she was worth the risk.

Colby slid up beside him. "You nervous?"

"Does it show?"

"A smile might help."

He forced his mouth to cooperate.

"That's better. Katherine is waiting for everyone to be present. You should've seen the guests. They were most disappointed when she didn't join me to greet them at the door."

Colby's rich laughter eased Theo's frazzled mind. "I can imagine."

"Loosen up, boy." Colby nudged him. "They'll be down soon."

Theo rubbed his hands on his trousers.

"I can see this is killing you. Come with me."

Theo followed Colby, who wove through the crowded room and out the door into the foyer. When they reached the bottom of the curved stairway, Colby pointed. "Stay here." He took the steps two at a time and disappeared down the hall.

First Katherine and Colby came down, then a vision of loveliness came into view causing Theo's heart to slam against the walls of his chest. Jeanette had loved her way into his family, into his heart, into that deepest part of his soul. Now, as he gazed up, he was unable to take his eyes off her.

She stood at the top of the staircase smiling down at him, slim and willowy with every curve accented. The dress she wore bedazzled from tip to toe. A thrill raced up his spine and exploded inside his head. Pure elegance floated down the steps. The light of the chandelier highlighted strands of auburn threaded through her thick brown curls. Never had he seen any woman look so beautiful.

"Well, are you going to stand there and stare," she asked, "or are you planning to escort me to the ball?"

The hypnotic lilt of her voice mesmerized him. "You look incredible." His eyes dropped to the scooped neckline covered only by the sheer material, and liquid heat seared through his body. His lips ached to claim hers, but Katherine and Colby were waiting for them just outside the ballroom entrance.

"Do you like it?" Jeanette twirled slowly, making the dress shimmer and sway. Her kind brown eyes sparkled with merriment.

"It's stunning"—he lowered to whisper into her ear—"but it's the one wearing the dress who's got me tongue-tied. I long to whisk you away and not share you with a soul."

"Come on, you two." Katherine laughed. "There'll be a whole evening for that."

Theo held out his arm, and she placed her slim fingers into the crook. Never had he felt more alive or more proud of a woman on his arm.

CHAPTER 38

Jeanette held her head high as they followed Colby and Katherine into the ballroom. If Theo's reaction was any indication, this was indeed going to be a wonderful evening. The music played, but the room hushed. Why were all eyes on her and not Katherine? She clutched Theo's arm.

"I'm right here," Theo whispered, as if reading her mind. "Dance with me."

"You may have to excuse a few missteps, but yes, please, I feel like a fish in a fishbowl."

He took her by the hand and led her onto the dance floor and into his arms.

She trembled beneath his touch.

"Relax, my darling. I have you."

Oh, the sweetness of that endearment…darling. No one had ever called her that before. She melted into his embrace. One hand held hers, warm and comforting, poised for the dance. The other arm curled securely around her waist. The feel of his large hand splayed across her lower back brought a jolt of desire. Headiness filled her being, but he was able to guide her with a confidence she could trust. They moved to the tempo of the waltz, Theo expertly gliding her around the floor.

"You are so easy to dance with," she whispered.

"And every eye is upon you."

"Thanks, now I'll stumble for sure."

He smiled. "No, you won't. I have you." He pulled her a little closer. "Keep your eyes looking into mine, and we will waltz through life together."

Now what did he mean by that? Was he inviting what she thought he was? A spike of thrill raced up her spine. "A song does not make a lifetime," she teased.

He said nothing but tiny hazel flecks of devilment flickered in the depth of swirling brown, and amusement crinkled the corners of his eyes. It was no hardship to keep her gaze riveted on him.

One song melted into another, and they kept dancing. It was totally against etiquette to not allow the filling of one's dance card, but Jeanette's had never been filled, no matter how long she'd stood in the shadows. Those days were over. Her handsome prince had found her.

Another song ended, and Jeanette was ready for a breather, having to concentrate so intensely on the steps to each dance.

"May I cut in?" Solomon faced them, took one look at Theo, and clarified. "As friends."

"Honestly, I need a break." Jeanette smiled. "How about the next one?"

Solomon's grin split wide. "See you in a few minutes."

Theo didn't seem to want to let go. "Guess he didn't get the message."

"What message?" Jeanette had no idea what Theo was talking about.

Theo didn't answer. "Let me get you a drink." With his hand on the small of her back, he ushered her through the crowd. Numerous men stepped forward as if to procure a dance but took one look a Theo and moved aside. Was Theo glaring at them? The thought that he could be jealous tickled her soul.

Theo guided her over to the side table where a large bowl of punch sat surrounded by tea, coffee, wine, and lemonade.

"What's your pleasure?" he asked.

"Punch, please."

While he filled her silver goblet, her eyes caught the tea board, which was filled with tantalizing cakes, tarts, and pastries galore. Biscuits, cheeses, cold meats, poached salmon, and savories crowded another side table beside it. Being that the whole town was invited, Katherine and Colby did not try to orchestrate a sit-down meal but had a continual supply of delicacies to enjoy.

She sipped her drink as daintily as she could, conscious of many eyes on her. Was this what Katherine had endured over the years? If so, then Jeanette pitied her sister. She had only wanted to look beautiful for Theo, not to catch the attention of other men. What a novel but annoying scenario when she only had eyes for one.

"My dear." Someone tapped her elbow from behind.

Jeanette whirled around. "Helen, I didn't expect to see you here."

The knuckles of one hand were whitened over her cane, and she motioned with the other hand to the nearby chairs. "May I have a moment of your time?"

Theo smiled down at Helen, reaching for her elbow to escort her. Once he settled her in a chair, he pulled out another chair for Jeanette. She slid in beside Helen. "I'll give you ladies a moment. Seems Colby is waving me over." He raised his hand in acknowledgement and headed across the room. Jeanette's eyes followed him. Wow, did she have it bad. There was no mistaking the love she felt for him.

"You look so lovely." Helen touched Jeanette's cheek with her cold hand bringing her back to the present. She turned giving

Helen her full attention. "What are you doing here? I know what an effort it is for you to come out these days. Especially in the cold."

A grin twitched on Helen's lips. "Sometimes, an old woman needs a little excitement in her life." There was a decided sparkle in her eyes.

What did she mean?

Helen reached over and squeezed her hand. "I want to tell you how proud I am of you for stepping out of the shadows."

Jeanette patted her heart. "I feel different right here. And it's not this stunning dress, though I do love it."

"I can see that, my dear. You've stepped out in faith and allowed God to give you the confidence to be all He created you to be."

"I have to admit, it's weird to be the center of attention. I don't like it much."

"Men are noticing because you exude poise and assurance. Looks like one is headed this way right now."

Solomon was moving toward them.

Jeanette whispered in Helen's ear. "But I only have eyes for a certain tall, good looking farmer."

Helen leaned close and chuckled. "It never hurts for a man to have a little competition."

Solomon reached out his hand and helped Jeanette to her feet. Before she knew it, she was whirling around the dance floor in the arms of her cowboy friend, who was smiling down at her. She kept sneaking peeks at Theo, who stood on the sidelines seeking out her face from one end of the ballroom to the other. Whenever they locked eyes, he smiled, and she smiled back.

Victoria appeared beside Theo. Jeanette moved her head from one side of Solomon to the other so she could watch the exchange. Victoria was not to be trusted. Jeanette didn't like the strained tension nipping at her neck. Theo shook his head, and

Victoria moved away. Jeanette caught Theo's eye and he winked at her.

"I can tell you're not with me," Solomon said.

Jeanette pulled her gaze from Theo. "Hmm?"

"I get the distinct notion I best return you to the man you love."

Jeanette stumbled in his arms. "I'm sorry, Solomon. Am I that obvious?"

"As it should be. I wanted a moment to tell you how glad I am that the two of you found each other. Seemed the only way I could do that was to ask for a dance."

"And I've noticed that you and Daisy Mae have been kicking up a storm."

"Yes. She's very mature for her age, yet fun-loving. I like her, a lot."

"I'm so happy for you, Solomon."

"And I, you." He guided her to the sidelines, where Theo waited.

"I'm bringing your girl back to you. Right where she belongs." He smiled at Theo and walked away.

Jeanette lifted a cold palm to soothe her burning cheeks. "'Tis true," she whispered. "All I could think about was you."

"I do like the sound of that." Theo didn't waste a moment. He whisked her onto the dance floor and across the room, nodding at Katherine and Colby, who stood next to the platform where the chamber orchestra played. The soprano singer's soft voice cooed out a ballad in velvety tones. Everything but Theo faded as she gazed into his warm eyes, not caring a whit if the world saw her unabashed love.

"You are beyond lovely," he whispered as the song came to an end. "Good thing there's a crowd or I would be in trouble."

"What kind of trouble?" she asked with a grin.

"I think you know."

Katherine and Colby walked up on the platform. Katherine raised her hand, and the crowd quieted.

"I know you're used to our annual speech thanking you all for being part of the wonderful community of Lacey Spring, but tonight we have something far more exciting to share with you than our boring ramblings."

The crowd laughed.

"We would ask that you all clear the dance floor, all except for one special couple."

Jeanette tried to move toward the edge of the dance floor, but Theo held her firm. "We are the couple."

Jeanette's pulse galloped at a speed that made her head feel light. "What?"

Theo leaned forward and whispered into her ear. "Shh. All you have to do is listen."

Jeanette's hands trembled in his as the crowd gathered in a wide circle around them.

Theo dropped to one knee and pulled a ring from his pocket. He cleared his throat. "Jeanie Rose, my love, my best friend, my soulmate, and the woman of my dreams…and wow, have I been dreaming about this moment."

Laughter filled the room.

But Theo wasn't laughing. His Adam's apple bobbed.

Jeanette raised her hand to her mouth, choking back the lump flowering in her throat. Happy tears slipped down her cheeks.

"I love you more than I have words to express. I love everything about you, from your stunning beauty to your heart, the kindest heart that has ever beat, and even to your no-nonsense ways, which brought order out of chaos in our home. You are the only woman for me."

"Children." Theo's gaze moved from hers up onto the platform. "Children." He waved them forward from their bird's eye view.

Now where had they been hiding? Jeanette had not noticed them earlier.

Jacob, Charlie, Sarah, Laura, Ben, and Tessie split through the crowd. They lined up in birth order behind their father, who was still on his knee.

How beautiful they looked, every bow and ribbon in place, shoes spit-polished clean, hair groomed or curled beautifully. Even Ben, who hated dressing up, had on his best trousers and a perfectly knotted bowtie.

Theo nodded at the children then turned back toward her. "Will you be my love, my wife, the mother of our children…the children you have already taken under your wing and loved with such generosity of soul, and the children, Lord willing, who may come in the future? I feel like you and I were created for this moment, for this family, for our story. I pray you feel the same. Will you marry me, my Jeanie Rose?"

In unison, the children asked, "Will you be our mama?"

Jeanette was so overwhelmed with emotion that she couldn't speak. Were her dreams coming true right before her eyes?

Stillness filled the room. It was so quiet she could hear the beat of her thumping heart.

"Please?" Tessie's small voice pierced the silence.

Jeanette found her voice. "Yes. Yes. Yes!"

Theo stood and swept her into his arms.

The room erupted as he swung her around and lowered his lips to hers. He pulled back from their kiss and lifted her hand, sliding a ring on the finger she thought would never wear one.

"It's so beautiful."

"It was my mother's," he whispered in her ear, stroking the back of her neck. "It was the one thing I refused to sell. I was saving it for one of the girls, but then you came along, and I found myself dreaming again."

The children gathered around, and Jeanette lifted Tessie into her arms. Her chubby little hands touched Jeanette's cheeks. "You'll be my mama, for real now?"

"Yes, sweetheart. I'll be your mama for now and forever."

Tessie nuzzled into her shoulder.

Jeanette's heart was so full it felt ready to burst.

Katherine clapped her hands above the din.

"If Jeanette is willing, we have the whole community here, and a beautiful wedding gown... Doesn't my sister look amazing?" The whole room clapped.

Heat flooded Jeanette's face.

Katherine looked at Jeanette and laughed. "Now you know why that dress had to be perfect."

Jeanette turned to Theo. "This was all planned?"

"I botched the first attempt at asking you to marry me, so I wanted to do it right. Your sister was only too happy to oblige."

Colby joined in. "And we have food, music, dancing...the perfect evening for a wedding celebration. Even Reverend William is here."

Theo took her hand. "When your sister suggested that there was no better time for a wedding than the annual ball, all I could do was hope and pray you would feel the same, because I'd love to marry you right here, right now. I don't want to waste another day"—he lowered his voice and spoke just to her—"or night apart. I feel like I've already waited a lifetime for you."

"And me, a lifetime for you." Jeanette lifted her lips to his. Oh, how she understood now why she'd had to wait. To think of all the worrying, the wondering if God had somehow forgotten her, when He'd had this planned all along.

Tessie wrapped her arms around them both and giggled.

"One more surprise." Katherine's singsong voice filled the room, her expression bright and excited.

"What! I cannot take more." Jeanette touched her heart.

Theo took Tessie from her arms.

Katherine was thoroughly enjoying herself. "'Over snow and bumpy trail, in carriage and by rail, what would a wedding be, without all the family?'"

Lucinda and Joseph, with Sammy, Tommy, and Emma, stepped forward from the crowd. Amelia and Bryon with Jenny, Pearl, and Jonathon came out from a side room. Matthew and Gracie, holding their baby daughter, Lorabeth, followed. Katherine and Colby stepped down from the platform. Seth, Jillian, Georgian, and Geena joined them, with Pa bringing up the rear.

Tears poured down Jeanette's face. A joy she didn't know could live inside her bubbled up and out.

"Happy tears?" Laura asked.

"So happy," Jeanette said, squeezing her hand. "So happy."

Mariam bustled out of the crowd with a long flowing veil made with lace that perfectly matched the dress. She pinned it in place.

Jeanette was handed a bouquet of red roses. "From my solarium," Katherine whispered. "To my beautiful sister, Jeanette Rose." She gave a fierce hug.

Theo put Tessie down and took Jeanette by the hand. He nodded at his family, and they followed him up to the platform. They stood in front of Reverend William as if the whole thing had been rehearsed. The girls on Jeanette's side each holding a single red rose, and the boys on Theo's side with wide grins.

"Dearly beloved," Reverend William said, "you thought you were gathered here today for a Christmas ball, but God had this day planned long before time existed."

CHAPTER 39

Theo waited for his bride. The farmhouse was quiet and theirs for the weekend. His kids and Pa were staying at Colby and Katherine's, their many rooms a haven for all the relatives. The two of them could come and go at will over the weekend. Visit if they felt like leaving their nest, but chances were slim they'd be seeing anybody.

A fire burned low, giving off warmth and just enough flickering light to make the bedroom dangerously romantic. Theo had never felt more alive as he reclined against the stack of pillows on the bed.

Another wedding night filtered into his memory. A drunk bride who wanted to spend more time drinking than being with him. He pushed Louisa out of his head. She would always be part of his history, and he loved the children she had given him, but he was thankful she was not part of his future. His beautiful, brown-eyed Jeanie was his future. How did he ever get so blessed?

Jeanette stepped out from behind the dressing screen. She wore a long flowing gown of shimmering satin that clung to every curve. His eyes feasted on the most beautiful woman in the world. For the first time, he got the pleasure of seeing her hair free and long, cascading around her.

"My darling." He held out his hand, and she moved across the room to the edge of the bed. She seemed unsure.

He stood and gathered her in his arms for a hug. "You won't be needing these," he said, drawing back and removing her spectacles. With a smile he kissed the tip of her nose and placed the spectacles on the side table. He touched his lips to her hair and drew in the scent of wild roses. His fingers worked through her glorious thick hair. He'd waited so long to touch it like that.

She stammered. "I-I don't know what—"

His mouth met hers, and he kissed her until she relaxed, pressing her body against his. Desire ignited into passion. Between that kiss and one look, his plan to take things slowly was sorely tested as he slipped the outer gown from her shoulders. Only a sheer gown remained, revealing every beautiful secret.

He lifted her in his arms and lowered her slowly to the bed. "You are beyond lovely."

She pulled his head down to hers. "Kiss me, Theo. Make up for every lonely moment. Teach me how to love you."

"You, my dear, are the teacher. You've brought so much love into my life. I will spend a lifetime learning from you. But as for the beauty of being a couple, we shall learn together."

He kissed the pulse in her throat, which fluttered beneath his lips, then brushed her mouth with a whisper of a caress. Her breath was intoxicating. Her lips deliciously enticing. He covered her mouth, ensuring the kiss was warm, pliant, needy, seeking out her response.

She didn't disappoint. Every move he made, she mimicked, until they were both dancing in flames of searing sensation. As natural as the rise and fall of waves, they found their cadence, their rhythm, their song. He had never experienced anything so potently powerful in his entire life. They were far more than husband and wife. They had been created for each other.

～

*J*eanette fought between the worlds of foggy and familiar. She had experienced the most beautiful dream—a ballroom, a dance, a marriage. She squeezed her eyes shut, begging to return to that place of peaceful slumber.

"Good morning, my Jeanie."

Her eyes popped open. It had not been a dream. Theo was lying beside her wearing a big goofy smile.

"So yesterday really happened? Not just my wild imagination?"

"I certainly hope not, or your pa will be outraged to find me in your bed."

She was so happy, her joy almost felt like a slow ache. "Pinch me. I'm sure I'm dreaming."

He rolled on top of her and smoothed the tousled hair from her face. "Oh, I can do something much more enjoyable than pinching you."

Jeanette giggled. "And what might that be?"

"Well, Mrs. Wallace…"

How she loved the sound of that—Mrs. Wallace. She was a missus to the most amazing man in the world.

"How about I show you rather than tell you?"

She wrapped her arms around his neck. "For as long as I can remember, I've longed for someone to look at me the way you're looking at me now."

He kissed her forehead with aching tenderness. "And for as long as I can remember…" He brushed each eyebrow with his lips. His stare crackled with heat. "I've longed…" He kissed his way down her nose, his warm breath fanning her face. "For someone…" He cupped her cheeks in his hands. "To love me…" His lips traveled slowly from her neck to her chin. "The way you so genuinely do." His lips landed softly on hers, and he moaned to the movement her body instinctively sang.

"You are a quick learner, my Jeanie."

Her giggle was stifled by a loving kiss. Her body tingled with life, and what began as a gentle touch blazed into passion.

EPILOGUE

SPRING 1882

Jeanette clapped her hands above the loud chatter around the breakfast table. Heads swiveled to where she stood at the woodstove flipping flapjacks. Her stomach fluttered in excitement. "I have a surprise."

"As long as it's not like the last one," Jacob said.

The last one? Jeanette couldn't remember announcing a surprise. She walked to the table with a full flipper in her hand and plopped another stack of flapjacks onto the platter. They were quickly snatched onto the plates.

"Last one?"

"Yeah. Pa's surprise asking you to marry him in front of everyone at the ball was a great one, but yours...not so much."

For the life of her, she didn't have a clue what he was talking about. "Do tell."

"Last summer when you announced a surprise and pushed that widow Victoria dragon lady on us."

Jeanette laughed. "I agree. Not one of my better ideas."

"That's for sure." Theo got up from the table, kissed her on the cheek, and headed to the stove to refill his coffee. "Pa, you want a warmup?"

"Sure do." Pa held up his tin cup.

"Ben." Laura's voice was shrill. "Don't take all the strawberry jam. I want some too." Laura sat beside him on the bench and gave him a good nudge. She held out her hand.

Ben slathered on an extra scoop and then handed her an empty jar.

"See what he did?" Laura whined.

"He's always picking a fight in some way," Charlie piped in.

Ben's face turned red. "And you can never mind your own business."

"Children, I can open another jar." Jeanette smiled at her rambunctious family. She would not trade a moment, not even moments like these. She turned back toward the stove. "I guess no one cares to hear my surprise."

Tessie got up from the table and ran over. She tugged on Jeanette's hand. "I do, Mama. I do."

They all called her Mama, and it never ceased to warm her heart, but she was especially blessed by the way Tessie used it on every occasion possible.

Jeanette put down her flipper and moved her hot pan to the cooler side of the stove. She gathered the affectionate Tessie in her arms and sat in her chair next to Theo.

"What's your surprise?" Pa asked. "You look like a cat that just ate the canary."

"She does not," Theo said. "She looks stunning, albeit somewhat mischievous." He leaned over and kissed her on the cheek. "I'm most interested in your surprise, my darling."

"Tell us, tell us," Sarah pleaded. "I love surprises."

Jeanette looked around the table at each curious expression. She finally had their full attention. She turned toward Theo and touched the side of his face with her hand. "Well, dear man, you're going to be a father, again.

His eyes widened. "You mean...you mean...?"

"Yes. That's exactly what I mean."

She turned to the children. "And all of you are going to have either a baby sister or baby brother." Her eyes scanned the bunch, then returned to Theo.

Theo lifted Tessie from her knee and spun her around. "Did you hear that? I'm going to be a papa again, and you're going to be Mama's big helper." He set Tessie down and then pulled Jeanette to her feet. "There is no happier man on earth." He kissed her full on the mouth, then lifted her off her feet and twirled her around.

The children gathered around with cheers and hugs aplenty.

Pa clanged his spoon on the side of his tin cup, adding to the racket.

Jeanette's spirits soared, floating up and away like a hot air balloon high above the surface of the earth.

Theo set her down. "Goodness, in all my excitement I wasn't thinking. I should be more careful." He touched her midsection gently.

She placed her hand over his. "I'm not going to break."

"What did I ever do to get so blessed?"

A bubble of sass slipped free. "You are blessed, indeed, dear husband."

He laughed, and light twinkled in his eyes. "Well kids, shall we have a little fun? Will this little one"—he patted Jeanette's abdomen—"make the boys outnumber the girls, or the girls outnumber the boys?"

The girls broke out screaming. "It's a girl. It's a girl."

"No. It's a boy," Jacob yelled over the commotion.

"Darn tootin', a boy for sure." Charlie echoed.

Ben nodded, for once in agreement with his older brothers.

Jeanette's laughter filled the room. "Well, that's a surprise we won't know until at least the end of summer."

"The end of summer?" Laura's face fell. "That's so far away."

Tessie tugged at Jeanette's dress, her eyes wide and glistening. "Will I…will I still be your sweet pea when the baby comes?"

Jeanette pulled her up into her arms. "You'll always be my sweet pea, sweet girl." She kissed her forehead. "You and I will pick out a new nickname for the baby."

"Like, honey bunny."

"Honey bunny is a very good choice, but we'll have lots of time to think upon it."

Theo kissed Jeanette's head.

She gazed up at him.

"You're the best mama any child could ever have," he said.

The way he looked at her made her feel like she was falling off the edge of a cliff. She was happy, truly happy. God had not forgotten her. In His providence, He had known all along how much this family would need her.

And how much she would need them.

Did you enjoy this book? We hope so!
Would you take a quick minute to leave a review where you purchased the book?
It doesn't have to be long. Just a sentence or two telling what you liked about the story!

∼

Join Blossom's monthly newsletter where you can win prizes, receive a new recipe, or get a peek into her life: https://blossomturner.com

∼

Receive a FREE ebook and get updates when new Wild Heart books release: https://wildheartbooks.org/newsletter

BOOKS IN THE
SHENANDOAH BRIDES SERIES

Katherine's Arrangement (Shenandoah Brides, book 1)
Word Guild Semi-Finalist

Amelia's Heartsong (Shenandoah Brides, book 2)

Lucinda's Defender (Shenandoah Brides, book 3)

Gracie's Surrender (Shenandoah Brides, book 4)

Jeanette's Gift (Shenandoah Brides, book 5)

ABOUT THE AUTHOR

*I write because I can't **not** write. Stories have danced in my imagination since childhood. Having done the responsible thing—a former businesswoman, personal trainer, and mother of two grown children—I am finally pursuing my lifelong dream of writing fulltime. Who knew work could be so fun?*

A hopeless romantic at heart, I believe all stories should give the reader significant entertainment value but also infuse relatable life struggle with hope sprinkled throughout. My desire is to leave the reader with a yearning to live for Christ on a deeper level, or at the very least, create a hunger to seek for more.

Blossom Turner is a freelance writer published in Chicken Soup and Kernels of Hope anthologies, former newspaper columnist on health and fitness, and novelist. She lives in a four-season playground in beautiful British Columbia, Canada, with gardening at the top of her enjoyment list.

She has a passion for women's ministry teaching Bible studies and public speaking, but having coffee and sharing God's hope with a hurting soul trumps all. She lives with her husband, David, of forty years and their dog, Lacey. Blossom loves to hear from her readers. Visit her at blossomturner.com and subscribe to her monthly newsletter.

Don't miss Blossom's other book, *Anna's Secret*, a contemporary romance and Word Guild semi-finalist.

WANT TO JOIN BLOSSOM'S SUPPORT TEAM?

If you enjoyed this book and love reading and would like to be a part of my Support Team as the next book launches, contact me through my web page at https://blossomturner.com, under the "Contact" heading.

A Support Team member will receive a free advance copy of the next book *before* it is released and promises to support in the following ways:

• Read the book in advance and have it completed by release date.
• If you enjoy the book, leave a review on Bookbub and Goodreads before release date as soon as you are done reading. Right after the release date, copy that review onto the other retailers, Amazon.ca, Amazon.com, Kobo, Barnes and Noble, and Apple Books. I will send you all the links so it is super easy.
• Promote ahead of time on social media, FB, Twitter, Instagram, or where ever. (I will send you memes to post before release date so everything will be easy. I will not inundate you with too many.)

WANT TO JOIN BLOSSOM'S SUPPORT TEAM?

I will have numerous prize draws for the support team members, in which your name will be entered to win gift cards from Amazon. I will try and make the process as fun and painless as possible, and hopefully you will enjoy the read. Those of you who have joined my team before and left such wonderful reviews, I thank God for you and consider you a part of my writing family.

I thank you in advance for joining me on this journey!

(Sorry, open to residents of Canada and the USA only.)

ACKNOWLEDGMENTS

To put in words my thank you to the amazing team at Wild Heart Books is next thing to impossible. To publisher/final editor Misty M. Beller and edit team Erin Taylor Young and Robin Patchen you have my sincerest thanks for elevating my work way beyond its original first draft. Wild Heart Books is a pleasure to write for, the company is well-run and the professionalism second-to-none.

To my critique partner Laura Thomas who spends hours fine-tuning my story, thank you from my heart. And to my amazing support team who read the book before it hits the market and then encourage others to read by your wonderful reviews, as a new author your gift of time is invaluable. I thank you.

And as always, but by the grace of God go I. Without His outstretched hands of help each day when I sit down at the keyboard, I could not accomplish half of what I do. Thank you, Jesus, for being a living, breathing, wonderful part of my every day. Thank you for the gift of imagination. You are the best co-author any girl could ever have.

Want more?

If you love historical romance, check out the other Wild Heart books!

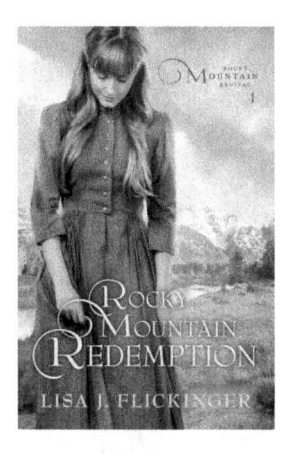

Rocky Mountain Redemption by Lisa J. Flickinger

A Rocky Mountain logging camp may be just the place to find herself.

To escape the devastation caused by the breaking of her wedding engagement, Isabelle Franklin joins her aunt in the Rocky Mountains to feed a camp of lumberjacks cutting on the slopes of Cougar Ridge. If only she could out run the lingering nightmares.

Charles Bailey, camp foreman and Stony Creek's itinerant pastor, develops a reputation to match his new nickname — Preach. However, an inner battle ensues when the details of his rough history threaten to overcome the beliefs of his young faith.

Amid the hazards of camp life, the unlikely friendship growing between the two surprises Isabelle. She's drawn to Preach's brute strength and gentle nature as he leads the ragtag crew toiling for Pollitt's Lumber. But when the ghosts from her past return to haunt her, the choices she will make change the course of her life forever—and that of the man she's come to love.

Marisol ~ Spanish Rose by Elva Cobb Martin

Escaping to the New World is her only option...Rescuing her will wrap the chains of the Inquisition around his neck.

Marisol Valentin flees Spain after murdering the nobleman who molested her. She ends up for sale on the indentured servants' block at Charles Town harbor—dirty, angry, and with child. Her hopes are shattered, but she must find a refuge for herself and the child she carries. Can this new land offer her the grace, love, and security she craves? Or must she escape again to her only living relative in Cartagena?

Captain Ethan Becket, once a Charles Town minister, now sails the seas as a privateer, grieving his deceased wife. But when he takes captive a ship full of indentured servants, he's intrigued by the woman whose manners seem much more refined than the average Spanish serving girl. Perfect to become governess for his young son. But when he sets out on a quest to find his captured sister, said to be in Cartagena, little does he expect his new Spanish governess to stow away on his ship with her six-month-old son. Yet her offer of help to free his sister is too tempting to pass up. And her beauty, both inside and out, is too attractive for his heart to protect itself against—until he learns she is a wanted murderess.

As their paths intertwine on a journey filled with danger, intrigue, and romance, only love and the grace of God can overcome the past and ignite a new beginning for Marisol and Ethan.

∽

Lone Star Ranger by Renae Brumbaugh Green

Elizabeth Covington will get her man.

And she has just a week to prove her brother isn't the murderer Texas Ranger Rett Smith accuses him of being. She'll show the good-looking lawman he's wrong, even if it means setting out on a risky race across Texas to catch the real killer.

Rett doesn't want to convict an innocent man. But he can't let the Boston beauty sway his senses to set a guilty man free. When Elizabeth follows him on a dangerous trek, the Ranger vows to keep her safe. But who will protect him from the woman whose conviction and courage leave him doubting everything—even his heart?

CPSIA information can be obtained
at www.ICGtesting.com
Printed in the USA
BVHW032024021022
648513BV00007B/71